PRAISE FOR A DRI

MW00582609

"When Matthew Willish wakes ι got there, he begins desperately seaι realize, however, is that this is only _____ ....g of a journey that will ultimately send him searching other worlds for the answer to numerous profound questions, the most pressing being: is he living in reality or in a dream? Or is he just an insane man who desperately needs help? A Dream of Waking Life is a philosophical and psychological thriller that tells the story of one man's journey through space, time, and mind to not only discover his true identity but also the love of his life—a woman who keeps slipping through his fingers and into another reality. A thought-provoking meditation on the thin line between what is real and what is not, A Dream of Waking Life will leave readers questioning how far they would go to understand the nature of their own existence and how much they would sacrifice for love." - Advance Reader Review

"A mix between Lathe of Heaven, Inception, and The Three Stigmata of Palmer Eldritch. I simply could never have foreseen this story's trajectory. What a heartrending yet satisfying and impressive journey! The plot kept me guessing at every turn; every time I thought I figured the grand mystery, the author threw me for a new, profound curve. The characters jumped right off the page, and the love between Matt and May felt tangible. The ending left me in tears, and months after reading it, I still can't get it out of my head. A love story, mystery, grand philosophy, incredible suspense – A Dream of Waking Life stands in a category of its own. By far the most impressive work from E. S. Fein so far." - Advance Reader Review

"What is reality? What do we really know about what is REAL? Is this waking life? These are probably the questions you will be asking yourself as you read this wildly impressive story! Navigating through the maze of Matt's mind felt all at once exhilarating and puzzling...how did it get to this? You will be questioning your own sanity as you continue down the rabbit hole. Dream of Waking Life delivers a fantastical ride filled with drama, action, and suspense! A psychological thriller that would make Philip K. Dick proud. Definitely cannot stop thinking about this one! Am I awake...?" – Advance Reader Review

"A Dream of Waking Life takes the seemingly straightforward question "how do you know what is real?" and turns it into a mysterious and suspenseful story. Blending elements of philosophy and science fiction, ES Fein has created a narrative that will draw you in and have you speculating until the very end. At times, the tone of the story veered into surprisingly dark territory almost reminiscent of a Black Mirror episode. However, the story avoids feeling depressing or oppressive as these elements are well juxtaposed with other instances of intentional absurdity and humor throughout the book. As the name suggests, dreams are central to the plot and setting of the book...While obvious parallels to the movie Inception can be made, A Dream of Waking Life stands on its own and treads entirely different and more introspective ground. I loved how much this book kept me thinking and every chapter renewed my curiosity. I could not put it down!" – Advance Reader Review

"The kind of novel that stays with you long after you read the final word on the final page. It left me thinking about how real my dreams sometimes seem and what that might mean for me when I'm awake. If you enjoy stories that keep you guessing about the plot and how it might connect to your own reality, then A Dream of Waking Life is for you." – Advance Reader Review

"This is a super interesting fast-paced read. After every chapter, I was left wondering where the story would go next. The characters are so flawlessly integrated into the story that it was more than halfway through before I realized how attached I really was to them and their outcomes. A true mystery until the end, this book is sure to keep you on your toes and make you think. I don't say this often, but A Dream of Waking Life is also a great reread with so many easter eggs along the way! Would recommend to all!" – Advance Reader Review

"Right from the start, I felt projected into the main character's exciting and chaotic journey through dreams and waking life. This book had me questioning the realness of reality and driven to find answers in E.S. Fein's cleverly-written novel. The characters felt so real that I found myself yelling and screaming at them throughout the story and even long after I finished reading." - Advance Reader Review

OTHER WORKS BY E. S. FEIN

Points of Origin
Ascendescenscion
The Process is Love

OfficialESFein.com
Instagram.com/AuthorESFein
Patreon.com/OfficialESFein
Facebook.com/AuthorESFein

A
Dream
of
Waking Life

E. S. Fein

A Dream of Waking Life
Copyright © 2022 by E. S. Fein

Author: E. S. Fein
Publisher: Feinbooks
Editor: Nichole Paolella Petrovich
Editor: Melissa Feinberg
Formatter: Claire Krauss
Cover Illustrator: Leraynne

Ebook ISBN: 978-1-7323069-4-3
Paperback ISBN: 978-1-7323069-8-1
Publication Date: May 2022
Library of Congress Catalog Number: 2022908029
First Edition

Thanks

Thank you to all my family, friends, and fans for your love and support. To my closest friends, thank you for your patience and acceptance of my mind.

Special thanks:

To Jesse, for pushing me to continue my writing and take it to the next level. I genuinely appreciate your honesty and your critiques of my work. We go so far back that it precedes the beginning of memory. You've always been a part of my life, bro, and you always will.

To Rachel, for your support and incredibly deep understanding of me. You have provided incredible comfort and helped me attain deep levels of acceptance for myself. I will always be grateful to you.

To Brad, the Dungeon Master of the greatest DnD campaign anyone has ever experienced. You were the first official beta reader to finish the book, and your feedback gave me a ton of confidence to share this story with others.

To Marcin, for encouraging me and pushing me to finish this story and to give the whole of myself to it even when it meant a great deal of confusion and torment for me. You are my brother, and I know with complete and utter certainty that I can always count on you.

To Melissa, for your invaluable edits, of course, but also for your understanding of the overall vision I was going for with this piece. Your changes to the language of my story were expert and thorough. Nichole and I built a great house, but you gave every square inch of it the deep clean it needed. Your editing career will have no limits. You are the best of the best. (Secret handshake).

To Nichole, for always being by my side, especially when it comes to my writing. We both know the truth is that my stories wouldn't be worth half as much as they are without your guidance and vision. You are basically coauthor of my stories — that's the way I see it. Especially when it comes to the characters. I have evolved and grown into the author I am today specifically and very directly because of you. You have my eternal gratitude. And though I'm sorry the story didn't end exactly as you and I would have liked, it did end exactly as it needed to.

To Mom, for fostering my passions and for always encouraging me to write. I can't believe how many hours and days you spent listening to me tell the most random and bizarre stories as a kid. And the whole time, you would just smile and encourage my creativity. Life was not easy for us, Mom, but you made it seem easy. You always made life as wonderful an experience as possible for a very confused and angry and wild and pained child. And now, seeing you with Leif, my son, I understand why there is so much joy deep down inside me that I can turn to whenever the darkness in my mind closes in and threatens to consume me. You gave me that foundation of joy. I will have that until the day I die. And maybe beyond. Who knows, right? The universe and love are capable of anything.

To Claire, truly my other half. I cannot imagine my life without you. I don't want to. I was searching for you for years before I met you. We started practically living with each other within weeks of me asking you out, and 13 years later, I still get excited each day that you love me and want me and thrive with me. You are my clarity. You are my rock. And I am yours. We have overcome every obstacle. We are meant for one another. We are truly yin and yang. I'm grateful I found you all those years ago and convinced you to come back to my place with my grandma's frozen homemade spaghetti sauce. You are my inspiration, and you never cease in your support and belief in me. And as for this story, you were there when I first started planning this story as we hiked random trails in New Zealand over a decade ago. You were there when I gave up writing it. You were there when I started again. And you were there for the countless other times I gave up. You were there for the years of piecing it together. And you were there to see its end. This story would not exist without you by my side. I would not exist without you. I love you forever and a day.

Author's Note

I've been a lucid dreamer since I was 13. I'm 33 now. That's two decades of living other lives and exploring other worlds. That's tens of thousands of other personalities I've met and engaged with. That's thousands of surreal experiences that are simply unavailable to waking life. I even have persistent dream characters who are more like friends at this point. Some are even lovers. The point is, I spend a great deal of time in my dreams. Stephen LaBerge, one of the pioneers of studying lucid dreaming as an empirical science, once said, "If you must sleep through a third of your life, why should you sleep through your dreams, too?"

Approximately 13 years ago, in my early 20s, I woke to a remarkably vivid world full of carnage and chaos. A random group of people shuffled me into a room and we hid there for a moment, listening to the terrible sounds of death outside. With my history of lucid dreaming, it was at this point that I realized I was dreaming. However, when I did reality checks, they all passed. I did four separate reality checks, and all of them told me I was awake. My heart raced. I am in tears now recollecting that pang of perfectly real dread. I told this group of people, "this is just a dream," and the look they gave me is still seared into my brain. They looked at me as if I were truly insane. One of the doors to the room burst open, and a large man started spraying me and the rest of the group full of bullets using a giant assault rifle. As I lay there dying, my blood pooling out of me as I hacked on strings of fluid in a futile attempt to breathe, I just kept wondering how this could happen. How could any of this be real?

Of course, it wasn't. I died in the dream finally and woke up utterly startled. Only, I wasn't able to move my body. My body was old. It was clear I was on my deathbed. Giant windows in front of me showed that I was in outer space. Again, my mind raced in confusion. Aha! I finally remembered that I was probably still dreaming. Again, I did some reality checks, but they all passed. I felt my heart racing so fast that I was certain I would have a heart attack. And I did. As I lay there dying, I reached out an arm and begged for someone, anyone, to help. But I was all alone on my deathbed. Again, I experienced death.

I woke up utterly startled in this normal reality. Your reality. Our reality. I felt creeped out by those intensely vivid dreams, but I had to go to work, so I tried to brush them off. I went about my morning routine, showering, coffee, eating, brushing my teeth. All of it. I even watched some YouTube videos. Then I hopped in my car and drove to work. It wasn't until halfway there that I noticed the sky was an odd purple hue. I looked down at my hands and saw that they were longer than usual. I eyed my tattoo on my forearm, which normally says "Awake?", but it was all hieroglyphic-looking. I realized then that I was still dreaming. I pulled the car over and started crying. Will I ever get out? And even if I get out, will I ever know if I'm really out? I screamed at the top of my lungs, and then I woke up. Really woke up. At least, I think so. For all I know, any moment now things could unravel and all these years could have turned out to be a dream. In 5 minutes I might wake up and be 12 years younger. This is always a very real possibility for me. Especially as a person who suffers from bipolarism and for whom delusions are the norm, it is easy for me to become confused about reality. You wouldn't know it. I keep the really problematic stuff to myself or just between me and my partner. The alternative is to seem stark raving mad. But I will tell you now. This is all a dream. I don't mean you're going to wake up at the end of this life (though maybe you will). I mean this might as well be called a dream, because we don't know what it is. We don't know why reality exists, or what it really is, or where it's all going. We don't know anything. Nothing. We are like dream characters who confidently believe themselves to be real. But what does *real* mean? Can you prove the realness of your reality? Of course not.

Though *A Dream of Waking Life* is listed as fiction, most will be surprised to hear that it is not entirely a work of fiction. And it is not a work of nonfiction either. I went through a great deal of existential confusion and emotional turmoil writing this story. It is very much a story about me as much as it is a story about these characters whose lives I have become intimately involved with.

I hope you enjoy this story. I really do. It is something I've wanted to write ever since I had those series of vivid dreams 13 years ago. I hope this story makes you wonder about reality and yourself. I hope it thrills you and leaves you constantly guessing and wanting to know the truth. I hope it sticks with you long after you read it. But most of all, I hope it convinces you what is most important, regardless of whether or not reality is real or just a dream of waking life. I promise you, there is only one thing that matters beyond all else. I can guarantee it. I would stake everything on it. And I do.

There is only one thing that matters. Nothing else. Nothing.

Contents

A
Dream
of
Waking Life

1. Try Again

Viscous heaviness coursed through Matt, numbing his awareness with cloying, sluggish satisfaction. His mind was empty, but behind that emptiness lingered some great urgency. *No*, Matt demanded, wanting only the emptiness forever. The emptiness tasted sweet, even familiar somehow. Maybe he could linger...*maybe*, he thought. But Matt's senses were already pulsing with life again. The emptiness was filled by vividly lucid sensation.

Matt rolled over and pressed the naked skin of his back against a cold, steely floor. He let it sting with an icy pinch and absorbed his surroundings, forcing himself to remain calm for the sake of caution despite franticness stabbing his mind's periphery from every direction.

A handful of people moved about casually like hulking shadows, towering over Matt within a dimly lit, ten-by-ten-foot cubic cell. He let them loom, savoring the cold, metal floor sucking at his heat as if for sustenance.

Something warm wrapped itself around Matt's shoulder. He turned and was met by the unreasonably serene grin of a slender, naked woman. As she pulled her hand away and nodded sweetly at him, Matt instinctually tried to place her sharp Eastern features to a specific country, but he came up blank. Her lips were pleasant curves asking to be kissed, and Matt was suddenly taken aback by his overwhelming attraction to this woman he'd never met before. There was something else too – a familiarity about her that filled his heart with a heaviness not unlike sorrow.

With jarring abruptness, the reality of his situation injected itself into Matt's awareness. "Where the fuck are we?" he heard himself say, his heart quickening with appropriate rapidity for finding oneself locked naked in a tiny, dark cell with strangers. "Who –"

1

Before Matt could ask more questions, the woman knelt and put a hand on his shoulder again. She displayed her open body as casually and innocently as a toddler. She didn't seem to take notice of Matt consciously covering his genitals with both hands.

"Everything'll be all right," she said with enrapturing warmth, stealing Matt's breath. She had a slight accent, but at least she spoke his language. He hoped the others did too.

Why don't they seem worried? Matt wondered anxiously. *Are they the ones that brought me here?*

The woman's lips were so close to his own, and in response, Matt felt his body and mind galvanize against the shock and confusion of the present moment. Just by staring deeply into Matt's eyes, the woman somehow steadied his heart rate and slowed his breath to a pace that filled him with overwhelming calm.

What did she do to me? Matt wondered nervously. Her cherry lips widened, and he couldn't help an intense craving for her.

I don't even know this woman or what the hell is happening! Matt scolded himself harshly, feeling even more lost for experiencing such misplaced lust given his predicament. Yet the feeling would not relent. Her every feature was like a siren song beckoning him to breathe her very presence.

Stop it! Matt demanded of his mind. With jarring terror, he realized in that moment that he had no concrete recollection of his past. He racked his brain, desperately trying to recall something about himself other than his name, but his mind could provide nothing outside of racing confusion and the constant threat of his heart exploding out of his chest. It was the woman's presence, somehow, that kept Matt's fear from overwhelming him.

Who is she? Matt pleaded, certain that he must know her somehow. But she was a stranger like the others.

It's like I'm a stranger even to myself.

The woman rose and walked to the others, all of them naked and preoccupied. They were illuminated by a single dim light source at the base of the far wall. Matt watched with cautious intrigue as a well-built man with flowing, black curls cascading over an intricate, dazzling peacock tattooed across his entire back stretched at the hips and flexed his wrists in tight circles. In awe of the man's nearly tangible aura of

2

strength, Matt turned and was even more impressed by an olive-skinned, giant of a woman seemingly made of pure muscle and covered in scars and patches of burnt skin, squatting up and down, up and down, breathing rhythmically and forcefully like the exhaust of an overworked furnace. Beside her, a colossal man with skin as dark as the shadows of the cell performed slow, methodical pull-ups, one after another, using only his fingertips and a small steel ledge jutting from a high portion of the wall that Matt couldn't have jumped to even if he tried.

"Loki's awake. He seems...weird though," Matt heard the lithe yet delicate Asian woman say to the others.

"That's just Loki," the peacock-tattooed man explained casually with a thick Indian accent. The others nodded in agreement as if those three words explained the entire situation.

"What the fuck is going on!?" Matt demanded. He pulled himself up but kept a hand over his genitals in a futile attempt to retain some dignity. The others took no such actions, appearing to fully accept their predicament.

The serene woman offered a gentle smile and walked toward Matt. She cupped a hand around his shoulder and said, "Everything will be all –"

"– No!" Matt interrupted and waved her hand away. The overwhelming attraction he felt for her was replaced by a measure of disgust.

Is she toying with me? Matt wondered seriously. He analyzed the others with equally grim suspicion. *Is this all their doing?*

"What the hell do you want!?" Matt barked, backing away until his back finally hit the wall behind him. He desperately attempted to place these people, but he was certain he didn't recognize any of them. The single light was pointed directly at Matt, and he stood agape, shivering in the darkness as silhouettes stared back at him, a naked and horrified spotlit man.

"Tell me!" Matt ordered, balling his fists with mounting fear that not even the beautiful woman's smile could totally assuage.

"Shut the fuck up!" the large black man growled back. His accent was African of some sort, though Matt had no idea which country or tribe. *These people are from all over the world. They all speak English, though,* Matt noted, unsure how that might help him.

The monstrous, scarred woman smirked. The tattooed man openly

3

chuckled. But the Asian woman looked concerned for Matt.

"No, something's not right, Igwe," she said to the large man. "He's...strange, don't you think?"

Igwe shrugged his boulder-sized shoulders and went back to his methodical pull-ups. As he lifted his great mass, his arms exploded with vein-popping musculature. Each of the minor connective muscles was bigger than both of Matt's biceps combined. He was almost cartoonishly hulkish.

"What do you think, Putch?" Igwe said, offering a nod to the scarred woman who was nearly as massive as him.

Putch grunted neutrally, never breaking from her squats.

"What about you, Kartikeya?" Igwe asked with an obvious air of jest.

The tattooed man pulled at a tip of his finely sculpted mustache and yawned obnoxiously. "He's probably toying with us," Kartikeya concluded simply. "Mu can't help worrying about us. He knows that." Kartikeya turned his attention to Matt. "Why you messing with Xiwangmu? Huh, Loki?"

Matt shook his head. "You're all confused. My name is Matt," he urged, certain only of his name and the ominous, misplaced attraction to Mu that he was forcing himself to ignore for the sake of surviving this nightmare. "I'm...I'm not supposed to be here." A moment of silence, then the others burst into laughter.

But Mu wasn't laughing. She looked at Matt disappointedly. "I hope you're not messing with me," she lamented.

Matt gawked at these naked people, like anachronistic warriors stripped of their time and clothing and then tossed into a fathomless bin. He tried desperately to recollect how he got here, but his mind kept coming up blank.

"I need to get out of here," Matt ruminated aloud.

The wall to Matt's left and the group's right began to hum with activity, and a small red light at each end of the wall popped to life.

"Damn, Loki, right on cue," Kartikeya purred, rolling his R's with captivated amusement. "The show's about to start."

Igwe, Kartikeya, and Putch turned to face the wall. Igwe pushed to the front while the other two took a synchronized step back. A second red light was illuminated at each end of the wall directly after the first,

4

moving toward the center.

Mu offered Matt her hand. "Come on, we should take our positions behind the others."

Matt pulled back like a scared field mouse. "What's going to happen?"

Mu offered a half-smile. "Something really is wrong, isn't it, Loki? I can tell when you're just joking around, even if the others can't."

A third red light was added to each side.

What happens when the lights reach the center?

"Please," Matt pleaded. "I have a terrible feeling. We need to get out of here. You understand me?"

It was as if Mu was totally accepting of whatever fate might befall her. "We'll do our best," she offered sweetly.

Matt lunged and grabbed her shoulders in desperation. "Please!" he tried, unsure what else to say. There were too many questions and too many unknown variables. *And they think I'm toying with them?*

"We have to stay positive. Okay, Loki?" She calmly grabbed his hands with hers and whispered something in a language unknown to Matt, filling him with tranquility inside and out. Suddenly the shadows of the room felt comforting rather than menacing. Another pair of lights appeared at either end of the wall, nearly at the center now, but his panic had totally subsided. Worry threatened to rear its ugly head but was immediately subdued by Mu's voice resounding in his mind like a songbird's dulcet mating melody.

"What did you do to me?" Matt whispered through a fog of calm.

She smiled wide and kissed him with her eyes. "Everything will be all right, Loki."

An ominous, single bellow like a blood-filled war horn shook the room from all sides, and a pair of yellow lights appeared instead of red.

Matt wanted to demand more answers, but Mu's intoxicating calm kept him debilitatingly fulfilled.

Mu turned while still holding Matt's right hand with her left, leading him to a position behind the others. It was clear she was intending to use their massive, powerfully built bodies as a shield for...something, and Matt was meant to do the same.

Another pair of yellow lights jumped in front of the last.

"Come on!" Igwe roared, and he slammed his fists like iron war hammers against the humming wall.

"There is time enough for death, Igwe," the normally silent Putch announced playfully.

"Fuck death. Life is my mistress," Kartikeya practically sang.

Death. Death. Death. Matt repeated to himself with a feeling of dread in the distant background of his mind.

"Death is coming," Matt whispered, uncertain if it was better or worse that Mu's words allowed him to experience only a fraction of the overwhelming fear bubbling in his brainstem.

The other four nodded in placid agreement. "It always is," Mu confirmed softly, and her sweet smile forced Matt to look away.

Is she a psychopath?

"You're all insane!" Matt yelped as a spurt of internal dread escaped his lips. "This is insane!"

Again, the bellow resounded through the cell, threatening to consume them.

"Here we go," Kartikeya said, flashing his teeth with excitement.

Putch licked her lips. Mu breathed deep. Igwe rumbled with impatience.

A single green light appeared at the center of the row of lights, and in a flash the wall lifted to reveal a towering figure twice the size of Igwe and a whole story larger than Matt. Its featureless, matte black skin shone sinisterly in the single light of their cell. Its limbs were long and wrapped around its torso like braided rope around a neck, and each hand held a perceptibly sharpened blade.

"Fuck!" Kartikeya cried, his excitement suddenly replaced by contagious fear.

Behind the figure, Matt saw a giant room the size of a hollowed out skyscraper. Endless cells lined the walls of the dark hollow, some of them open and others still closed.

Matt gritted his teeth and fell against the wall, his legs giving out completely.

Igwe roared and charged at the giant figure, battering his fists against its body, but his sledgehammer fists bounced uselessly against what might as well be thick titanium. Putch and Kartikeya dove in to help, but their jabs and kicks and punches looked to be hurting them more than the towering figure.

The figure's red eyes opened, and in an instant its blades swung round and eviscerated the three warriors' flesh, vaporizing them like a gale through fog. Matt felt his bladder empty down his legs. He moaned, unable to actually form words.

Why? Please! Why? His mind fluttered erratically.

Mu closed her eyes and uttered the first few syllables of a chant before the figure removed her head cleanly from her body. Her body slumped, and her head rolled directly into the light. She stared pleadingly at Matt as blood drained from her severed skull, lips still chanting their enveloping warmth.

Wait! Matt thought just as a blade pierced his forehead.

2. The Procedure

A torrent of air forced itself down Matt's throat, and he heard himself gasp desperately with rasping heaves.

"Help!" he cried miserably from an all-white hospital bed. Still gasping for air, Matt forced his eyelids, heavy like lead, fully open and gaped frantically about the room. Fresh white sheets clung to his paralyzed legs, and beyond his bed, a plain white wall lined with large windows was all that separated Matt from the star-filled void of outer space scintillating with an unnaturally dense spray of luminosity.

I'm in space? Matt gawked in a terrible panic, realizing now that he couldn't remember how he got here or even who he was beyond his own name. He turned his neck left and then right, hoping and searching for someone who might be able to help him. An infinitely curved corridor, identical in nature across its entire observable length, extended on both sides of Matt. Behind him, an assortment of office-looking doors lined the wall.

I'm alone, Matt gawked in horror, and then he suddenly remembered the towering figure and the woman's sweet smile and the spray of blood and the blade passing through his brain. He reached for his forehead but stopped short when he saw the skin of his arms.

Old! Old! Old! Matt repeated madly in his head. His arms were littered with clustering liver spots, and his skin sagged helplessly on his withered frame.

"Someone!" Matt pleaded, and he noted with horror that his voice was that of an old man. "I need help!" Matt heard the old man say once more, and he painfully forced himself to accept that the voice was his own.

Tubes and wires and braided cords of endlessly varied gauges and colors grew like exotic follicles from Matt's sagging upper arms, and he followed them weakly to find them attached to a hulking machine behind his bed that blinked and flashed and strobed with numerous hues. Indecipherable text streamed across multiple monitors.

A door opened to his left, and a shapely young woman emerged and began jogging toward Matt. She wore a traditional nurse's uniform, all white, along with a white mask that covered her entire face below the eyes.

"Mr. Willish!" she called, visibly distressed by Matt's state. *At least she knows my name*, Matt noted with a spoonful of relief amidst total confusion.

"Help me!" Matt called back, uncertain what he should say. *I...had a bad dream? But that was more than a dream. And...I don't know what's going on.*

"Where am I?" Matt croaked, his voice strained by oppressive age. "What's happening?"

The nurse nodded knowingly and stroked Matt's head compassionately. "Everything will be all right."

She removed a syringe from the front pocket of her uniform and uncapped it. "This'll put you back to sleep, don't worry," she said with serene calm despite Matt's hysterical state.

"No, I don't want to go back to sleep!" Matt explained with frustration, "I don't know what's happening. I'm an old man!"

The nurse pulled back, hesitating for a moment as she seemingly processed Matt's warning about his age. *How can you not see I've turned into an old man!*

Her concern turned back to sweetness. "I see. That's very good, Mr. Willish. The procedure is coming right along. You just need to go back to sleep, and then we'll keep going with everything."

Matt reached out to grab at her uniform and demand answers, but his arm was too weak for any more movement.

"There, there," she said, patting his head as she injected the contents of the syringe into one of the dozens of IVs hanging from the machine behind him, all of them snaking into his veins, ravenously consuming him.

"Please!" Matt repeated once more before his mind finally submitted to sweet release.

3. Home Base

M att woke in a flurry of limbs and gritted teeth and screamed out, "Please!"

But he had his own voice, not the old man's. He wasn't in a cold cell with naked strangers either. He was back in his bed. Back in the real world.

Just a fucking dream, Matt assured himself, but he didn't feel any of the relief normally associated with returning to reality from a nightmare. The dreams about the cell and the old man – they weren't just dreams. They couldn't be. They were as vivid as reality – in the case of the old man, maybe even more so.

Matt touched his forehead and inspected his arms. Everything seemed to be in place.

"It was a fucking dream, Matthew," he told himself aloud with an authoritative tone, forcing the words into the deepest recesses of his unconscious awareness. He often felt like his mind was a battlefield to be conquered, only it was himself with whom he was locked in eternal battle.

I remember that, Matt realized with relief, remembering that in his dreams, he couldn't recall anything outside his own name.

Attempting to soak in what should be his familiar apartment, Matt suddenly paused uneasily, noticing an air of foreignness weaved into every detail of the room.

This is my apartment, isn't it?

He looked at his hands, checking to make sure they looked normal. It was a reality check he hadn't used since attempting to lucid dream as a kid.

He inspected them carefully, but they were just normal looking hands.

Knock it off! Matt told his mind, unwilling to do battle this morning. His right hand instinctively probed a small night table and came up with an empty prescription bottle.

My meds! Matt remembered finally. *I ran out. When did I run out?*

Matt looked for a date on the bottle and found one at the bottom.

February 10. 30 pills. Serotel. 100 mg.

The name of the drug didn't sound familiar.

What's the date today? Matt looked around for a phone or calendar to check, but again he felt a surge of foreignness, as if this were some makeshift simulacrum of his actual room. The bigger problem was that he couldn't fully remember how it was supposed to look or even feel in the first place. He considered that maybe his own memory was the simulacrum, and he felt suddenly like an invader in his own reality.

What the fuck is going on? Matt ruminated at the threshold of panic, gritting his teeth harder as his legs went as numb and heavy as the old man's from his dream. Then it came to him in a flash: the cell with the naked people – he remembered now. It was his game...*the* video game. *Room Reaper* was soon to be the most popular game on the planet. It was Matt's game. He was an indie video game developer. He was poised to make millions. He lived in Chicago. He worked in an office. He lived alone. He had a therapist.

Yes!

Matt rejoiced at the rush of memories finally filling in the necessary details of his life. *I need to go back to Dr. Heron. I need more meds. That's right*, Matt told himself. *Everything'll be all right.* He remembered that both the naked woman, Mu, and the nurse had said those words to him. His mind centered on Mu, focusing on her lips and nipples.

Enough! Matt scolded himself. *Get out of bed. Go to work.*

He remembered the empty bottle, and he wondered forlornly how long it had been since he ran out of pills.

Few days at most, he reasoned with nervous skepticism plaguing his every thought.

Swinging his legs over the side of the bed, he saw his phone lying on the ground. Grogginess still filling his eyes, he picked it up and tried to turn it on, but it was dead.

Shit! I must've forgot to plug it in.

As he plugged his phone into the open charger, something across the room caught his eye. Beyond his dresser, a *Room Reaper* poster signed by his coworkers practically buzzed, beckoning his attention. All the characters were there, posing with illustrious armor and intricate weaponry. Igwe stood at the vanguard, his raised fists covered by gauntlets emitting lightning. Mu crouched just beside him, black filigree patterns painted across her skin and her armor like flowing water connecting her to the ground. She held a hand close to her face, displaying sharpened kunai between each finger. Putch stood apart from the rest of the group and brandished a giant, misshapen boulder carved into a makeshift bat. Kartikeya hovered above the group with spread peacock wings while brandishing a spear multiple times the length of his body, pointing it at the viewer as if he was about to charge at them. Behind the entire group was a small figure wearing a cloak of shadows. Only his eyes could be seen, like tiny spotlights in an infinite void.

Yes, Matt sighed with a measure of relief as he absorbed the familiar faces of the poster. *I just dreamed of my video game. Just a dream!*

Below the poster was a photo he took with his father at a beach when he was a kid. They were both smiling at the camera, and Matt couldn't help staring at the young man in the photo.

Is that really me? Matt was reminded suddenly of the Serotel. *I'm not even recognizing myself*, he thought, tightening his grip on the prescription bottle still held in his left hand.

Call Dr. Heron! Matt ordered himself.

He tried his phone again, and now it had just enough juice to power on. The phone stirred to life, and its welcome message asked, "Are you awake?" Matt chuckled to himself with grim humor as he continued to shake the vividness of his dreams and false awakenings from his mind. *Maybe I should get back into lucid dreaming and try exploring those dreams,* Matt pondered seriously, but the thought was forced out of his mind as soon as it entered, replaced by the jarring realization that he would be late for work if he didn't get a move on. The phone said it was already 8:00 a.m.

He swiped at the screen and pressed the calendar app. The date glared insanity at him, leaving Matt blinking in confusion. *July 24. No — that's not possible. The Serotel was prescribed in February. There must be a more recent bottle around here. That has to be it,* Matt reasoned as his breath skipped a beat. *No way I've been off the meds for that long.*

He felt his heartbeat quicken and a flush of sweat fill his pores. Was it possible that multiple months had already gone by?

Matt checked his head with his fingers and came back with a smear of red.

Blood.

He raced to the bathroom and peered anxiously into the mirror. Sure enough, there was a small gash on his forehead. All of a sudden, he saw the giant figure behind him through the mirror, its twisted arms and death blades like flesh-rending hurricanes. Falling back and screaming as the blade lunged at his forehead, Matt felt a flow of blood force its way out of the wound. Then the giant figure was just gone, and Matt was once again alone in his apartment.

Fuck! Fuck! Fuck! was all Matt could think as he stood and rinsed away the blood. *It's just…just a hallucination,* Matt reasoned in his mind. *I just need meds,* he assured himself unconvincingly as he applied pressure to his head with one of his bathroom towels. The blood seemed perfectly real, as did the searing pain emanating from the gash.

Psychosomatic symptoms, Matt probed in a weak attempt at objective rationality, trying to calm his shaking hands and breath. *Or maybe I cut my head in my sleep somehow. Or…*

Matt pulled the towel back and looked in the mirror. His mind staggered as he saw that the gash didn't look as bad as it did only a few moments earlier. But the gash was still deep enough to warrant a single stitch, and though it was bleeding profusely, he knew that head wounds always bleed worse than they actually are.

It'll be all right, Matt told himself, wondering suddenly about the fate of those naked people in the cell. *Are they really dead? Will they be there if I go back to sleep?*

He thought of the beautiful Mu and the way she had openly displayed herself to him. *Will I see her again?*

No! Matt grabbed his head. *Stop it! A dream. Just a dream!*

"It was just a dream," he told himself aloud, shaken suddenly by the youthful sound of his voice.

No, he remembered. *I'm not an old man. I'm me. I'm me!*

14

He lifted the towel again and jumped back in shock.

No gash. Not even any blood.

Just get more meds. Matt urged himself, feeling dizzy with confusion as he let the unstained towel fall to the floor.

But first go to work, another part of his mind urged, clawing him away from the obvious psychological break he was currently experiencing.

Work will have to wait, he weighed, considering that he might only be a liability at work while undergoing an episode.

An episode, Matt considered, ensnared by the terrible familiarity of the word.

This has happened to me before, Matt realized with dread. *And I need to get back on my meds.*

He forced himself to return to his phone to call his therapist or even an ambulance if that's what it would take to get more meds. The phone remained lifeless as he attempted to power it on, and he looked down to find that the cord had fallen out somehow.

Fuck! Matt groaned, but then he recognized in that moment that everything seemed normal. *Maybe I'm okay enough to get to the office and just call my therapist from there*, Matt considered, doubting every word of his thoughts. But as he breathed, the world seemed clearer, and something inside him assured him that he would be all right.

Biting his lower lip, Matt eyed his phone one last time before leaving the apartment without it.

I'll be all right, Matt urged his mind. *I go to the office. I call my therapist from there. That way no one will worry about me.*

The bus stop was at the corner only a few buildings down. As he walked to the corner, a wave of relief washed over him; he felt like his world was finally returning to him as if from a haze. The dreams had been so jarring and vivid, and having two right in a row like that made the experience truly horrifying – like he would just keep waking into endless dreamscapes, each one more varied and strangulating than the last.

Maybe I'm still dreaming. The thought fell into his mind like a precision bomb aiming right for the heart of his psyche. He checked his hands, but they were still his normal hands.

Maybe my hands just happen to look normal because I'm in a dream of waking life. He felt his heartbeat quicken again, and his head pulsed with phantom pain.

How can you ever really know for sure? His mouth went dry at the thought, and he felt sweat build in his armpits and palms. He scratched an itch at the base of his nose and tried to hum away the possibility that he was still dreaming, but it was no use.

Shit! Matt scolded himself. He tried to recollect the other reality checks he used as a boy.

A light switch, but there was no light switch around.

A clock, but there was no clock nearby. He searched frantically with his eyes and through his memories.

A wall! Matt tried to push his hand through the brick edifice of the wall he found himself leaning against. It was as solid as any old brick.

That's two, Matt confirmed. *That's two reality checks. I'm awake. This is real.*

He hoped pleadingly that he wasn't falling into a new cycle of psychosis.

Or maybe I'm in it now — knee deep in an episode of insanity, Matt thought in horror once more. *Yes, that has to be it. And Dr. Heron is the solution.*

Get to work. Check in with everyone. Call Dr. Heron. It'll all be all right, Matt thought, treating the words like a handhold for his mind to grasp for survival.

As Matt arrived at the bus stop, his eyes looked among the others already waiting. A bearded man spoke lovingly to his little girl; an old woman held a phone unsteadily as she scrolled through a series of pictures. A teenage boy nodded his head to a beat that could be just slightly heard over the din of slow traffic. Everything was so normal — these people and their activities. The simple joy of these people living their lives while waiting at a random bus stop in a random city of the world filled Matt with an unquenchable but ineffable longing. Something about these people...it just seemed right. It was as if every moment of the universe had conspired to create this singular moment, and Matt got to observe it — he was a part of it. He imagined that there were these scenes and moments all over the world happening all the time, and he breathed deeply, reminding himself again that this was the real world and not a dream within a dream.

The bus turned a corner and screeched to a halt. Matt let the others get on first, then made his way into the vehicle. He reached into his pocket and then realized he didn't have his pass on him. He opened his wallet, revealing that he didn't have any money on him either.

"I'm so sorry," Matt started saying as he brought his eyes level with the bus driver. A large woman with a scar stretching from the left side of her forehead to her right cheek stared at him with surprise. Then she furrowed her eyebrows and looked him over head to toe inspecting him. Matt, on the other hand, recognized her immediately.

But that's impossible, Matt told himself, wavering again in his certainty regarding reality. It was the woman from the cell – the one called Putch. Here she was overweight instead of rippling with muscle, but the rest of her was identical.

"Do I know you?" the bus driver asked, her voice identical to Putch's down to the Brazilian accent.

Matt shook his head, uncertain of what to say.

"I don't think so," he lied uneasily, telling himself it couldn't be a lie if it only happened in a dream.

She'll think I'm crazy if I tell her the truth. I...I am crazy!

"I'm...I'm positive I know you from somewhere..." she said, trailing off despite her claim of certainty.

Matt wanted to say something clever or anything at all, but he couldn't even bring himself to move.

"Let's hit the fuck'n road, lady!" a passenger barked from somewhere in the back, and a murmur of agreement from various other passengers followed.

"Come on then," the woman told Matt with a disappointed sigh, but she offered him a half-smile. "It's okay just this once."

Matt hesitated, uncertain what she was referring to. Then he remembered he was still holding his empty wallet as if intentionally displaying it to her.

"Oh, oh, yeah," Matt stammered, and he looked away suddenly to avert her gaze. "I mean, thanks," he said finally.

She cocked her neck back, indicating he should get on. Then she turned back to face the road.

Feeling suddenly old and heavy, Matt pulled himself through the bus using the backs of seats and avoided eye contact with anyone else. The bus rumbled into movement, and Matt finally arrived at an open seat. He plopped into the chair and kept his gaze to the ground, terrified that the passengers might look like the other people from his dream.

Look, damn it! Matt scolded himself. *You have to look!*

He finally looked up and scanned the passengers, but no one else struck him as familiar.

Shit! I need those meds. This is too much.

Matt gritted his teeth and held his eyes tightly shut.

Those dreams were too vivid, Matt ruminated. *That wasn't normal. None of this is normal.*

He wondered if the Serotel had ever made things better for him, but it must have, or else he wouldn't even have a job. Who could possibly live without being able to distinguish dreams from reality with absolute certainty? How long could the average mind withstand being deprived of its own existential validity?

I do have a job, Matt told himself with sudden uncertainty. He tried to think of his coworkers, but no names or faces came to mind. He could remember the office, at least how to get there and what it looked like. But he couldn't remember his coworkers now that he actually tried to.

When I see them, it'll all come back to me. It has to, Matt assured himself grimly, wondering if his memory would always be this patchy and hazy.

Matt consciously slowed his breathing to a steady rhythm and let his body rock with the bus's soft turbulence. He felt like he hadn't slept in weeks, and exhaustion filled every pore of his body as the bus's whirrs and thumps and rocking lulled him to the edge of sleep. Hypnagogia began to trickle into his conscious thoughts, and he saw a vision of the beautiful, lithe woman from the cell standing before him. She smiled at him, and he felt his own lips curl into a smile along with hers.

A chant formed on her lips in the same foreign language she had used in Matt's dream. Tangible calm flowed through Matt's cells, and he began to fall easily into a heavy slumber.

"Everything will be all right," she said just before Matt's mind slipped fully into unconsciousness.

4. Time to Play

M att woke in a slumped position, arms outstretched over his legs as if he were a deactivated action figure. He found himself back in the dark cell with the naked people.

Shit! I'm back here. I fell asleep on the fucking bus.

But this time Matt remembered falling asleep. This time he knew it was only a dream, though that didn't assuage the confused feeling that still lingered from his dreams to waking life and back to this dream.

I should warn them, Matt thought, remembering the giant creature that had pierced his skull last time.

"There's a giant homicidal maniac standing right outside that door," Matt warned simply, pointing to a wall indistinguishable from all the others without the count-down lights.

The others looked at each other and shrugged.

"Whole lotta killers out there, Loki," Igwe rumbled. "Same as us." The large man snarled with ecstatic expectation for the door to open.

"You don't understand." Matt laughed at the futility of convincing the others and almost resigned himself to the dream's inevitable course. "When that door opens, there's going to be a giant creature with blades standing there. It's going to slaughter us all in the blink of an eye."

"You think the Reaper is right outside already?" Mu asked seriously.

Putch grunted, discarding Matt's words without a second thought.

"Fuck does he know?" Kartikeya scoffed. "He's fucking with you, Mu."

Mu let her body sulk and twisted her lips in consideration. "Are you...messing with me, Loki?" she asked innocently, avoiding the use of slurs.

She was beauty incarnate; every one of her features was implemented and designed to nano-perfection, and Matt couldn't help feeling that he might lose himself to his desire for this dream woman.

She's only that beautiful because she's a character from a video game, Matt reminded himself. *My video game. And this is a dream.*

But the reality of his situation didn't stop his dream body from producing hormones of attraction. He felt an intense urge to grab her hand and bring her close enough to kiss, but the shadows and the smell of cold steel and the knowledge that he was about to watch her die and then be impaled by the same dancing, murderous specter stayed his body.

"It'll be right outside that door," Matt warned, desperately trying to keep calm and serious despite being the only one in the room focused on covering his genitals with his hands.

A red light came to life at both ends of the wall, and the immersive reality of his surroundings injected Matt with the sudden recognition that this felt far too real to be just a dream.

This is more than just a dream, Matt gasped inwardly. *This is...I don't know what it is. But I know it ends horrifically.*

Matt shuddered at the memory of being impaled by the Reaper's dancing blade.

I could just get this over with...or...

Matt looked about the cell with forced confidence, allowing the ink-black shadows to claw at his periphery alongside his tangible fear of death despite knowing none of this could be real.

Or I could try exploring this dream that feels so much more than just a dream.

He gulped at the thought of having to face the bladed demon on the other side of the wall, but his curiosity had to be satiated.

I have to know what's really going on. But I have to stay alive longer than the first few seconds.

"We should huddle up into one corner. Maybe we can trick it – make it think our room is empty," Matt offered.

"Coward," Igwe rumbled, and Putch grunted in pleasant agreement.

"It's not a bad idea," Kartikeya said, his eyes never leaving the lights on the wall. "If we want victory, we should gain it by any means."

Putch rumbled in consideration, and Igwe gave a half-hearted shrug.

20

"It's a coward move. But so be it. I'll leave the strategy to you, Kart."

Kartikeya winked at the large man, and the group walked over to Matt's side of the cell.

Mu slid her hand into his and hugged his arm gently against her torso. Matt gripped back and audibly gasped at the warmth of her skin.

"I think it's a great idea," she whispered to him as the others laughed over some grotesque taunt at death. "Might as well be safe."

The alarm bellowed a single note, and a set of yellow lights appeared. Mu gave his hand one last squeeze, then let go. She began chanting her words of magic, injecting resolve into her party. For Matt, it had a calming effect, and for the fighters, it gave them strength and fearlessness.

Thank you, Mu, Matt thought genuinely as he felt the fear fade from his every nerve; the welcoming softness of her palm was now the only thing on his mind.

Another pair of yellow lights appeared, and the group huddled closer to the inside corner.

The alarm bellowed a final time.

This might work, Matt thought with an ounce of actual hope.

The green light appeared. It was time to play.

The door lifted instantly into the ceiling, and the group pulled back against the wall in unison.

Kartikeya couldn't help peering around the corner, but Putch elbowed him back against the wall.

"Damn it, Loki!" Kartikeya said, pushing away from the group. "You were fucking with us the whole time?"

Matt shook his head, nervous to leave the fickle sanctuary of the corner, but the others were already breaking away from him to find that there was no Reaper standing outside their cell.

Mu looked betrayed and glared at him for just a moment, then let her gaze fall away just as fast.

"I swear I thought it would be out there," Matt said.

The dream is different, Matt thought, unsure about the implications. *Why did I expect it to be the same?*

He wished he could convince Mu that his warning had been genuine, but it was no use.

"We've wasted enough time," Igwe announced. "Let's start looting."

The others jogged out of the cell, leaving Mu and Matt to themselves. Mu cocked her head for him to follow.

"Something's weird about you, Loki. I can tell when you're just messing with us even when the others can't," she mused.

Matt nodded with equal frustration and relief. "I wasn't lying, Mu. Last time the Reaper really was out there."

Mu furrowed her eyebrows in consideration. "Last time? What do you mean?"

Cries of battle and desperation resounded from somewhere distant, injecting urgency into Mu and paralysis into Matt.

"It's out there," Matt said, and the thought of a blade passing easily through his skull made him audibly yelp.

Just a dream! He reminded himself, but everything felt perfectly real. There was no slowness or vagueness or detachment like a typical dream.

He held up his hands and did a reality check. They looked perfectly normal. He pushed against the cell wall, but it was perfectly solid. It was all exquisitely detailed – maybe even more real than the real world.

No! Matt insisted to himself. *It's just a dream!*

Mu smiled serenely and uttered a few words, returning feeling to Matt's legs. She took his hand and clasped her fingers through his. "The Reaper is always out there," she said. "Always."

She pulled him away from the wall, and together they ran toward the others. He felt totally unable to resist her.

As they ran, Matt noted that the expanse outside the cell felt remarkably familiar; he was the lead designer after all. A cubic area measuring two miles on each side was partitioned into hundreds of smaller cubes measuring an average of 100 feet on each side. The walls of the larger structure and smaller cubes jutted seemingly forever into the sky, disappearing in an area of impenetrable darkness two miles overhead. The smaller cubes were aligned so that they formed straight or zigzagging streets filled with blind spots.

Matt and Mu jogged down one of these streets as they caught up with the others, passing countless open and closed cell doors. Weapons and armor lay in wait behind the closed cell doors while the open doors represented cells from which other players had emerged. It was almost comforting to remember so much about the game, and Matt felt invigorated that the whole of his memory might return to him once he went back on his medication in the real world.

This is real, a detached part of Matt's mind demanded he accept, and though Matt's senses agreed, his rational mind knew better. Attempting to nullify his mind's insistence that this was no mere dream, Matt reminded himself of the game's mechanics. *Every cell has a chance of containing varying equipment to help us survive against the Reaper and other players,* he recollected as if from a rule manual. *The objective of the game is to be the last survivor, no matter how close to death. A torso could win as long as it was still breathing.*

You see? Matt insisted to himself. *This isn't real. I can't be inside my own video game. That's not possible.*

"Come on!" Kartikeya urged from fifty feet away, breaking Matt from his thoughts. Kartikeya, Igwe and Putch stood outside the doorway of another cell lined with golden lights.

Mu's eyes lit up with exultant excitement.

"You found it!" she gushed at Kartikeya.

Putch grunted, and Kartikeya shrugged. "She found it. I'm just here for the spoils."

"Hurry up, Loki!" Igwe grunted, looking up and down the expanse for others. "We won't be this lucky for long."

Matt hurried toward the door, but he couldn't place the meaning of the golden lights.

"What is it?" he asked. In response, Mu soured and shook her head.

Putch flashed her teeth and grabbed Matt's neck with scorpion-strike quickness. "Open!" she demanded.

What do they want from me?

"I don't know what you want!" Matt told them, pleading with them to believe him so that Putch would release her indomitable grip.

This is real. This feels real.

Grunts and shouts of battle could be heard from somewhere in the distance, followed by screams and yelps of horror.

No! This is a dream. This is just a fucking dream.

"Kill me!" Matt told the group. "Just kill me and be done with -"

"- just open the door, Loki!" Mu said pleadingly from outside Matt's field of view. He was still being held immobile at the neck by Putch.

What do they want? How do I open it?

"How?!" Matt pleaded. "Just tell me how!"

Putch grunted and threw him to the ground. Mu and Kartikeya shook their heads in disappointment, but Igwe offered him bellowing laughter.

"I respect you, Loki," Igwe said. "You laugh at death. But damn are you an asshole."

Igwe opened a tiny panel in the wall just beside the door that Matt had overlooked in his disorientation. There was a keypad and number pad below a monitor with text that asked a single question: *Are you awake?*

There were more screams from somewhere distant, but this time they were ominously closer.

Matt shook his head. *Is it a riddle?*

He typed *yes* and pressed enter. The door's golden lights flashed a foreboding red three times then changed back to gold.

The others groaned, and Matt turned to see that Mu couldn't even look him in the eyes.

"He wants us to lose!" Kartikeya suggested coldly.

Blood curdling screams resounded so closely that the group could hear the ensuing spray of fluid against steel with each of the Reaper's strokes.

Igwe shook his head. "Bastard," he said, and he stretched his arms wide, preparing to wage battle without weapons against an invulnerable enemy.

"What am I supposed to say? 'No?' I mean, how else can you answer that question?" Matt urged.

"You know we can't see the question, Loki," Mu said grimly, likely already thinking of the best chant to help her group just accept their inevitable death.

"We should at least start running," Kartikeya suggested. "This fool won't open the door. We might still evade the Reaper. We might still win."

Matt shook his head and input the answer *no*. The door flashed red three times then remained red.

"Motherfucker!" Igwe shouted at Matt.

Am I awake? What was I supposed to answer? Riddles on doors — that wasn't part of my game...

The others, including Mu, abandoned Matt and ran fifty feet away to a cell lined in green lights. Igwe hit the cell door, causing it to lift on its own.

Matt forced himself to join the others, expecting the whole time that the Reaper would turn a corner and pounce on him in a heartbeat, but the screams seemed to be getting further away.

We evaded it, Matt told himself through a veneer of comfort that didn't even last a heartbeat. *For now.*

The others hastily equipped themselves with armor and weapons lying in several heaps within the cell. Unable to totally dispel his fear and accept everything as a dream, Matt hastily rummaged through the items haphazardly strewn alongside the others. Matt found a cloak large enough to fit Igwe, and as he wrapped it around his body like a makeshift robe, Kartikeya went directly for a thin javelin that was more like a child's toy in his grip. Igwe fitted his fists with what appeared to be brass knuckles. Putch inspected a large wooden bludgeon. Finally, Mu chose a satchel filled with throwing knives.

The others moved methodically in the foreboding silence, but Matt couldn't help a nervous shaking in his hands as he frantically searched for a weapon of his own.

"Any weapons for me?" Matt asked, feeling silly now for caring so much about being naked as death inevitably hunted them down one by one.

"No," Igwe announced simply. "Besides, what do you care? You won't even do your job."

My job?

"Opening cell doors, you mean?"

The others shook their heads in disappointment, still taking him for an insincere prankster named Loki.

"Let's go," Kartikeya announced. The others followed him down the hall, and Matt noted that none of the others had bothered to cover their bodies still.

"Why didn't any of you take the armor back there?" Matt asked as he tightened the cloak around his body in a futile attempt at security.

"What's the point?" Kartikeya called back. "It's not real armor. That cloth and leather armor is only for half-wits who care about aesthetics more than glorious battle."

Putch grunted satisfactorily.

Igwe stopped suddenly and held up a hand for the others to stop as well. They pressed themselves against the wall and listened, but Matt didn't hear anything down the corridor that Igwe was presently peering at with incredible disdain. Cautiously, Igwe took a step toward the edge of the wall to get a look around the corner. Another step and he was close enough to risk a quick glance.

He turned slowly to the others.

"Nothing," he whispered with a rumble. "I think we –"

A blade suddenly protruded from Igwe's open mouth, spraying the others with shockingly warm fluid. An arm whipped around the corner, pulling the blade out of Igwe with a sickening crunch. Then, as if toying with them, the Reaper took one long stride into the open just as Igwe's lifeless body hit the floor.

Matt braced himself.

Just a dream! It's just a dream!

But the sordid glint of fresh blood on impossibly sharp blades filled Matt with engorging terror, and he couldn't help but fall back against the wall, losing sensation in his legs and suddenly feeling anciently old. As he fell to the ground, he noted that the Reaper was covered in bloody gashes and tears from battle with other players, revealing that it wore a black suit and didn't just have black skin.

There's a living creature beneath that suit. Maybe it isn't invulnerable.

Kartikeya and Putch charged fearlessly forward, and Mu backflipped to Matt, throwing several knives directly at the Reaper's featureless head with perfect accuracy, an action that only angered it. She chanted words of strength that filled Matt with enough resolve to stand on his own two feet. The other two began hacking at the Reaper's bloody limbs, and Matt thought that the Reaper might even be slowing down. Then, in a flash, the Reaper went from tired to tireless and diced Kartikeya's and Putch's bodies into a crimson cloud of death.

"Run!" Mu screamed at Matt, and the Reaper dove at them with its hungry blades outstretched.

Just a dream! Matt thought, desperate to override his mind's insistence that he was truly about to die forever.

Just a dream!

He took Mu's hand and pulled her to him, holding her tight and wishing he could make this singular moment stretch into eternity. Embracing Mu felt like home – it felt perfect – and it could have been were it not for the two-foot blade that skewered both their brains at once.

5. Stuck Inside

His lungs clawed and scraped to fill their present vacuum, forcing a curdling yelp from his lips, but Matt was quick to silence himself. He lay silently in the hospital bed and stared at the scintillating stars outside to steady his mind and breath. He wanted time to look around — time to understand.

There has to be a reason this all seems so familiar — a reason this all seems so real. And my dreams, he realized, *they're clearly occurring in a cyclical pattern. Yes,* Matt told himself, absorbing his surroundings as his mind raced to process his existential predicament. *One dream leads invariably to the next. I wake up from the video game, then I fall back to sleep in the life of the video game designer.*

Matt nodded to himself. *Yes. I'm starting to remember.*

No! Matt shook his head and began to tremble.

This is the dream. The next world is the real one. This is still a dream.

But everything was perfectly real, and when he thought of the video game designer, it was so obvious that younger man wasn't actually him, but a reflection of who he once was.

No! Matt urged his mind. *That's wrong. I'm me. I'm me!*

"What is happening!" Matt demanded with a decrepit groan.

He heard shuffling to his left, but when he turned all he saw was the endless, curving corridor — windows and stars on one side, doors on the other. Matt stiffened his body and pretended to be asleep.

I need more time to think. I need to figure this out.

He saw movement in his periphery. It was a nurse poking her head out from one of the doors. She stared at him for a few moments, then, satisfied, shut the door and returned to something else.

Am I just a dream character, or am I the dreamer?

He glanced at his old hands full of webbed discoloration and naked veins. Except for being old, they seemed normal. He pressed against his bed, and that seemed normal too.

I'm not dreaming. But I did reality checks in the video game world too, and I wasn't dreaming there either. And it was the same when I woke up as the video game designer. If reality checks fail and a dream seems perfectly real — if they all seem equally real — how can I ever know which one is the true reality?

Matt tried to calm his breathing, but he felt claustrophobic and stuck inside his own mind.

Maybe all three worlds are a dream.

Matt gulped, not wanting to consider the possibility.

Or maybe all three dreams are real, he thought, uncertain which possibility was worse.

Matt swallowed hard and forced himself to try anchoring his mind to his current reality.

I need to get up — figure out what's going on.

He tried to lift his tired, time-worn flesh, but it was no use. He could barely hold his arms up for longer than a few seconds at a time.

So old, Matt gasped. *How much time do I even have left here?*

Just a dream!

The thought injected itself into Matt's awareness.

This is just a dream.

No! Matt urged, certain that couldn't be true.

This is the real world. Those other places are the dream. But that's exactly what the video game designer thought in his world.

His world?! Matt checked himself, volleying with his mind.

He is me. I am him. This is...this is just a dream...isn't it?

Matt audibly whimpered, unable to stifle his dread and confusion any longer.

"Help me!" he called out. "Nurse!"

He suddenly found the strength to lift his body high enough to look out the window in order to survey the land outside. But there was no land. There were only stars and endless black.

No! Matt revolted, unsure of the implications or why the infinite starlight filled him with such indelible panic and terror. Matt spun his head round. Directly behind him was a set of perfectly ordinary hospital doors with small glass windows.

No! Matt panicked again, foreboding and profound disquiet welling from deep within him as he looked through the windows.

Not that!

A world of ice and darkness raged silently outside the doors, tugging at eldritch fears within the deepest pits of Matt's being.

Matt experienced a snap of detachment and wondered at the intensity of his aversion to the icy landscape for just a moment before snapping back into the unfurling chaos of himself.

What is happening? Where am I? Matt probed like an imprisoned alien.

"Help me!" Matt screamed.

Multiple doors burst open simultaneously, and a platoon of nurses converged on Matt. They were all identical, right down to the most minute feature. Though he felt like he might be in hell, the nurses glided to Matt like angels, and he couldn't help feeling immediately calmer seeing them come to his aid.

They will help me, Matt assured himself with quivering fright. *Everything will be all right.*

"Mr. Willish!" the nurse at the head of the group called out casually as she came within a few feet of him. "You're awake again?"

Matt shook his head. "No, that's not the problem. You have to help me. I don't...I don't know where I am and I don't..." Matt stopped short, realizing what he was about to say: *I don't even know who I am.*

Matt began to weep pitifully.

I'm crazy. In every world I'm crazy.

One of the nurses uncapped a syringe while another two talked hurriedly among themselves. Another handful ran back to their respective rooms with looks of concern.

"There, there," the first nurse said, patting Matt's head softly. "Everything will be just fine, Mr. Willish. This is all part of the procedure."

"Please!" Matt urged. "Make it make sense. Please tell me what's happening."

The nurse smiled from beneath her mask, and Matt imagined that the nurses might all be Mu, just with shorter hair. The rest of their features, at least those Matt could discern, were close enough.

"Mu," Matt pleaded. "Will you please help me?"

The nurse nodded to the nurse holding the syringe.

The injection flowed into his veins and reached his heart.

No! Not yet! I don't want to go back to the dream yet!

"Everything will be all right, Loki," the nurse said serenely, but Matt wasn't sure if it was his own mind or the nurse who said those words.

6. Her

A firm grip shook gently at Matt's shoulder, and he opened his eyes to see the scarred woman wearing a bus driver's uniform, shaking him awake with a look of great consternation.

"Lady, let the bum sleep!" someone demanded.

"You okay?" she huffed at him as she squeezed her large body between the seats to check on him.

No, Matt thought. *I'm not.*

But he said, "Yeah, fine," then lifted himself quickly to save her from the ridicule and shouting of other passengers.

"Sorry, I..." Matt started, but he wasn't sure what to say. He wasn't even sure where he was.

"I remembered your stop, so I just figured..." she said, struggling for the right words. "You just looked really out of it when you got on."

"You know me?" Matt asked, his heartbeat quickening.

"I remembered you after you got on, yeah. You used to take my route all the time. You always said hello to me. Then one day you just weren't at the stop anymore."

"You want me to drive so you can talk, lady?" a passenger shouted as the busload of people grew tangibly impatient.

She nodded to Matt and walked back to the driver seat. He followed along, avoiding eye contact with the other passengers.

Meds! Matt urged himself. *Call Dr. Heron and get a script for meds right when you get into the office.*

He felt better with a sense of concrete direction, but he still couldn't shake the disorientation of his current state.

Get the fucking meds.

"Thanks," Matt said again, almost calling her Putch. "What's your name?"

She blushed a deep crimson and smiled softly. "Fernanda," she answered, beautifully accentuating each syllable. "Yours?"

Maybe not her musculature, but her finer features — she's almost identical to the character in the dream. And she's identical to the character on the poster. I must have designed the character based on her…Yeah, that has to be it.

"Matt Willish," he said, hoping she might be able to mend some of the missing details of his life.

Her smile vanished and she cocked her head in confusion. "As in...Matthew Willish?"

"You do know me?" Matt checked. "I mean, beyond just being my bus driver."

The bus's groans were turning into an uproar. "We all know you, Mr. Willish!" a red-faced man called out with terrible anger. "Now get the fuck off the bus before I drag you off, eh?"

Fernanda smiled half-heartedly at Matt and nodded to him. "I'll see you around, uh, Mr. Willish," she hesitated, acting as if he truly was insane. She looked embarrassed and stared through the windshield, pretending to focus on something. She seemed to want nothing more to do with him.

What did I say?

"Sorry," Matt stammered as he dragged himself off the bus and onto the sidewalk.

Fernanda closed the door and accelerated away.

Through the open windows, Matt heard the uproar of the bus simmer back to murmurs. "He's one of *them*. The motherfucker said he's Matthew Willish," a passenger laughed hysterically with another. "Matthew fucking Willish!"

The bus clambered with wild laughter as it faded into the distance.

What the fuck.

Matt stood in place, trying to piece together what had occurred. His forehead throbbed, and he expected the bandage would already be damp with blood, but when he checked it with his finger, it seemed perfectly dry.

At least there's some good news, Matt thought. *Now, get to the office. Call Dr. Heron. Get your —*

"Mr. Willish?" came an elderly woman's voice filled with genuine surprise.

Matt turned to find a woman dressed in a formal suit standing like a guard outside the large, tinted glass doors of a polished skyscraper sparkling amidst other glass towers. The handles of the doors were golden and styled as an *M* and *W*, which merged together into a seamless symbol exuding power and luxury. The woman gawked at Matt as if she had just witnessed him return from the dead.

"Mr. Willish...is that really you?" She looked more horrified than surprised now as she visibly processed information in her mind that she found unsettling. "But I thought..."

She knows me!

"I'm sorry. I don't remember you," Matt admitted. "But...can you help me?"

The woman shook her head in complete bewilderment.

"Help you?"

"Yes," Matt confirmed. "I...I seem to have forgotten a great deal...and..."

She stared at him as if he were a compelling, exotic film.

"Can you help me?" Matt asked again.

Something isn't right.

She nodded finally, breaking herself of her stupefaction. "I don't understand, Mr. Willish. Or —" she gasped suddenly. "You're one of those imposters, aren't you? These fakes that keep showing up! You're one of them, aren't you?"

Her confusion transformed to vehement indignance.

"Shoo!" she ordered, waving him away. "Get outta here, you...you...you baddie! You cretin!"

Matt backed away, shaking his head the whole time.

"You don't understand," he tried to explain.

No! Matt corrected himself pitifully. *It's me who doesn't understand. Someone help me. Please!*

35

His mind reeled with anticipated madness, but he grabbed it back from the edge.

No! I'm not crazy. I just need my meds.

Matt pictured himself in the old office, sitting at his old tower computer in the RGB glow of numerous computer fans.

I can remember that, Matt rejoiced bittersweetly. He needed to get back there – back to normality. Back to reality.

He peered at the old guard standing between him and sanity and couldn't help a twinge of anger.

She thinks I'm an imposter at my own office? This is my office!

Matt walked confidently to the door, not giving the guard any opportunity to stop him.

The woman moved aside in seeming fear of whom she seemed to view as a crazed "imposter." She grabbed the radio at her hip and began warning someone of an intruder.

"This is my office!" Matt asserted with sudden uncertainty despite his previous surge of confidence.

This is my office, isn't it?

He pushed the heavy door open and walked into the foyer of a lavish building. Waterfalls and ponds and live plants and koi fish filled every inch of the room except for a single walkway covered in golden carpet, a set of elevators at the rear, and a reception desk at the center. Suspended multiple stories above the reception desk was a gaudy looking chandelier in the shape of the MW symbol. That chandelier alone must have cost a small fortune. The symbol was also displayed in front of the reception desk and again on the door of each elevator.

MW. Matthew Willish. Is that what the symbol means? He looked about the lavish room with newfound disgust. *Is all this mine? All this gold and luxury – is this my personal empire of dust?*

A young woman with a green ponytail and numerous piercings jumped up as Matt approached her. She wore a golden blouse of sequins and matching leggings.

"Mr. Willish," she gasped. "This is...you're alive!"

People think I died and just left behind all this? Matt tried to recollect his past and what she might be referring to, but the furthest back he could remember was the first time waking up in the video game dream. Everything else seemed so hazy still.

The woman from outside walked in and lifted her hand in warning.

"He's one of those imposters, Linda! The back room is off doing god knows what. They aren't responding. Call the police. I left my phone in the back."

"Alice. Good lord, woman. Calm yourself," Linda said, obviously familiar with Alice. "It's him, Alice. Just look at him," Linda confirmed with a streak of genuine relief. "You ever seen an imposter this convincing?"

Alice considered it. "Yes," she confirmed stiffly. "Poor Mr. Willish is dead, Linda. Dead! This man is insulting the great Mr. Willish's legacy."

The great Mr. Willish, Matt echoed inwardly with apprehension as he reexamined his wastefully luxurious surroundings. Few people in history ascribed the title of "great" could ever be thought of as genuinely great outside of things like conquest and power.

"Can you please just help me?" Matt asked Linda, clasping his hands together. "I need to call my therapist. I need my meds. I don't have my phone on me."

Linda didn't look at all suspicious and said in an excited rush, "Okay, Mr. Willish. Okay. Do you want to use my phone or...do...do you want to go up to your office? I just...this is just...just so unexpected, Mr. Willish. I hope you understand."

Matt almost laughed at the irony of her hope, but he just wanted this ordeal to be over with.

"I understand," he lied. "Yes, take me to my office. That'll be fine."

Alice threw up her arms. "He's an imposter, Linda!"

"That's enough, Alice. Mr. Willish has obviously been through a lot." She turned to him and offered a supportive grin. "Don't worry, Mr. Willish. We'll figure all this out. You seem...a bit off. Like you said, I'll take you up to your office, okay?"

"Sixth floor still, right?" Matt checked.

Linda blushed. "I can't tell if you're joking," she said, but the confusion on Matt's face must have been obvious. "You own the building, Mr. Willish. Your company used to rent out the sixth floor just a few

A DREAM OF WAKING LIFE

months ago, though. Maybe you're just misremembering?" she offered sweetly.

Matt nodded, unsure what to say.

Misremembering reality itself, apparently.

She brought him to the elevators and used a keycard to open the one at the center. They both walked in, and again, she swiped her keycard.

"One-way trip to the executive suites," she announced as if she might be an old-time lift operator. As the elevator ascended Matt's building, heading for the 81st floor, Linda glanced at Matt, and he could see a longing in her stare.

I'm rich, Matt thought with equal amusement and despair. *How? Did the game get big? Did I miss the release?*

He remembered that the calendar said it was July. *It's like I just wasn't here for a few months. Like I died, just like Alice said. Maybe...she was right?*

Matt thought of the old man suddenly and remembered his realizations.

Or maybe this is just a dream? No! Matt stopped the thought immediately. *No!*

"So…" Linda said, unsure how exactly to form into words whatever she wanted to ask. "What...happened exactly? Where were you, Mr. Willish – if it's okay to ask."

"I don't know," Matt said honestly.

Linda nodded herself into silence, taking Matt's honesty as an attempt to brush her off.

"Are we friends?" Matt asked, truly unsure since he had no memory of her or anyone else he worked with.

She giggled and hit his arm softly with her palm. "I asked you out for drinks, remember? You said, 'maybe one of these days when I'm not working my life away.'"

I don't remember that at all. Am I a fucking imposter after all?

"That's right," Matt lied. "We should do that some time."

Linda's smile disappeared in a flash, and she looked completely disarmed.

"Sure," she blurted. "I mean…yeah…I mean…that sounds great, Mr. Willish. I mean, Matt. Can I call you Matt?"

She likes me. I just asked her on a date. Fuck.

"You can call me Matt, of course."

She tried to stifle more giggles, but her bubbly excitement was overflowing.

She must be half my age.

"So, when should we…I mean…do you want to…err…I mean –" Linda stammered excitedly.

"Things are…crazy right now," Matt said, and Linda nodded rapidly to show her understanding.

"Of course, Mr. Willish…err…Matt, of course. I was just, I mean, I just wanted to see if –"

"Let me just get my life in order, okay?" Matt offered gently, not wanting to hurt her feelings but also not wanting her to be suspicious that he was one of the imposters Alice warned about.

"How did you know it was me, by the way?" Matt asked uneasily. "And not an imposter."

Linda scoffed at the idea. "Everyone's been trying to get at your fortune – even getting plastic surgery to look more like you. These last few months…well, anyway, it's not like they ever look anything like you. You're actually cute, but the imposters are always ugly old saps."

She glanced up at him to check his reaction to her compliment, but Matt couldn't help going silent and wide-eyed as he imagined swarms of others wearing his face as they each demanded ownership of his single identity.

"You okay?" Linda asked with concern.

The elevator slowed and finally came to a halt.

Floor 81.

The doors opened, and Matt turned to Linda with a smile, ignoring her question for both their sakes. "I'll talk to you soon, okay?"

She looked rejected and tried to say something more, but she simply said, "Okay, Mr. Willish," before the elevator doors closed.

I'll have to actually take her out for drinks now, Matt noted to himself, feeling terrible for leading her on.

But the meds come first, Matt thought with freshly mounting urgency.

The executive suite floor consisted of a short hallway with a head office at the very end and several offices lining each side of the hall. Plastered on every window was the *MW* symbol.

"Matt?" a familiar male voice asked with incredulous surprise. "Matthew?" he repeated with just as much disbelief.

Matt turned to see a group of five or six people in the first office to his left sitting around a large conference table. There were a few faces on laptops as well – people working from home or a different office. They all gawked at him in shock.

"Matt?" came the familiar voice again, and Matt pinpointed it to a well-built man beginning to droop in his middle age. He wore black slacks, a sky blue, button-down shirt with a pocket full of pens, pencils and a pocket protector, and a golden bowtie with a crimson *MW* at the center. His dark black skin stood out against the blue of his shirt. Matt traced the man's face and absorbed his hauntingly familiar features.

It was Igwe. Unmistakably.

"Igwe," Matt gasped, reeling at the unreality of seeing another character from his dreams and game.

The man howled with laughter and jumped out of his seat, pushing the others aside to reach Matt.

As the man approached, all smile and open arms, his real name finally came to Matt. *It's Chike!* Matt rejoiced. *I coded the Igwe character based directly on him. He's a good man. He started the company with me. We dormed together in college. We were childhood friends. This is Chike. Chike!*

"Chike!" Matt gasped with a childlike moan, and he embraced the giant man, feeling like he might sink securely inside him.

He can help me! Chike...my friend! He can help me, finally!

"I need help!" Matt cried, letting it all out now.

Chike recognized the seriousness of the situation and nodded at the others in the office to carry on without him. He closed the door and held Matt by his shoulders.

"What happened, Matt? I figured you just ran off to some island with a few hotties, ya know? The whole world thinks you died, though. What in the heck happened?"

"I don't fucking know!" Matt sprayed, tired of asking himself the exact same question without ever getting an answer. "I don't fucking know!"

Chike nodded hastily and walked with Matt down the hall, half-carrying him as Matt's mind throbbed with the bittersweetness of finding a familiar face amidst utter confusion.

Tired. Weak. Thin.

Someone opened an office door as they walked past, but Chike nodded to them that everything was all right. Matt heard the office room break into a flurry of whispers and gossip before the door closed.

Meds. I need meds.

"Come on then," Chike said, taking on more of Matt's weight.

Another office door opened. A man dressed in a leather jacket and a stylish button-up shirt featuring peacock-like, polychromatic geometries peered out. He wore a meticulously sculpted mustache and goatee, and his hair hung naturally about his head in lustrous, black, Adonis-like curls. His mocha brown skin shone with a supernatural aura.

Kartikeya! Matt gasped. *It's him.*

He looked at Matt in shock, then looked to Chike for an explanation.

"He just showed up," Chike explained hastily.

"But...what the hell, man!" Kartikeya demanded.

"Souvik, just help me, will you!?" Chike scolded the younger man.

Yes! I know him. Matt gawked as more memories flooded his still hollow mind. *Souvik. I hired him. He's a programmer. He looks like a fucking celebrity.* Memories of Souvik sleeping with every other woman in the office returned. *That's right. I was jealous of him. He's the best programmer there is other than me.*

"Souvik!" Matt said with sweet recognition.

"Matt! My man, I..." Souvik stopped himself and grabbed Matt's other arm.

The two men easily carried him to the single door at the end of the hallway. Chike opened it, and they brought Matt into an expansive, lavish room that was a near replica of the building's foyer: lavish gold and crimson carpeting, mahogany desk at the center, living plants and softly frothing pools of water filled with fattened koi, and the MW symbol everywhere he looked. The windows at the far wall looked out over the Chicago skyline, filling Matt with an intense feeling of déjà vu.

I've been here. I've stood at those windows. I've looked at and pondered that sky-line.

"I've...I've been here," Matt stammered to the others as they carried him to a small couch.

"I'm not sure you have, actually," Souvik said with uncertainty. "You disappeared before this room was finished. People were saying —"

Chike cut Souvik off with a forceful grunt.

"You found him?" a familiar female voice asked with painful incredulity. All three men looked to the other side of the room to see a petite woman sitting barefoot in lotus position on a crimson couch surrounded by ferns and daylilies and various other plant life. A butterfly fluttered from one frond to another as she unwound her legs and hurried over to inspect Matt. She wore a dark-purple sports bra beneath a slate denim jacket that only came halfway down her waist, revealing most of her midriff. Thick leggings made of a soft fleece material quieted her move-ment. Her black hair was shaved close to the skin on one side, but it cascaded freely down the other side. A small, high-quality diamond nose ring in her right nostril glimmered with the same spectral light of the three diamond studs lining the top of her left eyebrow.

"Mu!" Matt almost cried, desperate for her rejuvenating words of magic.

It's her. It's absolutely her.

She stopped short, seemingly dumbfounded.

"Did he just call me...?"

Chike nodded. "He's confused. He needs our help. Matt, that's May. You remember her, don't you?"

Yes. May! It's her! Matt nearly burst, tears welling his eyes as her beauty filled his blurred vision and her presence stilled his aching soul. She was like a blazing fire amidst arctic cold.

Her! Matt rejoiced as the memories returned all at once. *She's our mar-keting specialist. She was hired in the early days. I had a crush on her. I'm in love with her. I've been in love with her for years...maybe a whole decade. But I don't re-member the details. I don't remember our love — just the idea of it. How can I not remember?*

42

"I don't understand," Matt pleaded with them, on the verge of breaking down and crying. The room took on an air of steely darkness, and Matt was suddenly reminded of the cell from the video game.

"Honestly, bro, we don't either," Souvik said, looking at the others helplessly.

May strode to the phone on the desk at the center of the room and began dialing a number as if from memory.

"I'm calling his doctor," she said, seeming to force herself to remain calm despite her shaking hands.

All three men nodded in agreement.

"Dr. Heron! Call him!" Matt urged. "I just need my meds. I'll be fine if I can get my meds."

May nodded with understanding. "I know, sweetie. We're going to figure this out, okay. Everything will be all right."

Tears streamed from Matt's tightly shut eyes. His body started shaking, shivering with overwhelming convulsions.

"What's going on, bro?" Souvik asked, raising his hands with uncertainty.

"I don't know," Matt said through gritted teeth.

So tired. Weak. Frail.

"Yeah, this is May Anh. I work with him!" May explained, retaining her calm composure.

Chike gripped Matt's hand and stroked his forearm with brotherly affection. "We got this, Matt. Just relax, okay? We got you now."

So confused.

"He's here, yes! We found him!" May urged, breaking from her perfect calm.

"This is nothing, bro," Souvik said, nodding rhythmically and trying to keep his cool. "You're back. That's all that matters."

"I don't fucking know!" May shouted, all composure tossed away. "Just tell us what the fuck to do!"

Matt cracked a smile. *Yes,* he remembered. *May had a temper when something was urgent.*

May…

She hung up the phone and reached into her pocket. She removed several small baggies, inspecting each one carefully before confidently choosing one. "Help is on the way. In the meantime, this'll do the trick."

Matt's body was shivering intensely now. He felt totally stripped of life.

Help me. Somebody. May. Help me.

She removed a small blue pill from the baggie and crushed it with her thumb on the polished mahogany desk. Crushing the pill further with her manicured, unpolished nails, she finally lined the powder into a small ridge on her thumb.

"It's just some low dose Xanaxi. Snort a bit. It'll calm you down."

Chike pushed May away from Matt. "Are you crazy? He needs his meds, not drugs."

"Meds are drugs, Chike!" May insisted. "They're .25 milligram Axies. He's freaking out, man! This'll help him."

Chike shook his head in exasperation. "No! No drugs!"

Anything! Yes, anything!

Matt reached for her hand and brought her closer.

Both May and Matt looked to Chike for approval.

"Bro, I snorted, like, six times as much in one line at that Tokyo convention," Souvik told Chike. "He'll be all right with this amount."

Chike huffed with disapproval, but nodded at Matt to go ahead. Matt snorted hard, inhaling the blue powder, forcing it through the loose congestion leftover from crying beforehand. Coughing just a few times and wincing away the burn, Matt finally lay back and felt the room become lighter.

A rapidly increasing weight blanketed Matt in enrapturing warmth.

I need to let go. Shut my eyes. Just for a second.

He stopped shivering. His heart slowed to a state of deep sleep.

"It'll all be all right," May said, her words like a magic spell.

Or is that Mu? Am I dreaming? Am I awake? Am I...something else?

He wanted to know the answer, but a quicksand heaviness was bathing him in calm, whisking the worry softly away. He felt the silent darkness lick at his heels and fingertips, and then it enveloped him whole.

7. Perfect Darkness

Matt woke, as usual, with the cold steel floor pressing like a vice against his naked body. But this time there was no light source to illuminate the cell – only perfect darkness. With nothing to focus on, phosphenes fractaled across Matt's vision, filling the darkness with buzzing madness.

"Hello?" Matt called out.

"Quiet!" the unmistakable Igwe rumbled back.

"But what's going on, I –"

"*Shhh!*" someone sprayed, likely Kartikeya.

Matt remained silent, waiting in the perfect darkness for something – anything.

What seemed like several minutes passed, but the light never came on, nor did the count-down lights on the door.

The drug she gave me, Matt realized suddenly. *It knocked me out. That must have influenced the dream.*

Matt tried the group again. "Something isn't right. I think –"

"You don't do the thinking!" Igwe roared at Matt. "That's Kart's job."

Matt shrugged in the darkness before remembering they couldn't see him.

"This isn't how it normally happens. That's all I'm saying."

If everything is shut down, then maybe the Reaper is too. Maybe I can finally explore this place.

Matt squeezed his fists, taking in the realness of this reality despite it clearly being based on his real-life video game.

"Normally?" Mu asked sweetly, a bodiless voice in the darkness.

"Yes. This is just a dream. You're all just dream characters —"

"Shut up, Loki," Putch said with a voice like pressed metal.

Should have been obvious that would happen, Matt groaned to himself.

"Come on," Igwe said from somewhere in the cell. "Putch. Kart. Even Mu and Loki. Help me with the door. All of you."

"Think about it!" Matt jumped. "How do you even know there's a door there?"

There was silence, then, "Shut up, Loki." This time it was Kartikeya.

"Really!" Matt urged, feeling silly for urging dream characters to consider their reality. But it seemed like the perfect opportunity to test the dream's boundaries.

"Everyone knows there's a door," Mu offered, taking what the others perceived as obvious bait from the trickster Loki.

"Who is everyone?" Matt pressed.

"Us. And the others behind the other doors. What are you getting at, Loki?"

"But…" Matt hesitated. "Okay, let's put it this way. Where were you and all the others before you were in these rooms. Does it really make sense that you just appeared in this room like this?"

"Does it really make sense that we listen to you at all?" Igwe retorted.

Damn it! Matt cursed himself and the character the others assumed him to be.

"Just tell me!" Matt nearly shouted in the perfect darkness. "What do you remember before being in these rooms?"

Mu's unmistakable grip curled around Matt's shoulder as she bent down to whisper calming words into his ear.

"If you can't remember anything about your own reality," Matt winced and painfully whispered to Mu over her chanting, speaking more to himself than her, "doesn't it stand to reason you may very well be a dream character who just popped into existence in the dream of an unknown dreamer?"

Is that what I am? Matt pondered his own words as Mu's chanting finally calmed his nerves. *A dream character in someone else's dream?*

"The hell are you on about anyway, Loki? Dream character? The phrase doesn't even make sense," Kartikeya ruminated.

"The door!" Igwe bellowed. "We can deal with Loki's riddles once we find the Golden God Door and win."

Matt heard the others shuffle to a single point, and he followed.

"I'm just curious," Kartikeya said, exhausting his breath as he bent at the knees, attempting to manually lift the steel wall with the others. "What do you mean by that phrase? What other dream or goal is there but to attain victory?"

They don't know what a dream is. They don't sleep. They are dream characters, and they don't realize it!

"A dream is what happens to your brain when you sleep. It's something you imagine in your head and experience, usually without realizing it's a dream." Matt laughed to himself, knowing he was traversing a dead-end discussion. "But none of you know what sleep is, let alone dreaming."

Putch rumbled, considering Matt's words, then said, "I don't get it."

The others offered nothing in response, probably assuming he was toying with them, as Loki was apparently inclined to do.

Matt laughed stupidly to himself. *What am I doing? What is the point of this? Why is this happening?*

"Lift!" Igwe huffed. The others began lifting, and Matt did his best to help, though it felt like he and Mu were mostly just getting in the way.

The door moved a millimeter, then another.

"Come on!" Igwe cried, demanding the door open.

Mu hummed three enchanting syllables, injecting strength into all five of them.

The door gave way, shooting up into the ceiling once it was lifted a few inches. The open door unfurled endless darkness, though not perfect. A single dim, reddish light emanated from somewhere distant. None of the other cell doors were lit, and there were no sounds of others doing battle.

It's dead. The Reaper is dead!

"Is it just us out here?" Mu asked.

"Doesn't that mean we win?" Kartikeya said.

"Maybe," Igwe offered.

"Now what?" Putch asked.

"You all seemed to know everything about everything back in the cell," Matt said sardonically. "You don't know what happens when you win?"

He could just barely make out the figures of the others in the dim light now that his eyes were adjusting to the scant luminosity.

"You just win," Kartikeya explained.

"And then?" Matt asked.

"What *then*?" Kartikeya scoffed.

"Tell us," Mu said. "What happens, Loki?"

"Let's go," Igwe said, trudging toward the dim red glow without waiting to hear Matt's response.

The others began to follow, but Mu held back and kept to a slow pace with Matt.

"Server reset," Matt told her.

She shrugged. "What's that mean?"

A wave of frustration followed a surge of corrective recollection that she was just a dream character without a rudimentary concept of dreaming. Her ignorance wasn't her fault. Technically, as the designer, it was his fault.

"Never mind," Matt said, enraptured by her voice and the allure of her every movement.

"I saw you in the real world," Matt said, not caring that she was a dream character. He would have to settle for this, though he just wanted to talk to the real version of this woman whom he clearly loved and longed for but whom he had somehow forgotten about entirely.

Can you just forget about someone you love? Just like that? Is it really love, then?

"You were just as beautiful there, you know," Matt whispered longingly.

He could feel her beaming smile through the darkness like a vibrating, braided strand between them.

"You are too kind, Loki," she responded modestly.

Now you're going to try to make it with a character in your own head? Matt asked himself sharply. He didn't want to admit his excitement regarding

48

the possibility. She was simply so beautiful, even without being able to see her fully in the darkness. She was like an iron anchor of certainty in a torrenting sea of unknowns. She felt exactly like...*home*, Matt told himself, uncertain what it really meant.

Matt grabbed her hand and held it as if it were a delicate heirloom that could easily turn to dust outside his grip.

"If the Reaper is dead," he said, "maybe we can just stay here." Matt checked himself. "At least for a while. I don't want to be stuck in this dream forever. But...I just —"

He suddenly pulled her close, embracing her naked body against his own. He gasped at a fluttering in his stomach that was now permeating his veins and every cell of his body, consuming and reciprocating her warm touch. Tears streamed from Matt's eyes.

I know you. Matt gasped inwardly, though his mind was still a network of dizzying self-ignorance. *You're important to me. You're everything. How...how could I have forgotten?*

She hugged him back and offered a few friendly pats on his back before loosening her grip. Matt's shoulders dropped as he realized that none of the same emotions were inside her.

She feels nothing for me.

No! Matt corrected himself as they pulled away.

She's not her. And you aren't him — that video game designer. You're an old man on his deathbed.

"No!" Matt shouted as he pulled away.

I'm not that old man! I'm not! That's a dream! The real world is real! The real world is —

"Are you okay?" Mu asked, startled by his sudden outburst.

Matt laughed to calm her, but inwardly he reeled at his confusion.

Or maybe this is real. Or maybe it's all a dream.

"Sorry," Matt said, doing his utmost not to scream.

You need your meds.

No! That's a dream, Matthew. You're not young anymore.

No! I'm not that old man either! I'm me. I'm —

"Hey! Over here!" Igwe bellowed from at least a thousand feet away, his voice echoing ominously through the hulking, shadowy corridors.

Matt's mind halted and centered on Chike's voice.

Not Chike! Matt corrected himself. *This is just a dream. Just a dream. Just a dream!* he repeated over and over again, demanding his legs to move toward Igwe.

There may be something I can learn here, Matt hoped desperately. *There may be a way out of this...this madness. A way out of...myself.*

Mu bent low at the waist and waved for Matt to follow. Despite the emptiness of the room, she still remained cautious by staying low and running swiftly.

Matt followed her through the darkness, the shadows intensifying as they neared the light source.

Just a dream. Just a dream. Just a dream!

"We found something," Kartikeya announced jovially. He pointed downward towards the light. "Look."

Matt walked carefully toward a slab of golden metal lying beside a circular hole in the ground. Igwe huffed deeply, catching his breath from what Matt assumed was the removal of the golden cover from the circular hole. Peering over the edge, Matt couldn't help gasping.

No fucking way!

"What is it?" Mu asked, holding onto Matt for added stability as she craned her neck to look over the edge.

"My...office," he stammered, stunned by the level of precise detail. Directly below, the crimson carpet buzzed with supernatural energy, and the koi fish swam with frightful urgency. Even the plant life seemed on edge somehow. The only difference was the absence of a door to enter or leave; there was just additional wall space. On the grand mahogany desk there was a laptop with its screen open to an old-school DOS prompt. In front of the desk, in a lifeless heap, the Reaper waited like a sleeping bear in fruit-laden woods.

"It looks dead," Igwe said.

"But maybe not," Mu considered. "It might be trying to trick us."

"This is a strange cell," Kartikeya said.

"It's my office," Matt reiterated. "And if I can get to that computer, I might be able to...change things in here. Maybe."

Matt wanted to jump down, but the sight of the Reaper kept him paralyzed as it injected memories of violently dying into his consciousness. Dream or not, the experience of dying was still painful and shocking enough to make Matt think twice about jumping headfirst toward death.

Putch knelt down to the edge and shook her head at Matt's words, then let out a powerful huff before jumping down into the room. The others held their breath, all eyes on the Reaper.

It didn't move.

Putch lifted one of its rope-like arms and let it fall back to the ground.

"Dead," Putch stated stoically.

Igwe jumped down, followed by Kartikeya.

Matt offered to help Mu, holding out his hand to her, but she just smiled and backflipped gracefully into the room, landing directly beside the lifeless mass of the Reaper.

She lifted her arms in presentation, and Matt nearly applauded her landing. She smiled at him, catching his eyes with hers.

May...

Matt yearned for a woman he still could not fully recollect outside a few basic facts.

Mu kept her gaze locked on Matt, but her smile began drooping like superheated wax. Her mouth gaped open, and a torrent of crimson fluid spilled onto the identically colored crimson carpeting.

Mu's knees gave out as she fell, revealing a blade protruding from her head, which was attached to a snaking, elongated limb.

"Bastard!" Igwe roared, and the Reaper came fully to life at the same moment that the normal lights of the facility powered on.

The drug is wearing off! I took too long! I wanted more time with her, and now she's dead —

— Just a dream! another part of Matt's mind interjected.

But the whirling dervish of death below didn't seem at all dreamlike to Matt.

This is real! Matt urged himself as the Reaper stood fully upright, its head only a foot away from his own. Its skull looked human enough, and Matt saw the terrible creature for a moment as a suited slave to some worse master of its own.

"*This is just a dream!*" Matt shouted as the Reaper leered at Matt with its featureless, ink-black head.

The others had already been converted into a crimson fog of blood and brain and bone, their very essence indistinguishable from the original crimson glow of the office.

Matt breathed heavily, and he could taste the concentrated iron from the blood of the others.

This is real! Matt confirmed finally as the Reaper swung its arm in an elegant upward arc, piercing Matt through his open mouth and passing through his brain with incredible poise and purpose.

8. A Dream Within a Dream

C *alm*, Matt told himself as he woke from the dream. *Stay calm. They can probably see my heart rate from those offices.*

He kept his eyes closed and breathed steadily. He needed time to consider everything – to critically analyze his very existence.

This feels real, Matt considered. *But the middle-aged game developer sees his world as the real world, and though the video game character recognizes his world as a dream, his world seems perfectly real too.*

Matt gulped hard. *And when I go back to being them, I'll think back to myself now, and it will seem perfectly obvious that I'm just a dream.*

His heart rate threatened to quicken, but he willfully slowed it with his breath.

Breathe. Just breathe. I need to understand!

All three of these people...they are all me. They all seem perfectly real. But...I am me. I'm not those others. They're just dreams...

Matt opened his eyes momentarily, taking in the stars shimmering in mad defiance against the infinite darkness outside the windows.

When all reality checks fail, then what? When a dream is as real as reality, is it not true reality? The only reason we call reality real is because we can compare it to our dreams – the unreal – and because when we die, there's no coming back. So then, by that logic, the video game world can't be real. I can die there and come back. But that leaves me and the video game designer. Neither of us have died...as far as I can remember. Is that the only way to know for sure?

Matt couldn't help his heart rate this time. He looked back at the machine and saw a small yellow warning light flashing beside scrolling cardiography lines.

Do I have to die to know? Matt searched his mind, wishing it could answer him on its own accord.

He lifted his arms and let his eyes scan the length of an azure vein extending like a braided cord from wrist to inner elbow.

Am I the dreamer? Or am I the dream that wakes to being the dreamer?

He lifted himself onto one arm and peered through the windows behind him. A small distance separated the windows from what appeared to be a glacier wall of ice blocking the entire view of the sky from where Matt was lying. Between the ice wall and the corridor's exterior, a blizzard raged so violently that he thought he could hear the arctic gales, but then his mind would return to the near perfect silence of the infinite corridor, reinforcing that those sounds were all in his mind.

His eyes locked on something in the blizzard. There were figures out there. Other people. Two others.

Who?

Matt lifted an arm in an unlikely attempt to get their attention. To his surprise, they waved at him.

Are there really people out there? Or is this just part of my mind's corroded confusion?

Doubting the reality of people just standing and waving as an unearthly storm raged around them, Matt lowered his arm, and the figures did the same.

Will I ever know what's real? Matt begged his mind, but it could offer no reprieve from the chaos of ignorance.

"You're up," a nurse said cheerfully, approaching Matt without him noticing. "Let's just take care of that," she practically sang.

"Just...just give me a moment," Matt pleaded weakly.

"I'm sorry, Mr. Willish," she said with genuine-sounding regret. "You know we can't do that. You've got to remain asleep."

Asleep! So this is real! The other selves — they're just dreams! This is...the real world?

Matt thought of May and saw her in his head, walking toward him to offer him the powdered blue pill.

May...that means she's a dream? She can't be...just a dream.

Matt gasped, his chest pounding in protestation against the possibility.

"Tell me," Matt said evenly, not wanting to alarm the nurse into urgency as she worked slowly and pleasantly, preparing her syringe. "Is this the real world? Am I...awake?"

The nurse smiled with her eyes and placed a gentle hand on Matt's shoulder, imbuing him with supernatural warmth.

"I can only imagine how disorienting this must be, Mr. Willish," she offered sweetly. "But we're very close. "Doctor Heron thinks we're almost there. So, just lie back, okay? It'll all be all right."

"Doctor Heron?" Matt gasped as she injected the syringe into his IV.

My fucking therapist?

The nurse smiled with her eyes, offering only beautiful confusion.

9. Sanctuary

"Matthew!" someone scolded, jarring Matt awake. He twisted at the neck and absorbed his surroundings.

A man in his early fifties, just slightly older than Matt, sat across from him in an overly padded, black leather chair. He wore a black tweed jacket over a black shirt, black slacks, and black shoes – all black. Even his tightly cropped hair was black. The man stared at Matt through large black glasses with incredible disappointment – a look of *I told you so* spread across his scowl. Behind the man was a large abstract, black-and-white painting that looked like a giant Rorschach inkblot test. It took up most of the wall behind him.

"Did you nod off again, Matthew?" the man across from him asked with more disappointment.

"Dr. Heron!" Matt gasped, remembering the nurse's words.

Just a dream, Matt reminded himself. *I just need my meds.*

The thought strobed suddenly in Matt's mind, telling him this was exactly the sanctuary he'd been searching for.

"Meds!" Matt blurted out.

"Oh, we'll get to that," Dr. Heron assured him didactically. "You haven't even been taking them, Matthew!"

Dr. Heron seemed genuinely disturbed by Matt's behavior. There was something else in his tone too, an incredible anger from somewhere deep inside him.

Matt nodded vigorously, pushing away every thought that didn't pertain to the meds.

"I ran out!"

"Over four months ago!" Dr. Heron nearly barked, releasing a tendril of indignation from some fathomless pit inside him before collecting himself. "I'm sorry, Matthew. I am. I've just been so worried about you. Everyone has."

Matt shook away his observation. *Of course he's angry with me. I'm his patient. He's just worried. He can help me*, Matt told himself, basking in the oasis of the realization amidst his desertous despair.

"I'm confused," Matt began telling him, but Dr. Heron held up a hand for Matt to stop.

"Of course you are. You've been off the Serotel for what might as well be a lifetime."

"But —"

Dr. Heron shook his head. "But what? Why do you do this to yourself, Matthew?"

Matt shook at Dr. Heron's words, uncertain of what he meant exactly.

"My dreams," Matt began telling him, but again, Dr. Heron waved away his words.

"I'm writing you a new prescription of Serotel. I'm doubling the dose. Just for now. We need to get these hallucinations under control."

So I am hallucinating. There's something wrong with me. Has there always been?

"Am I crazy?" Matt asked him, unable to remember if there had even been a diagnosis at some point in his past.

How long have I been like this? How did I get here? Where are the others? Matt saw May in his mind. *Where is she?*

Dr. Heron finished writing the script, then answered Matt. "No, not crazy," he said simply. "Just chemically imbalanced."

Dr. Heron rose from the colossal black chair, allowing it to swing round and reveal the whole of the abstract inkblot. Matt imagined braided white cords overlaying a black background; then his mind shifted, and he saw the inkblot as fathomless black spills over a barren white background. He forced his eyes away from the painting, not wanting to lose himself in it.

Dr. Heron fished for something in his top desk drawer, then removed a bottle of Serotel.

"This will hold you over for at least a month," he said. "Here. Take one now."

Dr. Heron removed a single large crimson pill from the bottle. Terrible paranoia coursed through Matt's veins at the sight of the pill, and he had to use every bit of himself to stifle the sudden urge to run.

Something isn't right, Matt warned himself.

"Matthew…" Dr. Heron said, offering him the pill like a parent to a child.

"I'm just confused, I just –"

"I know," Dr. Heron confirmed. "That is exactly why you must take this pill, Matthew. This will help you."

Yes, Matt confirmed inwardly.

No! Another part of him shot back. It was the old man. *The medicine,* Matt thought in horror through the mind of the old man from the dream. *That's exactly what caused all this confusion, making me think my dreams are real.*

"I don't want it!" Matt shouted, standing in anticipation of some unknown threat.

"Matthew!" Dr. Heron ordered, furrowing his dark brows over his pitch black glasses. "You are in my care. Do you understand that? You signed over that power the last time this happened. I am telling you to take this pill for your own good. Do you understand me?"

"No!" Matt shouted back, half pleading. "This is just a dream!"

Just a dream, Matt told himself, now seeing the obvious unreality of this world with ease.

"I'm an old man. I know the truth!" Matt said, nearly laughing at the impossibility of it all.

Matt caught Dr. Heron's eyes, and his stare was like blades plunging through the depths of Matt's soul.

No! No! No! This is the real world, Matt realized. *The old man is the dream. This is real! The old man is the dream! He's the dream!*

"No!" Matt screamed, reeling at his own terrifying certainty just a moment ago that he was a dream character.

"I need help!" Matt cried to Dr. Heron.

"Take the pill for goodness sake, Matthew! Free yourself from this torment, will you? Take it now!"

Dr. Heron's words seemed to inject themselves into Matt, controlling him like a puppet. Matt felt himself reach for the crimson pill, grab it, pop it into his mouth, then swallow it.

No, you fool! Matt told himself as the old man. *This is just a dream!*

Matt fell to his knees and grabbed at his skull full of electrifying chaos, wishing he could just know for sure what was real.

Dr. Heron let out a great sigh as Matt began sobbing into his own open palms.

"You are already on your way to getting better, Matthew."

"What's wrong with me?" Matt asked solemnly as Dr. Heron gently lifted him back onto the couch.

"We've been over this, Matthew. We don't know. No one does. Some kind of schizophrenia. You disassociate yourself from reality, and you disassociate your dreams from your self-image. This time, though, you are displaying signs of amnesia."

"This time?"

"Yes. You go through cycles, as do most with serious psychological conditions. Fortunately for you, there is a medicine that works. You only have issues when you stop taking it. So, Matthew, why did you stop taking the Serotel?"

"I —" Matt began, but he still couldn't remember anything before the first time he woke up confused in the cell of the Reaper world. Sure, there were a few flashes from childhood — walking in a park, attempting to lucid dream, fishing with his dad — nothing concrete or profound, though.

"I really don't know," Matt admitted. "I woke up this morning from a series of nightmares, and when I reached for the meds, the bottle was empty and dated from February. I..." Matt trailed off, uncertain what to say.

"The obvious correlation is the success of your business. You stopped taking your meds almost exactly when you signed the deal with Congo-Rayo."

Dr. Heron offered Matt a moment to speak, but Matt could only shake his head in continued confusion.

"Who?" Matt struggled, unable to recall ever hearing that name before.

Dr. Heron cocked his head. "Okay. I admit, I didn't anticipate this level of amnesia. You forgot a few people's names and a few parts of your life the last time you stopped taking the Serotel, but this is different. You're forgetting basic facts of your life now. Do you understand what might happen if you stop taking your medicine again? Missing a day or two, okay, that might happen. But Matthew...this is serious! You forgot about the largest tech conglomerate in the world — who you signed a contract with." Dr. Heron let out another exhaustive sigh. "I can't imagine what might happen next time, Matthew. Do you understand?"

Matt shook his head. "No," he said simply.

Dr. Heron nodded gently. "Right. That's fair. Everything will come back to you in a few days, Matthew. As long as you stay on the Serotel. Do you understand? I'm going to be sending you text reminders to take your pill each morning. I'm going to need you to text back after you take it. And if I don't hear from you within a couple hours, I'll have to notify the authorities to start looking for you."

Matt nodded with grim acceptance. "Sure...okay, sure," he said, desperate for a reprieve from the madness. "I just want this all to stop."

Dr. Heron nodded with newfound understanding. "You really don't remember. Okay, I'll remind you. I saw you at the beginning of March, and you left my office after telling me you didn't need a drug to make reality make sense. And then you just disappeared. There were talks about holding your funeral. No one was really sure what else to assume."

Matt saw an incredible strain for emotional control in Dr. Heron's features.

"I'm sorry," Matt said, feeling guilty for making so many people worry. "I wish I hadn't done that. Because now I'm so confused. Now everything is...I'm just not sure what's real..." Matt shook his head, feeling like crumbling again.

This is a dream.

No! This is real! May is real. I'm real!

"I need something to help me fall asleep without dreaming while the Serotel kicks in," Matt said. "I can't do this anymore. I'm too confused. I'm just so —"

Dr. Heron held up a hand for Matt to stop.

"Not to worry, Matthew. We've been through this before. Take these."

61

Dr. Heron suddenly held three small white pills in his hand as if they had always been there, just waiting for Matt to ask for them. This time Matt didn't hesitate. He grabbed the pills and swallowed them.

"I'm not sure how you swallow pills so easily without water," Dr. Heron chuckled, and Matt felt strangely comforted by the grounded simplicity and familiarity of his words.

"Lie back, Matthew. Those will knock you out. I'll have your body-guards carry you back to your apartment and make sure you get safely to bed. Now's not the time to leave anything in your control. You just go to sleep."

Matt didn't even try to ask about the bodyguards he had never seen before, or why he still lived in his old apartment if he was supposedly a rich man now.

So tired. So goddamn tired. He wasn't sure if it was the sleeping pills or his panic, but Matt felt as heavy as packed mud as he sank slowly into the couch.

"Very good," Dr. Heron said, the giant inkblot directly behind him. The strips of black looked as if they were moving of their own accord, and Matt thought suddenly of the Reaper's wild arms flailing death at naked flesh.

No! I don't want to go back there! I don't want that!

"Go to sleep now, Matthew. No more dreams. This will knock you out."

Yes, Matt thought. *No more dreams. No more!*

No! Matt realized suddenly. *This is the dream. I'm an old man in some strange corridor. This isn't real.*

"It's okay," Dr. Heron said, curling his lips into a rapacious grin that bordered on evil. "They're all dead anyway."

"What…" Matt managed, but his mouth could barely move, and his vision was already blurring into darkness.

"Sweet dreams," Dr. Heron chuckled to himself maniacally.

That's just in your head, Matt told himself. *That's just a hallucination.* But Matt couldn't be sure.

10. There Is No Way Out

Spiraling vertigo coursed through Matt's consciousness like a chrysanthemum unfurling its thousand individual petals, depositing him onto solid ground. He opened his eyes and suddenly fell over before he even realized he was standing.

The sudden closing of bus doors directly behind him forced him stumbling back onto his feet. He turned to see a bus driving away, and he could just make out the oversized woman at the steering wheel.

He turned back to see that he was standing outside his office building.

How did I get here?

Matt probed his mind, desperate to recollect what had occurred between the therapist's office and this moment, but all he could remember was darkness.

At least I didn't go back to the video game dream, Matt noted hopefully. But that still didn't explain how he got here.

Matt reached into his pocket and found the full bottle of Serotel. He popped it open and looked inside the bottle, just to be sure. It was full of large red pills, and he sighed with tepid relief.

Now what? Matt wondered, looking up and down the street as if the world itself might offer an answer. *Back to work?*

He had his pills. He was back on track. He had a company to run. Matt nodded to himself, hoping against a torrent of doubt that as long as he kept popping a Serotel each day, everything would be all right.

Back to work then, I guess.

There was no guard outside the building this time, so Matt walked in without resistance.

"Mr. Willish!" Linda gushed, practically jumping to her feet.

Matt reached out a hand, not wanting to alarm her.

"It's okay, uh, Linda. Please, you don't have to get up."

She half-ran to him anyway, but Matt didn't break stride.

"I got the text, I mean, we all got the text that the other executives sent out."

Matt nodded, pretending to understand.

"So you're totally back, then? You're okay now?" Linda checked with genuine concern.

Matt offered her his most convincing smile as they approached the elevator, and she swiped her card, opening the elevator doors without him even having to ask.

"Mr. Willish, did you still want to, I mean, did you..." Linda said, struggling to find the right words.

"Drinks," Matt said, and Linda chuckled and rolled her eyes playfully.

"Sorry," Linda started, but Matt quickly interrupted.

"No, I'm sorry, Linda. We'll have to put it off just this one more time, okay?"

Her smile vanished and was replaced by a heart-rending look of rejection.

"Sure," she said simply.

She swiped her card again, giving him access to the executive suites, but she didn't ride up with him this time. The elevator doors closed without her giving Matt a second glance.

Idiot, Matt scolded himself. *Stop playing with the girl. Next time just tell her it isn't going to work out.*

Matt felt heavy suddenly, and he was forced to brace himself against the wall as the elevator ascended.

Get out! a voice said inside his head. *This is a dream! A fucking dream!*

"Shut up!" Matt said aloud to his suffocating mind. "Shut the fuck up!"

But the feeling wouldn't relent. The pill bottle in his pocket felt like barbed wire wrapped around his thigh.

The meds! the voice told him. *It's the fucking meds.* The voice was the old man, and the old man was Matt.

64

Get out of my head, you old bastard!

The voice didn't answer back, but a feeling of complete dread was deposited into him, diffusing across every cell of his body with each quickening beat of his heart.

Maybe this really is a dream, Matt ventured, trying out the thought as if to check its solidity.

He squeezed his eyelids tightly. *May isn't a dream,* he told himself. *Fuck you for even thinking that way.* He rolled his eyes at his internal blaze of emotion, remembering the heart-rending attraction and impossibly deep love he felt for May.

May's just your employee. You don't even know her that well, Matt admonished himself.

You don't know what you know, came the old man's voice.

He slowed his breathing, forcing his mind into the present moment. But, despite everything seeming perfectly real, he couldn't fully cleanse himself of the haunting feeling of unreality.

The elevator slowed then opened its doors to the executive suite hallway, jolting Matt back to reality.

Or maybe unreality, he reminded himself grimly.

He stopped, for he felt that if he didn't, his mind might suddenly give out. The elevator might suddenly drop. All the world might suddenly explode into a trillion scintillating fragments of nonsense.

"What is going on?" Matt asked the world and himself and everything. "I should be in a hospital. Dr. Heron...he..."

He's part of the dream, the old man's voice explained. But this time, Matt didn't strangle the thought into silence.

Maybe, he reasoned. *Or maybe you're just in my head.*

There was no answer, and as the elevator doors closed again due to inactivity, he felt a chill as the two sides of his body in the door's foggy golden reflection became one.

Are you in my head? Matt asked the old man. *Or am I in yours?*

Or maybe we're both inside the video game character's head, Matt considered even more horrifically. *Why not? Nothing makes sense anyway. So why not?*

Matt shook his head and let it fall into his open palm. He sobbed silently.

I just want to understand.

Peering into his past was like catching glimpses of burnt, grainy film of another person's life. He tried to picture his dad's face clearly in his mind, but the image kept contorting and shifting through an array of possibilities.

What about my mom? Matt wondered. *Siblings? Grandparents?*

It was as if the memories had been haphazardly torn away and every attempt to piece them together only fogged the scant clarity that remained.

Would Dr. Heron really let me be on my own if I weren't capable of being alone right now?

Matt realized that he still had no recollection of how he ended up in front of his building.

If I walk through these elevator doors, can I be sure I'll end up in the right place?

The thought made him almost laugh in horror. It was something only a lucid dreamer would think to consider.

I can remember that, at least, Matt noted with a trace of solace. *I used to practice lucid dreaming. I mean, I still do – I think.*

Just a dream, the old man interjected through a whisper.

I know, Matt admitted to himself painfully, breathing heavily against the horrifying implications. *Maybe this is all just one giant dream.*

Matt groaned into his palm and began wiping tears from his eyes.

The elevator doors opened suddenly, and Matt lowered his head at the sight of a man and woman wearing fine tailored suits standing side by side. They looked like upper management, but Matt wasn't sure if he had ever met them before.

"Hey there, Mr. Willish," the woman said uneasily, clearly unsure if he was okay.

Matt nodded and walked immediately through the door, hoping they would chalk up his insanity to eccentricity.

"Have a good one," the man called out to Matt, and the woman hushed him as they stepped into the elevator.

"He –" the man began, but the woman hushed him again, waiting for the elevator doors to close before the gossip started.

They think I'm crazy, Matt told himself before laughing wearily and admitting the obvious truth again and again. *I am fucking crazy.*

He walked straight ahead to his office. He didn't know what else to do. He didn't know where he could find answers, and he didn't know what answers he was looking for. He didn't know where to start or if any of it would ever end. He didn't know himself nor his other self nor his other self. He didn't know anything.

Matt opened the door to his office. It was just like the last time he was here, but also just like the dream. He couldn't help checking to see if May was sitting on the couch in meditation, but the room was empty, save the fountains, fish, fixtures, and a large desk with a single laptop on it. Just like in the video game dream.

He checked the door, half-expecting to see it replaced by a solid wall, but the door was still there. He looked above the desk and checked for the circular golden cover leading to the *Room Reaper* battlefield, but it was just drywall embedded with golden-hued lights.

Everything was perfectly normal, except Matt's mind.

He pulled himself to his desk through a swamp of fatigue and sunk into the oversized red leather chair.

Half his mind recognized the office with casual certainty, and the other half peered at the room of a total stranger.

He let the sound of the running water pierce and dilute his confusion with a forced calm, but his thoughts wouldn't relent.

Who even decided to decorate everything like this? Was it me? Did I do all this in February before I ran out of medicine — before all this madness? Will I ever be okay again? Was I...ever okay?

Someone was walking toward the office, so Matt opened his laptop in an attempt to look busy.

Three quick knocks broke the calming sound of running water, and Matt knew somehow that it was Souvik.

"Yeah. You can come in."

Souvik opened the door but kept to the side of it, hiding his body playfully. He peered into Matt's office with a huge grin.

"Hey, buddy! Back in action, huh?"

Matt nodded.

Don't act crazy, he told himself.

"Okay! Okay!" Souvik said cheerfully, treating Matt's silence as endearing. He strolled into the office and balanced on a single foot, pretending to nearly fall into the pond before easily correcting his stance. He took a half-seat on the end of Matt's desk and smiled wide again.

"You're feeling better though, right?" he said with seemingly genuine concern.

Matt nodded and glanced at the computer screen. There was a prompt. It said: "Are You Awake?"

Realizing he must have been the one who input the question, Matt's heart skipped a beat. He remembered giving the wrong answer when the Golden Door asked him the same question.

That was a dream! Matt had to remind himself. He quickly typed, "yes," but the password was denied.

Souvik forced some laughter under his breath and pulled an inch away from Matt.

"You still mad at me, man?" Souvik said with a crack in his voice. This was clearly his true purpose in coming to see Matt. He was seeking forgiveness for a past slight of some sort.

"I'm not mad at you," Matt said without knowing what he should be mad about. *Whatever issue we had is the least of my worries right now.*

Souvik nodded hesitantly and let out a deep sigh.

"I hope you're not just saying that, man."

Matt nodded absentmindedly and tried the password again. He typed "no," but the password was denied once more.

"Look," Souvik said, forcing Matt to finally give him his full attention. "I know you said you wanted to be left alone. We all got the text this morning. But...I just don't want bad blood between us, you know?"

Text?

"What text?" Matt asked nervously. He reached for his phone to check.

"You sent it at like 4:00 in the morning. You don't remember?"

He checked the messages. Sure enough, there was a group text sent to dozens of numbers at 3:52 a.m.:

"Thank you for your hard work. I ask that I not be disturbed until I send another text notifying you otherwise. Thank you."

No one had responded, though based on the content of the message, they probably just saw responding as an unwanted disturbance.

These people just listen to me. I shouldn't even be in charge of my own life, yet I'm responsible for dozens of other people?

He scrolled up and saw a message from Dr. Heron at exactly 8:00 a.m.:

"Did you take your pill?"

And there was a response from Matt that said:

"Yes, doctor, thank you for your concern. All is well."

That doesn't even fucking sound like me. Matt noted with horror. *It's like half the time someone else is in control of my life.*

"Anyway," Souvik continued, "I just…"

Matt let him struggle with whatever he was chewing on and tried the password again. In exasperation, he typed, "Imstuckinadreamwithinadream." The password screen faded to a standard-looking interface full of apps and file shortcuts.

Why did that work?

On the right side of the screen, there was an internet browser called *Rayo* open to an array of headlines from various news outlets all under the category of *Rayo News*.

"I feel bad about it, Matt. The whole thing. I feel fucking terrible, man," Souvik said finally, letting his words gush forth from some cavernous pit pooling deep within his mind.

Matt nodded, but his primary attention was drawn to the news headlines displayed on his laptop:

"Matthew Willish: The Elusive Billionaire Is Back?"

"*Room Reaper*: Your Guide to Class Selection"

"*Room Reaper* and the Man Behind the Global Phenomenon"

"Willish Enterprises Closes at All Time High for 80th Straight Day!"

The news was all about Matt and his company. The spotlight of the entire world was on him. *Room Reaper* was even bigger than he could have ever imagined.

Room Reaper spread worldwide. And I'm apparently a billionaire?

"Matt," Souvik lamented, "she's not into me, okay? She's into you. You hear me, man?"

Matt could barely discern his words. His full attention was now devoted to the headlines:

"#roomreaperislife Chirped by Over 1.2 Billion People in Single Day"

"The Golden God Door: What's the Secret to Its Secrets?"

"Analysts Say Willish Enterprises to Remain Bullish Through Third Quarter"

"Scientists Say *Room Reaper* Is Better Than Intercourse"

"Matt?" Souvik said, forcing him away from the news. "Okay?"

Matt nodded.

Souvik exhausted a heavy sigh, obviously not satisfied with Matt's answer.

"Come out with us tonight. May'll be there."

Matt finally perked up.

May...he felt that intense longing for her again. She was important to him somehow. She was...everything.

What does that even mean? Matt probed his mind, but all he could know for sure was that he felt an unnerving level of comfort just hearing her name.

"Is...she here now?"

Souvik's sad eyes widened, and his lips curled back to child-like glee.

"I knew it!" he said. "Is she why you came back, man? I knew you had a serious thing for her." Souvik reeled himself in and tightened up. "Sorry, that's...that's exactly why I'm sorry, you know, man?"

Souvik's words and facial reactions finally made sense, and Matt realized in a flash what all this was about. *He slept with her. That must be it,*

70

Matt noted, but he didn't feel any of the upset that Souvik assumed he must.

"May's her own person, Souvik. If she slept with you, it's because she wanted to," Matt told him sincerely, though he couldn't help wondering how May felt about Souvik.

"No, of course, man. I didn't mean otherwise. I just..."

Souvik shook his head, treading carefully with his words.

"I knew you had a thing for her, and I still went after her. And I'm sorry for that."

Matt nodded. "Okay," he said and then looked back at the screen in a subtle attempt to let Souvik know that he had more important matters to consider.

Like the validity of my own damn existence.

Souvik nodded back, dissatisfied with himself and the result of this conversation that he'd probably played in his head a thousand times.

Maybe it would be better if the other me took over, Matt thought. *I don't know the emotional dynamic of my own life. I don't know if I should really feel jealous. I don't know how I act when I'm...not me.*

"Okay," Souvik said finally, lifting himself off the desk. "Okay, okay," he repeated. "So you'll come out with us tonight?"

Matt shook his head, his eyes still on the computer screen. "I don't know. I...have a lot to work out." *At least that's not a lie,* Matt told himself.

Souvik nodded, offering visible understanding. "Sure. Yeah, that makes sense, man. I'll let you get back to it."

Souvik walked straight for the door, hesitated for a moment to speak, then thought better of it and opened the door.

He was halfway through the door when he said, "She's not here, by the way. May and Chike had to fly to Atlanta to check up on one of the pilot offices. Some run-of-the-mill stuff, but I guess it was important enough for them to check it out."

Matt nodded, and Souvik nodded back.

"Okay then," he said. "See you tonight, I hope."

Souvik left and closed the door with incredible care.

Matt placed his fingers on the keyboard and felt familiarity in its texture. This was his tool. This was how he could make sense of the world.

If there's any sense to be had, he noted with dread.

He began searching for information about the company and himself, filling his mind with data that must already be stored in the inaccessible recesses of his memories.

Matt was surprised to learn that over just the few months between his last bottle of Serotel and this one, the company's only game, *Room Reaper*, had become more of a global pastime than mere recreation. The game and its unparalleled ability to integrate a multitude of IPs into a single dynamic server spawned a new term: Grand Scale Maps. One article explained that tens of thousands of players competed on the same map in official tournaments while hundreds of thousands of players competed on the same map in unofficial tournaments that could last days or even weeks. Another article celebrated that if a team of five couldn't be formed, missing teammates would be replaced by some of the best AI the industry has ever seen.

A total of 3.9 billion people play Room Reaper, Matt gawked as the statistic filled his mind with profound awe. *That's nearly half the world.*

Matt performed another search and learned that the game cost only fifty dollars, but there were a multitude of payable cosmetic options for each character. Furthermore, it cost only a single dollar to try out for an official tournament, but if someone made it to the final forty thousand or so players, they had to pay an additional thousand dollars just for the opportunity to compete for the million dollar prize. Willish Enterprises held tournaments every single weekend.

That's pure exploitation, Matt winced. *My company is pilfering the pockets of half the world using a scheme that would make a used car salesmen squeamish.*

Matt continued reading and learned that *Room Reaper's* unexpected success allowed the company to go public, making Matt worth exactly $32 billion as of one week ago, though virtually all of it was tied to unrealized assets in the company's stock. Official reports anticipated that he would be the richest man in history before the end of the year.

I'm a fucking asshole, Matt gawked as he learned about the man he had become. *I'm exploiting the world. I'm preying on billions of people for…*

He looked around his office – at the fountains and gargantuan water-hungry plants and shimmering gold trim around every little feature.

I'm a grade-A asshole.

72

He felt dirty.

Am I really capable of being...this person?

He remembered having a small office. A small team. A small life.

Not this.

A folder on his desktop called *Patch Notes* flashed red, indicating that it had just been updated in real time. Surprised he could remember what the flashing meant, he clicked the folder and read through the recent issues and fixes released for the game. He absentmindedly scrolled through the patches, allowing his mind to wander.

Did I really do all this? If I'm rich, then do I really have bodyguards?

"There was a major issue with the servers last night, 07/25, around 23:00. But the issue has been resolved."

Should I be concerned for my safety? The whole world knows who I am...

"The issue involved a total disabling of all lights, along with the Reaper."

What?

Matt stopped to read the rest of the internal report.

"Servers continued to function otherwise normally, but only a single team of four NPCs and one player were able to access the servers.

"The player, who chose Loki, utilized a client-side program to mod the game on the fly. The player engaged the character Mu in a sexual manner before attempting to access the company's system files via a remarkably clever backdoor created when the player logged in to the server.

"Player is believed to be an experienced hacker. Admins, please be on the lookout and report any suspicious activity. The last thing we need is a horny little schoolboy programing prodigy throwing a wrench in the spokes of our golden wheel."

Matt tried in vain to keep his breathing even.

That was my dream. That was me!

His mind reeled at the possibility.

No! It's not just a possibility, Matt corrected himself. *I have the proof right here in the logs. The logs recorded exactly what I experienced in my dream.*

He expected the old man to interrupt his thoughts, but he was alone inside his head.

That might mean I can control the dream from here. Maybe I can program the dream from this desk.

That's actual crazy talk, Matt considered. *That's absolutely fucking crazy.*

But he couldn't deny what he was reading in the logs.

Matt took out his phone and texted Souvik:

"Are these logs about the hacker accurate?"

All Matt could do was stare at the phone. He wasn't sure which reality he preferred: the one where Souvik said, "What the hell are you talking about," or the one in which Souvik confirmed the accuracy of the logs.

Souvik texted back:

"Crazy shit, right? We need to hire the guy."

Matt turned off his phone and pushed it across the desk. It was like a vial of poison, and he didn't feel safe even holding it.

What does this mean? Matt urged his mind helplessly. *I'm dreaming myself into the game? Or there's some weird psychic connection happening? Or…*

He reached for the Serotel bottle in his pocket.

I'm just fucking crazy. I'm just fucking crazy!

But the logs said that he was perfectly sane. The logs proved that the world was crazy, and to be crazy in a crazy world – that seemed like sanity, or at least some form of it.

I'm not crazy. I just have to figure out what's going on.

There was another icon on the interface called *Source*. He clicked it.

Code streamed across the screen, unfurling the inner mind of *Room Reaper* into Matt's eager consciousness. Queries and commands and numbers and symbols were translated effortlessly by his mind, and rather than disjointed code, he saw, with perfect clarity, the impossibly complex yet brilliant intricacy of what he and his team had constructed.

It's fucking perfect, Matt marveled, probing his creation with a mind both perfectly acquainted and perfectly foreign to its landscape.

It's a masterpiece.

Concise, clever, efficient, sleek: the array streaming through Matt's consciousness was the programming promised land. The digital infrastructure they had written, synthesized, and parsed would be used as the evolutionary prototype of every digital species born in the future. It was as if they had created the very first cell in a chain of multibillion year evolution that would eventually grow into intelligent life.

This masterpiece is just the beginning, Matt marveled.

His eyes stopped when he saw the code constituting Mu.

It's May, he confirmed, seeing this woman he longed for, possibly even loved, in every little detail of the code that brought Mu to life.

I'm sorry, he told her in his head. *I have to make changes to your world.*

He knew what he had to do, regardless of the beauty of Mu's world. It might be the only way to know for sure what was real and what was only a dream.

I have to change things. I have to mar this masterpiece. I have to experiment.

Matt absorbed the code, surveying it like a satellite over an endless landscape. From satellite, he changed his perspective to that of a hawk, scanning the ground for its miniscule prey; he spotted the perfect place to start making changes. Smiling and diving at full speed, Matt felt free for the first time in as long as he could remember.

He burrowed and bounced and consumed and digested the digital world without any sense of final destination at first. Then he began to reform the digital world, atom by atom. His fingers raced to keep up with his mind. The outside world was no more; there was only code and this world of his own making. Time became a foreign construct, dwindling in the recesses of his consciousness and eventually disappearing altogether. He felt one with the digital construct, as if it were his own body he was exploring and altering.

He had to be careful not to change it too drastically – only just enough to make a difference, but not enough to kill it.

Yes, Matt confirmed to himself with a bleak stain of hope welling in his gut. *If this works and the system doesn't automatically revert to the last stable patch, then –*

"Matt!?" Souvik said, standing in the open doorway with a look of total surprise. "What are you doing, man? I've been knocking for like ten minutes now."

Surely ten minutes was an exaggeration, but Matt hadn't heard any knocking whatsoever.

"Sorry about that," Matt said, saving his work and closing the laptop in one swift movement.

"What are you doing, bro?" Souvik pressed again with a tone of worry.

"Work," Matt said simply. Souvik didn't push any further.

"You've been in here for ten hours straight, man. Or did you leave at some point without me noticing?"

Ten hours? Was it possible?

Matt turned and glanced outside the windows behind him. It was dark outside. He felt the sudden, intense urge to urinate, and his mouth became extremely dry.

I'm certain it's only been a few minutes since I started coding.

Time had been burnt away in an instant, and this wasn't the first occurrence.

He felt the bottle of Serotel in his pocket and reasoned that the medicine just needed time to really kick in.

Souvik waited for an answer, but Matt just shook his head, uncertain what to say.

"Well...okay," Souvik stammered, then shook his head and let go of his curiosity. "Anyway, you still coming out with everyone tonight?"

Souvik recognized Matt's hesitation and quickly noted, "She'll be there."

May...

Matt shrugged, not wanting to reveal his true feelings. "I might. Yeah."

Souvik nodded and offered Matt his classic wide grin.

"That's the best I'm going to get, isn't it?" Souvik laughed.

Before Matt could respond, Souvik held up a card connected to a lanyard.

"Linda said you still don't have a keycard, so here you go, man."

Souvik handed Matt the card. Matt grabbed it, but Souvik had something to tell him before he let go. They were connected through the

76

card, and Souvik demanded Matt's attention with his desperate eyes.

"I'm really sorry, man. Okay?"

Matt nodded easily. This *bro code* that Souvik clearly subscribed to was plaguing him at the very foundational levels of his being.

"Just let it go, Souvik. I'm okay with it," Matt told him sincerely, not caring how he actually acted when he wasn't in control of his own body.

Souvik nodded furiously to himself, hoping, despite his doubt, that Matt's words were authentic.

"Thank you, Matt," Souvik said with incredible gratitude. "Thank you, thank you, thank you."

He let go of the keycard.

"It's a block east of here. The place is called LaBerge's Dream Lounge."

Matt laughed inwardly at the twisted synchronicity of the bar's name. *Of course that's what it's called.*

"Hope to see you there, man."

Souvik still wore a subtle etching of self-inflicted pain at the edges of his being, but he visibly forced the feeling away and left Matt's office without another word.

She'll be there, Matt repeated to himself.

May…

He'd been disrupted before he could put the final polish on the changes he'd made to the game's source code, but it would be enough. The next time he went to sleep, he would at least have a purpose in being there. If the changes worked, he would know for sure that the video game dream was in fact a dream. And, he would also be able to gain access to the replication of his office they'd found last time.

If I can get back to that laptop, maybe I can make changes to the old man's world. That will at least prove I'm the real one. Then I won't have to, Matt gulped hard as the words slithered into his mind, *die to find out for sure.*

He felt an all-consuming rush at the thought of dying with no waking dream on the other side.

Matt pondered true death. He knew people killed themselves time and time again in the depths of mental illness.

Is this how it happens? Are some of them just trying to…wake up? Or is it only my fucked up mind that's like this?

Matt stood, and in the same instant, the lights in the executive suite hallway flickered off, leaving only dim bulbs to light his path back to the elevator.

Matt turned and peered outside the window, wondering if he could see the bar from his office. Even if he could, he was too high up to discern anything at the ground level.

May, his mind interjected forcefully. She filled his every thought, and he felt suddenly as if there were a braided cord connecting the two of them. The now tangible draw to her was so intense that he could feel exactly where that braided cord, extending from his chest to hers, finally ended.

So strong, Matt noted in horror. *This pull — she's everything to me. So how the fuck could I have just forgotten about her?*

Matt rose and breathed in the sweetness of the koi fish and the butterflies and the viridescent fronds of numerous technicolor fauna.

It was the very definition of tranquility, and yet it filled Matt with loathing.

It's an illusion, Matt forced himself to admit. *The truth is horrific, and all this does is hide it. The truth is…*

The truth is that you're dreaming, came the voice of the old man, and Matt felt his breathing suddenly constrict.

Get out, Matt told him. But he could still feel the old man somewhere in his consciousness peering at him with condescending pity.

You aren't even real, the old man told him.

"Get out!" Matt shouted.

The old man was gone suddenly. His office softened, and the tranquility it was meant to fill him with became more apparent.

The rush of water filled Matt's mind, blocking out the old man as if it were a powerful mantra.

Stay out, Matt warned him.

He breathed deeply and stepped into the dark hallway, leaving the crimson sanctuary of his office behind.

Each of his steps seemed to ground him, reminding him of the connection he could still feel tugging at his chest.

He swiped his card at the elevator, then waited as it ascended to meet him.

He stared at the *MW* symbol, and he felt it burrow inside him, forcing itself into each of his cells as it filled him with disgust.

I don't want it, Matt thought.

He closed his eyes and waited for the elevator. He didn't want to open them again until the doors parted and the symbol disappeared into the walls.

That isn't me!

He strained to breathe as he centered his thoughts on May. He could feel the tangible pull at his solar plexus. The elevator dinged at the same moment the invisible braided cord tugged at his chest so hard that he was yanked forward. Intense vertigo threw his mind into panic as he plummeted from the 81st floor into the pitch darkness of the empty elevator shaft.

No! his mind wailed futilely against the fall as an image of his broken body at the bottom of the shaft stabbed through every thought with strobing panic.

Matt clenched his fists and jaw, but his legs flailed wildly on their own. He wanted to scream, but he could only grunt in shock.

Then everything changed.

The darkness beneath him coalesced into a chrysanthemum-shaped, undulating, RGB-glowing field and immediately unfurled to reveal a quickly approaching sidewalk beneath glass towers and a placid night sky.

Just as he was about to hit the sidewalk at terminal velocity, Matt's speed slowed to a crawl without any inertia, and he was regurgitated from the darkness of the elevator shaft. His body rolled haphazardly onto the sidewalk, battering his limbs against the solid ground with enough force to bruise but not break.

He gritted his teeth against the pain and pulled himself onto a bench just a foot away. Lifting his head, he saw the bar directly across the street.

Fuck! Matt thought in total shock. He looked back at the place where he first hit the ground, but everything looked normal.

The chrysanthemum pattern that stopped my fall and brought me here — it felt

79

like I passed through something similar when I woke outside the office this morning, Matt observed eagerly, hoping the connection might elucidate precious information regarding his insanity. *Is that how I got from Dr. Heron's office to my office so quickly? A…chrysanthemum portal?*

Does that not prove this is a dream? came the voice of the old man.

He's got me there, Matt thought. *How can I possibly explain that away?*

Then he remembered. The message sent to all the other executives. And the message from Dr. Heron.

I didn't portal to my office this morning, Matt urged himself to believe. *I fell asleep at the doctor's office. My bodyguards took me home. I slept through the night and somehow sent some messages without remembering.* Matt winced at his memory lapse and wished desperately that his life would return to him from the void of amnesia.

Not remembering those messages could just be a side effect of the sleeping pills, Matt told himself, but the reassurance his reasoning brought him was like an anchor attempting to find the ground of a bottomless sea. *And this morning,* Matt continued, trying to piece together the jigsaw of his existence with only a few useless puzzle pieces, *the bus was driving away when I finally…woke up. I clearly took the bus to my office, not a fucking portal.*

Matt nodded vigorously to himself, forcing acceptance that the portal was a hallucination. Like Dr. Heron said, he was dissociating himself from reality. The portal was his mind, not the world. The world made sense. The world was normal.

It's me. I'm the problem, Matt accepted fully. *So what do I do?* he thought to himself, almost whimpering.

Laughter filled his mind. It was the pitying laughter of the old man.

Matt tried to shake him away, but he wouldn't leave.

I'm going to get to the control room in the video game dream, and I'm going to erase you, Matt told him.

The laughter stopped.

What makes more sense? the old man asked evenly. *That you're crazy? Or that you are simply a confused dream character inside my head?*

Crazy! Matt seethed. It was the only thing he was really sure of.

Then why aren't you in a hospital? the old man asked with a slap of seeming sorrow. *Should a person who travels randomly through flower-shaped portals really be on their own in the big world?*

I should be, Matt admitted, more to himself than the old man. *I should be in a hospital.*

Do you know where I am? the old man asked, this time with seemingly genuine condolence for Matt's condition.

"A hospital," Matt said aloud, and it suddenly made sense. The dream of the old man represented Matt's deep understanding that he belonged in a hospital until he could get better.

No! the old man scolded. *I'm not your dream. You're mine.*

A pang of dread torrented down the length of Matt's spine. He gripped the Serotel bottle in his pocket.

This will take care of you for now, Matt told the old man. *And over time, I'll get better, and you'll be extinguished from my mind like a forgotten thought.*

Matt felt suddenly resolute in what he would do next.

I'm going to see May. I'm going to tell her I love her. I'm going to apologize to her for everything – for myself. And then I'm going to a hospital to have you erased from my mind. For good.

Matt opened the bottle, removed three pills, then swallowed them.

Fool! the old man told him.

Matt smiled, though there were tears in his eyes.

You're in my mind, not the other way around. Now leave me alone. Hurry up and die, old man.

He could feel the old man shaking his head with profound disappointment.

Fool, the old man repeated, and then he was gone.

Matt sat there, relishing the silence for just a moment. He evened his breathing and focused on the air as it moved in and out of his nostrils. In and out. In and out.

Now I know what to do, Matt told himself. *Everything will be all right.*

"Hey," someone said, jolting Matt from his thoughts. "You okay, pal? You say you need a hospital? We saw you trip over there."

A man and woman stood over Matt with looks of incredible concern.

"You mean I didn't fall out of a portal?" Matt said with a smile, and he laughed at himself with incredible, freeing joy.

The couple realized that he was joking and laughed along with him.

"Okay, okay," the man said. "As long as you're okay."

Matt nodded and thanked them with his eyes. The couple waved and went on their way.

See? They said I tripped. I'm just crazy, Matt told the old man with an ounce of happiness, and he chuckled miserably at himself for even entertaining the voice in his head.

You'll be gone soon, Matt urged.

He stood and walked across the street to the entrance of the bar. A soft neon coursing glow from the small, innocuous *LaBerge's Dream Lounge* sign filled the air.

Matt's solar plexus throbbed with coursing energy.

She's here, Matt confirmed, butterflies filling his stomach and rising into his chest. They seemed drawn to the braided cord.

"Mr. Willish," announced a young man at the bar's entrance. "We've been expecting you."

The young man wore a tailored suit, fine gold necklaces and bracelets, and slicked-back auburn hair. He didn't look large enough to be a bouncer, but he made up for his size in presence. Matt could tell that his smile and frame were a facade hiding lethal danger just below the surface.

Maybe ex-military, Matt wondered.

"The others told you I'd be here?" Matt asked.

The young man just winked and opened the door for Matt. A trance beat could be heard in the distance, and the interior buzzed with a soft crimson glow, not unlike Matt's office.

The man nodded for Matt to enter and winked once more.

"Enjoy yourself," he said as he waved Matt through the threshold.

"Thanks," Matt said, genuinely thankful for the seemingly friendly face, despite the danger he had felt emanating from the man.

The bar reminded Matt of something that might actually be pulled straight out of someone's dream. A soft spray of roaming lights oscillated steadily between red, green, and blue hues, filling the air with an aura that reminded Matt of the RGB lights of his old computer and the terminal-like room he used to work in as a fledgling programmer — at least, that's what he felt to be true.

I still can't fully remember. It's just…a feeling, Matt thought, struggling with the right words. *I can't trust my mind.* Matt gulped with grim under-

82

standing.

Something floral and pungent filled Matt's nostrils and drew his mind back to the here and now. Matt traced the billows of smoke to their milky roots at the first table in front of him. A small group of people bobbed their heads to the trance music and lounged around an ornate, golden hookah at the center of the table, taking pulls of the floral smoke between smiles and nods. A large bulb hung above them and emitted a soft ochre light from a glass shade featuring a green field with numerous peacocks, their wings outspread. The birds seemed to be staring at Matt with incredible intensity, though none of the people at the table took any notice of him.

Matt's eyes darted left to a large oil painting of a blizzard-white ram's face in front of a solid blood-red background. The ram's eyes were the same blood-red as the background; it was as if they had been removed by the artist as an afterthought. A pair of eccentrically dressed people wearing swami-like robes sipped mixed drinks and took no notice of the ram staring straight at them.

On the far right, a man and woman with near-identical cascading dreadlocks tended to the bar. On the wall behind them hung a gargantuan oil painting, at least six feet high and nine feet wide, of a furious-looking tortoise. It stood erect next to crisscrossing rivers and roared with its mouth fully open. A handful of assorted animals stood at the tortoise's colossal feet in seeming obedience to its power.

Matt's eyes finally came to a table tucked into one of several small alcoves cut into the long wall every fifteen feet or so. There was a table in each nook with a hanging bulb and peacock lampshade emitting either an ochre or crimson hue, but Matt only had eyes for the nook closest to him. A sizable oil painting at the back of the nook featured an ancient Chinese castle surrounded by a large moat of water filled with abstract, swirling fractals. Peach trees filled the courtyard outside the castle, and a single jaguar prowled beneath the peach trees, scanning the other side of the moat for intruders. Beneath the painting, Mu tucked her raven hair behind an ear and nodded easily to another woman Matt had never seen before.

That's May, Matt corrected himself, not wanting his mind to shatter before he had the chance to finally talk to her. *Get yourself together.*

He saw now that Souvik and Chike were also sitting around the circular table with a couple other people, likely other executives.

Matt listened for the old man's return, but he seemed totally gone. He felt for the Serotel in his pocket and was filled with a tangible boost of confidence.

I'm going to tell her how I feel. And then I'm getting you out of my head, Matt said, more to himself than the old man.

Matt was on his way to the table when Souvik turned and noticed him. He jumped up and waved Matt over, beaming his wide smile for all the bar to notice.

Chike and the others turned and greeted Matt, while May stared him down as if she were the jaguar in the painting's peach orchard. She sipped her drink and never broke her enchanting gaze.

Matt wished the others would leave him and May to themselves.

But what am I supposed to say? Hi, I barely know you and forgot all about you for a while, but I love you. You mean the world to me, but I'm going to the hospital now. Bye.

Yeah, that'll go great, Matt scolded himself as his mind raced for a reasonable alternative to those words. But he was already at the table.

"Hey," Matt said directly to May. She didn't nod or smile or do anything to acknowledge him. She just kept staring and sipping at her drink.

"He only has eyyyes...for youuu!" Souvik sang to May, mimicking the Garfunkel version of the song.

May lowered her drink and turned slowly to Souvik while the rest of the table waited for her reaction.

"Look!" May pointed with mock excitement to the bartenders and the tortoise painting. "There's some unattended women at the bar. Go say hi. Just don't start humping their legs like a cute little puppy."

May winked, and the three diamond studs lining her eyebrow sparkled with ochre brilliance from the light above.

Souvik smiled even wider and put his hands up in defense.

"I'm not that bad!"

The whole table quickly looked among themselves, looked at Matt, then returned their eyes to Souvik in clear disagreement.

"Shoo, pretty boy," May told him with an easy wave of her hand.

Chike bellowed with the laughter of a father observing a sibling tiff.

"Come on everyone," Chike said with a sudden joyful burst. "Drinks on me. Let's do some shots at the bar."

Matt wasn't sure if the other executives agreed out of obedience or genuine desire to drink with Chike, who Matt assumed was their superior, but they all rose in unison and shuffled out of the booth. May was the only one who didn't move a muscle.

Chike gripped Matt's shoulder with brotherly affection and forced him to sit at the booth.

"Talk to you soon, buddy boy," Chike told him. Matt watched as Chike made a fist and pretended to wind up to punch Souvik, who chuckled and tucked his arms to his chest defensively. The other executives laughed along with their playfulness and found seats at the bar.

"They're like animals at the feet of the almighty Putch," May said with casual amusement, staring at the others along with Matt.

Putch, Matt repeated to himself in sudden horror that she was referencing his dream. But then he remembered Putch was also just a character from the video game they had built together.

"You okay?" May asked him, her voice like silk across his skin.

Matt shook his head in a painful rhythm and moved closer to May on the bench.

How can I possibly even begin to answer that question?

"What did you mean by that? About Putch?" Matt asked, trying to redirect the conversation away from his sanity.

"You're the one who taught me about Putch the tortoise god. Remember?"

Matt nodded along with her, pretending to remember. He recounted painfully again that he had no concrete memories of May whatsoever. None. It was the same for the others too – Souvik and Chike. Objectively, he knew their relation to one another and himself, but beyond that, he couldn't recall any memories of them in even the vaguest sense. There were just flashes of emotion. He could feel in those flashes the brotherly affection for Chike. But most of all, he felt the intense beaming love for May. No matter where his mind turned, even in his dreams within dreams, there was that incredible longing for May constricting and releasing his every thought – like a beating heart pulsing through braided networks of living tissue.

"All the animals flock to the feet of Putch when she roars," May re-

85

counted, lowering her voice and adding an air of authority as she mocked some version of himself that he couldn't remember.

"Not like Xiwangmu," May said, and she winked at him while sipping from her cocktail. The jaguar in the painting was just behind her, as if readying itself to pounce.

May looked back at the jaguar and nodded with approval.

"The art really did come out spectacular," May marveled. "You made the right choice in artists."

"I commissioned these paintings?" Matt gawked, and he had to stop himself from admitting the truth that he could remember virtually nothing of his life before just a few days ago.

May offered a half-smirk, then peered at him more closely, catching just a glint of the seriousness of Matt's mental predicament.

"You're not really feeling better, are you? That text was just you placating us, wasn't it?" May sighed with something like disappointment or maybe even worry. She pursed her lips and peered deep into his eyes as if searching for something.

Matt shrugged honestly.

I'm not here to lie to her. I'm not here to trick her. I'm here to tell her the truth.

"May..." Matt began with trepidation, not wanting to shock her with the impossible depths of the chaos and confusion that constituted the endless, haunting caverns of his mind.

"I'm glad I'm here with you right now, May," Matt said, grasping for her longing stare with his own.

She furrowed her brow and looked away from him for just an instant before placing her hand on the bench and moving a few inches closer.

"I'm glad you're here too, Matt. But, what exactly —"

Souvik's howling laughter suddenly jolted their attention to the bar, breaking the moment. Souvik had his arm around some young girl and was regaling a crowd of people with some story that seemed to be making them genuinely laugh.

May shook her head in disappointment.

"You like him?" Matt asked bluntly, feeling wrong for even putting her in the position of having to explain her relationships to another man.

May rolled her eyes, tilted her head back, and laughed a few forceful beats.

"Sure. In a reckless, disappointing little brother sort of way."

May shook her head and rolled her eyes again in Souvik's direction.

"He can't help it. His brain is used exclusively for coding. The rest of his neuronal networking is rerouted to his dick."

Matt didn't stifle his laughter, and she encouraged him to laugh with some of her own.

"He's harmless. You know that. More like a little puppy dog than a man, though."

May turned suddenly and eyed Matt with suspicion.

"Did he put you up to this, Matt? Coming out tonight. Showing up out of the blue. Talking to me like this. I mean..."

She trailed off, but Matt wasn't entirely sure what she was getting at.

"Never mind," she said, not letting Matt consider the matter. "I think he feels like some weird bro-code was destroyed between you two just because we slept together."

Matt nodded casually, conscious to not show any reaction. But inside, his mind raced with possibilities.

So they did sleep together. Maybe she cares more about Souvik than she's letting on.

Matt glanced at Souvik.

He looks like a celebrity. He's even better looking than Kartikeya, the CG version of himself. Of course May likes him...who wouldn't?

"I wish he would drop it," May continued. "I'm the one that instigated it. I just had to know what all the fuss was about. He's an entire topic of conversation all on his own when it comes to the other women in the office."

May drew closer to Matt and cupped her hand in front of her mouth, offering to tell him a secret.

"He's a great guy, but my god is he a boring lay."

Matt chuckled, and she straightened herself into a more comfortable position.

"So you and Souvik aren't..." Matt began, but May interrupted him with more liberating laughter.

"Sleeping with someone doesn't have to mean you like them." She laughed to herself and eyed Matt with a newfound realization. "You have a traditional mind, you know that?"

Her drink was empty, so she replaced it with the half-finished drink of one of the other executives.

"I'd offer you some, but I'm not sure you should be drinking on the medication you take, right?"

Matt felt paralyzed. Reference to his mental illness – here it was. He would have to admit to her sooner than later that he was far further down the rabbit hole of insanity than he was letting on.

"Serotel, right?" May asked. "I saw the bottle the other day when I called your therapist, or psychiatrist, or whatever he is."

Matt nodded, unsure how to tell her.

"I'm surprised I've never heard of it," she finished.

A traditional mind, Matt wondered, recounting her words. *Is that true?*

Tell her, he urged himself, forcing his mind away from distracting tangents.

"I have a broken mind," he said finally.

May cocked her head and looked physically hurt by his words.

"You have a beautiful mind! A beautiful mind!" she said, nearly scolding him.

Why does she seem so angry? Matt knew there was something he was missing – something between them.

Why can't I just remember? Matt seethed at his mind. *Damn you.*

He grabbed one of the cocktails closest to him and downed it in a single gulp.

"Whoa!" May said with incredible concern. "Easy, Matt. Is that even safe?"

"I don't know," Matt said. "I don't know," he repeated in reference to absolutely everything.

May tenderly removed the glass from his grip, set it on the table, and took his hand in hers.

"Just relax with that, okay? Let me be your poison and let's just talk. No more alcohol, okay?" she said, squeezing his hand.

The tangible bubbling in his chest, like a tethering to her soul, surged as they made contact.

Can she sense it too? Matt wondered, his heart fluttering in anticipation. But she didn't give any indication that she noticed the connection.

She let go of his grip and offered him a half-smile of assurance.

"This is the part in the movies when you profess your undying love for me," May chuckled, and she placed the back of her hand on her forehead and pretended to swoon.

Matt nodded at her, desperately wanting to tell her.

I do love you, May. I do love you.

May took his hand again, and this time she held it more comfortably in hers as if she didn't plan on letting go.

"Just tell me. Where did you go, Matt? All those months. You just disappeared. Just...where did you go?"

She looked deeply hurt, and Matt could tell that his willingness to be honest with her was paramount in this moment.

She's right, Matt told himself with painful admission. *If you love someone, you wouldn't just leave like that.*

"I don't know," he told her honestly, his voice cracking with the realization that she would see that answer as anything but honest.

She pulled her hand away from his and nodded with some painful resignation of hope.

"May, I –" Matt started.

"You know," she interrupted, "I've always been straight with you. And you always stay totally hidden. I know you do it to everyone, even Chike, but..."

"I really don't know," Matt urged, wishing that he could directly show her the events of his life over the last few days to help her understand.

Matt removed the bottle of Serotel from his pocket.

"I think I'm going crazy," he told her evenly.

Wrong! his mind shot back.

Matt nodded in agreement with himself. "I *am* crazy," he said.

"I know," she said with enrapturing warmth, and the smile she offered him was full of pain and longing in equal measure. "You're a fucking loon," she chuckled at him as if it were their personal little secret. She squeezed his hand tighter. "I know that, Matt, but I wouldn't be in love with you if you were normal. Normal people bore me."

In love? Matt repeated the words in his mind in rapid succession.

"Don't pretend you don't remember," she said evenly, but Matt could see the strain in her eyes and the tightness of her lips and understood that he had been the cause of a great deal of hurt in her life. "I told you about my feelings after all those times you led me on so hard you practically gave me a rash," she said with restrained but tangible pain in each syllable. "And then eventually you just brushed me off," she finished, waving her hand in front of her face as if shooing away a persistent fly.

"I didn't –" Matt started, but May cut him off again.

"Sure, you didn't exactly brush me off. You blamed it on your work. And your mind – my two favorite parts of you."

She still thinks I'm lying. She thinks I'm just playing her. Who am I in this world when I'm not...me?

May turned and nodded in the direction of the Ram painting. Matt followed her eyes and saw Linda stealing glances at Matt from behind a beer bottle.

"Seems like you have eyes for the young ones nowadays anyway," May said with a sneer in her tone. She sighed, loosened her grip, then reshuffled an inch or two away from him.

She was giving me a chance to tell her the truth. She thinks I'm lying to her. May...please believe me.

"No," Matt said, shaking his head. "That's not it. I –"

"Then tell me where you went," she demanded with finality, letting everything hinge on his answer.

Matt continued shaking his head, unsure if he should just make up a story to appease her. But even if he wanted to, he didn't know what he could possibly say to rectify the damage done to any potential relationship by the Matt who took over his life for whole days and months at a time.

May removed a small pink pill from a shallow pocket in her red cropped denim jacket. She popped the pill, then removed a joint from behind her left ear that Matt hadn't noticed until now.

"Sorry," she said, laughing to herself and shaking her head self-scoldingly. "You don't have to tell me anything. Why would you? I'm just a coworker, right? Just an employee."

She stood and Matt lunged, reaching for her arm.

She cocked her head, and her look of warning made him stay his hand.

He pulled back and lowered his head.

"Please," he said, wishing he could redo the whole conversation. "I love you, May. I love you. Please don't leave."

May kept her gaze on the exit to the bar for a few seconds, then rolled her eyes and let them fall back on Matt.

"Sure you do," she offered with a cruel, facetious stab.

"Please don't leave," Matt pleaded, not sure if he would ever see her again after tonight.

There's no telling how long I'll be hospitalized...or if they'll ever let me out again once they understand how bad off I am.

May hesitated, sighed, then said, "I'm going for a smoke. I won't leave if you don't. Deal?"

Matt nodded with relief and felt the sudden, intense urge to urinate. He stood and May turned around.

"Matt," she said almost beneath her breath, "let me just have a minute to myself outside."

"Sorry," Matt said, "just going to the bathroom."

May laughed at herself and shrugged. "Of course. Sorry, this is all just...a lot all at once. I'll see you in a few, okay?"

Matt nodded and smiled at May, and her smile blossomed back.

He watched her leave the bar, and he marveled at her incredible poise and beauty. She was like a spotlight amidst darkness.

She can have any guy she wants. But she said she loves me.

It was the last thing Matt expected: they already had some kind of relationship, and Matt had been the one to end it.

Why would I leave her? Why the hell would I do something so stupid? If I could just remember...

He caught Linda's gaze suddenly, and she averted her eyes immediately, pretending to be busy in conversation with a group of young people. Matt felt genuinely horrible.

I'll have to explain everything to Linda once and for all. Enough screwing around with her emotions.

But it would have to wait. He needed to get to the bathroom first.

He quickly scanned the room, looking for a sign, and he spotted the bathrooms near the bar. Making his way over, he caught Souvik's attention, who nearly pounced on him with a series of excited thumbs-up and jeered violently with dramatic fist pumps of approval. Chike pulled Souvik back to the bar and held him lovingly in place by the neck. Souvik laughed with child-like glee. Chike just raised a single large hand and offered Matt a thumbs-up without even turning his head.

These are my friends, Matt told himself, demanding his mind release its hold on his memories.

But his mind refused.

While the bar itself had an ambience befitting its name, the single bathroom was anything but special. There weren't any pieces of art or posters or ads on the walls. It was just a tiny room containing a sink, a mirror, and a stall with a toilet inside. There weren't even any paper towels or an air dryer.

The intense need to urinate was bordering on painful. Thankful that it wasn't occupied, Matt locked the stall and was finally able to relieve himself.

Any longer and I would have burst, Matt thought with a pang of worry. *Does the other me just never pee? Or was it just because I lost track of time on the computer?*

As he urinated with incredible relief, he stole a curious glance at some of the writing on the stall's walls:

A dream has no true beginning or end.

Funny, he told himself without laughing. *The universe really does have a grim sense of humor.*

He looked down at the large green lettering to his right:

Endless is the maze.

I guess they're really going for the lucid dreaming vibe.

There was writing everywhere. Some of it was short scribbles while other parts were more like poetry. He read another one written in blue marker:

Silent and empty is the way of heaven. Full and vibrant is the way of Earth. Tao is neither.

He was still urinating, and it didn't feel like it was letting up in the slightest.

This is a fucking world record, Matt thought with a twinge of concern, and he wondered if he might have damaged his bladder by holding it in so long.

He read another longer one written in bright red:

Treating everything as a dream liberates. As long as you give reality to dreams, you are their slave.

Matt closed his eyes with mounting worry.

How the fuck am I still peeing?

It wasn't slowing down. He estimated that more than a gallon of liquid had already streamed out of him without pause.

In a panic, not knowing what else to do but give it more time, he read another scribbling:

She is all that matters.

Who is "she"? May? Matt shook his head and tried to force his mind to calm down. *It's just writing on a stall wall, you loon.*

He remembered that's what May had called him in a strangely endearing way. *A loon. She knows I'm crazy. She said she loves me for my craziness. That really happened. That was real!*

She is all that matters, Matt told himself. He read the line on the stall again:

She is all that matters.

No, the old man told him miserably, sorrow welling in his voice as if he really was sorry that Matt's existence was nothing more than a transient idea in an old man's dying head.

This is all a dream, the old man told him just as Matt read another piece of text on the stall:

This is all a dream.

What the fuck? What is happening? he demanded inwardly, and his eyes darted to another piece of writing:

What the fuck? What is happening?

His heart jumped and he momentarily lost control of his stream, peeing on the back of the toilet.

"Will it ever end?" he yelped aloud, panicking in full force now.

He closed his eyes and tried to will his body to stop peeing, but it seemed to only make it worse. The pressure of his urination was ramping up, and he felt like he was going to explode.

"FUCK!" he screamed, and his forehead ejected a fount of blood from the same spot the Reaper first stabbed him.

He grabbed at his forehead and came back with crimson-slick fingers.

"FUCK!" he screamed again, but his urination was finally coming to an end, providing a shallow measure of determination that he could keep himself alive long enough to just get to a hospital.

In his terrible panic, he glanced another piece of writing:

There is no way out.

Call: "16180339887"

A number, he gawked, holding his hand against his head for pressure. His clothes and the entire bathroom were covered in blood and urine, and he felt disgusted and cold, like a misplaced piece of litter among corpses. He began trembling, and he wondered if he was losing too much blood.

My head, he remembered. *It was bleeding the morning this all started. I bandaged it up. And then suddenly the bandage was gone and my head was just fine. I...just didn't notice, I guess.*

No, Matt admitted. *That doesn't make any sense. None of this makes any sense.*

He forced himself to remove his hands from his forehead, letting the blood flow freely over his eyes. He closed them, replacing the sanguine flow of life with pitch black darkness.

None of this is real, is it? he asked the old man.

He felt the old man shake his head.

I wish it were, the old man said.

Matt couldn't help tearing up.

There is no way out.

Maybe that's true, Matt forced himself to reconcile with total horror. *Maybe there is no way out of this madness. Maybe even the hospital can't help me. Maybe nothing can help me.*

Blood freely poured from his skull, and there was a flash of objective observation in the madness that told him it was simply too much blood

94

to lose without passing out or even dying on the spot.

It isn't real, he seethed to himself, spiteful of his mind for betraying him so devilishly, for abandoning him without a hope of refuge.

Refuge, his mind raced.

Matt grabbed at the Serotel bottle. It was his only hope.

He brought the bottle out, blood still flowing at an oddly even pace, his hands and the floor and maybe the whole room covered in his thick red insides.

The bottle was empty.

No! Please, No!

The hopelessness of his situation injected him with a defeated and helpless form of acceptance.

There is no way out, he repeated to himself.

Matt opened his eyes and read the message again.

There is no way out.

That's when he finally noticed that all the messages were in his handwriting. It was like this exact stall and this exact moment amidst all of space and time was a meeting of his own subconscious mind with itself.

There was a black marker on the floor. Matt picked it up and wrote:

Somebody help me.

He glanced left and saw the same message.

Somebody help me.

It was identical. It was absolutely his handwriting.

"Somebody help me!" Matt screamed, slamming hard against the stall as his legs went weak and he lost his balance.

The door to the bathroom opened suddenly, and the strobing RGB glow of the bar flashed inside the stall. Matt felt sober suddenly. His head stopped gushing, and he watched as the blood and urine-soaked floor steadily vanished like slowly burning grass.

"You okay, bud? You say something?" someone asked from outside the stall.

Matt swiped at his forehead, but his hands came back clean, and except for a splash of urine on the backside of the toilet, everything seemed perfectly ordinary. Except for the writing. All the writing remained. Either it was real or it was a hallucination, and the person outside the stall could tell him.

Matt opened the stall and tried playing it cool, nodding in a futile attempt at assurance to the twenty-something surfer-looking dude.

"Can you see the writing in there?" Matt asked him, readying himself for the man to look at him with bug-eyed skepticism.

"Yeah, bud. That stall is pretty intense on a mescal-run or a k-drop, or sometimes I lock myself in there for a while on some good 'ol acid, you know?"

Matt had no idea what he was talking about, but he could discern they were all drugs of some sort.

"So you can see the writing in there right now?" Matt asked with greater urgency, but the young man kept his zen demeanor.

"For sure, bro. It says stuff about dreams and how there is no way out of a maze or something – some trippy shit, bro."

"Yeah," Matt nodded, unsure if it was better or worse that this man could see the writing.

"Oh shit!" the man said suddenly. "Marker!" he said, pointing excitedly at the marker in Matt's hand. "My dude, you for real just wrote all that? You like, a poet or something?"

"No," Matt started, "I mean yes, but –"

"Don't worry," the young man said, holding up his hands in assurance. "It's all good, bro. I mean, that just adds to the trip next time I get lost in the stall. So thank you, you know?"

Matt shook his head. There was no point trying to explain everything.

"Thanks," Matt said, dragging his voice. He turned and saw the number on the wall. He took out his phone and snapped a picture of it.

"You going to call that number?" the man asked, sounding genuinely curious.

"Probably," Matt admitted forlornly, knowing that he would at least try it on his way to the hospital.

The young man clearly recognized that Matt didn't want to get any deeper into what had sparked the man to enter the bathroom in the first place. He patted Matt on the back, and Matt moved to wash his hands.

The young man left without any further comment, and Matt breathed deep.

Say goodbye to May. Then go to the hospital. Enough is enough.

He shook his hands of excess water, then opened the door. May was seated in the alcove. She waved her head to the trance beat and eyed the people of the bar with measured interest.

Matt felt suddenly that the air was different. There was a heavy humidity in it. It felt like a late-summer day.

Surrendering to the well of total insanity he had fallen inside, he took out his phone and checked the date. It was August 21st.

He looked back at May and saw that she was still wearing the same outfit.

Is this the same day or isn't it?

Matt didn't lose himself to the panic this time.

How much worse can it all get? Maybe I jumped a month forward somehow. That isn't new, he told himself in a defeated, sordid resignation that his mind might never actually be whole.

But May is still sitting right there. There is no way out. She is all that matters.

Matt could feel it now with acute certainty: he would never see May again. He would never see any of them again. He was too far gone. Reality was bent too far out of shape, and there was nothing strong enough to bend it back nor any way to even know what the original shape looked like.

Say goodbye, Matt lamented inwardly, wondering if it would be better if he just left without saying another word. *Maybe that would make it easier for her. Maybe I've already caused a problem by even getting this involved with her.*

No! another part of his mind that was not the old man reminded him. *She said she loves you. That's what matters. You walked away once – apparently. Don't do it again. Don't do that to her again.*

Matt waited for the old man's take, but he remained silent. Not that it mattered – Matt knew what the old man would say anyway: *This is all a dream.*

Fine, Matt said inwardly in defiance of the old man and reality itself. *If this is all a dream, then fine.*

He strode forward to May. She smiled with her eyes and pursed her lips.

"I saw you check your phone by the bathroom," she said playfully. "You getting bored?"

Matt existentially ached for this woman who was but an ever present shadow in his mind. The braided cord between them pulsed with incredible energy. He hesitated for only a moment, then offered her his hand. She smiled, elusive but endearing, and allowed him to lift her to her feet.

He gently pulled her close, and she let him wrap his arms about her.

She is all that matters, he knew with perfect clarity despite nothing else making any sense. His lips were drawn to hers, and as they kissed, the braided cord pulsed with such intensity that Matt had to pull away just to breathe.

She smiled with her eyes first, then she let her lips curl with profound elation.

"Fuck yes!" Souvik jeered from beneath the giant tortoise painting before being strangled into silence by Chike.

May chuckled and rolled her eyes despite an attempt to keep her gaze locked on Matt's longing stare.

He pulled her close again, embracing her fully as the connection pulsed back and forth between them.

"Can you feel that?" Matt asked her, hoping that it was anything but a hallucination.

"Everyone staring at us, you mean?" May snickered.

Matt pulled away and saw that the entire bar was watching them. He glanced back to where Linda and her friends had been standing. Her friends were there, but Linda was gone.

"Your place or my place?" May asked bluntly, and she curled the fingers of her right hand around his left hand, squeezing him to let him know she had no intention of letting go.

Matt knew the right answer: *Take me to a hospital.* That's what the rational part of his mind wanted to say.

"Yours," he heard himself say with equal relief and horror.

I can't just leave her now. Not now. Not again. Not ever.

They left hand in hand.

When they were outside on the sidewalk, May said, practically giggling, "Quite the show of confidence, Mr. Willish." She let go of his hand and removed her phone from a shallow pocket at her waist. "That was fun. I see you're going for the romantic movie theme like I suggested earlier."

She glanced at him, smiled, then went back to her phone. Matt didn't break his gaze from her. He didn't want the world to crumble and portal him to some far away corner of the world or anywhere at all if it wasn't by May's side.

"I'm getting a Mega back to my place. You can pay me back."

Matt just stared, absorbing her every movement.

Don't let this end. Please don't strip me from this moment, Matt pleaded to the world. But everything seemed normal. *Too normal for having just had a complete psychotic break in the bathroom.* He knew it was only a matter of time before his mind snapped again.

The hospital, Matt urged himself. But here was May. The hospital would always be there. He didn't have the same assurance with May.

She glanced at him again and this time let her stare linger. "That was a joke. I know you're rich, but I work with the numbers every day, and I have more money in my bank accounts than you do. You'd have to sell some of that precious stock. So until then, I'll just look after your broke ass, okay?" May said, cracking another joke.

Matt removed his wallet and showed her that it was completely empty. It didn't even contain his ID.

May reared her head back and let out a hoot of laughter.

"Not a dollar to your name, Matthew. What am I going to do with you? I'll teach you about finance back at my place, how does that sound?"

Matt allowed himself a shallow chuckle.

"Okay," he managed.

May furrowed, unsure how to read him.

"Is everything okay? You want to go back in?" she asked evenly, pointing back at the bar.

No! Matt almost yelped aloud. He shook his head fervently and closed the gap between them.

"No," he told her with an obvious pang of dread in his tone. He moved to kiss her lips again, and May pulled him hard against her, kissing him passionately.

After a few seconds, May pulled away, but she let her lips linger half an inch away from his. He could feel the warmth of her breath mixing with his own. She kissed him twice on the chin, then pulled far enough away to take in his sad, longing eyes. She offered him a smile identical to Mu's.

"Everything will be all right," she told him.

Her words were meant to comfort, but they filled Matt's mind with the grotesque memories of Mu being decapitated or shredded to pieces or skewered.

"I'm not sure about that, Mu. I mean, May," Matt said, looking at the ground out of embarrassment. "I'm crazy, May. I'm...I'm not..." Matt said, unsure how to express that Alice's trip in Wonderland was like a walk in the park compared to what he was enduring.

"You're right," May told him pleasantly. "Kissing me in the bar like that was a pretty crazy thing for you to do. But I'm glad you did."

She doesn't understand just how bad off I am. And if I explain it to her, that might ruin everything. But I can't lie to her. And I can't just walk away.

Matt removed the empty bottle of Serotel from his pocket.

"It's empty," he said as he formulated how to explain his predicament without *really* explaining it.

"Don't you have a script for it? I thought you went to see your therapist after you...came back."

"It's not a prescription," Matt began, "or, maybe it is. But Dr. Heron gave me this bottle from his office."

May looked slightly alarmed. "He just...gave it to you? Where do you usually get your prescriptions filled?"

Matt shrugged. "I would tell you if I knew."

May shook her head in consideration, then began searching for something on her phone.

"Serotel? Like, s-e-r-o-t-e-l?" May asked incredulously.

"That's what the bottle says."

May huffed in frustration. "I can't find anything at all. Did he refer to it by a different name?"

What the fuck is he giving me? Matt pondered with dread.

"There isn't even any information on the bottle. It just says *Serotel,*"

May confirmed with greater surprise. "But what happened to the pills? You drop the bottle somewhere, or…?"

Just tell her the truth, Matt demanded of his mind.

"It was July and then I went to the bathroom and it was suddenly August. And all my pills were gone. Just like that."

"You probably just spilled them in the bathroom, Matt. I'm so sorry," May offered, overlooking Matt's statement as some form of strange exaggeration.

"I'm not sure I can trust Dr. Heron," Matt said finally, admitting it more to himself than May.

"Why?" May asked, her eyes wide.

How will she react when she sees just how far down the well of insanity my mind really is?

Matt shrugged, unsure how to explain it.

I should be in a hospital, Matt reminded himself. *A fucking hospital. But I can't tell her that. Not now. Not yet. I don't want this to end.*

"Well, I admit it's weird – this Serotel he's giving you," May said. "The pill just says the drug name and to take one a day."

"I took three earlier," Matt admitted.

May nodded with a casual understanding, as if everything suddenly made sense.

"Okay, well, there you go, Matt. Maybe you took too much?"

Matt shrugged. It was certainly a better theory than anything he could offer.

May stroked his temple with her palm, and Matt closed his eyes momentarily, letting his head fall into her hand.

"Maybe we should take you home," May offered tenderly.

"Please!" Matt begged, his eyes still closed. He felt that all he needed was her gentle caress. "Please don't leave me. Let's just go back to your place."

"Matt…are you sure?"

"Please don't leave me, May."

May went on her tiptoes and pulled his head down to meet her lips. She kissed his forehead.

"I'm not going anywhere. But tomorrow we're going to get your meds filled. We'll go together, okay? I'd like to ask your therapist about this Serotel," May said, sounding like a concerned spouse.

Yes, Matt told the world. *Give me tonight. And then the whole world can fall apart. Just let me have tonight.*

The Mega arrived, and May checked with the driver to make sure he was the right one. After confirming the information, Matt opened the backdoor and let May get in first.

"Very gentlemanly," she told him playfully, but then she smiled seriously and said, "You're sweet, Matt."

Matt took his seat beside May and folded his grip into hers. She nestled her arm atop his and crossed her legs. Her tight black jeans did nothing to stop the warmth emanating from her legs, enveloping Matt's arm like sweet nourishment. She slowly caressed the outside of his hand with her thumb, gently rocking his mind into a blanketing calm with just the subtlest caress.

The driver, an elderly man wearing a brown beret, finished working haphazardly on his phone, then put the car into gear. He drove slowly and easily, seeming to be in no hurry.

The city lights streamed by like smeared starlight, and Matt was reminded of the starlit space outside the windows of the circular laboratory from where he assumed the old man must be watching him.

Get out! Matt ordered at the presently silent old man. *I don't want you ruining this.*

He breathed in May's very presence. *This is perfect,* Matt rejoiced. *This is what I've been searching for.*

May kissed the outside of his ear, and a pleasant tingle ran down the length of Matt's spine. He smiled and leaned into her lips, and she giggled and squeezed his arm into her chest.

"That young love, *oohwee!*" the elderly man beamed at them from the rearview mirror. He smiled and nodded to himself, recounting happy memories of what Matt assumed must be his long-lost love.

May smiled back at the man through the mirror. Matt couldn't take his eyes off the man's drooping eyelids and sallow cheeks as the memory of old, sagging skin filled his mind.

Is that really who I am? Is May just...a dream?

Matt swallowed the idea away, pushing it as far down into the recesses of his being as he could manage.

Matt marveled at how normal everything was in this moment. He wished there were a way to make sense of all the confusion. Though he knew he would have to go to the hospital tomorrow, that didn't solve the present moment.

I should ask her about the inconsistencies, he thought, *like the logs and the time jump and...even the bodyguards. Dr. Heron told me I have bodyguards. Why would he say that if I don't?*

"Do I have bodyguards?" Matt asked her bluntly.

May considered it, then said, "I don't know. Do you?"

"I've never seen any," Matt told her.

"Me neither," she laughed. "Why? Do you want some bodyguards? I'm not enough protection?"

A wave of realization pummeled Matt suddenly, and he was reminded that this would all come to an end. It was only a matter of time.

But maybe it doesn't have to end. Maybe May will be there on the other side of the hospital, if there is an other side. Maybe...

"Last time I was at his office, my therapist said that he would have my bodyguards take me home."

May shrugged. "I'm really not sure, Matt. But I definitely don't like the sound of this therapist. Let me go with you tomorrow, okay?"

Matt squeezed her tight, and he couldn't help tearing up.

"Thank you, May. Please don't leave me."

"You okay, buddy?" the driver asked.

"He'll be all right," May answered. She looked back and smiled at Matt. "Right, Matt?" she said and stroked his temple the same way she had outside the bar.

"I'm not leaving, sweetie."

Matt nodded fervently in thanks.

Everything'll be all right. That's what May and Mu always say. But everything does seem all right when I'm with her. Everything is staying normal. Everything is all right. Maybe I won't have to go to the hospital. Maybe I can just stay with May. Maybe...

"You ever feel like maybe everything is just a dream?" Matt asked grimly.

"Of course. It *is* all a dream," May offered sweetly, taking his question in stride.

"I'm serious," Matt told her.

"So am I," May said, and she went back to caressing his hand with her thumb.

"You don't think that's crazy?"

May shrugged. "I don't know. It's something I think about all the time, Matt. I just feel like saying reality is a dream is no crazier than calling reality real. What do we even mean by that word — reality? That it exists? So do dreams. So, by that logic, are dreams not real since they exist?"

Matt nodded rhythmically. "Exactly," he said, impressed by her succinct use of logic to easily disprove the so-called realness of reality using reality itself.

May went on with a painful, dragging tone, speaking as if she had been through all this in her mind a thousand times over. "The atomic structure of reality is mostly free space, and that free space is made up of other subtle energies and fields, and none of it has any real, objective solidity outside of what our brain convinces us is true." She shook her head and stared into the distance as if recounting painful memories. "But our brains are made of the same stuff. We don't really know what's going on in reality. Science just categorizes and observes. It can never derive meaning because there is no meaning." May lowered her head despairingly, then she turned to Matt and smiled. "So it might as well be a dream."

Tears streamed from Matt's eyes in full force. "Exactly," he said, and he turned his head to wipe his eyes, embarrassed to be crying in front of her.

"Merrily, merrily, merrily, merrily, life is but a dream," the old driver sang, waving his finger as if he were a composer.

May removed a tissue from one of her many small jacket pockets and offered it to Matt.

"It's okay to cry," she offered with what seemed more like empathy than sympathy.

Matt nodded in gratitude. She was right. *What do tears matter anyway?*

"What happened between us?" Matt asked. "Will you tell me? I...can't really remember much."

May kept her hand entwined with his, but she pulled away a little to catch his eyes.

"Are you for real right now, Matt? You're not just saying that?"

Matt nodded miserably.

"Okay," May said, accepting his words. "Tell me what you do remember."

Matt sighed heavily. "I woke up confused from a series of strange dreams. I went to the office. You helped me. And then I came back the next day and –"

"I mean, what do you remember about us?"

"I…" Matt began, and he tried to remember something. Anything.

Please! he begged his mind. But his memories remained encased in some unreachable portion of his psyche. He stared into her inviting eyes and breathed in her every feature.

Nothing. I don't remember her. Not a single memory.

"I remember that I love you," Matt said in a whisper, ashamed that he couldn't remember anything specific. "I remember that you mean everything to me."

May looked disappointed and shrugged with defeat.

"But Matt...why are you saying all this now?" she demanded.

"Why the hell didn't I say it before is a better question," Matt said with no other explanation.

"You were always busy coding," May said, flipping her hand as if tossing the words away. "Coding everything. Every minute. And the rest of your time spent alone doing...who knows what. But...you made *Room Reaper*. I mean, we all did. But really it was you, Matt. You're like Doctor Manhattan – you can just work your fingers and create life. You created, line by line, the biggest...*thing* in the world. *Room Reaper,*" she repeated with actual awe in her voice. "So I guess it was all worth it, huh?"

Matt slumped in his seat, feeling heavy from the hapless realization that his programming masterpiece was one of the major causes of May's affection, but also one of the major reasons they hadn't been truly together until now.

"I don't want any of it," Matt lamented. "Nothing is worth being without you, May."

"Beautiful," the driver rasped.

"It is beautiful," May admitted bittersweetly. "I just wish you would have told me all this sooner."

Matt prepared himself for some forlorn ultimatum from May. Maybe she would say he was just too late.

I can't possibly matter that much to her, certainly not as much as she does to me. Can she not feel that cord between us — our connection? Even a little? It's so damn strong!

"But that's okay," May told him, providing sweet relief. "We have this moment and all the rest."

She kissed him on the forehead and wiped away a stream of his tears.

Matt continued sinking into the seat. He felt so heavy, but he refused to fall asleep.

Not now! Matt demanded his tired mind. *Not yet. Not yet!* He remembered that he had made changes to the source code of the game. So, he had a reason to fall asleep. He had a mission, finally, and it might even lead to some semblance of understanding...of something.

Stay awake! Matt shouted in his head, and the car drove over a small bump, knocking them an inch into the air and jarring Matt back to alertness.

"Don't let me fall asleep. Not yet, okay? I don't want to lose you again," Matt told her, his voice rasping with exhaustion.

"Lose me again?" May asked, trying to understand. But then she let go of trying to understand his words and just offered him her sweet caresses.

She pinched him on the hand suddenly with her nails.

"Ow!" Matt gasped playfully.

"You told me to keep you up," May beamed.

The Mega came to a stop.

"This is it," May told the driver. "Thanks."

The driver smiled and waved goodbye as if he might actually miss them.

Matt's legs felt like hardened muck, and May had to help him out of the car.

"Merrily, merrily, merrily, merrily, life is but a dream," the driver sang pleasantly as he waved goodbye.

Matt felt terrible and downright pathetic that May was holding up so much of his weight, but there was so little strength in his legs now.

She helped him up the steps to the front door, and May placed her finger on a biometric scanner. Several bolts slid open in what Matt now understood to be a large steel door painted to look like wood. The door swung open on its own, welcoming them inside.

"Are you sure this is okay," Matt asked her, giving her a chance to be rid of him and his endless burdens. "I don't want to impose on you like this. My legs are just....and –"

"Shut up, Matt," May cooed as she helped him up the steps of one of Chicago's classic Victorian two-flats and into the foyer of her home.

"You own the whole building?" Matt marveled, realizing they had walked through the front door and right into her home without having to take stairs or an elevator.

"Of course," May said reasonably as she helped him find a place on her plush ochre-colored couch. He breathed deep, and he felt a small measure of life return to his limbs.

"Don't you own your own flat?" May chuckled with surprise.

"Maybe," Matt admitted, "but I woke up in my old apartment. Just my old, small apartment."

And I'm not even sure how I know that it's my old apartment, Matt reminded himself, still in surrender to whatever might come next. *Some things I just know. But it's all useless information. Why would I not have any memories of May? Why would I not remember her beyond anything else?*

"We'll have to buy you something that more accurately reflects your wealth, then," May said, spreading her arms wide to present the whole of her luxury house. Matt estimated that it must have cost her at least a few million to buy something this large so close to Lake Michigan. It probably cost at least half as much just to furnish it.

It was obvious now who designed the foyer of Matt's office building and the decor of his personal office.

"Who feeds the fish when you aren't here?" Matt asked aimlessly, not sure what to say to deflect from the madness of his mind and the world that was like a desert outside the oasis of May's home. May filled a glass with water from a small nozzle near the sink, and as she walked to Matt, the light above and the shimmering of her diamond piercings made her seem otherworldly. Matt absorbed her and the surroundings all at once, and for a moment, he felt like he might be back inside his office. The crimson carpet, the luscious green fronds, the gently swimming koi – it was all the same, except here there was no *MW* symbol to be seen. Matt was thankful for that.

"The house feeds the fish. A lot of it is automated. Nice feature to have when I'm out of the state or country," she explained, handing Matt the glass.

He gulped it down in a single movement, unsure of the last time he actually drank water.

"I didn't realize how thirsty I was," he told her, wiping his mouth.

She giggled and refilled his glass. "Plenty of water. Don't feel bad for drinking an ocean's worth. I'll just add it to your running tab."

She returned to the kitchen and poured a drink for herself – a mix of whiskey and some mixer he couldn't make out.

Matt tried not to blink, fearing that everything might suddenly flip back to insanity. *Please don't let this end.*

She took a seat on a chair opposite the couch he was sitting on and crossed her legs.

"Did you make me one?" Matt asked, pointing to the drink.

May swallowed half the drink in a single gulp, then said, "Drink the water and get comfortable. That couch will be your bed for the night – or what's left of it. It's already past three."

The energy surged through Matt's solar plexus so suddenly and so intensely that he winced and gripped at his chest for just a moment before pulling his hand away and digging his teeth into his bottom lip to hide the...not pain, Matt thought. *Intensity. That's the only way to describe this feeling. Like pure energy.*

"Oh my god, are you okay?" May said, jumping to her feet at the sight of Matt's wincing. "Did you just have a heart attack?"

Matt shook his head vigorously. "Sit next to me," he managed, trying to will the coursing energy into submission.

With worry strewn across her every feature, she came to his side and slid her hand into his. The flow of energy finally began to wane, leaving

Matt gasping for breath as if he had nearly drowned.

"Just stay by my side, okay?" Matt pleaded.

She nodded and held him close.

"Okay, Matt. Okay. Everything will be all right," May said, putting down her drink and rubbing his back.

"You're worse than you were letting on, aren't you?"

As long as we're close. She's all that matters.

"I'm okay if you're by my side," he said, and it seemed like that was true, for the braided cord's vitality was no more than a soft hum, and the world was just the world, not a mind-shattering trip.

He opened his eyes and read a tattoo on her forearm that he hadn't noticed before: *Awake?*

He rubbed the tattoo, ensuring its realness, and he kissed it, savoring the sweet yet sweat-laden scent of her skin.

"What's your answer?" he asked her.

"I'm stuck in a dream within a dream," she answered without hesitation.

"That's my computer question and password," Matt whispered, knowing that was the least insane connection of anything that had occurred thus far.

"Well, yeah, I set up your computer. I set up your whole office. It's basically just my house all over again," she laughed. "It wasn't like you were using it."

Matt nodded into the nape of her neck, still staring at her tattoo and holding onto her tightly. "Of course, I'm glad you took that liberty. Who wouldn't want an office full of lush plant life and fish?"

May seemed pleased with his answer. "Good," she said snarkily. "Besides, your office is first and foremost my meditation room. It is your office exclusively on a secondary basis."

She kissed his head, then the tip of his ear, and then his neck.

"But we aren't having sex, Matt. Not tonight. I'm not taking advantage of you while you're in this state."

He didn't even need to have sex with her. Of course he wanted it, but all he really needed was her presence. Everything was so calm in her presence. Everything seemed serene and exactly as it should be.

"If you don't want to, then I understand. But if you don't want to only because you think I'm crazy – that I'm too far gone, then –"

"No!" May insisted. "Not that. That's not what I'm saying. I just...I want to make sure you're okay, Matt. I would just feel selfish if we had sex."

His mind was filled with images of May in orgasmic ecstasy beneath him, then above him. The energy in his chest pulsed, and he felt his penis pulse with it. He glided his fingers over her forearm, then moved his hand to her thigh and relished her warmth in his grip. She clasped her hand over his hand and issued an unintentional moan beneath her breath, gyrating her hips for just a moment to some internal tantric rhythm that Matt realized she was actively suppressing despite every signal in her body telling her to do the opposite.

"Then let's make love," Matt offered simply, and he gently kissed the inside of her neck and then her exposed collarbone.

May kicked back her head and laughed a few loud beats before hugging him even closer to herself.

"Matt, I want you too. Just not tonight, okay?" she told him despite clearly stifling an intense desire to have him in that moment.

"Sure," Matt told her, not wanting to push the subject. "It's just that...now...right now we have this...each other...and later is...so out of reach," he explained grimly.

"Don't say that," May volleyed, not wanting to even fathom the meaning of his words.

Matt pulled away and looked her straight in the eyes. "Am I crazy, May? Am I...is it all...will there ever be..."

He couldn't think of the proper words. There was something in the back of his head growing louder with each second. Then he heard it clearly. It was the old man's subdued, pitiful laughter.

Call the number, the old man told him.

Matt had forgotten all about it.

"Will you do something for me?" Matt asked.

May was caught off guard and gave him a hesitant look.

"Are you going to say, 'Have sex with me?" she chuckled.

Matt didn't laugh. He took out his phone and showed her the picture.

110

"Will you call this number on your phone? And let's use your phone. I can't...trust mine."

She eyed him suspiciously for a moment, then shrugged and dialed the number.

"That's the golden ratio," she told him simply, inputting the numbers into her phone with just a few easy glances at the picture. She put the phone on speaker.

"Have you really never done this before?" May snickered.

The phone began to ring, and Matt shook his head in total shock.

"You...have?" he checked.

"Of course. That number has been up in the stall for a while. Here, watch what happens," she explained with a measure of excitement.

The phone stopped ringing, and May brought the phone closer to their ears.

Maybe it will be nothing. Maybe normality will continue for a while longer, Matt hoped beyond all hope.

There was something on the other line. Beeps of machinery. A heart rate monitor. Heavy breathing.

May brought her ear closer and so did Matt.

"Nurse!" an old man said from some distance away. "Am I dreaming? Nurse!" the old man shouted with incredible urgency.

May looked at the phone with excited surprise.

What the fuck? she mouthed.

But Matt just stared wide-eyed, for there was nothing surprising about what he heard.

"That's me," Matt admitted to her, knowing that his statement wouldn't make any sense.

"You recorded it?" she asked incredulously, cocking her head.

The old man shouted for the nurse once more, and then the call ended abruptly.

"No. That old man on the phone call. That's me. I'm the old man."

May set her phone back on the table.

"It's just a random generator, Matt. Every time you call, it's something different. Watch."

She picked the phone back up and redialed the number. Sure enough, a loud whistle could be heard, and a train conductor said, "all aboard!"

But why would it randomly play exactly my dream? That doesn't make any sense.

May hung up the phone and set it down once more. She took his hands in hers and offered an uneasy smile.

"You heard it though, right?" Matt checked. "You heard the old man scream for a nurse?"

May nodded evenly. "Yeah. I heard that."

"It's me," Matt persisted, not caring anymore how crazy he might sound. He felt like these were his final moments anyway. Nothing made sense and nothing ever would.

"Every time I go to sleep, I wake up in a dream...I wake up in *Room Reaper*. You're there too," Matt gushed, and May allowed him to let it all out. "And I see you die over and over again in the most horrific ways."

Matt verbally whimpered and winced at the images of Mu being brutally murdered. May kissed the top of Matt's hands for comfort and allowed him to continue.

"And then we all die, and I wake up as an old man. I'm in a hospital, but it isn't normal. It's...huge...and there are stars outside...and on the other side there's a blizzard and...there are people out there...and..."

Matt stopped. *Holy fuck*, he told himself. *Holy fucking shit, I sound so batshit crazy.*

May kissed his forehead. Matt looked up at her and saw tears in her eyes.

"What?" Matt asked, tears welling in his own eyes.

"I don't want to see you like this. I don't want you to suffer like this. Promise me you'll go with me tomorrow to the hospital."

Matt nodded with total assurance.

"Promise," she repeated stolidly.

"I promise," he answered, truly resolute that it was his only real option.

She kissed his forehead and hands again, then she lifted herself onto him, straddling and wrapping her legs around his thighs. She sniffed hard, stifling her tears.

Their bodies intertwined, she lowered Matt's head into the crook of her neck and rocked with him. He could feel the intense heat from between her legs as she slowly gyrated and rocked against him. He pulled her closer, and her soft hip movements continued, grinding softly into his groin.

"I don't think you're crazy, honey," she said, her voice hoarse and full of buzzing desire. "I'm the crazy one because I'm fucking crazy about you, Matt. I think you're just you, and I'm mad about you."

She lifted his chin and locked lips with him, kissing him passionately. After a few seconds, she broke away and said, "If a little craziness comes with the package, I'm okay with that."

"What about a lot of craziness," Matt offered, his breathing heavy with the same desire overtaking May.

She nodded vigorously and licked her lips. "I'm okay with a lot of crazy too. You let me in your life, finally, and I'm not letting go that easy. I want to know you, Matt. The real you. If the real you is crazy, then so be it. That's who I want."

The braided cord swelled at her words, and he felt the overwhelming urge to have her in that moment. He lunged with incredible desire and so did she, locking lips and bodies. This time the braided cord's energy did not abate but surged with orgasmic power. Matt moaned as pleasure flooded his cells, and May beamed at him with eagerness and exhilaration. They tore at each other's clothes between impassioned kisses placed upon every inch of skin they could reach.

"But you're out of it, Matt. Is this okay?" she checked, sensually gripping his inner thigh with her sharp nails.

"Yes!" he practically pleaded. "The only thing that makes sense is you. The only thing I understand is you. I want you, May. I need you!"

It must have been exactly what she wanted to hear, for she pounced like a jaguar prowling through sweet fruit trees.

She pulled at his thighs and practically forced him inside her, moaning with overflowing emotional and sexual desire for Matt.

His mind raced, wondering what she could possibly see in him, but her body and moaning and grabbing at every part of him forced his mind to focus only on her. The connection's energy swelled with an impossibly forceful rush. They both screamed in ecstasy, and Matt was forced to arch his back, desperate to counter the raging rush of energy between them.

"Fuck, Matt!" May moaned through rapid breathing, clinging tightly to Matt as he groaned and arched and nearly cried at the power of the braided cord. The whole room began to tremble, and he felt the energy explode inside him, spreading through him like a nuclear reaction.

May's moaning, ecstatic face was steadily washed away by mounting luminosity so bright that Matt had to shield his eyes.

"Fuck!" he heard May scream in ecstasy, and then her weight was suddenly gone. There was total silence. He opened his eyes and found himself laying on his back in a pitch-black room surrounded on every side, even above and seemingly below, by RGB LED lights flashing in sync with his heartbeat.

Amidst the perfect silence of the room, his heart beat madly in his ears. He thought he might scream, but he couldn't move his body. Not even his eyes. He felt a great buzzing mass protruding from his chest, but he couldn't move or look to investigate it further.

There was nothing he could do except observe and attempt to understand or maybe even recollect what it all might mean.

May! Matt pleaded, searching frantically for her inside and outside his mind despite being unable to move. But he was alone.

This might be a dream, Matt thought with familiar trepidation, and he realized that he still thought of himself as the same Matthew Willish who had just slept with May Anh.

Not the old man, Matt told himself with some amount of relief. *Not the video game character. I know who I am. I'm still me. I'm...*

He tried to do a reality check by looking at his hands, but he couldn't move his neck to observe his own body.

Sleep paralysis, came a thought from the recess of his mind, and he realized that's exactly what it felt like.

Did I wake up? Is this the real world? Was all that just a dream? Absolutely everything and everyone?

He recollected May moaning in ecstasy and gripping him intensely with sweet release.

No, he demanded. *She's not a dream. She's not a fucking dream.*

"Can he hear us?" an elderly woman asked, and despite her age, Matt knew who it was.

May, he tried screaming. *May, I'm here!*

But it was no use.

"Matt, my darling," the elderly version of May sobbed. "I wish you'd just wake up."

May! Matt raged inside his mind, but there was just the darkness and the endless blinking of reds and greens and blues all around him.

I'm stuck inside a dream within a dream, he wanted to tell her. *I love you,* he wanted to tell her even more.

"Goodbye, Matt," the elderly May said through painful sobs. "But I wish you'd just come back to me."

I'm here! Matt pleaded.

The lights began flickering off one by one.

Please! Matt sobbed within himself.

There were only a few lights left.

Everything will be all right, he heard from inside himself. It was Mu and his May at once, both their voices melding into a harmonized melody.

The final light went out.

11. Server Reset

H e felt the cold floor's icy bite first, and then he gasped violently for breath. He gripped his chest, probing frantically for the braided cord, but there was no cord or pulsing energy.

"You okay, Loki?" Mu's concern perfectly contrasted the uncaring attitude of the other three stretching silently in the single light of the grimly familiar cell.

I'm back here, Matt realized with frustrated horror. *Not just this dream, but all this madness. I'm back in it. I thought I got out somehow. I thought...*

Mu just smiled at him, waiting pleasantly for a response. Still on his back, he crawled away from her and tried to process what had occurred at the moment of orgasmic climax with May.

I went somewhere else. The cord. There was a cord coming out of my chest.

He stopped and gripped at his chest again. *No. I couldn't see my body. But I could feel the cord. And the lights. And May...her voice...*

Mu took a soft step toward him, forcing Matt to throw up his hands.

"Stay back," he told her, total confusion welling inside him. "None of this is real!"

Mu halted her approach and Matt could see that she was consciously stopping herself from reaching out a hand to help him. The others just shook their heads and laughed at him disappointedly.

Matt took in the whole of Mu's naked form, and his mind was infused with May's moans of ecstasy. He wanted to go back there. He needed her. It was the only thing that made sense or had ever made sense or ever would make sense.

She is all that matters.

It's all a dream, came the old man. *This world. May's world. And that world of RGB lights you went to – that too. It's all just a dream, Matthew.*

Matt groaned maniacally and rolled his head.

"Fuck you!" he shouted, slamming his fist against the steel floor as he seethed and gritted his teeth against the intense, emanating pain.

"How the fuck can that hurt so much?" Matt vehemently demanded from the others. "It's all just fucking code!" he screamed frantically. "I fucking programmed you! I programmed my own fucking hands and the fucking pain – even the particles of fucking light in this piece of shit cell!"

A dream, the old man whispered like a javelin piercing Matt's tirade.

"You're a dream!" Matt shouted aloud to his mind. "Fuck you!"

He was tired. Of everything. He wanted something to make sense, and for a short while, that something was May. But as he recollected May through Mu – her petite breasts and slanted smile and sharp chin and every inch of her skin – he could feel the truth: she had to be a dream. Not because the old man said so, but because it was too perfect. All Matt wanted was May, and now he had her in the real world. It was just too good to be true.

Because it's not the real world. It's a dream come true, but it's all still a fucking dream, Matt forced himself to accept.

He remembered the distinct feeling that he would never see the others again, including May.

Is that because she isn't real? Is that because...I woke up?

The alarm blared, but Matt didn't move into position with the others.

Mu seemed to wrestle within herself as she patiently observed Matt's outburst. Though her brows furrowed, she still offered him her cherry-lipped smile. She outstretched her hand to him, like a single buoy a thousand miles from shore. Matt shook his head and huddled further into the corner.

So maybe I didn't wake up, Matt reasoned, returning to his thoughts. *I'm back in this fucking dream. So what was that other place I went to then? What was that cord?*

He felt his chest again, rubbing his solar plexus. The feeling was totally gone.

He pictured May again, and with a flare of longing, he recollected the feeling of being inside her.

118

May, Matt sobbed. *You showed me something. Did you help me wake up? Was that really your voice I heard in that other place?*

What you experienced was just another layer of the dream, the old man explained stolidly. *May is a dream character. And so are you.*

"No!" Matt shouted aloud at his mind, and he inwardly caught a glimpse of the light that had filled the world during his climax with May. The light seemed to scare the old man into submission. Matt was also reminded that he had a mission here. He had made substantial changes.

"I'll find out once and for all what's real," Matt whispered beneath his breath.

"What?" Mu said, still centering her attention on Matt.

The alarm blared, but Matt knew there was nothing to fear.

"The Reaper is dead," Matt told them, not caring whether they believed him or not. "And look," Matt said, kicking the lower half of the back wall. The wall opened to reveal the God Weapons and God Armor that could normally only be accessed by unlocking the Golden God Door.

The door to the cell slid open, but the other players were frozen in confusion.

"But how?" Kartikeya inquired first.

"Who cares!" Igwe snapped. "Who cares!" he repeated, bellowing with murderous excitement. "Loki has his tricks. Let's just win!"

The others nodded in simple agreement, satisfied with confusion as long as it brought them closer to victory. They began searching for their respective weapons and armor. Fighting the Reaper with the God Gear would be an even battle in a one-on-one match.

But if this worked, Matt reasoned, marveling at the literally sparkling equipment while he simultaneously pictured the Reaper's twirling blades, *then the other changes I made worked too. The Reaper is erased. I wanted to lock out all other users, but Souvik interrupted me before I could make the finishing touches. Still, there should only be a handful of other people able to access the game.*

Matt shook his head at the thought of other real people being in his dream. *But the logs,* Matt remembered.

That might just be a dream, Matt reminded himself cruelly, speaking for the old man in his apparent absence. His mind was flooded with images of May rocking back and forth above him, grinding hard against him as her eyes glistened with pleasure.

Fine, Matt confirmed to himself. *It all might be a dream. Everything might be a dream. I don't fucking know anymore. But I can't think that way. For May's sake. I have to believe she's real.*

His eyes turned to Mu. She found her respective item first, and he watched as she garbed herself in a sparkling robe of gold and crimson. The robe tightened around her slender body on its own accord as intricate black eyeliner filigreed at the outside corners of her eyes, extending to her cheeks and temples and continuing into her hairline.

"Yes!" Mu practically moaned, and she sounded identical to May in ecstasy. Curved kunai seemed to be growing from between her fingers. Mu parted her lips and exhaled with sultry delight. Her tongue danced across her lips with an insatiable hunger for rapturous movement and murder.

She looks devilish, Matt thought in horror. *Any selflessness she had in her is just rabid lust now.*

A shockwave of thunder pinned Matt to the ground, but the others didn't seem to take any notice. He cocked his head and saw that the sound was coming from Igwe. He wore oversized pearl-white gauntlets that boiled the air around them with visible tendrils of lightning bolts. His already oversized grin swelled as he slammed the gauntlets into one another once more, shotgunning Matt with more forceful energy that seemed to have no effect on the others. Blood-red war paint lined Igwe's face in a simple geometric pattern while pear-white armor grew over his body like living flesh.

Putch appeared frozen and just as solid as the gargantuan tapering stone slab she rested her hands on. The stone grew over her hands and arms and continued to shell every inch of her skin with impenetrable armor. As stone stretched to coat her body, what was once a uniform slab took on the shape of a giant club. She appeared more like an earth-elemental creature than an actual person.

A moan of pleasure turned Matt's attention back to Mu. She was pressing the tip of one of her kunai into the exposed part of her left breast.

"May!" Matt screamed, rising to his feet at the sight of a small bead of blood dripping down Mu's cleavage. She opened her eyes slowly and bit her lip at the sight of him, looking as though she might pounce on him and have him for herself as the others watched.

"I want to feel life drain from someone's body," Mu purred, then she backflipped and corkscrewed in the air with perfect ease, leaving the cell in a flash to hunt down anything and everything she could find.

She's like the Reaper, Matt nodded to himself with terrible understanding. *That's not May. It's not even Mu. It's...just code. Just a game.*

Just a dream, the old man said from somewhere incredibly distant. The light from May was still suppressing the old man's voice somehow. *I'm going to find out the truth,* Matt repeated to himself with newfound resolve. *I just have to get to the office and the laptop before the dream ends. Then I'll know.*

With an animalistic roar, Igwe charged out of the cell, and the fully rock-armored Putch followed, each of her steps like an earthquake tremoring through the very structure of the dream itself.

Kartikeya wore an easy grin and winked at Matt as he lifted a golden spear carved with intricate, fractaling patterns. The spear was multiple times the length of his body and too large to hold upright in the cell, so Kartikeya allowed the majority of its length to stretch numerous feet outside to the battlefield. He pivoted to face the door, and the peacock wings tattooed across his back began to stretch out of his shoulders and fill the cell with dizzyingly ornate feathers.

"Your job is done, Loki. I don't know how you did it, but you did. We'll take care of the rest. You just stay here," Kartikeya said, his voice stolid and booming with a godly echo. With that, Kartikeya bent at the knees, then jumped out of the cell and into the air, his powerful wings rocketing him with a force that filled the small room with a hurricane gale, pinning Matt against the wall.

Who knows how long I have. Get up! Matt demanded of his body, and his legs unwound and rose easily as if in detached response to his direction.

There was only a single item left from the original pile, and it was meant for Loki.

A near-invisibility cloak, Matt reminded himself, remembering what he had learned from navigating the source code in the real world.

Yes! Matt said inwardly, assuring his mind and combating the old man simultaneously. *The real world...with May. That's the real world. And I'm going to prove it!*

He wrapped the cloak around his shoulders and it came to life. Swimming shadows sprang from the material and blanketed the whole of his body. Any enemy onlooker would have to be keenly investigating his position in order to actually discern that he was there.

He peered outside the cell. He didn't see anyone, but he could hear cries of horror mixed with shouts of savage excitement.

I might not have long, Matt reminded himself resolutely. *Once my team kills all the others, that might reset the servers and my dream along with it.*

Matt began sprinting in the direction of where they had found the entrance to his office the last time.

A flash of gold struck his vision suddenly, and he fell backward in shock as Mu, naked and defenseless, was impaled against a wall by Kartikeya's inhumanly long spear.

"Take that!" Kartikeya shouted almost politely from at least twenty feet in the air. There was no savageness or lust for death in his voice – not in this form. There was just the insatiable drive for victory. His groin and torso were covered in illustrious feathers identical to those of his wings, which flapped regularly and easily to keep him in the air. Ebony hair floated freely above his head as if swayed by an unfelt breeze. As Kartikeya bared his teeth and removed his spear from between Mu's ribs, his hair whipped itself in the same direction as his arms, seeming to afford him some kind of supernatural strength.

"Having fun, Loki?" Kartikeya inquired pleasantly. Without waiting for an answer, he ascended back into the thick shadows above, readying himself to divebomb another unsuspecting victim from invisible heights like an owl hunting for starved field mice.

Mu, Matt almost screamed before realizing it wasn't *his* Mu. This Mu had various small neon tattoos imprinted on her, along with numerous facial piercings and a single pink streak of hair on one side. One of the tattoos imprinted across her right thigh said *Congo-Rayo.*

Wait…isn't that the company I partnered with? Matt realized.

This other Mu bled profusely from her wound, and as life drained from her body, Matt noticed the other tattoos:

Cosmos Coffee. Pear Enterprises. Monty's. Freemart.

They all sound like companies, Matt gawked grimly. *Sponsorships maybe? From…the real world. This is fucking real!*

A wave of nausea stampeded his insides, and Matt had to force himself away from the now motionless Mu player.

This is a video game in the real world. I'm in a real video game right now!

The old man's uproarious laughter echoed through the furthest reaches of Matt's mind.

Listen to yourself, the old man demanded pityingly. *What makes more sense? That you psychically connected to a video game or that this is all just my dream?*

Neither, Matt told him in equal horror and self-pity. *Neither option makes any fucking sense.*

From where I'm lying, one of those options makes perfect sense. You'll feel it when you wake up and return to your senses...when you become me again, the old man explained with a twinge of sadness. *What is this going to prove anyway? How can you ever truly prove the unreality of my reality or the reality of your unreality?*

You'll see, Matt told him simply, and he realized with greater horror that the old man could be heard in both the video game and the real world.

Which...is the same world, Matt grappled inwardly to accept. On the other hand, when he thought back to his memories of waking as the old man, he remembered that the old man couldn't hear him.

Because you're a dream, the old man told him as if in response to his realization.

"Shut up!" Matt barked, and he visually beckoned May's light to silence the old man back into slumber. It seemed to work, but the old man's point remained steadfast in Matt's mind.

Go! Matt urged himself with existential reluctance. *Just get to the office!*

He turned a corner, uncertain precisely where to find the circular hole in the ground. A naked version of himself covered in company logos turned a corner and sprinted frantically past him, turning another corner as if changing his mind at the last minute.

Matt felt a pang of dissociation seeing the different version of himself run past, but he didn't allow his mind to slow him down this time. *Just go!* he demanded, holding on to May's light with all his mind.

He could almost see the light as he sprinted forward, certain the hole in the floor had to be close.

"Where'd he go?" a deep feminine voice lashed with wickedness. Matt turned and saw his Mu smiling with venomous satisfaction, her armor and skin a glistening spray of someone else's blood. Every bit of revealed skin not covered in a thick layer of fluid was imprinted by intricate black lines extending all the way from the corners of her eyes.

Matt shook his head, terrified of the malevolent predator demanding her bloody sacrifice.

Matt pointed haphazardly in a random direction, just wanting to make it to the room before the dream's end. He realized with dread that he accidentally pointed in the direction the other version of himself had actually been running.

"Thank you, sweetie," Mu winked devilishly, and she darted around a corner, leaving behind a crimson haze.

Hurry! Matt urged himself.

He isn't real, anyway, came the subdued voice of the old man. *None of this is real.*

Matt gritted his teeth and ignored the old man. He could feel time running out. Searching frantically for the hole in the floor, he felt totally lost among the high walls of the zigzagging streets. Then he saw it out of the corner of his eye – an unsuspecting solid gold circle inlaid almost randomly in the floor.

That's it, Matt knew somehow. *That's my office.*

He got on his knees and tried to find some way to pry out what amounted to a solid gold manhole cover, but it was perfectly flush with the ground. He stomped hard on it, but it felt even more solid than the normal steel ground.

"Damn it!" Matt cried, and he closed his eyes and scraped his fingers through his hair with desperate fingertips and knuckles. "Let me in!" he demanded of his mind. "Let me in!" he screamed again at the top of his lungs.

Opening his eyes, Matt found himself standing in front of a small pool of water filled with koi swimming frantically. Fresh green plant life grew from and surrounded the pool with dense, overhanging fronds. He jumped back in surprise, half-expecting the scene to change again, but everything remained in place. He looked up to find the golden circle inlaid in the ceiling of his office.

I got in! I...teleported on command, Matt thought excitedly. Achieving powers like flight or teleportation was part of the natural process of gaining greater and greater lucidity. First, one had to become aware of the dream, then, with practice, they could begin exacting control of their mind with increasing degrees of creativity and freedom.

Am I becoming fully lucid in this dream? Matt pondered, looking at his hands as an instinctual reality check. *But I thought...*he gasped, *I thought this was real.*

It's a dream, the old man corrected with a subtle whisper.

You're the dream! Matt volleyed desperately. *You have to be. And if I can become lucid here, then I can become lucid in your world too.*

He turned toward his desk and nearly fell over again in shock. May, not Mu, sat in lotus posture, eyes fully open and unblinking. She was surrounded by freely bobbing fronds and fluttering butterflies of varied hues. She took no notice of him and appeared to be staring at the laptop on his desk.

"May!" Matt gasped, wanting to take her in his arms. But she was unnaturally frozen as if by a spell.

Focus! Matt reminded himself. *For her sake. Ignore that dream illusion and focus!*

His lips were dry and cracked, and he felt incredibly thirsty from the nonstop rush of adrenaline. He felt increasingly heavy and sleepy as if the old man's age had suddenly caught up with him in this dream.

Not now! Matt demanded, jolting himself back to wakefulness.

He glanced once more at May. She looked exactly the same as when Matt had first stumbled back into her life...and his own.

"May," Matt checked once more, but her enchanting eyes didn't move with him, nor did her seductive lips part to speak.

Matt opened the laptop and was prompted with the familiar question: *Are you awake?*

He typed: imstuckinadreamwithinadream. The interface opened to an old school DOS prompt with a single flashing cursor.

What should I write? Matt thought, unsure how to access the source code of his own mind and the old man's world.

He typed: *<pathsearch> dir*

The cursor flashed a few beats, then displayed a single directory file: *source.*

Too easy, Matt thought grimly, and he glanced back at May. Though her beauty undulated through the room, she remained a perfect statue staring at the laptop.

"May," Matt checked, but not even the butterflies seemed to take notice of him.

He typed: *open / source*

An endless cascade of code streamed across the interface with exponentially increasing rapidity. Each character shifted dynamically with each additional line so that the code was never precisely the same from one moment to the next. To most people, the streaming symbols would look like nothing more than gibberish – maybe even a concerning error. But for Matt, it was something much worse. It wasn't the source code of the video game world or the old man's world. It was the source code for his own world – for what he desperately hoped was the real world.

His chest tightened and his hands gripped the edges of the desk as his body's internal drive for survival tried desperately to break his mind away from what he saw.

"No!" Matt shrieked. Sinking into the oversized chair, he still couldn't loosen his grip from the desk. It felt as if he might fall forever into an invisible void.

"May…" Matt groaned through gritted teeth and freely flowing tears. As he continued sinking slowly into the chair, paralyzed by this new layer of insanity, he watched as the laptop's interface aligned with May's unflinching face, displaying every detail of her form and her mind and her very essence with perfect precision.

"Is it so surprising?" May said sweetly, moving naturally all of a sudden as if she had never actually been frozen.

All is lost, Matt told himself, his wide eyes glazed with horror. *The source code…it's the code to the real world, not the old man's world. That means I can…I can rewrite the real world from this laptop.* He gazed dreadfully at May and the identical code streaming alongside her. *I can even rewrite May. She's just code. It's all just code. It's all –*

Just a dream, came the old man, but rather than pity, he sounded filled with remorse.

May blinked, and the butterflies fluttered away at the behest of her expanding smile. She untangled her legs and rose in a single movement, then she took a frond gently in her hand and breathed in its scent.

"It's so real," she marveled. "Just like the 'real' world," May said, casually making quotation marks with her fingers around the word *real.*

"But is it so surprising, Matt?"

Matt felt transfixed.

"Why are you here?" Matt pleaded. "Why is any of this happening?"

"You have to know for sure, Matt," May said bittersweetly. "Just as you made changes to this dream, you have to try out some changes in the other dream too."

"The real world, you mean," Matt pressed, but May didn't let up.

"A dream," May and the old man corrected Matt in unison as voices both inside and outside his head.

"No!" Matt demanded, pushing himself and the chair away from the desk.

"This is all in my head! This is just —"

May interrupted him with pursed lips and narrowed eyelids. She strode to him and glided the back of her hand over the overworked veins in his temples.

"You have to know for sure, my love," she explained gently. Then she nodded at the laptop and said, "Go ahead. Nothing substantial. You don't want to erase me, now do you?" she furrowed seriously at the idea of being erased from the very source code of reality itself.

She's right, Matt admitted pitifully, taking in the whole of May for just another sorrowfully sweet moment. *I have to know for sure.*

He raised his fingers and placed them one-by-one into position.

"Something small," May repeated again, and she kissed Matt atop his head multiple times, lingering lovingly with each placement of her grazing lips.

Something small, Matt repeated to himself, and as his mind considered potential changes, he watched in helpless dread as the code reformed and reconfigured itself to match the intent of his mind.

He imagined May with shorter hair, and then the May in front of him had shorter hair. He imagined her with purple eyes and then watched as her chestnut-brown eyes transformed, taking on a deep-violet sheen.

"No!" Matt demanded desperately, and the code constituting May reverted alongside the physical May. "I don't want to change you!" Matt told her.

"Then change something else," she said simply, squeezing his shoulder with her gentle grip.

A mammoth weight slammed against the ceiling, causing both May and Matt to jump in surprise.

"Hurry," she told him despite total calm in her tone.

Matt held his eyes shut and focused on the changes he would make.

Couldn't I just change myself so that I'm sane? Can't I just rewrite my own mind from here? Matt considered, but nowhere in the streaming code could he find anything pertaining to himself outside of what amounted to place-holder text as if he had been planned into the world but never fully fleshed out. *I'm like a body out of space and time. It's like I'm some unnatural part of the world. It's like I don't really...or fully...exist.*

Questioning the validity of his own state of being so directly remind-ed him of Dr. Heron and the Serotel.

That's it. That's the change I'll make. Three Serotel bottles. One containing seven pills. One containing two pills. Another containing no pills. All three bottles will be in the bottom drawer of Dr. Heron's filing cabinet. And when I wake up, I'll be in his office. And...

Matt gazed at May, trying to come up with something about her past, but his mind was still empty of her existence.

"Tell me something that would be impossible for me to know," he said as she slowly kissed his temple.

May considered it a moment, then said, "When I was eleven, I lost my favorite toy when my family and I went camping. It was a little gray cat. It looked like this." She held out her hand and offered him a small gray plastic cat no larger than her thumb. "I called her Katsy. I cried for three days after I lost her." She emptied Katsy into Matt's open palm, and he placed it in his pocket. He eyed the code and willed a final change.

"When I wake up to the real world," Matt told her, "if this works, then I'll have the toy cat in my pocket. I'll give it to you, and you'll know I'm not crazy. You'll know that...the whole world is crazy, not me."

May nodded. "I hope so, Matt."

Another colossal slam to the ceiling ejected the circular golden door-way into the room with the velocity of a bullet, leaving it half-embedded in the crimson floor of the office. Matt and May jumped back in startled surprise, then looked up to see Igwe peering into the room, his fists boiling the air with electric bolts of monstrous power.

"What in the fuck are you doing down there, Loki? And...is that Mu? Xiwangmu, that you?"

"So you can see her?" Matt shouted at Igwe. Igwe shrugged and nodded, then waved a gauntlet at Matt with sudden realization.

"You're still playing games, Loki? We're about to win! You two should get up here. There's only a few stragglers left."

A ground-splitting shockwave pummeled the far corner of the ceiling, and Igwe grinned with excited brutality.

"Oh, never mind!" Igwe said, unable to keep himself from battle. He pushed up off the ground at least ten feet into the air before diving fist-first toward his prey.

"He could see you," Matt confirmed to May, unsure what to make of it. "You're not just a hallucination then," Matt hoped painfully.

"Or it's all a hallucination," May and the old man reminded Matt in unison.

"Will I be locked forever in these endless layers of madness – these endless Matryoshka coffins of insanity?" he asked May and the old man at once. He sank back into the chair, energy evaporating rapidly from his body now that he had completed what he came to do.

"Maybe," May and the old man answered as one.

Maybe, Matt repeated dreadfully, his voice like rabid violence in his mind.

"Maybe there's a source code for the old man's world in that other place I woke up when we had...I mean...when we made love," he hoped, not caring that he was conversing with this dream character as if she were the real May.

"Maybe," May repeated simply. Then she smiled sweeter than ever and asked, "Are you dreaming?"

"I don't know!" Matt nearly yelped. "I don't know what the fuck's happening, May. You...you're part of this dream. And you're part of the...the real world. And you're in that other world. I heard your voice. And you must be in the old man's world too. It's always you, May. You're always there. You're always –"

"Are you awake?" she repeated smoothly, undaunted by Matt's panic.

"I don't know!" Matt screamed with abandon this time.

May appeared unphased. She just smiled wide with seemingly perfect understanding of Matt's predicament and knelt down to align her ravishing eyes with his.

"Exactly," May said, her presence like an impenetrable fog capturing Matt's attention. "You don't know. You can't ever know. No one can. That's why I had to leave. You know that, Matt. You just couldn't accept the truth."

"I got him!" Kartikeya screamed from above. "We won! Holy hell, we did it!"

The room began vibrating, and a soft rumble could be heard in the distance.

"The truth!" Matt pleaded with her, uncertain where she was going with this or if it was just meaningless dreamtalk. But as always, everything seemed perfectly real.

"What's the truth, May?" Matt pressed as the vibrating continued.

The server's going to reset, Matt realized. *We're almost out of time.*

The others were cheering maniacally, even roaring with blood-fueled ecstasy. The rumbling intensified, and the room's subtle vibrations turned into visible shaking.

"Tell me, May. Please," Matt begged.

May wrapped her arms around him and brought her lips a breath away from his left ear. She whispered something, but Matt couldn't hear her over the now thunderous rumbling.

"May!" Matt shouted frantically. "Tell me, please!"

He could feel her breath against the tip of his ear, and though it sent waves of pleasure up and down his spine, it offered nothing in terms of actual meaning. The rumbling was so loud that he couldn't even hear his own voice. He slid off the chair and instinctually crawled beneath the desk as if the tremors constituted a transient earthquake. He pulled May close, and they braced themselves against the now torrenting ripples undulating through their bodies and the room as if everything, including themselves, constituted a single homogeneous fluid.

He screamed her name once more, but it was no use. She clung to him as if she really would never let go, and he held her just as tightly, never wanting to lose her again.

All of a sudden, they were tossed like unstrapped freight against the far wall, and Matt couldn't help screaming in abject horror, though his voice was drowned out by the tumultuous rumbling of reality and the barbaric shouts of victory from the others.

They slammed hard against the opposite wall, and the very fabric of reality began pulling apart, splitting spacetime from endlessly fractaling seams like gaping scar tissue. There was a void-darkness hiding behind it all, and the tearing of reality forced the very atoms of Matt's body into painful separation.

12. Back to Sleep

ho was that old man? Matt wondered. It was his first thought upon waking once again to the infinitely curved corridor. He kept himself calm to avoid the nurses putting him back to sleep so quickly. *That old man in the video game designer's head — that's not me. So who was he talking to?* Matt probed what he remembered from the dreams. *Was the old man's voice some imaginary version of me?*

The dreams lasted so long this time, and Matt felt exhausted from the extended jaunt through his mind.

The dream lasted longer this time because the video game designer took those pills in his therapist's office, Matt remembered. *Did that make the dream last longer and...skip over me and the video game character in what is normally a cycle? Was that just...random?*

The stars and darkness outside reminded him of the Reaper and of Dr. Heron.

That's right, Matt remembered. *The last time I woke up, one of the nurses referred to Dr. Heron.*

He raised a hand to call over one of the nurses and ask for the Dr. Heron of the real world, then thought better of it. There was still so much to consider, so many unanswered questions.

But those are all questions pertaining to my dreams. Just dreams! Matt wished he could accept fully. *They're so convincing,* yet *whenever I wake up, it's so obvious those other people and places are all in my head.*

May filled his mind, and he reached for his chest, half-imagining that the braided cord was there.

That's right — the braided cord, Matt remembered, following the thought to the newly revealed layer of his dreams. *But that was still in the video game designer's head. That was still just a dream*, Matt ruminated grimly. *Even the characters themselves confirmed it's just a dream. The video game character found the source code to the designer's world and vice versa. Those are both just dreams. And the dream with the cord in my chest, that's just a dream within a dream. But…*

May's slanted smile filled his mind once more, and he nearly sobbed.

But that would mean May is nothing but a dream.

He shook his head, and he saw the glowing flashes from the monitors behind him, warning the nurses and other presumed staff that Matt needed another shot of whatever it was they injected into him to keep him asleep.

That can't be, Matt pleaded in horror. *I love May. I know that. She is all that matters. I know that with absolute certainty.*

He closed his eyes against May's unreality and the consequent unreality of his love for her and her love for him.

Don't I? Don't I know that? Can something like love just be dreamed accidentally?

A pair of nurses emerged from one of the many doors and walked swiftly to Matt, smiling pleasantly with their identical eyes.

Those eyes, Matt realized, and he thought himself stupid for not realizing it sooner.

"It's you," Matt called out to them. "Both of you. All of you. You're all her."

The nurses looked at one another with measured concern, then finished their walk to Matt's bedside. One nurse reached into her pocket and took out the syringe. The other took Matt's hand into her own and rubbed the inside of his thumb just like May had in the car.

"Everything will be all right, Mr. Willish," she assured him.

"Take off your masks, will you?" Matt asked bluntly. "Both of you."

The nurses exchanged glances, then removed the large white coverings. Both nurses were absolutely identical. And they were both May, only without the piercings and carefully plucked eyebrows.

"So you are here," Matt nearly gushed, grasping the nurse's hand and never wanting to let go. "It's you, May," Matt confirmed, his old voice cracking as tears streamed down his face. "But you're so young, and I'm so old!" Matt gasped.

May squeezed his hand for comfort, and the other May continued preparing the needle.

"Oh, Mr. Willish," May sighed regretfully, patience and compassion in her voice. "Not much longer now, okay?"

"May!" Matt gasped, realizing in full force that he was about to be thrown back into the dream world and back into the mind of a character who thinks himself fully real. "Help me," Matt pleaded.

The other May set the syringe's plunger, sending a spray of liquid through the needle.

May cocked her head and smiled at Matt as if he were just another patient in an endless ward of dying men.

Distant. Cold. Why is she so detached? Like I'm nothing to her.

"Are you really her? Are you really May?" Matt begged to know despite recognizing that May could very well be either of the nurses.

"The real May?" the nurse checked incredulously, and she kissed the old, bony knuckles of Matt's hand.

"You're just confused, Mr. Willish. But Dr. Heron said we're just about there. So we really shouldn't be talking like this, okay? Not until we finish with the procedure, at least."

"Dr. Heron!" Matt demanded. "I want to speak with him."

"Okay," May agreed simply. "We'll let him know."

Both Mays nodded sweetly at Matt.

"Back to sleep now," May said with a confident smile.

"Everything will be all right," the other May assured him with equal sincerity and sweetness.

He could feel the heaviness coming on, and as the nurses refastened their masks over their ears, the lights behind them began to blur, and his thoughts slowed and stuttered.

Focus! Matt urged himself, imagining himself becoming the video game designer and the video game character all over again. *Remember that it's all just a dream. Just a dream. Just a dream. Just a dream...*

13. Running Out

"**J**ust a dream," Matt felt his lips mouth of their own accord. He opened his eyes and picked up his head from its slump. Dr. Heron glared at him, and his void-black glare burned beneath Matt's skin.

"You," Dr. Heron snarled. "You just nodded off there, didn't you?"

Matt shook his head instinctually, then he remembered that he was not actually this man in a therapist's office. This was just a dream.

It has to be. I proved it, Matt told himself resolutely. *This world is just a dream. The old man is right...I mean...I'm right,* Matt thought as his mind's disposition turned to existential horror, then finally changed again, settling on a nearly perfect confidence that he was merely lucid in a dream of waking life.

Matt remembered that he had made changes to this world – May's world – just to be sure of its unreality.

"This is just a dream," Matt told his therapist with the tried-and-true wisdom of an old man on his deathbed.

Dr. Heron shook his head and sighed deeply, considering his words carefully.

Matt rose and pointed to the bottom drawer of Dr. Heron's filing cabinet before the man could speak.

"There's three Serotel bottles in that drawer. One of them has seven pills. Another has two pills. And the last one contains no pills. If I'm right –"

"Enough, Matthew!" Dr. Heron barked, and Matt was caught off guard by the harsh tone in his voice. The inkblot painting seemed to pulsate behind Dr. Heron, inducing a feeling of falling toward it.

"No!" Matt barked right back. "You listen. If I'm right...if that's what I find in that drawer —"

"Do not touch my desk, Matthew Willish," Dr. Heron warned, his voice like the edge of a sheathed blade ready to be drawn.

Fuck you, Matt thought, and Dr. Heron went wide-eyed as if he could read Matt's mind. Matt strode to the desk and pushed away the man in all black, taking hold of the drawer's handle. He tried to jerk it open, but it was locked.

"Matthew!" Dr. Heron shrieked. "How dare you!"

"Open it," Matt told him resolutely.

"Sit down, Matthew."

"Open it!" Matt shouted this time.

Dr. Heron didn't seem phased by Matt's threatening tone. "Just five minutes ago. You don't remember just five minutes ago?" Dr. Heron offered with forced composure.

He's stalling, Matt realized, and his heart ramped up with the expectation that he was right about the contents of the bottom drawer.

"Five minutes ago I was awake in reality. Now I'm in a dream. Open it," Matt demanded.

"Five minutes ago you asked me how much Serotel I have on hand. I told you not much. You asked for specifics. And I told you that in my bottom drawer there are three bottles: One of them containing seven pills. Another containing two pills. And the last bottle empty."

Matt shook his head, but already he was starting to feel mentally unstable rather than lucid.

"No," Matt demanded. "That can't be."

Dr. Heron removed a key from his pocket and unlocked the drawer. Inside, Matt saw three bottles. Dr. Heron offered him all three.

"All yours," he said, "just don't invade my space like that again, Matthew."

Matt licked his dry lips and took a cautious step backward.

"No," Matt said again, his voice cracking and pleading. "This can't be."

Dr. Heron finally rose and put a stiff arm around Matt's shoulder.

"Matthew, we need to increase your Serotel dosage. And I'm putting you on a new medication as well. But for now, I don't think you're even

138

fit to be in public. You should be in a hospital. Do you understand?"

Of course, Matt confirmed to himself, remembering how resolute he had been about going to the hospital the previous night.

But May…

He could still feel May's gyrations and groaning and gripping.

Did any of that even happen? Matt considered helplessly. He went weak in the knees and fell back onto the black leather couch, tearing away from Dr. Heron's stiff embrace.

There was a sudden knock at the door, and both Matt and Dr. Heron turned their necks to investigate.

A man opened the door and poked his head through without asking for permission to enter.

"Sorry, Doctor, I just really need to get in here, you know?" The man smiled at them nervously, and Matt could see that there were others in the waiting room outside Dr. Heron's door. They all looked like poor imitations of…someone else. Then Matt saw it: they were all imitations of himself.

"You…look like me…" Matt stammered. "And…so do those others…"

Imposters, Matt realized. *It's like Alice said.*

"Get out!" Dr. Heron ordered.

The man clenched his teeth and pleaded, "I need more Serotel, Doctor. This guy's been in here long enough!"

"I said out!" Dr. Heron bellowed, his voice like a frayed whip.

The man nodded apologetically and closed the door. The others in the waiting room looked just as impatient.

"They're all imposters," Matt said, wanting confirmation.

Dr. Heron nodded. "They all want to be you, Matthew. Even down to the Serotel."

Dr. Heron looked nervous, darting his eyes from one area of the room to the next as if attempting to further conceal a cleverly hidden secret.

"Or," Matt began, nodding with forlorn realization at the obvious possibility he had overlooked, "I'm one of them."

Dr. Heron shook his head ardently. "No, Matthew. You are Matthew

Willish. They aren't. Do you understand?"

He's worried. He's hiding something. I...discovered something he doesn't want revealed. Am I...not me?

"Or...you're just saying that. I could be a particularly bad case. Why else would you be giving me Serotel along with them? You told me before that Serotel is custom made for me. But that's not true. And when May looked it up, she couldn't even find it!" Matt was working himself into a passionate fervor. "What are you not telling me? Am I not me? Am I an imposter of myself...of this man named Matthew Willish?"

"No!" Dr. Heron bellowed with stalwart certainty, cutting Matt off and rising to his feet. "Don't start thinking that way. You are Matthew Willish. Say it, Matthew. And then I'll have your bodyguards take you to the hospital. I'll meet you there. But first say it. Say who you are."

"I'm," Matt began, and he felt the environment hum and vibrate. His hands began buzzing. He lifted them, palms up, and observed them, checking them for strangeness as a reality check, but they seemed perfectly normal.

"Say it," Dr. Heron repeated, his black pupils aglow and consuming.Dr. Heron took on an air of anger, and at the same time, the inkblot began moving in slow undulations behind him.

Matt was frozen, locked to the surface of the couch like an animal cornered in its den.

"The hospital. Just take me to the hospital," Matt pleaded.

"Say it!" Dr. Heron snapped. "Say your name!"

The inkblot slid off the canvas, leaving a pure white field on the wall. It tightened and formed limbs and a distinct body – like chromatin winding into chromosomes. The eldritch ink-creature injected raw terror into the very molecules of the air. Dr. Heron took no notice as the inkblot continued morphing into a lanky giant behind him. Now its final shape was obvious.

"Reaper!" Matt shrieked, pointing at the creature in helpless terror.

"That's *my* name!" Dr. Heron seethed. "What is yours!"

The vibrating of the room intensified suddenly, and the ink-Reaper stretched its limbs, extending them like blades toward each of Matt's pupils.

Matt opened his mouth wide to scream as reality itself fissured open

140

along with him. The chrysanthemum portal curled its fractaling edges around Matt's body and deposited him directly outside his apartment door.

The vibrating ceased, and everything seemed perfectly normal and still.

Matt gasped and bent at the knees, holding the door with one hand and the floor with the other for support.

"Fuck this nightmare," he seethed.

There is no way out, the old man whispered in his head.

"Fuck you!" Matt lashed at his mind.

His bent knees stretched his jeans tight, and he could feel something small and hard in his pocket. He removed the item and inspected it in his palm. It was a small gray cat, exactly like the one May had described in the video game dream.

"Katsy," Matt gasped.

The old man offered only silence.

"That's right," Matt said aloud to his mind. "You got no explanation for that, do you?"

He wiped away tears, stood, then checked his pockets for keys. He didn't even have his wallet. The only thing on his person was the toy cat.

"You okay?" someone asked, making Matt jump back in shock.

"Sorry," a large woman said from his right, "I didn't mean to scare you."

It was the bus driver.

"Fernanda, right?" Matt checked, wiping his eyes and putting Katsy back inside his pocket to seem at least fractionally normal.

"That's right," she said, seeming grateful that he remembered. "Are you...okay?" she inquired again.

Why is she here? Matt wondered, and he found it odd that she was just casually asking him this question. *Does she live in the same apartment building?*

"Why are you...here? I mean —" Matt stopped himself, realizing too late how rude the question might sound.

She nodded with understanding. "Yeah, sorry, I didn't mean to alarm you. You just dropped your keys on your way in, I think."

The keys were there in her hand, and she offered them to Matt with a demeanor and comfortability that seemed like more than mere familiarity.

It's like she knows me...even outside of just being my bus driver. It's like...

"We have the same therapist," she admitted suddenly as if reading Matt's mind. "Today's my day off. I saw you at Dr. Heron's office...when you stormed out. And I...it's not that I followed you back to your apartment or anything, but I just –"

"I walked back here?" Matt checked, interrupting her struggle to explain herself.

"Well...yeah," she hesitated, looking at Matt with greater scrutiny. "You don't remember?"

Matt shook his head, and he couldn't help a deep sigh of helplessness. He let his back fall against the hallway wall, and he slid down, bending at the knees again.

"I need to go to a hospital," Matt told her bluntly.

"Do you trust Dr. Heron?" she volleyed just as directly.

"What?" Matt checked, caught off guard by her question.

"Do you trust him?" she repeated, locking eyes with Matt. She removed a pill bottle from her pocket. "Serotel," she groaned. "Does he have you on the same stuff?"

Matt nodded, and she nodded back.

"You ever think maybe it's this shit that's fucking us up?" she offered grimly, and her breathing increased as Matt's heartbeat intensified, filling his ears with the haunting drumbeat of his own life.

"Yes," Matt answered, simply and honestly. "But it seems like I'm fucked even when I don't take it," he said, remembering the first time he woke and realized that he hadn't taken his pills for months.

She nodded, seeming to understand.

"Do you trust him?" she asked again, and her eyes welled with quivering fluid.

"No," Matt nearly whispered, and he felt the old man shaking his head pityingly at Matt's despair and confusion. "But I can't even trust my own mind. And I feel like...there's no fucking way out of this...this madness."

"There's no way out," Fernanda repeated hollowly, as if it were some terrible lesson she had learned over and over again through a lifetime of suffering. She groaned in despair, then she threw the Serotel bottle down the hallway. It bounced against the floor and walls, finally settling near the entrance to the building. The keys hit the floor, and when Matt turned to look, Fernanda was suddenly gone, as if she had just disappeared through her own chrysanthemum portal.

Matt gulped hard, then exhausted a deep breath. He narrowed his lips and slowed his breathing the best he could.

The world…this place…everything is too unstable. Everything is madness here.

Because it isn't the real world, came the sorrowful voice of the old man.

Matt nodded in sullen acceptance.

"There is no way out," Matt said, and he felt the old man nod in agreement. "And May is all that matters," Matt continued, but the old man disagreed.

She's a dream.

Matt shrugged in horrible resignation.

"Whatever," he said, "dream or not, she is all that matters to me."

You're a slave to an illusion – slave to your dreams, the old man warned.

"Leave me alone," Matt told him, and he visualized the explosion of light that had overtaken his body during his time with May.

Simultaneously, Matt felt the old man retreat deep inside his mind just as he heard a ringtone coming from somewhere in his apartment.

He picked up his keys, opened the door, and saw his phone lying haphazardly on the floor of his small kitchen. He picked it up and answered it without even checking who it was.

"Matt?" May said with incredible urgency and worry in her voice.

"May," Matt nearly yelped, and though he couldn't help smiling, he also felt a pang of dread that his memory of their time together might very well be a fabrication of his madness.

"I sent you so many fucking texts, Matt. What's going on? Are you okay?"

Matt practically whimpered with relief. "So last night did happen. We were together?"

"Matt…that was two weeks ago. Are you…where are you?"

Two weeks.

The words battered his brain with more maddening fodder.

She thinks I've been avoiding her, Matt thought, but another part of his brain warned him that was the least of his worries.

No, Matt told the logical pathways of his mind pleading with him to call an ambulance. *She is all that matters.*

Everything seemed perfectly normal at the moment just as it did the entire night he was with May.

"Everything's fine as long as you're with me, May."

"Did you go to a hospital, Matt? Did you see your therapist? I can go with you. Chike and Souvik can handle things."

The ink-Reaper filled Matt's mind at the mention of his therapist, and he was also reminded of what Fernanda had said to him in the hallway.

"I can't trust him," Matt said.

"Okay," May said, accepting his words without the need for further explanation. "But you can trust me. So let me come pick you up. Okay?"

He remembered the toy cat in his pocket.

"I have Katsy," he said without context; he wanted to see if it would elicit the type of profound reaction he was hoping for. The May in the video game dream had said that it was a memory only she could possibly know.

"What?" May checked, her tone shifting to utter surprise.

"Katsy. Your toy cat as a child," Matt explained, and he stared into the alluring eyes of Mu on the *Room Reaper* poster as he waited for May's answer.

"Why would you say that, Matthew?" she said, sounding almost disdainful.

"So then it does mean something to you?" Matt checked desperately.

"Should I pick you up, or will you be coming to me?" she asked, ignoring his question.

"May, please," Matt begged. "Am I talking nonsense, or am I saying something that only you could know?"

"Are you toying with me, Matt?" May asked, choosing her words carefully and methodically.

"No! Of course not!" Matt pleaded. "May...I love you..."

"I'll come and pick you up, Matt. Then we can talk."

"Okay," Matt said with a sense of resolve.

If it meant nothing, she would have just shrugged it off, Matt considered. *But it means something to her. How else could I have this toy cat if I didn't change things in the video game dream?* Matt winced. *So this is...this is for sure all a dream, then. This is all in my own head.*

"Just stay at your apartment, okay?" May reassured him.

"Okay," Matt confirmed, and as he turned away from Mu's seductive smile to close his apartment door, the doorway's edges unfurled with the chrysanthemum pattern. The doorway shimmered with an ethereal fog, obscuring the hallway outside. Then the fog cleared, revealing that the hallway had been replaced by the sidewalk and trees and road outside of May's house. Matt peered out the window in his living room and saw that it was late afternoon, yet the sky through the doorway carried the ebony hue of late night.

"Actually," Matt said, almost grateful for the madness in this moment, "I'll be there in just a sec."

"No," May said urgently. "I'll come to you, Matt, you just —"

He walked through the doorway, unintentionally cutting May off. The temperature of the air plunged around him, dropping from room temperature to a brisk fifty degrees as he stepped from his apartment directly onto May's street some unknown number of blocks away.

"What if there is a way out?" came a woman's voice with a Brazilian accent.

Matt turned to look behind himself and found that it was Fernanda who had asked the question. She stood beside the shrinking chrysanthemum portal, taking no notice of it.

"What?" Matt asked. "I mean, what are you doing here now? You...followed me?"

"You told me to," Fernanda said in defense against Matt's admonishing tone. "Do you want me to leave?"

Either she's lying or I'm fully losing all sense of time and space or...

"You think there's a way out?" Matt pressed.

Fernanda looked caught off guard.

"I don't know," she admitted, "but you said it with such certainty back at your apartment. I just...I don't want to think like that."

Fernanda went wide-eyed and peered at the pavement below her, and

Matt saw her indelible gaze of madness. It was a look of confusion and helplessness and anger and awe all at once.

She's insane. Like me, Matt realized.

"Have you ever looked into the Serotel?" Matt asked.

Fernanda shrugged and shook her head.

"I did," Matt said. "It doesn't exist. Go ahead. Look it up."

"Dr. Heron said that it's custom made for me," Fernanda explained tepidly.

"He said the same to me." The pair stood on the sidewalk, neither of them sure where to go or how to move on with their lives.

"Maybe if we stop taking the Serotel —" Fernanda offered sadly, clearly not able to believe her own words.

"I tried that," Matt interjected. "The only thing that seems to keep me sane is being around May. She's my...coworker."

Fernanda cocked her head. "You said a few months ago that you're him. You think you're Matthew Willish, don't you? And May...you're talking about May Willish?"

"May Anh," Matt corrected.

"No," Fernanda interrupted with certainty. "The news said they married before he disappeared. Matthew Willish, I mean. May Willish controls his whole company — I mean, her company, now."

"My company," Matt corrected her, and he felt for Katsy in his pocket. It was still there — his floundering proof of sanity in a rudderless and insane world.

Fernanda nodded and shrugged. "You really think you're him?"

A surge of anger filled Matt, but it was only fair for her to ask that. Even he wasn't sure.

"Matthew!" May called urgently from her doorway.

Matt turned suddenly and took the whole of her in. She wore a loose, crimson silk robe, and her hair was pulled back and held in place with several chopsticks. The streetlight several houses down reflected off her facial piercings, making them sparkle radiantly. She lifted her robe and ran barefoot down her front steps to meet him.

"Matthew!" she repeated, this time with a mixture of worry and anger. "I told you to stay put. I went to your apartment and you weren't there. And you haven't been answering my calls or texts!" She gave Matt time to respond, but he wasn't sure what to say first. He turned to introduce Fernanda, trying to stall his explanation, but she had disappeared once more.

"Did you see someone out here with me?" Matt checked, becoming less certain of Fernanda's reality.

What's one more hallucination in an endless series of hallucinated realities? Matt considered despondently.

May ignored his question and latched onto him, squeezing him in her embrace.

"Matthew!" she heaved with equal relief and anguish. "I was fucking worried about you. All I fucking do is worry about you."

Her warmth enveloped his cold mind, and he breathed her in as if for sustenance.

I have to explain to her just how bad I am. I have to tell her somehow. But first thing's first.

Matt gently broke their embrace, then he reached into his pocket and removed Katsy, presenting the toy cat to May as if it were the world's greatest treasure.

May took two horrified steps back, her eyes never leaving the toy cat.

"But why? How?" she gawked, unable to avert her awe-struck gaze.

"Take it," Matt told her, wanting her to hold it to further confirm its reality. She hesitated a moment, then took it from Matt's palm and inspected it with incredible consternation.

"How?" she repeated breathlessly.

"That's what we need to talk about," Matt confirmed, and he felt a wave of relief at her reaction.

This is it. For better or worse, there's no way I could have this toy. The way she's reacting is proof alone. She might even...believe me if I'm honest about what I'm going through.

"Come on," she said, wiping away her tears. "Let's go inside."

She took hold of Matt's hand and squeezed it lovingly. He could see that she was squeezing Katsy tightly in her other hand, probably in continued disbelief.

"You didn't see anyone else out here with me?" Matt asked as they entered May's home.

"No," May said. "I saw you talking to yourself, which isn't exactly unusual for you," she offered gently. "Who...who were you talking to?"

"Maybe no one," Matt admitted, accepting May's words as the most likely truth. "But I thought I was talking to my bus driver, the one I based the character Putch's design on."

The hulking metal wall swung closed behind them. May allowed herself a shallow huff of laughter at Matt's words.

"You going to take credit for everything now?" she said with a jesting tone. She looked Matt over and saw that he was being serious.

"I designed Putch," May said. "You're right that you designed the others, but Putch was my design. I'm quite proud of her, thank you."

It wasn't a total surprise that May had designed Putch, but that didn't explain the uncanny similarity between Putch and Fernanda.

May must have based Putch on Fernanda.

"You've seen her then?" Matt asked. "My bus driver? She's practically identical to Putch, even down to the scar across her face."

May shook her head. "I've never seen a bus driver who looks like Putch. I just free-formed her design."

Matt sighed deeply and fell back onto the ochre couch, allowing his body and mind to sink further into the madness of it all.

What does it matter? This must all be a dream.

He felt the old man nod in approval.

"What about Katsy?" Matt urged.

May nodded. "Yes. What about her? I would love an explanation."

"An explanation," Matt repeated, marveling at the simplicity and hollowness of the word.

"Or you can just ignore me and disappear again like you always do," May lashed suddenly.

"I'm sorry," Matt said almost out of habit, but he really was sorry for everything, even his own mind.

"Just...just," May stammered, searching for the right words. "Just talk to me, Matt. Just...tell me what's really going on."

She'll think you're crazy, the old man offered.

"She already thinks I'm crazy," Matt told his mind aloud.

May nodded and easily shrugged off Matt's words. "Your mind is like an intricate, beautiful origami maze, and right now it's raining for you, sopping all that paper into a big mess. But maybe if you talk to me, Matt…maybe if you talk to me we can dry up that rain…together."

Her shoulders were huddled tightly together, and her eyes looked as though they might well with more tears. She held Katsy close to her heart.

"How is this possible, Matt?"

I have to tell her. Everything. For better or worse. I have to tell her now before everything melts back to madness again.

"You told me about Katsy. In a dream," Matt admitted, shaking his head at how ludicrous he sounded. "A dream that I keep having every time I go to sleep. And then there's another dream. And maybe…I think maybe this is really the dream world and the other dream world is the real world. Or maybe they're all dreams. Maybe –"

"Matt," May urged. "Just…just start from the beginning. Just…try to explain, okay?"

She sat beside him on the couch and wrapped her arms around his shoulders, kissing his temple tenderly as she placed Katsy on the table.

"You can tell me everything, okay? I'll suspend my disbelief for now. Okay?"

Matt sighed heavily. *Where do I even begin?*

He thought back as far as he could remember, back to the first time he woke naked in the cell with Mu and the others.

"Okay," Matt breathed. "I'll tell you everything I remember."

He told her everything. Every little detail and strangeness and impossibility. She listened the whole time, never asking questions or demanding further explanation. She just listened.

"And then I stepped through the door of my apartment and arrived here all of a sudden," Matt said, finishing the labyrinthine journey through his mind. "Time jumped again for the whole world, but only a second passed for me. Fernanda was outside. She said…she said that you and I are married. She said you took over the company. And then…then you came outside and found me. And…and here we are."

May stared into Matt's eyes with incredible compassion and sadness. After several long seconds, she finally said, "Okay."

"Okay?" Matt repeated, uncertain how to gauge her response.

May nodded and rose to her feet.

"The server logs. The Serotel. Katsy. Everything. It's all...it's all very overwhelming, isn't it?" May offered with sincere understanding, though Matt still didn't know if she believed him, or if it was even possible for anyone to believe him.

"But when I'm with you, everything is all right," Matt reminded her. "Everything is so stable. Everything makes sense."

"But you still need to go to the hospital, Matt."

Matt nodded fervently. "Yes. Yes, I do. But every time I try to go, reality turns to mush and everything is insane...until I end up back with you somehow. Everything is all right when I'm with you, May."

Matt felt astounded that his words were not hyperbole. Somehow, all of reality remained stable as long as May was by his side.

"I'm not going anywhere, Matt," May assured him. "I don't have an explanation for a lot of what you're telling me, especially Katsy. But you have to understand, for all I know, this is all an incredible ruse. For all I know, this is the other you right now – the Matt that takes over when you...lose yourself. You said so yourself, right?"

Matt nodded, admitting that she was right.

"I don't know what to believe for sure with you, Matt. You say so many different things and...well...you're right about you seeming like a totally different person sometimes. I don't know which one is the real you."

"I don't either," Matt admitted pitifully. "But I can tell you that the Matt you're talking to right now – this is the real me. I'm here now, May."

"Until you aren't," May retorted, revealing the pain involved with loving a man like Matt.

"I'm sorry, May," Matt said, pleading for forgiveness. "I'm sorry I'm like this. But I love you. I know that. I know that I love you."

May's shoulders sank in defeat, and she returned to the couch to sit beside Matt. He held her, and she allowed herself to sink into his chest.

"I love you too, Matt. I do...but..."

But, Matt repeated inwardly. *There's a but.*

"The effects are instant, and though it only lasts a few moments, it can feel like an eternity. When you smoke it as a crystal like this, it can make you die – I mean – not actually die. But you experience ego death."

Matt shivered at her mention of death, and he remembered how he had concluded, as the old man, that the only way to know for sure whether or not reality is actually real is to die.

Death, Matt repeated the word in his head with dreadful trepidation.

"If it's not death, then what is ego-death exactly?" Matt inquired as he attempted to stifle his nervous shaking.

"Ego-death is the loss of all anchoring to self," May said, and as she took another hit of the bowl, she looked as though she were coming to some impossible realization. She spoke as if on autopilot while the rest of her seemed to contemplate the fringes of some great madness that had just clicked in her mind. "During ego-death, there is no more separation between the atoms composing the countless eukaryotic and pro-karyotic cells of your body or the atoms composing the air exhausted by the eukaryotic bundles we call plants. There is just the field – the system itself. There is no more you. It's...it's not really possible to relate through language because it's beyond language," she said with a hint of sorrow, and as she turned to Matt, he noted that her eyes looked distant and afraid suddenly. "I'm sorry if this isn't making sense," she finished.

Though he felt entranced by both her beauty and intellect, he couldn't help noticing the subtle change in her.

May put the bowl to her lips and looked wide-eyed at the ceiling. Matt imagined she might be recollecting one of her egoless DMT dives, but he wasn't sure it was possible to recollect something that didn't involve a thing to do the recollecting. She pulled hard at the bowl's contents, burning far more of it than she had with the first hit. She held it for just a moment, then released it. This time she didn't cough.

"It only lasts a few minutes when you smoke it, but time becomes irrelevant. Those few minutes feel like multiple eternities. It lets you really step outside yourself," she said, and she seemed to sigh away a portion of whatever was irking her. "I think we all get the feeling sometimes of being trapped inside reality, you know? Of just...being stuck in something we can't explain or understand or even question meaningfully. But the thing we're really stuck in is ourselves. DMT lets you get outside yourself and the world and everything, even if just for a moment. It

153

shows you that...there's more. There's...there's more than just this...thing...this existence and this self that we will never and can never comprehend." She lowered her head suddenly, seemingly in shame and said, "I don't want you to see me as some kind of junkie, Matt. I just see substance as a tool for self-exploration and...much more. And these substances have served as exceptional tools throughout my life – maybe the only truly effective tools I know of."

Her words about being able to step outside the self resounded in Matt's mind. *She said...it lets you get outside yourself. Like...like a way out.* Matt nodded in an attempt to reassure her, but already his mind was considering how he might convince her to let him try it.

What could it possibly hurt? My mind is already shattered into a million pieces.

"I don't see you as a junkie at all, May. Actually, you're the most beautiful and intelligent person I've ever met."

"Funny," she told him with her slanted smile, "that's exactly how I feel about you."

Matt couldn't help blushing, a reaction that only deepened when he realized how childishly he'd reacted.

Maybe she'll just let me try some, Matt considered evenly.

"I could use a way outside myself," Matt told her, and he pointed to the largest of the DMT crystals half-buried in cannabis.

"Matt..." she hummed through a buzz of sorrow. "We should go to the hospital."

"Okay," he nodded, and he offered her a sheepish smile despite knowing what he had to do.

I have to try it. What the hell will the hospital do for me that hasn't already been tried? What the hell do I possibly have to lose?

"Okay," he lied. "I was just thinking out loud, that's all," he assured her.

May sighed, still wrestling with something inside herself, then she closed the gap between them. She pulled his head to her chest and stroked the back of his neck.

"I'm sorry, Matt, I –" she began, shaking her head at some great internal confusion. "I don't understand...I...I'm going to use the bathroom," she said as if suddenly many miles away. "What about you?"

Matt thought back in dread to the time in the bar bathroom, but he

154

felt fine. Besides, this was his chance. All she had to do was put the pipe back on the table.

May bent down, kissed the top of his head tenderly, then set the pipe on the table, just as Matt had hoped. Appearing grief-stricken, she shook her head; she seemed to be attempting to process some still foggy realization at the front of her mind.

"I love you, Matthew Willish," she said, still shaking her head. "I'll be right back."

He closed his eyes and breathed deeply in preparation for death, as May had called it.

"I love you too, May."

She broke away and strode to the bathroom. He waited a moment after she closed the door, then jumped at his opportunity.

She just trusts me not to do it? he wondered as he grabbed the bowl. *She doesn't understand how bad off I am. But if she understood...if she really understood...I'm sure she would agree with me that this might be my only way out...my only chance at some level of understanding.*

He unscrewed the metal cylinder and removed the largest DMT crystal. His fingers trembled with anxious trepidation as he placed it atop the remaining half-burnt cannabis in May's bowl. He wasn't sure how exactly it worked, but he had just watched May use it, and it seemed simple enough.

He picked up the lighter and brought the bowl to his lips. His heart pounded in terrible anticipation, and he had to breathe even deeper to try and bring it under control.

What if I have a heart attack? Matt considered, and his heart pounded even more forcefully, threatening him with his own reeling thoughts.

Then he felt it. The mounting vibration of reality that he had felt numerous times before losing himself to a dream within a dream. He realized that it had begun at the periphery of his mind just as he made contact with the DMT, but now the vibration was totally obvious.

I can't lose this chance, Matt thought, demanding that his fingers and lips and lungs obey his inner mind's desperate attempt at some semblance of self-understanding and self-stability.

He heard the bathroom door open, and May rushed out in tears.

Do it! he commanded his body.

"Matt –" May gasped, but she didn't rush to stop him as he lit the lighter and pulled hard, sizzling the crystal with the open flame. The smoke was thick and tasted like burnt plastic, but he ignored his lungs pleading for air and flooded them with more and more DMT.

May shook her head finally and sprinted to him. She smacked the bowl out of his hand, jarring him backward, but he could barely feel her hit amidst the intensity of the vibrations.

"Matt, no! Let it out! I'm sorry, Matt," she pleaded, looking him over from head to toe in directionless desperation.

The need for air became too much, and as Matt released the smoke from his lungs, he watched as the cloud merged with the background of May's apartment. Just as quickly, the smoke began undulating and forming into chrysanthemum crests and folds, overtaking his entire field of vision.

He felt something tug at his chest, and he realized that it was the braided cord.

Am I going back to that other world? Matt considered with equal parts horror and exhilaration. His body was paralyzed and totally at the mercy of the DMT.

May grasped his hand and kissed it.

"I'm sorry, Matt. I'm sorry, sweetie. But everything will be all right," she assured him unconvincingly despite her every attempt to remain calm.

The existential vibrations became more of a staticky buzz, and though the buzz nearly drowned out May's voice, he could still hear her as if from miles away. She was humming one of Mu's chants, and though it offered only a negligible softening of Matt's panic, it was at least something.

"You took a lot, Matt. Way more than I ever have," May said, her voice incredibly distant despite the pleasant feeling of her breath against the quivering skin of his neck. "But I'm right here. You'll be all right. You just…you have to know – whatever that means. I don't understand. But…but it's such an overwhelming feeling. It's like I had no choice, Matt…I'm sorry, sweetie…"

May…

All at once, the whole of his vision and his body and the room and May and everything solidified into a single chrysanthemum surging with hyper-real energy. The petals unfurled, and Matt's consciousness was stretched at light speed into the infinite, fractaling center of itself.

14. Possibilities

..
...
...
...

hyper infinite eternity forever flux transient

possibilities

confined body twisted decay

remade digital memory
expired run down entropy

damaged confusion dilute
altered experiment curiosity
departed ending rebirth
strayed dream numb eternity
dream
dream...
an idea an anchor
dream...
dream numb eternity experiment memory ending maybe
maybe...
possibilities
light dark self other thing
self other thing
self...
source self-other thing
source...
a self-other thing an idea a thing an anchor
self

self...

a thing

urgency

desperation a thing

terror

c
  o
   n
    f
   u
     s

finality   i

        o   death
         n

death?

a question self-other thing a question

death?

possibilities surge expanse infinite transition

death?

a question self-other thing a question

answer question possibility stream self-other thing

silence wash abate stillness eternal

...

...

...

..

.

.

.

.

.

.

.

.

.

.

.

.

..

...

...

...

decision

      desperation

achievement|

    fulfillment

          dream

            infinity

eternity

...

...

...

..

.

.

.

.

.

.

.

.

.

.

.

..

...

...

...alone

alone

abandoned connection false eternity reality.

false?

a question self-other thing source

false reality?

a question self-other thing source

ı

answer question possibility

stream self-other thing

silence acceptance abate stillness eternal consideration

...

...

....

..

.

.

.

.

.

.

.

.

.

.

..

...

...

...false reality possibilities dream eternity

...

...

...

..

.

.

.

.

.

.

.

.

.

..

...

...

                        ...alone

   alone…

       abandoned connection

               false eternity

 reality others

                  death

confusion

                        dream

   alone...

...

...

..

.

.

.

.

.

.

.

.

.

.

.

.

..

...

...

...alone

...

...

...

..

.

.

.

.

.

.

.

.

.

15. Body Guards

Painfully bright light pierced Matt's retinas, and he was forced to shut his eyelids and hold them tightly closed against the torrenting radiance.

He felt for May's grip, but he couldn't find her warmth.

Alone, Matt said to himself as he tried in vain to recollect the whole of the DMT trip. It was like a typical fading dream; he could remember that little bit of information about it at least.

I'm alone. In my own head. Everything is just...it really is all a dream...or something like that. But I'm alone. That much is clear.

He remembered what May told him during one of the dreams of the video game world.

She said that she had to leave. And now I'm alone. May is...

He struggled to finish the thought, and though he couldn't explain it, the DMT had revealed that reality was not at all real. *Whatever the real world is – May's world or the old man's world or that other world with the braided cord or something else entirely – it doesn't matter. Because she left. And I'm alone. And...*

"And there's no way out," Matt whispered aloud to himself.

He tried opening his eyes again, and this time the light seemed more bearable. He squinted until his vision finally adjusted to the room.

He was in Dr. Heron's office, seated on the couch. Dr. Heron sat across from him, staring him down with venomous disdain as if he had been observing Matt for some time.

"How did I get here?" Matt croaked, and he had to cough to clear thick residue from his lungs.

"How can you know for certain there's no way out, Matthew?" Dr.

Heron inquired with pain-filled scorn in his voice.

I keep ending up back here in this fucking office with this...monster, Matt considered in horror. *This office is like a repeating dead end in an endless labyrinth of madness, and he,* Matt eyed Dr. Heron with a shiver, *is the Reaper of that maze.*

The man in all black removed a typical prescription bottle from his jacket pocket, opened it, and held a red pill in his palm.

"Serotel," Dr. Heron mused sadly. Then he brought his palm to his lips, let the pill fall into his open mouth, and swallowed it.

What the hell, Matt gawked. *Is everyone taking this damn pill?*

"You have to know for sure, Matthew," Dr. Heron said with tangible regret. "Of course you do."

"Who are you really?" Matt demanded as his heartbeat quickened, flushing away the lingering fatigue left over from the trip that had launched him inside or outside himself – he couldn't be sure which. "Are you even my therapist?"

Dr. Heron grinned sinisterly and chuckled beneath his breath. "Why would a dream character need a therapist?" he laughed openly. "What a ridiculous notion."

Matt shook his head instinctually, readying himself for the deluge of insanity. But now Dr. Heron was finally agreeing with him.

"Death," Dr. Heron offered simply, "you know that's the answer. That's the only way to know with total certainty. But if you're wrong...well...there's no coming back from that mistake, is there?"

"You're telling me to kill myself?" Matt seethed at this man who was supposed to be looking after him.

No, Matt corrected himself. *He was never taking care of me. This is all a dream. A fucking dream!*

Matt lifted his hands to do a reality check. Then he checked the clock on the wall. Then he tried breathing through his closed mouth. Then he tried to taste the light. Then he closed his eyes and tried teleporting to a new location. When he opened his eyes, Dr. Heron smiled with childlike amusement.

"Seems perfectly real, doesn't it?" Dr. Heron announced with a mixture of dread and excitement. "I'm not telling you to kill yourself. I'm just agreeing that death is the only way to know for sure. That's how you know the video game world is just a dream, right? But how is that possible when the logs show that you really were in the video game? That would only be possible if even this world is —"

"A dream," Matt finished, and he bit his lip in an effort to keep himself from screaming out for existential help from some forever unknown real world.

"Yes," Dr. Heron nodded with seemingly genuine intrigue, as if he too was in this labyrinth with Matt and was just as desperate to get out. "That would certainly explain everything. And I suppose that means you're the dreamer. I'm just in your head. Is that it?"

Matt now recognized that piercing interest, bordering on all-consuming fascination, increasingly filled every one of Dr. Heron's words and movements.

"You have to die to know for sure," Dr. Heron repeated. "Or you can just keep taking the Serotel and sleep away eternity in a hospital. That's a possibility too."

Dr. Heron swallowed yet another Serotel and smiled with rapacious fervor.

Matt glanced at the undulating inkblot behind Dr. Heron and prepared himself for the ink-Reaper to come to life again. Dr. Heron's smile soured with a degree of something like agony as he appeared to be waging an internal battle. He sighed, composed himself, then removed another pill from the bottle and swallowed it.

"It's incredible," Dr. Heron mused with morbid interest, "that even after the DMT, your mind still can't accept the truth without actually dying." He let out a huff of pain-stricken laughter and threw up his arms. "But you're too attached to the illusion to let go. She is all that matters, right?" he mocked with deranged amusement. "So let's just get this over with and take you to the hospital. I'll have your bodyguards take you there now, Matthew," he said, smiling slightly as if savoring the bittersweetness. "We'll keep you there for observation and safety. Everyone's safety."

This is it, Matt realized in profound, existential anticipation as Dr. Heron swallowed yet another pill. *Everything is unraveling. This world is a goddamn dream, and so is the old man's world and the video game world and the braided cord world and even the DMT trip. Everything is a fucking dream. A nightmare!*

169

"And if that's true," Dr. Heron said expertly, addressing Matt's internal thoughts, "then we need to make sure nothing happens to you, the dreamer. Don't you think?"

Matt's heartbeat intensified exponentially, and he suddenly went as weak as the old man. *Just breathe,* he told himself, but it felt as though all the gravity in the universe was centered at his chest.

Dr. Heron rose from his chair, and Matt slumped into the couch, fighting desperately for air.

"Come on in," Dr. Heron announced to the door. "He's ready for you."

The door opened to reveal a retinue of Matthew Willish imposters. They shuffled into the room and crowded around Matt like ravenous wolves encircling their bleeding prey.

"Your bodyguards will take it from here," Dr. Heron explained despite being occluded by dozens of imposters at this point. Still, more men shuffled into the room, pressing against each other like liquid solidifying into a dense crystal.

Matt's vision blurred from lack of oxygen, and his mind raced in a desperate attempt to escape this nightmare.

Just let it happen, the old man suggested. *It's just a dream, after all.*

Matt processed the old man's words and knew them to be true, but the logical pathways of his brain were totally cut off now. Stars began flurrying at the periphery of his vision, and his survival instinct overtook every one of his thoughts.

"You have to know for sure, Matthew," Dr. Heron explained, and the voice seemed to come from both the outside world and inside his head all at once.

Because the world and your mind are the same place, the old man reasoned pityingly.

No! Matt objected, his eyes bugging with splintering veins as he teetered on the verge of total suffocation.

"Just let go, Matthew. Go to sleep," Dr. Heron said with a softened edge, but this time it sounded as though the voice was coming from Matt's mind.

Matt began convulsing as his lungs futilely pulsed against his iron-heavy chest cavity.

170

Help me! he pleaded in his mind, and he felt the old man shake his head stolidly, unable or unwilling to help.

The imposter closest to him removed a syringe from his jacket pocket and uncapped it.

No! Matt pleaded. *This is just a fucking dream!*

He felt the old man nod in sad agreement.

In his final moments of consciousness, he thought of May. He could hear her chanting Mu's calming words, and then he heard his own mind process thoughts on its own accord from some detached part of his consciousness.

This is all in my head, the thoughts announced. *These imposters aren't my bodyguards. They're doctors and nurses and medical staff. I must already be in the hospital.*

He could see May now as if through a window in the ceiling. She was busying herself with something in her home while humming one of Mu's chants under her breath.

Or maybe I'm still in her apartment, Matt considered as he watched May's movements like an audience marveling at a ballerina's perfect dance. *Maybe this is all the DMT,* Matt sobbed to himself in total defeat.

Just a dream, the old man explained sorrowfully.

Please! another part of Matt's mind pleaded desperately.

May is all that matters, another part of his mind concluded without him.

His lungs heaved against his chest with terrible intensity, flailing for the air just out of their reach. He opened his mouth as wide as possible and pulled hard, but his throat was blocked as if by some immovable mass.

The imposter stuck Matt in the thigh, injecting something cold into his veins.

He could still hear May's chanting despite his heartbeat machine-gunning his eardrums, and though he tried his utmost to hold onto her presence, the syringe's contents were already reaching his heart. His heartbeat suddenly slowed to a crawl, and the stars floating at his periphery scurried and multiplied, overtaking the whole of his vision.

16. Give Up

M att was ejected into the dark cell as if from a great height. Finding himself back in the video game dream was like ascending and escaping hell only to turn around and find himself back on the lowest, most sordid level.

He tensed his muscles and clenched his teeth and bellowed with anguish at the top of his lungs.

"Let me out!" he cried, his voice cracking.

Let me out! he screamed just as forcefully within himself.

Just a dream, the old man lamented.

I know! Matt pleaded inwardly.

"I know!" he shouted out loud. "So why won't it fucking end?"

"Shut up," Igwe rumbled simply. The others just stared at him as they stretched and flexed their rippling, naked muscles. Mu took a few steps toward him, then squatted, indifferently displaying herself to Matt. He couldn't help wanting her, even in that moment of total defeat.

He lowered his head to look away, but then it was May who filled his mind in turn.

Please, he pleaded with his mind. *She's just a dream. She isn't real. Please just...just accept that she's a dream. I need to wake up. I need...*

To die, the old man told him sullenly. *And ultimately so do I.*

Matt nodded in complete defeat.

"Are you okay, Loki?" Mu asked, oblivious to the fully shattered mind before her.

"I give up," he told her, unable to even look at her for fear of losing himself in her entrancing, impossible beauty and perfect likeness to May.

"What?" she checked.

I can't do this, Matt told himself, reeling in agony from the thorough understanding that dying here would just lead to a confused old man stuck in a dream within an endless series of dreams of waking life.

That term...waking life. It's meaningless. There is no waking life. Not for me. There's just these fucking nightmares.

He raised his head as the alarm sounded and the first of the lights on the door was illuminated. Mu smiled at him, her red lips like cherry fields in the spring against the ebony darkness of the cell.

"I can't do this anymore, May," he told Mu, wishing he was still in May's apartment.

Maybe I shouldn't have done the DMT, Matt considered, but he knew it wouldn't have mattered. *Even without the DMT, I'd still be lost in this endless maze. The DMT showed me something.* He thought back to the dream-like experience. *May said she left, and the DMT showed that I'm alone here. So, the May I was just with...is just a dream character. Does that mean there was a time when the real May was with me in these endless dreams...or whatever the fuck this all is relative to the real world?*

He winced, realizing the world he was certain was the real world, May's world, had to be just a dream.

But I have to die – really die – to know for sure, Matt thought, and a deep dread filled his inner being.

You might be stuck in a hospital in that world now, the old man warned, *like me. Dr. Heron said that's where he was bringing you.*

Matt nodded in agreement with the old man. *I'll find a way,* he told him. *Or are you scared that you might just be a dream too? If I die in May's world...you might die too.*

No, the old man interjected with an anguished sigh. *I don't think so. But you're right that there's only one way to find out for sure. And I'll have to find a way to kill myself as well.*

Matt felt his own trepidation filling the old man's tone. Then he remembered waking as the old man the last time and realizing that this old man talking to him in his head wasn't the same old man.

That's right, Matt remembered. *When I woke up as the old man, I knew right away that you, this voice, aren't me. You...are you just part of the dream? Like a...like dream character in my head?* Matt considered.

The old man shrugged. *Maybe. You're right that when you woke as the old man, you had no recollection of talking to yourself or saying anything that I've said to you. So...maybe I am just a dream. Or maybe you're the dream. Right?*

Matt nodded, hating that he was in full agreement with this voice in his head.

Mu shrugged in sheepish defeat at Matt's refusal to answer her. She began chanting her calming words just as the second alarm sounded.

No! Matt rebelled at her tranquilizing chant. *I can't do this anymore! I'm done! I give up!*

"No!" he screamed at her, anger and terror mixing violently inside him as he visualized himself far above the cell and away from these people. Mu instantly stopped chanting and fell back in surprise as the others went wide-eyed. In the next moment, Matt found himself suspended a mile above the cell.

He felt a sudden rush of vertigo and was filled with the fear of falling and splattering against the steel ground. But he didn't fall, and the fear coursing through him reminded him of the Reaper, then of Dr. Heron.

Just a dream, Matt demanded himself to accept, and the feeling of vertigo began to wane. He breathed deeply to calm himself, and then surveyed the field below. Even so high up, he could see and hear the mayhem that the Reaper was dispensing.

He remembered that the Reaper was more like a suited creature. *I want to know what this creature looks like beneath that black material,* Matt resolved. *And then you're up,* Matt told the old man. *You go first. And if we both don't disappear when you kill yourself and we wake up in my world, then it's my turn to kill myself, hospital be damned.*

The old man nodded in stoic agreement.

Images of May running to Matt and holding his lifeless hand as he lie on her couch filled Matt's mind.

No, that's just a dream, Matt knew, though he wished desperately that it weren't true. *That's just a dream. And so is this.*

The old man nodded, and Matt lifted his arm, beckoning the Reaper into the air. He watched as the giant creature rocketed upward then came to an abrupt halt directly in front of him.

Matt spread his hand, forcing the creature to splay its snaking limbs like a specimen beneath glass. With an easy wave, the material wrapped around the creature's head was stripped away, and Matt almost shrieked at what he saw.

Bone-white skin stretched over a gnarled, elongated skull that tapered to a human-like face full of hellish anguish. Wide, glossy eyes pleaded helplessly with Matt as lips repeated something frantically.

Dr. Heron, Matt gawked. He read the sad, twisted creature's lips. "I'm sorry, Matthew," the Reaper repeated over and over. "I'm sorry, Matthew. I'm sorry, Matthew."

What the fuck, Matt demanded as the warped, misshapen Dr. Heron pleaded for forgiveness.

Matt shook his head.

It's all a fucking nightmare, he concluded. *And I need to wake up. I need to...die...in every world.*

He gulped the fear of true death down into the pits of his being, then took one last look at the miserable creature before waving his hand, directing both himself and the Reaper to plummet.

I'm sorry, Matthew, the Reaper chanted as they fell with rapidly increasing velocity.

Matt gritted his teeth, mentally preparing himself for the painful collision.

Get ready, old man, he thought. *Get ready to die.*

The old man didn't respond, but Matt knew he could hear him.

Shouts of battle resounded below. Matt watched as the Reaper stretched its bladed limbs, reaching for him or anyone it could, and then they both splattered against the ground.

17. The Others

Jolted awake by the explosion of his flesh against the steel ground of the video game dream, Matt immediately willed himself into a state of calm, bringing his shallow breathing under control.

The old man I talk to in the other dreams isn't me, Matt reasoned carefully. *It's just a voice in the game designer's head — my head. And yet, I can't deny the voice's reasoning: I have to die in this world to know for sure if it's real or not.*

He pictured himself cutting his own throat with a scalpel or some other sharp instrument he could surely find in one of the rooms within the infinite corridor. Shivers ran the length of his spine as he imagined suffocating to death on his own gushing blood.

But I'm nearly certain this is the real world, Matt reasoned measuredly, not allowing himself to start thinking through the deranged mind of himself in the video game designer's world. He felt his heart beat at the pace of the beeping machine behind him. *I'm not at all certain,* he corrected himself, *but I think it must be true that those other places are just dreams. I just...I just don't know what's going on,* he concluded as always, and he damned his mind for failing him in its clearly advanced age.

He almost called out for a nurse, but the endless stars outside the windows directly in front of him caught his eyes, forcing him to turn and peer at the icy world outside the doors behind him. *I have to know what's going on,* Matt resolved. *And if I die,* Matt thought through a lens of detachment as he gawked at the cruel, obsolescent age of his sagging skin, *then I was going to die of old age anyway. How much time could I possibly have left?*

A failed attempt at picking up his shriveled body made him almost admit defeat and submit to his nightmares.

Up! Matt demanded of his frail bones. *Wake up!* he urged his decrepit muscles. He felt a bit of vigor, and he marveled at what the mind was capable of.

This old man has one last hurrah in him, Matt hoped, and his eyes welled at the pain involved in straining his body far beyond his age's limits. *I need to get outside this place. There were others outside. Or maybe there weren't. Maybe I dreamed that. But...I have to know for sure.*

With mountainous effort, he swung his atrophied legs over the side of the bare bed, but neither his arms nor abdominals had the necessary strength to hold him upright. He fell face first onto a hard ceramic floor, audibly cracking his forehead and shattering his nose, smearing it across his cheek like mere puddy.

He howled in pain and exhausted a forceful breath to flush the gushing blood out of his throat. Disoriented and dizzy from the physical trauma, Matt tried to stabilize his vision by placing his hands firmly on the floor, but it was slippery with his still-flowing blood.

A glance upward through the fluid, sanguine lens of his own life flowing across his field of vision told him that the icy world still raged outside.

Damn it, Matt lamented, reaching out his blood-drenched arm toward the doors. *Too much blood,* he noted in horror as blood continued pouring out of his body without any sign of slowing its pace.

I'm going to die, Matt realized. *Whether I like it or not.*

An alarm sounded suddenly, and the corridor strobed crimson and gold with urgent warning.

"Jus' le'me die!" Matt gurgled through painful sobs and free-flowing blood.

Nurses rushed out of doorways like an endless stream of identical hounds on a sacred hunt.

"Mr. Willish!" they yelped and screamed in a cacophony of urgency.

Let me die and know for sure, Matt pleaded with the world itself, though another part of him reeled at the thought of true death.

With a jarring slam and icy gust, the double doors Matt had been trying to reach burst open. Two nearly naked figures stood in the doorway, unaffected by the blistering cold already threatening Matt's fragile flesh with pinpricks of frostbite. The figures wore simple, neolithic-like scraps of cloth over their genitals, and one of them, the woman, wore a second strip of cloth over her chest. The woman didn't have the familiar scar across her face, but Matt still recognized both of them from his dreams.

Souvik and Fernanda, Matt realized. But they weren't old like him. They looked even younger and better built than the hyper-muscular video game characters. Matt no longer had the strength to speak, nor did he even have the ability to move his numb, lifeless body.

I'm dying, Matt told himself with mounting trepidation. He didn't want to die in fear, but the frigid cold and his still-gushing blood made it terribly difficult not to view his environment with absolute terror.

"What's he doing?" Fernanda asked Souvik.

Souvik just shrugged easily as Matt's vision of the others blurred into an actively mixing mosaic of quickly fading sanguine saturation.

"They fucked him up bad," Souvik mused with passive intrigue.

"Yeah," Fernanda confirmed simply. "But maybe it worked this time."

18. I'll Do It

M att awoke in a standing position in his apartment, and he had to catch himself before going weak at the knees and falling over. The *Room Reaper* poster filled the whole of his vision, and he realized he was standing only inches away from it. He could still vividly feel the sensation of his nose smearing across his face. Backing away from the poster, he felt frantically for his nose, but it was intact.

Did the old man die? Matt wondered, and he instinctively inspected his apartment for anything out of the ordinary.

Now it's your turn, the old man's voice told him from an incredible distance. *To die.*

Matt licked his dry lips with animal fear. He nearly asked the old man whether or not he died for sure, but then he remembered that the old man in his head and the old man of his dreams were not the same.

I need to think first, Matt reasoned through a mounting fog of panic, and he began to pace about the small apartment.

Fernanda and Souvik...they were both in the dream. And they weren't old. They were impervious to the cold, and they were more perfectly sculpted than their fucking video game character counterparts. He glanced back at the *Room Reaper* poster for assurance and caught Mu's stare.

*May...*Matt lamented with incredible longing.

A sudden knock at the door sent him jumping back. He regathered himself and peered through the peephole. Outside, May had her ear pointed towards the door and a look of incredible worry strewn across her face. Despite the numerous shadows, her features looked angelic and lustrous in the dim light of the hallway, and her diamond studs shone with an ochre hue that seemed impossible amidst the drab colors of the hallway.

"Matt?" May checked gently, and she knocked again. "You in there?"

Matt exhausted a heavy sigh. *Maybe that's why things aren't spiraling into insane oblivion right now...because she's here.*

He unlocked the door and had to immediately lower his head in fear of forgetting all about his objective to die in this dream of waking life.

"Matt..." May breathed, and Matt glanced up to see her shake her head, visibly in pain. "Have you been in there this whole time?"

What do I even tell her? What is there to say? He lifted his head and gazed at her as if from across a fathomless chasm. Tears were building at the corners of her eyes, and seeing her emotionally distressed was simply too much for Matt to bear. He reached out, and she immediately moved to close the gap. Holding her in his arms felt like sunlight in winter.

She buried her face in his chest and she couldn't help a series of sobs despite clearly trying to stifle her emotions. She gripped him hard around his back, and Matt gripped back, cherishing her presence.

You still have to die, the old man reminded him sullenly, and Matt mentally recoiled at the truth of his words.

But everything is okay when I'm with her, Matt pleaded with the old man.

You have to know, the old man volleyed. *You have to.*

Matt wanted to hold May for all time, but the sound of something smacking against Matt's living room window turned both their attention away from each other's embrace.

"What was that?" May checked, pulling away and looking as though she had felt equally enraptured and fulfilled by their embrace. She wiped away her tears with the back of her hands.

"I don't know," Matt said as he moved to inspect outside the window. He peered outside but was immediately forced to duck back out of view. A few stories down on the sidewalk, Dr. Heron and at least fifty imposters stood in a mass, staring at the apartment window like hungry automatons.

"It's him!" Matt shrieked, and he waved May over to have a look.

But maybe he's a hallucination, Matt reasoned cautiously.

May closed the apartment door, then strode to the window with her shoulders back as if preparing for a fight.

182

She peered outside, then jumped back just as quickly as Matt.

"What the fuck?" she screamed.

So, she can see them after all, Matt confirmed to himself with a sense of vague dread. He couldn't be certain if that was better or worse than the whole situation being a complex hallucination.

Another smack at the window forced Matt to turn his head. This time, he caught a glimpse of something small and red falling down to the ground. Another hit the window, and this time Matt understood what it was.

"Serotel," he seethed.

"Your medicine?" May checked, visibly attempting to stifle her nervousness.

Another Serotel hit the window and fell down to the sidewalk.

Peering outside the window again, Matt watched as Dr. Heron readied a pill in his fingers and wound his arm back to throw it before realizing Matt was showing his face again. Dr. Heron smiled sinisterly at him, and like marionettes, the army of imposters simultaneously smiled along with their puppet master. The imposters removed their own Serotel bottles from their pockets, and in a single movement, they poured the entire contents of their bottles down their throats along with Dr. Heron. They chewed their mouthfuls of pills like mad cows as their unblinking eyes stared at Matt. Crimson spittle leaked out of their overfilled mouths, but none of them took any notice, not even Dr. Heron. They were like battle-frenzied berserkers preparing for slaughter by ritualistically consuming living flesh.

What do they want? Matt desperately wanted to know.

Just a dream, the old man reminded him forlornly.

Matt absorbed May's distress-strewn features and rebelled helplessly against the knowledge that this all has to be a dream.

Maybe those are doctors and nurses here to help me, and I'm just seeing everything through my lens of insanity, Matt thought helplessly, not believing a word of it. *Maybe,* his mind raced desperately for rationality, *maybe they're here to take me to the hospital. Dr. Heron said he'd be keeping me there. So maybe...maybe I'm in the hospital already. Maybe this is all in my head,* Matt thought with desperate abandon, knowing that couldn't be the truth as he watched the horde of crimson-streaked mouths masticate and consume a month's worth of Serotel all at once.

183

Just a dream, the old man reminded him. *One that you have to die in.*

Matt winced and gulped down the truth of the old man's words.

"What are they doing?" May checked with mounting franticness. He was almost thankful she wasn't looking out the window at that moment.

Someone knocked at the door before Matt could respond, and he pulled himself to check who it was to save May from more madness.

"Who...who is it at the door Matthew?" May demanded as she moved nervously away from the door to look outside the window. "What the fuck are they doing?" May burst, but Matt could offer no reasonable explanation.

And there's no explanation needed, the old man urged. *All you have to do now is die and realize with total certainty that this is all a dream.*

Matt shook the old man off and looked through the peephole. Exhausted and shell-shocked, Fernanda stood outside the door drenched in sweat. The large scar stretched across her face shone a deeper red than the rest of her flushed skin.

"Fernanda?" Matt asked through the door, unsure if he could trust her or anyone for that matter.

"He's outside!" Fernanda warned, out of breath and barely able to hold herself upright. "You have to get to his office."

"Matt, please. What's going on?" May demanded to know, and she strode to the peephole to look outside the door for herself without waiting for an answer from Matt.

"It's...it's..." she stammered, backing away from the door and shaking her head. She removed a small baggie from her pocket and snorted a large amount of blue powder, shaking her head at the impossibility of what she saw.

"Under the carpeting in his office," Fernanda urged. "I found something, Matt!"

"Sorry," May said, shaking and staring at the ground before raising her stare to Matt and wiping the blue residue from her nostrils. "I just...am I going crazy too? That's...my character. Putch...I..."

Matt reached out to comfort her, unsure if she would accept him within the torrenting insanity that she was now a part of. She grabbed his hands and locked her eyes with Matt's.

"Matthew, what is happening?" she gasped.

It's all falling apart, Matt told himself. *Even being with her...the insanity is taking over. And Fernanda...what did she find? What did she mean?*

"I thought maybe as long as I stay with you," Matt croaked, stifling his oncoming tears, "but everything's still fucking crazy."

He nodded helplessly at the truth filling his mind like primordial muck.

I have to die.

He absorbed her scared features and tried to soften his own for the sake of calming her, but he couldn't push the thought from the forefront of his consciousness.

I have to die. I have to die!

"Matthew! Answer me!" May urged, squeezing his palms as if to extract him from his thoughts.

"Shit!" Fernanda screamed. "They're coming up!"

He heard Fernanda's heavy steps fade away down the hallway as May broke away to look outside the window.

"They're not out there!" she said, glancing back at Matt with wide eyes. "Matthew!" she screamed, too overwrought with panic to disguise it with a facade of self-confidence. "What do they want, Matt?"

Matt shrugged in perfect defeat. "Kill me. Please, May."

"Matthew Willish!" May shrieked. "What are you saying? Just...just help me here!"

She began pulling the large couch and inching it toward the door.

"If he takes me to a hospital...or does whatever it is he wants with me, it's only going to be harder to find a way to kill myself," Matt explained simply as May pulled frantically at the couch.

"Stop it!" May cried. "Just help me, Matt. Please!"

Matt couldn't help entertaining the suffocating and perfectly real possibility that she was just a dream character, but her distress was too much to bear.

That's May! a distant part of his mind urged. *This can't be a dream. She is all that matters!*

No! Matt shouted inwardly, but he still couldn't stop himself from helping May drag the couch in front of the door to use as a barrier against Dr. Heron and the army of Matts.

"You saw how many there are," Matt told her as they moved the couch into position.

"What the fuck do they want?" May demanded as she searched the room for more furniture to use as a barrier to the door.

"The police!" she realized far too late. "We need to call the police!"

Matt shook his head in painful resignation at May's despair. She shook her head back at him, giving up on trying to reason with him. She removed her phone and attempted to call, but evidently, she couldn't get a signal.

"What the fuck!" May screeched, terror welling in the deepest pits of her mind now.

It's just a dream, the old man reminded him pityingly.

What was Fernanda talking about? Matt urgently pleaded with the voice in his head.

The old man shrugged. *Go find out. But then you have to do it.*

Matt nodded, feeling a mixture of sullen and stoic.

In the hallway, footsteps could be heard filing outside Matt's apartment. May tipped over a small bookshelf onto the couch in a futile but desperate effort to add something more to the makeshift barrier. She backed away from the door, step by step, and reluctantly took Matt's hand in her own.

"I'm scared, Matthew."

Matt lifted her hand to his lips and kissed her alabaster skin, savoring the sweetness of her scent and presence and very soul.

It's just a dream, he repeated to himself, and he knew what he had to do.

"Me too," he admitted. "So let's get out of here."

All of a sudden, the door was battered with dozens of hammer-like hits all at once, threatening to splinter the wood right off the hinges. The door suddenly cleaved open as tireless, bloody fists continued widening the splintering gap in the wood.

May yelped in terror and almost fell back, but in a single movement, Matt caught her, closed his eyes, and visualized Dr. Heron's office.

The existential vibrations overtook the pair in a single crescendoing wave, folding and bending the space in front of them into a chrysan-

186

themum-petalled portal.

Opening his eyes, the last thing Matt saw through the gorge in the door was Dr. Heron. He smiled with typical rapacious delight as arms flailed around him, tearing the door open like frenzied insects excavating dirt to catch some treasured prey.

The petals enveloped them and then unfurled again, depositing them directly into Dr. Heron's office. They fell haphazardly away from each other, Matt slamming against the wall and May catching herself on the couch. Throbbing pain emanated from where Matt hit the wall with his lower back, and he grunted hard against the pain as he turned to make sure May was safe.

Just a dream, the old man reminded him.

"May!" Matt called out, lifting himself to his feet as he ignored both the pain and the old man.

Hunched over with both arms outstretched on the couch for support, May didn't appear to be breathing. She was dumbstruck with existential confusion, her mouth agape and eyes welling with tears.

"Please, May!" Matt begged. "Please just breathe."

He rubbed her back and drew her hair out of her eyes and over her ear. Her diamonds sparkled an impossible ochre hue despite the room only being illuminated by the particularly bright moon and stars outside.

"Please, May," he begged her, letting his lips linger against her cheek.

Just as Matt was about to launch into full-blown panic, May finally heaved a giant breath into her lungs as if surfacing from a mile beneath the ocean.

"Okay, there," Matt said, encouraging her with kisses against her temple as he continued rubbing her back for support. May pushed him away suddenly and pulled herself onto the couch.

"What's happening," she demanded, her eyes still wide and her mouth agape as she pulled at the air to replenish her body of precious oxygen. "What was that, Matt? Please. Please! Make it all make sense." She removed another baggie full of blue powder from her waist pocket, then let it fall on the couch, probably realizing it would do nothing to lift her from this pit of madness Matt had dragged her into.

"I'm sorry," Matt began, but May was quick to interject.

"I don't want sorrys, Matthew. What the fuck is going on?" she seethed on the verge of anger.

Matt nodded, sorrow filling his every feature as he wished desperately that everything could have just stayed normal and stable with May beside him.

"This is all a dream," he admitted reluctantly, knowing that it would offer her no reprieve from the insanity but would instead send her further down the rabbit hole with him. But it was the truth, and Matt didn't know what else to tell her, for the truth was more reasonable than any lie he could possibly conceive in that moment.

"You mean like, when we were talking in the Mega?" May considered, shaking her head in shock. "Matt, I wasn't serious about that. That was just...philosophy. I didn't mean to –"

"You didn't do this, May," Matt said, wishing now that he would have just stayed distant from her and never entered back into her life. *She shouldn't have to suffer this with me. No one should.*

"We just fell through a flower-shaped portal. You just saw a real-life version of the character you created. An army of my imposters, led by my therapist, just tried to break into my apartment. You experienced it too, May. This is...this is all just –"

"Stop it!" May shouted with wild abandon. "This is real, Matthew! This is real! Just stop it!" she snapped, rising to her feet as tears continued streaming from her quivering eyes.

She's terrified, Matt recognized, *and so am I.*

Stop wasting time, the old man warned. *Dr. Heron will surely be here any minute. And then...who knows?*

May eyed the door desperately, then collapsed back on the couch and let her head fall into her hands.

"If this is a dream, then I need to wake up," she reasoned through shallow sobs as she worked futilely to bring her breathing and anxiety under control.

Matt yearned to hold her and protect her and find a way to make everything make sense for both of them, but that wasn't possible anymore. He knew what he had to do.

He checked the top drawer of Dr. Heron's desk for something sharp and found a pair of scissors just waiting to be picked up. Scissors in hand, he got on his knees and began cutting the plush carpeting, wasting no more time.

"I need to wake up," May repeated, and Matt figured she was doing her utmost not to jump and run mindlessly away from him in any direction.

As he cut the carpeting and padding beneath it, he realized that it was freshly lain, as if it had been installed just a few hours earlier.

Hurry, the old man warned.

"Just a dream," May said, her voice low and distant now. Matt glanced up at her and nearly winced at the sight of her physically collapsed form.

"May," he whispered in an attempt to pull her from her mind's protective stupor.

What can you possibly do for this dream character? the old man demanded gravely. *Focus!*

"May," Matt whispered once more, but she wasn't even registering his voice.

"Just a dream," May repeated, her eyes glassy and her voice aloof and reserved.

Matt heaved himself away from his anguish over her despair and went back to cutting the carpet. After finally managing to cut a five-foot length with the office scissors, he stood and yanked the carpet, tearing it in new directions. As he pulled, a pitch-black trapdoor was revealed, only identifiable by a pearl-white handle.

Now what? Matt lamented inwardly. *What new madness does this nightmare have in store?*

It's just a dream, the old man assured him in direct contradiction to the survival chemicals coursing through Matt's veins with increasing rapidity as he took hold of the handle and pulled.

Straining against the immense weight of the door, Matt finally heaved it open and let it fall and slam against the floor like an ancient drawbridge loose from its chains. Peering inside, Matt instinctively withdrew his body from the edge of an infinite abyss so dark that it made the rest of the room seem bright.

"Fuck!" he yelped, backing further away from the edge. "Don't move, May!" he warned, for the couch was only a few feet from the edge.

She lifted her head easily and gazed detachedly into the abyss with puffy, tear-drenched eyes. She didn't avert her gaze from the impossibly dark depths beneath the floor.

"You should take a closer look," Dr. Heron said from across the room, sending Matt jumping and grabbing the desk for support. Just above him, the inkblot painting resonated with buzzing energy, threatening to come to life. Matt pivoted an inch away from the painting before recognizing that there was nowhere left to run.

May still sat on the couch, but now she turned her head away from the perfect darkness, finally acknowledging Dr. Heron's presence.

"We're in a dream," she told him simply.

"That's correct, dear," Dr. Heron said easily, offering a smile of assurance before turning his head back to Matt and allowing the smile to morph into cheshire delight. "Now," he bellowed, "take a closer look."

Dr. Heron removed multiple flares from his jacket pocket as if they were always there, waiting for this moment. He snapped them in one swift movement. They puttered with flames, illuminating his face with wicked, crimson radiance and shadows.

"Look," Dr. Heron said again, and he tossed the flares through the trapdoor.

The scissors, the old man urged Matt. *You can use them to kill yourself.*

Matt nodded in reluctant agreement and squeezed the scissors with surging dread.

"There's more than enough time for that," Dr. Heron said, still reading Matt's mind. "Just look!" he barked.

Matt glanced at May and noted in equal terror and relief that she looked almost placid despite her still flowing tears.

She snapped, Matt understood, and he wondered how he was still managing to continue wading through this nightmare delirium.

"Because you still haven't fully accepted the truth," Dr. Heron explained as he recklessly stepped over the trapdoor and sauntered to Matt's side. "Now, look!" he bellowed, kneeling down and squeezing Matt's neck in his constricting grip.

Forced forward by Dr. Heron's unnatural strength, Matt gripped the edges of the trapdoor and resisted being thrown into its fathomless depths. Dr. Heron pushed harder until half of Matt's body and the whole of his head were fully perpendicular with the opening. He was a hair's length from falling in, and Dr. Heron was the only thing stopping the plunge in that moment.

Gazing into the abyss, Matt's mind readied itself to reel in horror at the dizzying depths, but instead, he was filled with a wave of spiteful loathing for his own mind.

Why is this happening? This can't be, Matt gawked, but the old man sighed in an I-told-you-so manner.

"You see?" Dr. Heron inquired excitedly, his grip like a vice around Matt's throat.

The flares had halted their descent every thousand feet or so, and each was now frozen in place, creating a chain of lights illuminating the giant space at least a mile below, stretching to form a familiar steel ground and hulking walls lined with cell doors.

"*Room Reaper,*" Matt breathed, and though Dr. Heron removed his grip, Matt found that he was still frozen in place.

May rose, smiled sweetly, then stepped right to the lip of the door. The toes of her shoes hung an inch over the edge, but she seemed surprisingly stable. Still, Matt reached out in wordless warning, begging her with his defeated eyes to back away.

"It's our game," she told Matt whimsically as tears flowed freely across the lips of her wide, detached grin.

It's a dream, the old man urged Matt. *End it.*

May just smiled, staring into the maddening depths below like a child entranced by her first bonfire. Her mind was totally shattered, and Matt sobbed at what he had caused this woman, who was everything to him, to endure.

Dr. Heron stepped back across the chasm and into Matt's view once again. "Do it," he told Matt pleasurably, nodding to the scissors he still held in his hands like a nearly empty canteen in the middle of a desert. "Find out for sure, Matthew."

Matt glanced back at May, but she was still tranquilly hypnotized by the unreality of the world.

Matt let an image of himself slitting his throat with the dull scissors flash across his mind, and it sent chills down his spine despite the knowledge and concrete assurance below him that he was just dreaming.

He gritted his teeth, desperately demanding his arm to obey his higher mind and plunge the scissors into his own neck, but his body wouldn't listen. His drive to survive was still ever-present. But most of all, he couldn't do it – know for sure that everything was a dream – for that would mean not only the end of his reality, but also of May.

"She's a fucking dream, Matthew!" Dr. Heron urged with a twinge of agitation.

She's just a dream, the old man repeated sorrowfully.

May just stared, taking no notice of them.

Matt felt something undulate beneath his feet, and he backed away from the edge just as the inkblot slithered between his legs and pooled itself at Dr. Heron's feet like an obedient jackal. The ink rose up his legs like slow-growing vines, and another section of the pool lifted an object from somewhere unseen and placed it in Dr. Heron's hand.

"She's just a dream," Dr. Heron sighed with tangible scorn.

Matt squinted his eyes at the object and saw that it was a revolver. Dr. Heron leveled it at May's head, but she took no notice of the danger.

Grunting and heaving his body out of its prostrate position on the ground, Matt attempted to jump for Dr. Heron even if it meant falling through the door with him. But he was too late.

A devastating flash from the barrel and an ear-splitting roar stopped Matt in his tracks.

Matt screamed in unintelligible horror as May's skull exploded, splattering her brain into the air and across the walls. Matt fell to his knees and clenched his fists, screaming without sound as May's lifeless body slumped and fell through the floor like discarded meat.

He couldn't even bring himself to breathe, let alone move, but Matt's mind still injected him with visions of May's bloody body shattering like dense glass against the steel ground.

May! Matt pleaded, and her name was like an oasis burnt away before his eyes.

Just a dream, the old man reminded him.

"Shut the fuck up!" Matt scolded his mind with a gut-wrenching growl. "Just shut the fuck up!" he seethed again, and he placed the scissors against this throat. Pushing hard against his neck as he sobbed with terrible anguish, he was able to draw a small amount of blood, but something deep inside him still refused to let go.

Do it, the old man told him simply.

"May," Matt breathed desperately, blade pressed hard against the pulsing veins in his neck. He closed his eyes and visualized being in her apartment. He could see her now, readying a drink for each of them in her kitchen as she smiled seductively at Matt over her shoulder and swayed her hips to a melody only she could hear.

He could feel the portal vibrations already beginning at the periphery of his senses, and he held his eyelids shut, focusing clearly on his intended destination.

May, Matt pleaded, needing her presence more than ever before.

"Fine," Dr. Heron said with resigned disappointment. "I'll do it."

He opened his eyes, and Dr. Heron pointed the gun at Matt's forehead. Before Matt even had time to protest, the flash from the barrel illuminated the room with an all-consuming blaze. Time seemed to stretch and slow, and the roar of the gun's combustion and the sound of his skull and brain exploding inside his own head arrived at his ears as a single orchestrated wave.

The sound of death, he heard inside his head in the same instant that the bullet reached the center of his brain.

19. The Unreal

"May!" Matt wailed through his old, decrepit voice. Her brains exploded all over again inside his mind.

"Fuck!" he shouted inside the insidiously familiar, sterile corridor.

I'm not this old fucking man! Matt knew with total certainty. *May is real. May is all that fucking matters. I don't care about anything else.*

"May!" Matt wailed again in anguish, shutting his frail eyelids and replaying her death in his mind from a million sordid angles all at once.

"Where is he?" Matt seethed. "Heron! Where the fuck are you!"

Heaving his withered body upright, Matt swung his legs over the bed and stood without even giving it a second thought. The stars to his right shone with indelible, piercing wrath, and the icy world outside the doors to his left raged silently in chaotic anguish.

"Heron, you fuck!" Matt demanded, his wide eyes like smoldering embers at the pit of some long forgotten cavern. "I'll kill you!" Matt screamed, and he forced his body forward despite capillaries and veins bursting beneath his skin. His old body could only take so much, and Matt felt a detached shock that they were able to resuscitate his broken body after he'd split his face open last time.

No! Matt seethed in response to his shock. *This isn't real.* He reached for May in his desperate mind, but he could only imagine her lifeless corpse falling into the pit beneath Dr. Heron's office.

"Heron!" Matt barked, his voice cracking as he huffed to keep moving, though he didn't know where to. The corridor appeared infinite, but Matt reasoned once again that it must only be an illusion.

"Mr. Willish?" came the silken, sweet voice of one of the nurses.

Matt turned to see May — or at least one of the many perfect copies of her.

"She's dead," Matt told her as the exhaustion of his every cell finally caught up with his murderous rage. His knees gave out, and the nurse ran to catch him before he fell and broke himself all over again.

Her touch – it filled his body with blanketing warmth and security.

"But it isn't real," Matt sobbed in May's embrace. "You're not real," he told her sullenly.

"Come now, Mr. Willish. Back to bed. It'll all be all right," she assured him soothingly. More nurses entered the corridor from various doorways.

"You're all copies," Matt urged as the immeasurable exhaustion of his decrepit body caught up to him. Limp in May's arms, Matt cried, "Copies of an original. Do you understand?"

The nurse nodded with seemingly perfect understanding.

"I do, Mr. Willish. But we have to keep going. The procedure –"

"No!" Matt practically snarled. "That's enough! I want answers. Bring Heron. Now!"

The nurse holding Matt looked to the other nurses, then nodded, sending them in various directions.

"I think Dr. Heron will agree that we've reached an end point," the nurse explained, and she kissed Matt on his forehead. "You did great," she told him in a whisper. "I hope you'll assess our work as satisfactory, sir."

Matt shook his head. *She's speaking to me like I'm her boss.*

"Mr. Willish!" a familiar voice called out before Matt could answer her.

Struggling to twist his neck, Matt saw the unmistakable Dr. Heron approaching. Rather than his usual nightmare-black clothing, Dr. Heron was dressed in all white. Even his glasses had a translucent pearl hue.

A flash of Dr. Heron in the office gave way to May's body exploding against steel over and over again in his mind.

Kill him, every cell of Matt's body pleaded.

"You killed her! The only fucking thing that matters. The only –" Matt seethed, and his rage forced him to a standing position as if inflating a withered balloon. "I'll kill you!" Matt resolved.

"Mr. Willish," Dr. Heron issued with his arms held defensively. "You're going to end up passing out again if you're not careful with this form. Why not be..." Dr. Heron considered, searching for the right word, "less withered."

"What?" Matt demanded, caught off guard by Dr. Heron's question.

"Your body...I just mean...it looks so uncomfortable."

"Uncomfortable? To be old?" Matt checked, uncertain now if this was the man's attempt to stall him.

"Well, yeah. That's one way to describe it. I know this always happens with the procedure, but you can go back to something more comfortable now, sir."

Sir, Matt repeated in his mind. *Just like the nurse — he's treating me as if I'm his superior. But that can wait,* Matt told himself.

"How do I become young again?" Matt urged, breathing laboriously with each lead-heavy step toward Dr. Heron.

"How, you ask?" Dr. Heron almost laughed. Then his demeanor changed suddenly as a new understanding overtook him. He eyed the nurse who had been holding Matt.

"It...it worked?" Dr. Heron asked her.

"It seems like it," the nurse said cautiously. "In some ways, at least."

"What worked?" Matt growled before losing his footing and falling face first toward the hard tile floor. He braced himself for the familiar fatal impact, but the nurse caught him just in time.

He imagined that she would probably try to put him back to sleep once again.

"Don't!" Matt told her preemptively. "No more dreams!"

"Dreams," Dr. Heron repeated disappointedly. "So you do remember, then?"

Matt shook his head. "Remember what?"

"That...that this is the real world. That...everything else is a dream."

A dream, Matt repeated inwardly with seething anger.

"May isn't a dream, you fucking psychopath," Matt accused. "You killed her! And I already died here. I know this isn't real."

"And you died in the video game designer's dream too," Dr. Heron explained measuredly. "I monitor everything, as you know. May and

Chike and the Reaper and even me, the Dr. Heron that shot you, that was a dream, Matthew. But look at you. You really think that was the real world?"

The real world, Matt repeated to himself. *What the fuck does that even mean anymore?* He felt the forlorn confusion of every one of his identities cry out with pleading anguish all at once.

"I don't fucking know what's real," Matt admitted through sobs.

He used all of his remaining strength to lift his arm and remove the nurse's face mask. It fell away, revealing the only thing in any world that ever made sense.

"I don't know anything except that I love you, May. I don't fucking care what's real. I just..."

Rather than offer him her predictable, comforting smile, the nurse looked anguished, and she raised her eyes to meet Dr. Heron's equally concerned gaze.

"Not a complete success, then," Dr. Heron lamented. Then he allowed himself a final nod. "But at least we made progress, Mr. Willish."

The nurse nodded along with him and clung slightly tighter to Matt's utterly depleted body.

All of a sudden, Dr. Heron lifted his gaze to look behind the nurse at something occluded from Matt's vision.

"We made progress," Dr. Heron told someone, suddenly sounding like a nervous, young boy in the presence of a cosmic authority.

"Progress?" the unmistakable voice of Fernanda repeated with obvious sarcasm. "You mean like last time? And every other time?"

Matt wanted to call out to her, but it took all of his remaining energy just to breathe and blink.

"No," Dr. Heron huffed, and he lowered his head, seemingly in shame. "Although, the last procedure provided important and necessary insights that we utilized during..." Dr. Heron trailed off, apparently not impressing the importance of his work on Fernanda. "Anyway, the one in the tower will be satisfied with the results, I'm sure," Dr. Heron offered. "I mean, once we get this one reoriented."

They're referring to me as "this one," Matt considered. *Are there others like me? Is it May? The real May?*

Though he couldn't see them, Matt considered the last time he woke and saw the Fernanda and Souvik of this world; these people were titanous beings compared to the Fernanda and Souvik of the real world.

The real world, Matt considered hollowly. *Or the unreal world. It's all the same, really.*

"Matt," Souvik checked, evidently standing beside Fernanda, "did it work?"

What are these people talking about? Matt thought in horror. The infinity of space outside the windows shone with the dizzying brightness of equally infinite stars. Whether inside or outside the corridor or inside or outside his own mind, it was all the same. It was all inscrutable madness.

"Matt?" Fernanda checked.

"Come here," Dr. Heron offered, beckoning them closer with a pleasant wave. "Look for yourself."

What should I do? Matt wondered, hopelessness coursing through his decrepit but still-beating heart. *There's nowhere left to go. I already came to this conclusion, and it did me no good then. But it's still the truth. There's no sense to anything. Madness. It's all madness. Everything and everyone. Including me. It's all —*

"Holy shit," Fernanda cooed as she and Souvik came into Matt's field of vision. "He still didn't shake it off?"

"You see?" Dr. Heron offered. "He still doesn't understand how to change his body."

One of Fernanda's eyebrows popped up with incredible surprise at Dr. Heron's words.

"What else?" she checked with genuine intrigue, inspecting Matt as if he were an anomalous lab rat.

"He thinks the dreams are real, or rather, he doesn't know what's real."

"No one does," Fernanda reminded the doctor ominously. The nurses couldn't help lowering their heads, seemingly fearful of Fernanda's spoken truth.

"That's the whole point, isn't it?" Souvik added, which seemed to inflict Dr. Heron with a measure of physical pain.

"Still," Fernanda continued, "look at him, Souvik."

"Progress," Souvik admitted stoically, assessing Matt's nearly extinguished body and broken mind as some measure of sordid achievement.

"The one in the tower," Dr. Heron repeated, urging the point.

"Yes, yes," Fernanda said, waving him away. "We'll tell him."

"Him?" Matt croaked as he peered through the small slits of his dream-heavy eyelids.

Then it isn't May, Matt groaned inwardly. *Maybe Chike. Maybe he knows,* Matt considered.

"Souvik," Matt breathed, and a hulking, glowing version of the already Adonis-like man filled Matt's field of vision as the man pushed an ebony fountain of cascading locks over his right shoulder.

"Souvik, where's the real May?" Matt pleaded, using all his remaining energy to offer her name to this mad world. All he could do now was wait to be sent back to the real world...May's world...or for some new lashing of insanity to penetrate his mind.

Souvik ignored Matt's question and offered Dr. Heron a look of impatient disappointment.

Dr. Heron breathed deeply and stood his ground, though he still avoided direct eye contact while addressing Souvik.

"He will be pleased," Dr. Heron assured him. "Progress is progress. It's not like there's any rush."

No rush? What does that mean? Matt wondered as his mind flashed imagery of May straddling and kissing him in her apartment, then of her body splattering against unforgiving steel, then of her pleading anguish as she gripped Matt for safety inside his apartment as it was ransacked by Dr. Heron, then of her dizzying compassion as she called for help when Matt first resurfaced to his own mind and all this madness seemed to have first started.

But I don't know, Matt admitted, his newborn-like frailty and ignorance painfully clear to him at this moment.

Fernanda bent and lifted Matt's obliterated body into her arms as if he really were a newborn.

May, Matt lamented, absorbing every inch of the nurse as he was peeled away from May's physical embrace.

"Maybe," Souvik began, "maybe if I found a way to inspire urgency in you? Maybe then you'd be less relaxed about all this and start rushing a bit?" Souvik said, taking a single step toward the man a whole body length beneath him.

200

Dr. Heron physically cowered, though the nurses didn't seem at all threatened by Souvik's presence.

"We treat Mr. Willish's work with the utmost seriousness and urgency. It is our entire lives. You know that..." Dr. Heron finished, stopping himself from saying Souvik's name.

"We'll be taking him with us," Souvik announced, and Fernanda grunted at Dr. Heron, sending him jumping back a few paces.

"Of course," Dr. Heron offered, lowering his head. "But please. Take this with you. Just in case he wants to go back."

From his white laboratory coat, Dr. Heron removed a pill bottle filled with crimson pills and offered it to Souvik.

Serotel, Matt knew, but he couldn't tell Souvik to ignore the treacherous man from his dreams.

Dreams? Matt checked himself. *No. That's the real world. This is clearly the dream.*

Souvik shrugged. "I don't know why he wastes his time with you and this laboratory," he said, accepting the pill bottle.

"There's no such thing as a waste of time," Dr. Heron urged.

Souvik nodded, then shrugged with a sliver of capitulation. "Maybe," he admitted stoically.

Totally depleted, Matt allowed his eyelids to fall shut, but he was still perfectly lucid.

Now what? Now what? he wondered again.

The titanous pair turned and sauntered toward the exit doors.

"Or maybe not," Fernanda growled, glaring at the raging, icy world outside the lab.

"He'll die if we take him out there like this," Souvik reminded her.

"Counting on it," Fernanda said.

"You think it'll shake off the effects of the procedure?" Souvik asked.

"Only one way to find out," Fernanda finished resolutely.

They're going to kill me, Matt repeated to himself as they arrived at the exit.

The doors slid open, revealing a torrenting hellscape of ice with torturously penetrating gales whipping the world from every direction all at once. Matt screamed in total horror, and his eyelids were jolted open by the air instantaneously crystallizing the heat and vapor of his body.

I'm going to die, Matt said, preparing himself to return to May. *But this time there's no nurse or syringe. I'm really going to die this time…in this world.*

Fernanda and Souvik, despite wearing only thin loincloths, were unfazed by the frigid chaos.

Dark glacial walls towered over them on the left and right, and though Matt thought it was just a cloud formation at first, he realized they were walking toward an actual tower stretching above them to unseeable heights.

Matt began convulsing as hypothermia set in, making the world around him appear as if it were shaking with seismic vibrations. He was reminded of May's world and the existential vibrations that always preceded a portal.

I'm going to die, Matt repeated as the blood under his already purple skin began to crystallize, stopping his heart.

20. Flatline

M att was jolted awake by the feeling of his veins crystallizing into icy webs leading directly to his heart. But he did not find himself in that hellish dream world. Instead, the softness of May's ochre couch supported his back as he took in his surroundings, absorbing the sweet familiarity of May's apartment: there were the plants of every hue and shape, the koi fish, which were swimming in lazy swathes, and right in front of him on the coffee table were the grinder full of cannabis and DMT crystals and the pipe of DMT he had used seemingly a lifetime ago.

I'm back here, Matt gasped in electrifying horror, but the feeling subsided just as quickly as it came, and he couldn't help cherishing the sweetness of everything being so calm and stable.

So peaceful. So...normal.

The humming of a simple melody filled the air, and fingers caressed his skull and ran through his hair.

Turning slightly, Matt realized his head was in May's lap. She held her eyes closed as she hummed her sweet melody to soothe her damaged love.

That's Mu's chanting, Matt realized.

"What language is that?" Matt asked, jarring May with surprise.

Matt was about to apologize when she said, "It's a lullaby my grandma taught me. She was Chinese, but the language in the song isn't something I've ever encountered before. I think she might have made it up, though she always claimed it was some long-lost language of her ancestors, and all that's left of their entire memory and lineage is that single lullaby. It's meant to ensure that dreams don't become nightmares." May sighed, considering a stream of memories as she let her eyelids dip closed for a few seconds. "Anyway, you're back. How do you feel?"

Back, Matt repeated in his head. He recollected what occurred since he had smoked the DMT. *That was all just a DMT trip? Where is this even? Is this real? Is this just a dream after all?* Matt considered everything he experienced since ingesting the DMT and felt a wave of existential despair. *Was all that madness just part of the DMT trip? Or was the DMT trip part of the madness?*

May waited for Matt to tell her how he felt and offered him a worried smile as she clung tightly to him.

"How long was I out?" Matt asked.

"Just a few minutes," she explained with what Matt read as regret. "Though I'm sure it felt like an eternity. That's how DMT is," she said, sighing as if remembering some terrifying, minute-long eternity of her own. "I wish you wouldn't have smoked it, but that was my fault for leaving it out. That was stupid of me."

Matt shook his head and lifted himself out of May's lap to look into her eyes. "It was my decision to smoke it. Thanks for looking after me."

Matt breathed deep. *The last time I was here, we were going to go to the hospital.*

Obviously it was time to go to the hospital because his alternative was just more insanity forever and ever.

"You just smoked, like, a full gram of DMT. I didn't realize that was even possible. What did you see?" May urged, taking his hand in hers and pulling him ever so gently toward her.

"You died," Matt said, not caring about all the rest. He moved closer to May, wrapping his arm around hers as she gripped his leg tightly with her own.

"I'm right here, sweetie. I'm right here with you," May assured him, and she pulled his head down and caressed it like before.

Matt let himself fold into her embrace, and he felt a single tear fall down his cheek – a drop of cascading warmth lost in the endless maze of insanity only to dry up somewhere unknown.

What's going to become of me? Matt cried within. *What has already become of my mind?*

May released her grip first and looked Matt over.

"Do you feel okay to stand up?" she asked in a concerned whisper.

Matt nodded and lifted himself from the couch. *Everything is so wonderfully normal,* he thought. He lifted his hands and let his gaze linger on them for a few seconds. *This isn't a dream,* Matt considered. He looked at the wall full of plants and saw a semi-occluded painting of a jaguar sleeping beneath a fruiting peach tree under a midday sun. Then he turned to May and absorbed her every feature.

"You're real," Matt whispered, and he reached out his hand to feel the warmth of her skin. It was soft and alabaster, not bloody and glistening.

"You're not dead," Matt whispered, and May let her head fall into Matt's outstretched hand. No bullet wound in her forehead. No exploding flesh. No reddening and bursting of capillaries in her eyes.

"I love you, May," Matt admitted, holding back his tears.

May kissed Matt's open palm. "I love you too, Matthew Willish," she said, "which is why we should go."

"Go?" Matt checked, reminded of all the worlds inside his mind that she could be referencing.

"To the hospital," May explained.

Of course, Matt thought, nodding in agreement. But he couldn't help feeling that he should just stay with her instead.

"Maybe I should just stay with you," Matt offered bittersweetly, but May pulled back and lowered her head.

She doesn't want to be with me, Matt trembled, watching her move away from him.

"I do!" May answered, her eyebrows furrowed in sorrow and her eyes going red with tears. "I do want to be with you!"

Matt shivered. *Did she just read my mind?*

May looked at the door suddenly, then lowered her head, seemingly in shame.

"What is it, May?" Matt urged, glancing at the door with trepidation.

Three knocks resounded against the giant vault-like door, making both May and Matt jump to their feet.

Matt eyed May, wordlessly asking for answers.

"I'm sorry," May told him, and she fell helplessly back to the couch just as the door swung open.

Outside the door, Dr. Heron smiled devilishly, and a platoon of Matt's imposters smiled right along with him. Viscous red fluid leaked from the corners of their lips.

He found me.

No! This is a dream! Matt demanded himself to accept as his heart nearly burst out of his chest. He considered running for the window, but he couldn't just leave May to fend for herself.

I have to create a portal somehow. But…that still means this is just a dream.

"This really is just a dream?" Matt asked May, seeing that she hadn't even moved from her position on the couch.

Rather than respond, May softly sobbed.

Is this a dream or not! Matt asked, wondering if the old man's voice would respond inside his mind like it used to.

"Watch," Dr. Heron mused at Matt's dismay. Dr. Heron, dressed in all black as always in this world, removed from his coat pocket the same revolver he'd once used to shoot May. He cocked it, pointed it at May, and shot her in the forehead once more.

May's body slumped in place, twitching and spasming as her neck fell into her own lap.

Matt's knees buckled. The world stood still as he fell back against a wall and sank to the floor in defeat. He forced himself to look away from May's body and breathed deep, trying to ignore his anguish and recognize this illusory world as the dream that it must be.

He can't just go around killing people. He'd be arrested. He'd be put away forever. This isn't real. This isn't real!

"It's just a fucking dream!" Matt roared at the murderous spectre before him.

"Obviously," Dr. Heron stated simply with a measure of impatience. He walked easily into the house, then effortlessly swung the giant wall closed on the army of Matts. The wall latched, and in the same moment, May lifted her head, revealing a quickly shrinking hole in her forehead and no blood whatsoever.

"May!" Matt gawked, unable to suppress his love despite the knowledge that she couldn't be real.

"I'm sorry, Matt," May wept.

Matt shook his head and looked at his hands, then pushed against the wall, then tried breathing through his closed mouth, then tried feeling the existential vibrations that always preceded a portal. Nothing worked. Everything was stable.

"There's just nowhere else to go," Dr. Heron explained. He offered Matt a seat around the coffee table with a wave of his hand. "Might as well sit down and chat," Dr. Heron winked.

He's right, Matt admitted. *Where would I go even if I could teleport right now?*

Matt pulled a large ochre chair to the couch and sat down, Dr. Heron on his right and May on his left. May wept, and Dr. Heron smiled.

"I think we have some things to talk about. Don't we, May?" Dr. Heron said, keeping his stare on Matt the whole time.

May shook her head and whimpered softly, clearly not wanting to have whatever conversation Dr. Heron was referring to.

A glint from the steel of the gun on the coffee table caught Matt's eye, and he didn't waste a single heartbeat before making his decision and taking action. He jumped for it, cocked it, pointed it at Dr. Heron's sinister smile, and pulled the trigger.

The barrel exploded with a flash and the kickback nearly knocked the weapon against Matt's forehead, but Dr. Heron sat before him as if nothing at all had occurred. Matt's ears rang with a piercing cry.

Did I blow out all our eardrums from shooting the gun this close to our heads? Matt winced, though Dr. Heron and May seemed totally unfazed by the gunfire.

With a snap of his fingers, Dr. Heron stopped the ringing in Matt's ears, returning the world to its seemingly stable state.

"You can have control back right after this little conversation," Dr. Heron told him evenly. "Then you can kill me as many times as you want."

Matt dropped the gun back on the table and fell back into his seat. He felt like an insect caught in the predatory web of his own mind.

"May?" Dr. Heron said.

May just shook her head.

Dr. Heron sighed in disappointment. "She's been lying to you, Matthew."

He's lying! Matt thought. *He's the liar!*

Matt's nerves directed him to lift the gun once more. He fired twice at Dr. Heron's forehead, but this time the gun didn't even go off.

Dr. Heron just laughed.

"Tell him!" Dr. Heron barked at May suddenly, the Reaper coming out in full force.

"He's right," May let slip.

Matt shook his head, not wanting to accept any of it. "May…"

"I've been lying to you, Matthew."

"As have I," Dr. Heron admitted. "Though, I didn't play with your heart."

Matt looked back to May for confirmation, and she nodded in painful resignation to the truth.

"I know this is all just your dream," May admitted sullenly.

Just a dream, Matt confirmed in horror. His heart went wild. *Every fucking thing is just a dream.*

"So then…" Matt stuttered, unsure how to begin.

"This is all in your head. We're all just…dream characters," May said as if the words were daggers through her heart.

Matt didn't want to believe it, but he had just watched her die and be resurrected.

Just a dream.

"Then, then I…" he stammered, still not sure how to begin.

"We all represent your subconscious mind," Dr. Heron interjected, dropping his smile and replacing it with a look of professional seriousness. "Programs in the mind of the programmer. In the real world, the world outside this one, there is a Dr. Heron that I am in communication with. He told me about the procedure and your existential predicament in the real world."

"The real world?" Matt gawked. "You're talking about that icy hellscape and the infinite circular lab? That's just one of my dreams."

"The game is the other one, right? *Room Reaper.* He told me about that," Dr. Heron explained easily.

May clutched her shoulders and shivered at Dr. Heron's words.

Matt wanted to reach out to comfort her, but he was stopped by the undeniable reality that she was just his subconscious mind.

"You're not real, then?" Matt asked her, his voice cracking in agony.

May shrugged and let her shoulders fall with tortuous torment. "What does real even mean, Matthew," she urged, forced to defend the validity of her very existence. She pointed to Dr. Heron. "He claims the world outside this one is the real one, yet you call it a dream. I know this is all a dream, but I feel real, Matthew. I feel real." She started sobbing once more, but between each cry she said, "And…I wish that we…that we really could have a life together…here."

Matt took a heavy breath and stifled his anguished tears beneath the impossible, paradoxical weight of wanting to hold her while at the same time knowing she couldn't be real. But he couldn't help it. He went to her. Held her. Felt her. Breathed her.

He ignored Dr. Heron.

"Even if you're just a dream," Matt seethed against his mind, "I still love you. I love you, May."

She wept in full force and pulled him to her, but Matt stopped her. He thought back to the first memory of her that his mind could offer, as far back as he could remember, when he first stumbled into the office and knew with certainty that she could help him. That even though there might be no way out of his insanity, she was still all that really mattered in that moment and every moment that came after. The rest was unresolvable and pointless.

She is everything. She is all that matters.

Matt told May, "If the world outside this one is…more real, somehow, than this one…whatever that means…if there is a real world, then there's a real you. And…I need to find you, May."

May nodded as unstifled tears flowed freely down her cheeks and into her palms like cold rain. "I know. I know. But we can still have this here, can't we?" she pleaded.

Matt shook his head.

"He doesn't remember," Dr. Heron explained to May.

"Remember what?" Matt demanded, turning to face him.

"My counterpart in the real world explained it to me," Dr. Heron offered simply. "He said that you created him and the laboratory and everything in the real world to discover a way to make yourself believe that this world in your head is really the real world. You want to forget all about the world outside this one. You want to close it off forever and just remain inside your mind in this world. All this so you finally can be with her," he said, pointing to May, "without inevitably remembering that she is just a dream."

Matt shook his head in pleading disbelief. "I created the labs and...Dr. Heron? You? What do you mean?"

"The real world," Dr. Heron mused ominously. "It's your world. You've always had control over it. You may as well be God there."

"No," Matt interjected. "I'm just a weak old man in that world. I don't have control over anything."

Dr. Heron nodded. "That's exactly what's so exciting. You've undergone the procedure, Dr. Heron's procedure, countless times. And I mean countless. We're talking billions of times. More than that even. You can't die in the real world, so we're talking –"

"Then it isn't real," Matt interrupted.

Dr. Heron nodded as if expecting Matt to say that. "Yes, yes. That's always been your conclusion. But my counterpart and I believe it's the real world, and you just don't die in the real world. There's no such thing as permanent death. That's just an idea in your head."

"Death?" Matt gasped. "Just an idea?"

Dr. Heron nodded, seemingly excited to be sharing his theory on Matt's existential self-ontology.

"Yes. You've just gone mad after an eternity of being. You can't help imagining there's a world outside the real world."

Matt felt disgusted that his own mind was psychoanalyzing him and presuming him mad, but he couldn't resist the terrible, perfect logic any longer.

"But there is a world outside this one," Matt pressed. "Outside the fact that there's no way I just imagined all these people and the very concept of death, when I did the DMT and when May and I made love, I went somewhere. I...heard May's voice. There were lights and –"

"Yes," Dr. Heron said, waving away Matt's words. "You always go there the first time you make love to May after forgetting about her. And you always have the same experience on DMT – the realization, among endless possible realizations, that you are alone. Perfectly and utterly. But still, that's most likely just part of this dream. An unexplained part, I admit, but —"

"How do you know that?" Matt urged. "Maybe the DMT world or the world I went to when I made love to May — maybe one of those is the real world. Maybe they're the same real world. Something...something outside this solipsistic hell!"

Dr. Heron shrugged with open consideration. "Okay. Let's assume one of them is the real world. Then what? With regard to the lovemaking and the world it reveals, you always describe yourself as being stuck there. You can hear May's voice, and then you return here. That's it. What will you do with that information?"

Matt sat back, needing to hear Dr. Heron's words even if they were insanity.

"Tell me," Matt demanded of both of them, "how long have I been stuck in this series of unrealities?"

"Forever," they both said.

No!

"How long!" Matt demanded, refusing to accept their answer. "How many years!"

"Time doesn't pass like that," May offered quietly, painfully sniffing away her tearful sorrow. "The concept of time and years and all that — it's all just ideas you created. There are no years. There is no sun. We don't remember a beginning, Matthew."

"I didn't just make up the idea of time!" Matt nearly barked. "There's an outside world. There has to be! There has to be! How else could I know about anything? Doctors and dreams and pills and insanity!" Matt seethed at these people who might be mere personifications of his mind. "All of that is from a true reality. I didn't make up all that!"

May squeezed her eyelids shut with anguished force, clearly affected by Matt's outburst.

"As far back as memory goes," May told him regretfully, "it has always been like this."

Matt gulped down her words, then offered, "Or I'm just crazy, and I'm in a hospital right now, conjuring eternal insanity in my head as I wait to die."

Dr. Heron and May both nodded in agreement.

"You have also come to that conclusion many times," Dr. Heron explained.

Insanity. Dreams. Death. Will I ever know the truth? Will I ever get out?

Matt reached for May's hand like a ledge before the infinite fall. She intertwined his grip with her own and squeezed him for reassurance.

"I know that you are what matters," he told her, sure of nothing else. Not even his own reality. "The real May. She —"

He stopped suddenly, remembering what May told him when he had first discovered his office below the floor in the video game dream.

"You told me that you left," Matt ruminated to her miserably, "that you had to leave. But you wouldn't say why."

May shrugged sadly, unable to offer an explanation. "That might be true, but I don't remember saying that."

"Or are you still lying?" Matt wondered.

May winced, but said, "I deserve that."

Matt had to know. "So even when I first came back to the office," he said, "even then you were lying?"

May was quick to correct him. "No, of course not. We only remember who we really are once the world starts falling apart." She pointed a finger at Dr. Heron. "He's the one that's been lying to you the whole time."

Dr. Heron winked at Matt. "All part of the procedure. The procedure that you designed, Matthew. I do as you will, Boss."

Matt focused on his breathing. *In and out. In and out.* He didn't want to admit it, but everything they were saying made sense in its own terrible way.

But now what? Now what am I supposed to do?

"Once I die here or do DMT or whatever else, I'll go to the video game dream? With the Reaper?" Matt asked.

"No," Dr. Heron answered. "That dream was part of the procedure. There's the real world and then there's this world — that is, the world you go to in your head when you meditate, will yourself into your mind, or die in the real world. That's it. There are only these two worlds. The video game world is used in the procedure as a challenge for your consciousness, testing its ability to let go. You remember first becoming aware of yourself inside the video game dream, right?"

Matt thought back to the beginning of all the madness and could practically hear Mu's chanting in his mind. "Yes, that's when all this madness started," Matt admitted.

"Well, that's just the first time you remember," Dr. Heron continued. "During this last procedure, you experienced the video game dream eighty-one consecutive times before finally becoming consciously aware of it, representing the raging of your subconscious mind against an illusory existence."

Dr. Heron appeared excited to the point of jittery regarding the results of his work.

"What's the point of the procedure?" Matt pressed.

"I already told you. The purpose of your design is to make you forget about the real world and accept this world inside your head as the real world. You've spent eternity searching for May in the real world, assuming she must be there – somewhere – in infinity, as if she just left and will one day be found again. But deep down you know that isn't going to happen. So the next best solution is to leave that world and spend the rest of eternity inside your head where you can forget all about that fruitless search and just be happy with her here."

No! Matt seethed pleadingly against Dr. Heron's words. *That isn't the real world. It's just a dream. It's all just a dream.*

"The world you call the real world is inside my head too!" Matt demanded.

"Fine," Dr. Heron said, waving away Matt's concern. "We'll call it the world inside your head inside your head. It's all just semantics, Matthew."

"What about Souvik and Fernanda and the May nurses and the other Dr. Heron and –"

"You made them all."

No, Matt demanded inwardly. *I didn't make them. They're my friends. They're real. Somewhere they have to be real.* He stared at May, absorbing her into the foundations of his mind. *May is real!*

But it was no use fighting it. He had already admitted it over and over to himself. There was just no way anything here or in the other world was real. Even if there was a real world, this wasn't it. It couldn't be.

This is all just a dream.

"I made everything in that world?" Matt checked.

"You did. You even made copies of yourself," Dr. Heron said.

"Copies?"

Dr. Heron nodded, then sat back in his chair as if personally impressed by the information he was ready to divulge. "It's nearly mathematically guaranteed that you are a copy, as there can only be one original. But that doesn't mean anything. You are still real, unlike us."

Matt shook his head.

I'm just a copy? But I'm also real?

"How can I be real if I'm a copy?" Matt urged.

"In the real world, if you wanted to, you could wave your hand and erase anything and anyone. But you can't do that to a copy of yourself – a legitimate copy of consciousness itself. There is no death or erasure for the original Matthew Willish nor any copy."

"They're bringing you to the Tower of God, Matthew," May interrupted in seeming terror at the mention of there being an original Matthew Willish.

Dr. Heron exhausted an impatient breath. "He doesn't remember, May." He turned to Matt, and his eyes burned as he explained May's words. "It is believed that the one who resides at the top of the tower is the original Matthew Willish. He keeps to himself, sleeping at all times, guarded by reality itself, it would seem. He built the labs. He put you there under my watch. He built the tower outside the labs – the one we call the Tower of God. There is no way in except if he wills it."

Matt could barely believe the new layer of insanity they were introducing to him. *Tower of God? A version of myself at the top of the tower guarded by reality? What the fuck fantasy world are they talking about?*

"It's hospital time," Matt told them, stopping himself from engaging any further with his own existential confusion.

Dr. Heron and May looked at each other with actual surprise.

"Matt…" May began, unsure how to respond. She finally said, "this is just a dream, sweetie. You know that, Matthew. There's no point in going to the hospital."

"This isn't a dream!" Matt yelped suddenly.

It can't be. She's real. I know that May is real!

"You're real!" Matt barked, his words laced with pleading, desolate sorrow.

His throat constricted, suffocating him from the inside. He pleaded for help with his eyes, begging May to come to him.

"Maybe we should take him to a hospital just to make him feel better," May said, tears welling in her eyes as she knelt down to comfort Matt. "You know, until he remembers everything."

Dr. Heron shook his head stolidly, denying her request.

"I'm sorry for lying to you, Matthew," May told him, and she rested her forehead against his temple.

Matt's vision blurred, and he felt the subtle beginnings of existential vibrations mounting in the background of reality.

What does it matter? he thought as he felt the life drain from his limbs. *There is no way out.*

May exploded into a flurry of desperate tears. "For fuck sake, Heron, just kill him and let him wake up. This is terrible!"

Matt instinctively raised a hand to stop them from killing him, but Dr. Heron just shrugged at May's words.

"It's probably for the best."

With practiced ease, Dr. Heron removed the gun, cocked it, and pulled the trigger, only this time he shot Matt in the chest.

The force of a sledgehammer slammed against his sternum, sending bone and flesh flying and splattering all over his and May's faces. Matt gritted his teeth against the explosion of his torso, and the pain quickly subsided into an icy numbness.

"But I want you to experience death moment by moment, Matthew," Dr. Heron explained sinisterly. "Watch as this reality dissolves into the next. This is just a dream, Matthew. You need to remember that fully."

May clutched Matt's head and seethed at Dr. Heron, "You're cruel!"

"Reality is cruel, May," Dr. Heron snapped. "His mind is cruel. Cruelty is all there is. Cruelty is proof of existence."

Blood cascaded from the cavernous hole in Matt's chest and spilled over what remained of his torso. He was slipping into the other world as quick and certain as streaming rain.

The existential vibrations were replaced with howling, frigid winds.

The present world went dark, and he could see the other world like light at the end of a tunnel. He was being pulled toward it, and as the light enveloped him, he shielded his eyes against the blazing brightness. May's and Heron's faces stared at him, but they were no more than imprints of light against the darkness of his strained eyelids.

Frigid cold battered his skin, prying his eyes back open.

21. The Tower of God

T he world was awash in endless white – perfect void white spanning forever.

Matt twisted his head, bringing his eyes level with the ground. He saw and felt manicured grass, and he realized that the endless white was just the sky above. And in the distance, between the all-white sky and grassy earth, the blizzard raged. He was outside of it somehow, seeing the blizzard now as an all-pervading wall of torrenting madness. For Matt, brightness and relative calm replaced the blizzard's shadowy, howling chaos.

But the air outside the blizzard was still arctic cold. A stabbing squall forced him to grit his teeth and even threatened his body with hypothermia, but it passed and left him panting, trying to catch his breath.

Unlike the last time Matt had woken to this icy hell that Heron believed to be the real world, his skin was no longer crystallizing.

May! Matt's mind interjected against all else. *Is she just an act? Or worse, is her very identity just a figment of my imagination?* The dread of loving a mere illusion with every ounce of his being struck through him. *Is all this love I feel just a machination of my mind? Am I...is she...*

Matt shivered and contracted his old, decrepit body in a desperate plea for warmth. As he tightened his muscles, the cold world became more tolerable and a slight warmth lapped at his limbs. He realized then that he was wrapped in layers of some animal's thick fur. He further tightened the fur around his body and shivered, his teeth chattering against the frequent but random gusts and gales of below-zero temperatures.

But it was still better than dying in the crystallizing blizzard.

"He's back," Matt heard Fernanda say from somewhere unseen.

"Is he?" Souvik checked.

"Can't you hear his teeth chattering away?"

Souvik laughed. "Mind is a complex creature. He instinctively grew those furs to warm himself, but he still can't go all the way and just be warm."

Fernanda huffed in agreement. "It is quite interesting, indeed. Mind is capable of infinity, and infinitely capable of handicapping itself in an infinite diversity of ways."

"I guess finding ways to limit and transform himself is just another aspect of infinity though, right?" Souvik considered.

These people, Matt thought grimly. *According to Heron, they're just constructs of my mind. Yet here they are, contemplating the nature of my reality…their own reality… despite not being real.*

Matt didn't hear Fernanda offer an opinion, but he envisioned her nodding in agreement at Souvik's point.

"Hey," Fernanda goaded Matt, "why don't you try helping us here?"

Matt just stared at the sky and the blizzard and the grass. He didn't want to go any further. He didn't want to suffer through insanity a moment longer.

Why? he wondered simply. *Why is all this happening?*

"It's the procedure," Souvik explained simply, clearly able to hear Matt's thoughts. "That's why you forgot about this place."

"I mean everything!" Matt snapped, jolting his body upright. "Not just my goddamn forgetting of the past. Everything! Why is all this happening?"

Fernanda and Souvik knelt over a pile of twigs and kindling. They appeared to be attempting to light a fire. A gust pushed at his body, and Matt nearly fell back onto the grass.

"And are you reading my mind?" Matt accused.

"Well, of course," Fernanda shrugged.

"Well!" Matt seethed. "Don't!"

He turned to catch the pair shrugging.

"Fine," Fernanda agreed simply. "Now, your subconscious mind gave you furs and supplied us with this wood, but it didn't do the rest of the work. Why don't you try lighting the fire?" Fernanda issued. "It's for your own good, not ours."

Souvik turned at the neck to look at something behind Matt. Matt turned to follow and fell back with vertigo as the infinitely tall tower unfurled into the endless white above. They were a few hundred feet from its lustrous obsidian-black base. Matt marveled at its eldritch size and estimated that it must be at least a mile in diameter. The blizzard wall curved with the tower's base, extending around the edges to reveal that Matt and the tower were in the eye of the impenetrable blizzard raging on all sides.

"The other me. He built that thing?" Matt gasped.

"You and him both," Fernanda explained. "You're the same, Matt. You built the Tower of God as much as he did."

Matt tried to remember being a god in this tower, but he was still like an outsider to his own existence.

A gale pummeled Matt, slamming his frail body against the ground and knocking the wind out of his aching lungs.

"Try lighting the fire," Fernanda suggested again, not moving to help him.

This is my world, Matt told himself. *Just accept it. Please!* he begged his mind. He thought back to what he remembered about lucid dreaming. Somehow he could remember that at least.

Become the fire, he told himself. Gripping the icy grass blades, he pivoted and glared at the small teepee of sticks and kindling. *Ignite!* he demanded. *Burn!* he roared within, pleading with the world to abate its terrible cold. His skin began prickling, and he felt the pins and needles of warmth against his cold-rotten, age-bittered flesh. *Fire!* Matt demanded, and he felt his body ignite with warmth at the same instant the kindling combusted. A small flame gluttonously licked at the tips of the sticks, eager to be fed.

It worked! Matt thought with glee, forgetting for just a moment the insanity of his very existence.

Fernanda and Souvik smiled and nodded.

"You'll remember everything in time," Fernanda assured him.

He watched them add sticks and larger branches from a pile gathered near the fire. His smile soured as the obvious dawned on him.

219

Lighting the fire. Manifesting furs to cover my body. This so-called real world is just a dream. Like everything. And everyone.

"What's wrong?" Souvik asked him, seeing his frown and apparently obeying the order to not read his mind.

"It's all just a dream," Matt told him forlornly.

Souvik shrugged away the weight of existence with a wave of his arms. "Dreams. Reality. Existence. Being. Suchness – none of that has any real meaning, Matt. Not here, at least."

Fernanda exhaled a great sigh, like a bellow from the anguished Earth itself.

Matt turned back to the tower, not ready to explore the ontological nature of his existence with a personified part of himself.

"What will happen up there?" Matt asked, inching closer to the fire.

Fernanda shrugged. "Been a long time since we were here. Last time was the first time. The 'you' up there conjured us into existence, and then the 'you' down here stepped out of your own body, copying yourself into…well…you. Then you accompanied us to the labs," Fernanda explained with some difficulty. "You…are him," she continued, choosing her words carefully. "The man we brought to the labs, or rather, the man who brought us with him to the labs…there is no difference between him and the man in the tower – not in mind nor memories. You are you. You are him. You just don't remember."

Matt shivered and bundled the furs closer to his core.

"So he…I…all this…all this is my doing?" Matt craned his head around, referring to the world.

"And we're your creation too," Souvik reminded him.

"But you two must be real somewhere," Matt urged, thinking back to the real Souvik and Fernanda.

Or maybe the unreal, Matt considered grimly.

"You can't just be random forms I conjured at some point. You must be based on real people who…who matter to me!"

The pair just shrugged.

"Maybe," Fernanda offered. "You didn't explain our existence. You gave us a job. That's all. The job was to bring you to the labs and make sure Heron started the procedure and then bring you back to the tower if and when meaningful success occurred. We did our job, Matthew."

Fernanda seemed to be looking for forgiveness or recognition of some sort, but Matt could offer no such thing. Not because he blamed her in some way. After all, Fernanda was a stranger to him in this world. But it horrified him that these people didn't seem emotionally distressed by the ambiguous nature of their existence.

They're like the video game characters. Like programs. Only they're worse because they're sentient and dynamic, yet they still have no drive to understand. To know. To come to terms with the nature of their reality.

Matt was alone, and he felt the fullness of his solitude like concrete crushing him from every side.

Everything here is either me or a creation of my mind. And everyone and everything in the world inside my mind is the same. Even May, Matt winced, still unable to fully accept that as a possibility. *It's all just a dream within a dream. Everyone and everything. And there's no way out.*

Matt turned and gazed helplessly at Fernanda and Souvik; they could offer no solace. They were just fractaling mysteries within endlessly fractaling mysteries.

I just want to run away, Matt lamented. *I just want all this to be over.*

If he could regain control, he could part the blizzard and simply go somewhere else in this world. Away from these people and this tower and everything. He eyed the blizzard wall and gazed into its dizzying, tumultuous patterns of life-sucking air currents.

There's no way out. Not yet.

"What are we doing here," Matt seethed, aware that, until he could recollect the whole of himself, he would remain at the whim of whatever came next in this maze of insanity.

"We're waiting for the tower to open," Fernanda explained as she added another branch to the insatiable flames.

A gale kicked hard at the branches, but Fernanda quickly reformed the embers and unburnt wood with her bare hands. She was totally unfazed by the fire, and it didn't appear to burn her skin.

"Have you tried knocking?" Matt said, grimly half-jesting through gritted teeth.

Souvik shrugged and began walking toward the tower at Matt's suggestion. Matt shivered and bundled the furs closer around himself.

"Try being young," Fernanda advised again, forcing a surge of frustration into Matt that he still couldn't do something apparently so rudimentary for these people.

He tried. Just like with the fire, he tried feeling young, but it was still no use. The wind tore at his skin, and he was forced to inch even closer to the fire that he now realized was utterly smokeless.

Fuck! Matt cursed.

As he huffed with anger at his own mind, he noticed in his vision's periphery that icy webbing was encroaching onto the grass at the base of the blizzard wall like roots probing for nutrients.

It's closing in on the tower, Matt realized, unsure of the implications.

Three dull clangs emanated from the tower, and Matt turned to see Souvik beating his gargantuan fist against it.

The probing veins of frost beckoned Matt's attention back, hypnotizing him with undefinable urgency. This time, Fernanda noticed the subject of his gaze.

"The blizzard is slowly getting closer to the tower," she explained in awe. "During the time it took to administer the billions of procedures you underwent, it came maybe an inch closer, but it's still something. It's still a change," Fernanda marveled, letting her gaze fall on nothing in particular. "And now it's really starting to move ever since you came out of the labs. You can almost see it crawling. Like it's alive," she breathed in profound awe. Then she pivoted her gaze to meet Matt's eyes.

"Change," she told him simply. "And it's not something you're actively doing. It's your subconscious mind that's making it happen. Your idea with the procedure might just be working."

Matt found it difficult to follow her explanation, but one word stuck out beyond all others.

Change, Matt thought. *Something beyond the powers of the one in the tower...I mean...my own powers?* he wondered.

"Why doesn't he just stop the blizzard? Or let it consume the tower. Or execute whatever change you're talking about," Matt asked.

"It's part of your plan," Fernanda said without further explanation. "And I admit it's coming along. It...might even work, which just seems...remarkable to the point of hilarious in a way."

Souvik returned and shrugged with defeat. "Nothing," he said, referring to the tower.

"Hilarious?" Matt asked Fernanda.

"You've supposedly been looking for a way for…forever," Fernanda marveled with a chuckle. "Maybe it'll work after all."

"What?" Matt urged. "What's his plan…my plan…in all this fucking endless madness?"

A whole panel opened at the tower's base, revealing a dark interior.

"Ask yourself," Souvik offered before Fernanda could answer.

They stood and waited, clearly expecting Matt to walk along with them, or maybe even transport them if his powers really were limitless.

He tried to stand, but his legs gave out. The grass cushioned his fall better than the laboratory floor, but the slamming of his body against the ground still left him momentarily dazed.

I would have been dead from that fall if I were still as frail as I was back in the labs, Matt realized. He hoped that maybe he was slightly younger after all, but it still made no difference in terms of his ability to move himself.

Souvik and Fernanda lifted his frail body at the arms, then Fernanda pivoted and easily lifted Matt, cradling him like a newborn.

The tower loomed ahead, and with each of Fernanda's steps, Matt felt the environment warm slightly. By the time they arrived at the tower's base, Matt couldn't help loosening the furs and letting them fall to the ground. The blizzard seemed so distant; not even the wind seemed disturbed.

Impenetrable darkness filled the inside of the tower. Standing only a few inches from it, they still weren't able to see past the coal-black fog. Fernanda strode into the darkness without hesitation, but Matt couldn't help holding his breath and squeezing his eyelids into slits in anticipation for what might be on the other side.

The darkness turned out to just be an illusion, as they stepped through it and into a simple foyer, no more than twenty feet high, consisting of sharp metallic walls tapering to a single door a dozen or so paces in front of them. The door was normal sized, but in front of the door stood an actual titan whose head almost reached the twenty-foot ceiling. The titan's deep black skin perfectly contrasted his hulking pearl-white armor, and his mass made Matt feel like a lone ant in his presence. Even Fernanda and Souvik seemed like children in his midst.

"Chike," Matt gawked, taking in the giant's unmistakable features.

The giant gazed straight ahead, seeming not to even notice the tiny creatures below him.

"We come to speak to him," Souvik explained, having to raise his voice slightly to ensure the giant could hear him with ears so close to the ceiling. "The task he gave us appears to be arriving at a point of success...finally."

The Chike-like titan didn't say a word. With a single pivot of his whale-dense leg, he moved aside, sending tremors through the tower with even his most subtle movements. Eyes like lighthouse beacons stared into Matt's soul as Matt, Souvik, and Fernanda passed below the giant's waist and approached the office door.

Chike! Matt thought as he stared into the stoic yet profoundly present eyes of the man who he remembered as his best friend. *Are you just some hulking guard in a fantasy world, Chike? Or is all this just a grotesque version of reality?*

"Chike!" Matt called out to the giant. He stared and the giant stared back. "Chike!" Matt called again, but the giant did not respond.

"He's just part of the tower," Souvik explained, and then he opened the door before Matt could protest. The door was identical to his office door from the world inside his mind. The inlaid gold *MW* symbol adorned the door's mahogany, and as Souvik swung it open, flashing red, green, and blue light scintillated and reflected off the symbol's surface.

They entered the room, and Matt went wide-eyed at the sight of an amorphous area of space about six feet from the ground that undulated with a heartbeat-like rhythm. At its center, a point of perfect darkness, no larger than Matt's fist, churned and coalesced into itself while its periphery glowed and tendrilled with RGB-hued pure energy. Like a fissure in the fabric of reality itself, the energy flared outward, singeing the air near Matt. Still held by Fernanda, he shrank into her arms, feeling as though the reality fissure was both threatening and familiar somehow.

The world I went to when I made love to May, Matt thought, *that's what it reminds me of. That RGB glow...that's also the place I went on DMT. I'm certain of it.*

Then again, there was no way to be sure of anything. Like skirting the edges of a black hole's event horizon, Matt felt as though the flickering fissure might pull at him and rip him to pieces. He knew there was no real death in this world, and yet, the undulating fissure still filled him with the fear of existential finality.

He forced his focus away from the fissure and inspected the rest of the room. Though there was no other light to illuminate his surroundings except the glow of the coursing energy, it was still more than obvious where he was. The plants and the koi fish and the gold, crimson, ochre decor and everything.

"It's my office," Matt gasped, "and May's apartment. Down to every detail."

Except for that surging energy thing, Matt noted with trepidation.

Fernanda deposited Matt onto the ground then took her place beside Souvik in the doorway.

Matt caught movement in the corner of his eye, and he turned to see two figures in a king-size bed against the wall opposite the amorphous energy. One of the figures was still sound asleep, but the other was lifting itself out of bed.

"Quiet!" the figure whispered, more plea than demand. "He doesn't like to be woken up."

Though the figure's voice was unmistakable, as she walked out of the bed's shadow and into the light, the sight of May stole Matt's breath. It was May. His May. She was exactly as he remembered her from his dreams of waking life. Early 30s. Diamond piercings. Lustrous black hair down to her shoulders. A bright ochre gown of silk draped over her bare skin.

"May!" Matt shrieked, his skin aching to feel her. He could barely move from his place on the ground, but he still reached for her. Then he stopped at the sight of her backing away from him with a look of terror on her face. May cast a sorrowful, pitying glance over her shoulder at the figure still lying in bed.

"It's me, May!" Matt urged, wanting desperately for her to run into his arms and tell him everything would be all right.

May shook her head and offered Matt the same despair-filled, pitying face. Then she winced as the figure in the bed groaned in belligerent anger. "Fuck!" the figure roared from his resting place. "May! Where are you!"

May ran to the man in bed and guided one of his arms around her waist. "It'll be all right," she told him in a whisper that could soothe even a god's anger. May issued a soft chant, lulling the man back to sleep despite his series of indecipherable groans of protestation.

Is that the so-called Tower God? Matt wondered. *Is that...me?*

Souvik stepped back as if accepting that they would just have to wait an unknown amount of time for the man to wake up naturally. Fernanda, on the other hand, said in a subdued voice, "Sorry to interrupt you —"

The man interrupted her with a growl of exasperation. "Whaddya want?" he whined like an exhausted toddler.

May kissed the back of the man's neck, and in response, the man pushed her away so hard that she fell off the bed.

"May!" Matt croaked from the ground.

"Shut up!" the man in bed screamed through Matt's own voice. "All of you!"

That bastard, Matt seethed.

May lowered her head in shame, then returned to bed and allowed the man to wrap an arm around her torso and pull her tightly against his belly.

"Wake up!" Matt barked, barely able to hold his body high enough to see the pair in bed. "I said wake up!" Matt practically growled.

I'll kill him for hurting May. I don't care if he is me.

"I was deep in the dream," the Tower God seethed in a rumble that seemed to vibrate the very walls of his tower. "I was living in paradise with my love, and you come here and set fire to my Eden?" he asked with a threatening and barely controlled edge to his voice.

Souvik took a step back, and this time so did Fernanda.

"Please," Souvik pleaded, "we do only as you ask. The labs, they —"

The man in bed screamed with ghastly rage as he lifted himself into a seated position in the bed. "Get away!" he screamed with terrible cruelty, tensing his unclothed upper body with murderous rage.

In response to the Tower God's command, Souvik and Fernanda vaporized before Matt's eyes, their final expressions a mix of fear and confusion.

Backing away rapidly from the bed with his barely functioning body, Matt was unable to stop the despair and tangible fear he felt at seeing the extinguishing of Souvik's and Fernanda's familiar faces, illusory though they might be. He longed to escape this room, but his body didn't have the vitality to obey his will.

It's me, Matt confirmed, analyzing the man in bed for some subtle deviation. But it was him. An exact copy.

"You too! Get out!" the Tower God barked at Matt, pointing his finger at the door to the icy hellscape.

"What's wrong with him?" May asked, looking Matt over with sad, wistful eyes.

The man in bed shook his head. "I don't care," he said resolutely. He kissed May with equal depth and detachment. It was clearly an action he had executed countless times, but it still held meaning, no matter how disparately scant.

"He can stand there while we sleep for all I care," the Tower God exuded as he lay his head back on the crimson pillow.

Matt couldn't pull his eyes from May. And all the while, her probing, sorrowful stare never wavered from his eyes either. The flickering light of the amorphous energy cast swimming shadows across her face, rhythmically occluding and spotlighting her features.

"I feel bad for him," May admitted.

The man in bed huffed with impatience. "You," the Tower God demanded to Matt with vehemence bordering on disgust. "Leave. Make your own tower. Go away."

Go away, Matt repeated and nearly laughed in horror.

"I would if I could," Matt seethed, his body sprawled on the ground before them. "Just tell me how to be young again," Matt demanded. "I'm tired of this. Tired of everything."

May rose from the bed, leaving the Matt in bed grasping for her.

"No!" the Tower God demanded pathetically, his voice cracking in despair. "Come back to me, May. Ignore him!"

May peered over her shoulder at the petulant man-child shouting orders at her, but she didn't obey.

Is that really me? Matt thought in horror.

May sauntered to Matt, knelt down, and took his frail hand in her own. He felt his chest throb with desperate force, pulsing with energy that tugged him like a braided cord toward May.

"May!" the Tower God shrieked.

May reluctantly ignored his cries and beamed at Matt with her slightly crooked smile. Her eyes were slick with tears, but she hid her sorrow behind a mask of compassion.

"It's you," May confirmed to herself in pleasant surprise. "It's him, Matt," she said louder to the Tower God. "It's the one that went to the labs the last time we were awake."

"I don't care!" the man shrieked. "Just come back to bed, May! I don't want to be here!" he pleaded with urgent, desperate anguish.

May shook her head, then rose to address him head-on.

"Did you forget about the procedure?" May offered sweetly, exuding serene patience.

"The procedure," the Tower God repeated hollowly. "The procedure," he said again, this time even more distantly.

"Yes," May confirmed like a caretaker to an overworked patient. "We've been asleep a long while. But if he's back, that means Dr. Heron made progress."

"Dr. Heron?" the Tower God repeated with some confusion.

May turned to Matt, her smile blossoming. "He's just a little confused," she explained. "He doesn't wake up very often anymore, and when he does, it takes him a few minutes to recollect...well...everything."

"I'm the one that's confused," Matt cried. "I'm insane. This is all a dream. And I'm...I'm him. We're both me."

Can they make sense of all this? Can she help me? Matt wondered hopelessly.

"The procedure," the Tower God announced with an air of recollection. He rose from the bed and strode to Matt, taking his place beside May. He wore a pair of crimson boxers and a golden robe made of the same silken material as May's. He was like a totally different person from before. His wide eyes gleamed with a supernatural, directionless hunger, and each of his breaths was a focused, premeditated effort to respire. Every ounce of his being was directed toward Matt and Matt alone.

"This isn't an act, then?" the Tower God inquired of Matt with a glimmer of rage and a measure of amusement.

An act? Matt seethed inwardly. *A fucking act?*

228

Matt couldn't help laughing hopelessly at the very premise of the Tower God's question. Then his laughter turned to anger, and anger turned to rage.

"An act?" Matt roared at the younger version of himself standing beside the only person who really mattered to him. "Fuck you!" Matt growled. "Fuck you for existing. Fuck you for making me exist. Fuck you for dragging me into your insanity!"

The Tower God's eyes flared with equal wrath and intrigue. "I'm part of the chain too," the Tower God seethed. "You can't blame me for doing the exact same thing you'll do eventually. The same thing that was done to me!"

"You're just another copy, then?" Matt lamented.

The wild-eyed Tower God's lips twitched with ravenous anger. "Who knows. I don't remember being copied, but eternity makes you," he hesitated, searching for the word with miserable groans, "confused," he said, finally deciding on the right word. "No matter what I remember, the odds that I'm the original are one in infinity. So, I assume that, yes, I am also a copy."

"You assume?" Matt gasped, surprised that the Tower God would be satisfied with such uncertainty.

"What does it matter?" the Tower God exploded, making May jump to caress his shoulders in an effort to relax him. "Everything is unknowable. You know that," the Tower God concluded with grave finality.

"Where is the original?" Matt pressed.

The Tower God sighed and looked at May. But May smiled and even offered a tiny jump in celebration.

"Your plan's working!" May told him excitedly, and she clasped a hand over his, then turned to survey Matt.

The Tower God nodded with taciturn consideration at May's words and said, "Maybe."

"Please," Matt interjected, begging through his gritted teeth. "How do I become young again?"

"Just be young," the Tower God intoned simply.

Matt felt his skin contract suddenly at the Tower God's words. His muscles tightened and the aching pain emanating through his every cell subsided. Energy coursed through him to a hyper degree, tightening and strengthening his muscles to the point of vein-popping dehydration.

"Don't overdo it," the Tower God said with grim but tangible amusement. It was as if this were the first time he had ever experienced novelty through all eternity. "You'll constrict oxygen to your heart. Unless you convert your body to no longer run on oxygen. Not that it matters, really. You'll just die and reset to your subconscious self-image when you return from your inner world."

Matt didn't care that the Tower God's words released him from his old age, nor did he care what this original version of himself had to tell him. Not in that moment. Only one thing mattered.

Matt stood, easily lifting himself to his feet using his newfound form.

"Is she the original?" Matt demanded, pointing at May.

The Tower God shook his head, clearly enjoying Matt's confusion in the same way a sinister parent might prey on a child's ignorance. "What do you mean?" the Tower God checked.

"Is she the original May?"

The Tower God shook his head once more. "The original May?" he checked again.

"Don't play dumb!" Matt told his mirror image.

The Tower God nodded with some distant and terrible understanding. "There is no original May," the Tower God explained with torturous self-pity. "There's no original anyone. Everything. Everyone. It's our creation. We are alone. We have always been alone."

"You're not alone!" May urged the Tower God, and she hugged him tightly. The golden-robed man closed his eyes and breathed her in, moaning with terrible agony.

He's insane, Matt understood. *Like me.*

The other Matt clung to May and she clung back, embracing him as if Matt were not even present.

May is how he...how I...endure this eternity, Matt realized. He fell to his knees and let his head fall into his open palms.

"Who is she then?" he sobbed, forcing himself to confront May's existence.

The Tower God opened his eyes and looked upon Matt with blazing self-hatred. "A physical manifestation of our desires?" he offered without urgency. "A random algorithm of our mind?" he nearly growled. "I don't know," he seethed, churning each syllable with all-consuming rancor.

His words made Matt physically wince.

"A random fucking algorithm?" Matt repeated, refusing to accept that this soul-rotten specter could possibly be his own self.

"You've had enough," the Tower God announced like a hammer against lead. "Make a tower. Go to sleep. Let a copy continue with the procedure. You've done enough as it is." The Tower God's tone was authoritative, but the offer implied compassion.

It's not compassion, Matt told himself. *All this miserable being knows is himself. All he has is himself.*

May lowered her head seemingly in response to Matt's thoughts.

He doesn't deserve her, Matt concluded. He felt that his heart might rend at the implication that he didn't deserve May either.

"Just build a tower?" Matt repeated with disgust. "Like you did?"

The Tower God just nodded with reticent acceptance. "Like we all do eventually. To keep the world from disrupting sleep. Only now, things are different."

May had a sparkle in her eye. "The procedure," she explained with hopeful surprise.

"She's real," Matt demanded, ignoring everything else but May. "She is all that matters," he raged. "This is all just a dream, so who gives a shit about a procedure in a dream? We need to get back to the real world. I need to get back to her!" Matt proclaimed.

"Quiet!" the Tower God roared. "She isn't real, you addle-brained imbecile. The procedure made you forget. And that's a good thing. But I've already been through this over and over and over again to the foundations of infinity. There is no outside world. There is no reality. Not in the way we want there to be. There are only dreams within dreams!"

The fissure of coursing energy suddenly flared in brightness behind Matt, reminding Matt again of that other world.

"You're wrong," Matt asserted. "I've been to another world. I've heard May's voice. I've —"

"That's from *my* mind," the Tower God churned with scorn. "You *are* me."

Matt shook his head, wanting anything else to be true besides sharing

231

an identity with this broken man.

"We've been through this," the Tower God pressed like steam through metal slits. "Even if there is a world beyond this one, it is unreachable. But the world inside," the Tower God said, and he let his eyes glide over May with palpable, ancient pleasure. "The world inside is reachable. It is attainable. It is accessible. And you are proof that we are finally on the right track."

The Tower God lifted a hand and twisted his wrist, commanding a section of the tower to disappear. The outside world was still the same icy hellscape all around them as far as Matt could see except for the tower and the immediate area around it. In the distance, the veins of ice snaked their way toward the tower inch by certain inch.

"The encroaching ice is forcing the procedure to be successful," the Tower God stated, marveling at his own work. "And the success of the procedure, in turn, speeds up the ice. It's a looping feedback system. And it's working."

The Tower God took May by the shoulders and gazed deeply into her eyes as he spoke his next words. "Soon, the procedure will be a total success, and we'll go inside forever. We'll let this whole world crystallize to absolute zero in the path of the infinite blizzard. Everything will freeze to perfect stillness, and the more my mind crystallizes into a fossil of itself, the deeper into the dream I'll fall. There'll be no world for me to wake to. There will only be the inside world. There will only be May's world." The Tower God smiled with incredible elation, ecstasy smeared across his maniacal features. "No more interruptions. No more worry. No more guessing. No more eternal, existential, ontological bullshit," he sprayed, his arms outspread in practiced triumph.

The wall of the tower rematerialized, closing them off from the outside world once more.

Matt almost pitied this being forced to play chess against his own mind for all eternity.

And I'm just another chess piece, Matt realized in horror. *And I'm the chess board. And I'm the very concept of chess itself.*

"No!" Matt shouted, despite tasting a mere morsel of the insanity the Tower God had feasted on for all of time. "It's false. It's illusory. We can't give up on her!"

Matt turned to May and pleaded, "You aren't just a random algorithm. You're real, May. You are!"

The Tower God allowed himself a huff of amused laughter. "I love it," he breathed, watching Matt fail to wrestle with his own state of being. "This is incredible."

Matt felt like a slug being viewed under a microscope. All his actions and words were just part of this false god's experimentation.

"Did you name yourself God?" Matt asked in disgust.

"No," the Tower God answered easily.

"That's what the others call this place," Matt accused. "The Tower of God. And you are the so-called god."

"The denizens of this world, my mind, refer to me as God," the Tower God admitted. "They have sentience. They think critically. And it is a logical conclusion. You and I, us, we are God in this place. We are their creators...and destroyers," he said, clearly referring to his vaporizing of Fernanda and Souvik.

Matt nearly jumped at him, but the Tower God said, "Feel free to just recreate them."

Recreate, Matt repeated inwardly with profound, aching sadness. *They're just creations. Not my friends. Not my coworkers. They're just random dream characters.*

Matt balled his fists and gritted his teeth and squeezed at his existential anguish.

Why? he pleaded. *Why is this happening?*

The Tower God and May simply stared at Matt, one set of eyes a fiery blaze, the other a tranquil invitation.

The warping amorphous energy suddenly lashed out at Matt, singeing the air near his left ear and forcing him to move a few steps closer to his mirror image and his love.

"What is that?" Matt demanded, pointing to the warping, flashing energy.

The Tower God and May shared a confused glance.

"What?" the Tower God asked simply.

He's toying with me, Matt concluded.

"That!" Matt demanded, still aiming his finger at the amorphous space.

"It must be the procedure that is making him see things," May considered.

The Tower God nodded reasonably, as if considering this a minor side effect in the grand scheme of his ultimate design.

Can they really not see it? Matt wondered, unable to trust them any more than he could trust his own corroded mind.

The Tower God inspected Matt and sighed, coming to some forlorn conclusion. He closed his eyes and seemed to enter a momentary state of REM as his eyes moved beneath his lids with incredible rapidity. After only a second or two, a perfect copy exited the Tower God's body as if the Tower God were merely a mirror to walk in and out of. The copy was naked, though he didn't seem to take any notice.

The Tower God and the copy nodded to each other, then the copy waved his hand, materializing Fernanda and Souvik back into existence. Like before, their muscles rippled with impossible mass, and they wore nothing more than neolithic cloth across their genitals.

Then, without taking any notice of the reality fissure or Matt, the trio left the room, heading in the direction of the labs.

"More procedures?" Matt accused.

"Of course," the Tower God confirmed. "Yours was a partial success. No doubt Dr. Heron will find a way to achieve complete success. It's not like he can run out of lab rats. Or time. When the procedure is perfected, I will go to the labs myself."

Matt thought of Fernanda and Souvik and asked, "Why them? Why did you conjure them in particular? You couldn't even bother to give them proper clothing."

The Tower God actually chuckled at Matt's words.

"I've made them before. Why even bother thinking of something new anymore? And their clothes? What does it matter?" the Tower God snickered sincerely at Matt, enjoying his confusion with incredible elation.

"You should go inside for a while," the Tower God offered. "Inside your head, I mean. Until you remember everything, Dr. Heron can give you something to keep you heavily asleep. So, build a tower. Go inside."

Matt remembered the bottle of Serotel that Dr. Heron handed Fernanda before they left the labs.

"He gave Fernanda a pill bottle," Matt said.

"Fernanda?" the Tower God asked, clearly caught off guard.

"The large woman you vaporized!" Matt barked, loathing the fact that he didn't even remember her name.

"You named her?" the Tower God checked with further amusement.

"That's her name," Matt corrected. "From my dreams. Her name is Fernanda."

The Tower God shook his head in pleasant surprise. "I never named her. Interesting."

Matt was reminded that he was just a lab rat in the eyes of this other self.

But I'm changed, Matt seethed. *I'm not like him. I'm not him!*

He looked back with incredible trepidation at the coursing fissure in the fabric of space. The flashing RGB glow of the energy nearly hypnotized him and felt as though it were calling out to him, beckoning him with abject insistence.

Maybe that's what I'm meant to do, Matt considered in horror. *Maybe that's the way out,* he thought, imagining his body being shredded in an instant, atom by atom. He knew death meant nothing here, but the feeling couldn't be assuaged.

Why can't they see it, Matt wondered feverishly. *And if it's the result of the procedure, then what else did the procedure do to my mind?*

Matt shook his head in painful consideration and nearly forgot about the others for just a moment.

The Tower God bellowed, "Enough. I've had enough. Back to bed, May. Now."

May shook her head and gazed at Matt bittersweetly. "I want to help him. I –"

"I said now!" the Tower God ordered, jarring May and making her wince in pitiful submission.

"Don't talk to her like that!" Matt barked, and the sharpness in his voice created an unintentional shockwave that slammed against May, knocking her to the ground. The Tower God, however, was untouched.

"May!" Matt shrieked, "I'm sorry!"

Matt lunged for her, but in an instant, the Tower God was in front of

Matt, blocking his path.

"Move!" Matt ordered. He tried pushing the Tower God out of his way, but it was like trying to move an entire mountain.

I'm still too weak, Matt realized.

"You still have much to remember," the Tower God intoned. "Like that you and I can't destroy each other," he explained with disdain.

Matt ignored the mirror image of himself and checked on May. Seeming unhurt, she lifted herself from the floor and smiled at Matt as if in understanding that he hadn't intended harming her.

"I'm done with you," the Tower God issued. Lifting his arm, the Tower God placed his hand against Matt's chest, then he pushed with a fraction of his strength, sending Matt flying across the room despite Matt not even feeling the Tower God's hit.

As Matt's body whirled across the room, he flailed his limbs in a wild attempt to stabilize himself. His back slammed hard against the wall of the tower, but that pain was nothing compared to the searing agony pulsing through his hand in a heartbeat-synced rhythm that seemed to directly mirror the pulsing of the reality fissure.

Matt shakily lifted his left hand and gasped at the sight of blood freely pumping from jagged stumps of blood-slicked flesh that had once been his ring and pinky finger.

"Fuck!" Matt seethed. He looked up and followed the trail of blood back to the reality fissure.

My hand must have passed through it, Matt gasped in horror.

"Matthew!" May screamed as Matt cradled his hand to his stomach in a futile attempt to stop the profuse bleeding.

Absorbing Matt's incredible pain and confusion, May broke away from the Tower God's hold and strode to Matt. Her crooked smile tangibly washed away the searing pain, and as she took his blood-soaked hand into her own, he felt warmth emanating and flowing through him from the point of contact.

"It'll all be all right," May assured him, not caring that she was getting covered in his blood.

It's her, Matt gasped, staring into her eyes with longing desperation. *But it isn't,* he confirmed in the same breath, his mind like a mine-filled battlefield.

236

"Good god!" Matt shrieked in existential agony. He clung to May and sobbed as he buried his face in the crook of her neck. May clung right back, caressing his back with her hands and running her soft lips against the skin of his exposed cheek.

She isn't real, Matt knew. But it didn't matter. She was here in his arms.

May, Matt cried pitifully within, and she gripped him even tighter in response.

"Take her with you," the Tower God offered from behind them. "Maybe she can help with the hallucinations."

Take her with you, Matt repeated with mounting anger. *Like she's just property.*

Matt clung to her more tightly, to the only person in all of reality and unreality who mattered or could possibly matter.

He thinks of her as a random algorithm, Matt remembered with revulsion. *Something plumbed from his mind. A figment of thought.*

May! Matt cried within, then he pulled away and gazed into her eyes, into the core of her being.

"I don't know how I know for sure," Matt told her, "but I just know. I just know with total certainty that you are real. The real you is out there somewhere. And I will find you, May. I will."

Tears filled May's eyes, and she smiled and hugged Matt, cherishing every moment with him.

Matt let his eyes fall on the Tower God, who just stared at both of them with forlorn indifference. The light flashed across his features, reminding Matt of the inkblot and the Reaper.

Maybe the procedure is bringing me closer to the true reality, Matt considered hopefully. *Maybe that's what that energy is. Maybe that's why I can see it and he can't.*

The Tower God continued staring at Matt as if studying him down to the nano-level of detail.

He thinks I'm a broken version of himself. But maybe I'm closer to my true self than he is, Matt pondered.

"Why isn't your hand healing?" the Tower God inquired ominously. "How did the wall chop your fingers off in the first place?"

Matt shook his head at his other self with hateful scorn. "I told you.

It's that space of glowing energy. My hand passed through it when you hit me."

The Tower God shook his head with grim indifference.

"Go to sleep. Your mind is broken," the Tower God concluded more to himself than to Matt. Then he turned on his heel and got back into bed.

"You're just going to go back to sleep?" Matt asked.

"What else is there?" the Tower God intoned, and for the first time, Matt could hear in the Tower God a tributary of lamentation connected to an infinite ocean of helpless despair.

The Tower God lifted his arm, and a copy of May materialized beneath it. She cuddled up to the Tower God and smiled with a perfectly contented grin. Probing with his hand behind his pillow, the Tower God brought out a bottle full of red pills. He practically broke off the cap opening the bottle, then tilted back his head and poured the pills down his throat as if they were a free-flowing liquid. At least a hundred pills cascaded down the Tower God's throat.

The Tower God put his arm back around the new copy of May and let the pill bottle fall beside her, spilling crimson fragments of insanity across the crimson sheets and covers.

Matt could only feel disgust for his original self.

He gave up on her, Matt concluded. *He gave up on finding the real world and the real May.*

"You're just giving up?" Matt barked, but the other Matt was already fast asleep.

May squeezed Matt's unwounded hand and smiled her serene smile.

"Come on," she said, motioning toward the exit door.

Matt looked back at the tendrilling fissure in space, but May's pull convinced him to leave it behind with the Tower God.

They exited hand-in-hand into the foyer and the unreal world. Blood still flowed from his hand, and though May's touch had significantly numbed the pain, the ache was ever-present.

The titan wearing Chike's features still stood outside, silently guarding the sleeping Tower God.

Was it all in my head, Matt wondered sorrowfully, thinking back to what he remembered of Chike. *Were you never really like a brother to me? Are you just a fucking thought in my head?*

May's grasp brought his mind back to the present, and he shook his head, refusing to give his thoughts any credence.

She's real, Matt demanded his mind to accept. May smiled at him, her features like moonlight in endless darkness. *She has to be real somewhere.*

Chike stood as distant and enormous as the infinite world beyond the tower. Matt forced himself to step away from the giant, but he didn't know what to do next.

Should I undergo the procedure again? Should I just go back?

He looked out at the blizzard, and then he looked at his hands, which were young despite the fresh wound.

I can do whatever I want. I just have to remember that, Matt told himself. *I can heal my hand. I can go out into the blizzard. I can go out there and search for her, not just go to sleep and give up,* Matt thought resolutely as he imagined the Tower God with disgust.

"Are you out there, May?" Matt asked this woman of his dreams who he hoped, despite all doubt, was real somewhere, somehow.

"I don't know," she answered honestly, unfathomable pity and compassion for Matt filling her every cell. "But the other you in the tower…he thought so," she offered.

"What?" Matt checked, caught off guard. "But he called you a random algorithm."

May shrugged with understanding. "He gets frustrated. You get frustrated, I mean." She nodded to herself; clearly she had already gone over all this with herself. "Anyone would in your situation," she offered with sage understanding. "But deep down inside, he thinks the same way you do. He thinks deep down there must be a real world beyond all this. How could there not be? The alternative is that you created the very concepts constituting reality: the need to breathe, shape and form, even the very laws of physics." A wave of empathetic pain shot through her suddenly. "You're the result of his mind refusing to accept the alternative. It's too painful to even consider. It's too overwhelming to even fathom."

Matt considered the possibility that the very basis of reality and every concept within it were his own unique creation, and the concept of a real world on which all his creations were based was itself just another one of his concepts. Taken even further, his own individuality, his own identity, may very well be the idea of some greater machination with only a patterned and detached conceptualization of self.

No! Matt pleaded inwardly, pushing away the thought that his very self was just arbitrary, meaningless conceptualization.

May nodded, once again seeing Matt's existential horror an uncountable number of times. "That's why," she said with eyes full of tears, but her soothing smile never faltered. "That's why I'm happy the procedure seems to be working. This world is falling apart. It's been falling apart. It's a reflection of your own mind. What you need is a reset, and I'm hoping the procedure does that. I hope it just resets everything. This place wasn't always a form of hell," she urged. "It was a paradise once. A place of extraordinary interdimensional wonder and beauty. And before that – there was no before that. It was always a paradise. Until...until he...until you..."

"I'm not him," Matt rumbled.

May nodded. "Okay, Matt. You are separate now," she accepted, allowing him to believe anything that might bring him comfort. "Either way," May continued, "he thinks he can override his own mind and permanently stay asleep in the world within. But it's never going to work, Matt. The mind will always come back to itself."

That's what the Reaper dream was, Matt told himself. *My mind forcing itself back to this place.*

Reading his mind, May nodded in agreement with Matt's thoughts.

Because she is my mind, Matt told himself sullenly.

"The video game dream you experienced," May said. "That's right. The mind will always find a way to force itself to look at the light. To know the truth. You can only trick yourself for so long," May explained bittersweetly.

Matt considered just falling to his knees and crying out in helpless despair. He felt no closer to any actual answers.

What's the point? Matt mentally languished. *Of anything.*

May placed her gentle hand on Matt's shoulder, and he felt surging energy in his solar plexus coursing back and forth between him and May.

"Go inside," May told him gently. "Go be with her. With me. Leave this place for a while. We'll look after your body out here – not that anything can permanently hurt you out here."

We'll look after, Matt repeated in his mind. He felt their presence, and then he turned to see Fernanda, Souvik, and Chike smiling with open arms. They were exactly how he remembered them in the world inside his mind.

They took a step toward him, surrounding him with warmth and familiarity.

Matt couldn't help lowering his head and sobbing as a strangely comforting feeling of security washed over him. He was reminded of the video game dream – stranded in this infinite delirium, surrounded by his friends and his lover who were helping him overcome the impossible.

"There's no way out," he told them, shaking as he sobbed. Souvik placed a hand on Matt's right shoulder as Chike placed a hand on his left shoulder. Fernanda's hand gripped his back lovingly. May stepped forward and hugged her arms around Matt's torso, leaving no gap between them. The energy flowed through May, then spread through Matt to the others, making him moan with the tingling feeling of orgasmic pleasure mixed with pins and needles against his flesh. From behind him, Fernanda offered the pill bottle, holding it in front of him, level with his eyes.

Seeing the pills injected Matt with the grim, familiar possibility that he was just crazy – that everything was just a fever dream burning forever in the unquenchable embers of insanity.

Maybe this is all in my head, Matt reminded himself gratingly. *Maybe I'll wake up in a hospital and get treated with medicine that works. And maybe one day I'll actually die, and I won't have to suffer for eternity.*

Matt burst into tears. It was all too much. Everything. Everyone. His very self.

The others nodded with patient acceptance of Matt's mind.

The cap to the pill bottle popped off on its own, and Fernanda tilted the bottle, displaying the crimson pills to Matt.

Serotel, Matt lamented. *Just like in May's world.*

The energy surged and he pulled back, resisting the urge to scream out. The others seemed to take on some of the force of the energy's power as they grunted and braced themselves against it.

May caught Matt's stare, and with just her eyes, she offered him the whole of her being.

"I love you," he told her as infinity licked at the periphery of his mind with unrelenting savageness.

"I'm going to find you," he told her. "I'm going to find all of you."

They all nodded, placidly accepting his words.

"We know," May told him with tranquil certainty. "We're counting on you. We know you'll find a way and make everything all right."

The others nodded in agreement with May just as a bolt of energy lashed through Matt, making them all tense against the force. But they never let go of him.

"But go inside now," May continued. "Take a break from this world. Go be with her...with me. Maybe some of your memories will come back, for better or worse."

Matt envisioned sitting beside May in her apartment, but the thought was tarnished by the awareness that it might just be a reflection of the Tower God's room.

"I love you, May," Matt said in defiance of his own mind.

May pulled herself to him and kissed Matt passionately. The sweetness of her tongue and lips reached deep into his mind and pacified reaches of insanity that he was likely better off never remembering.

May broke away and eyed the pills.

With a nod and the cocking back of his head, Matt signaled to Fernanda to pour them into his mouth. He was reminded of the great flow of crimson that the Tower God had also allowed to fill his throat.

He gave up, Matt seethed. *He just gave up on May. But I won't.*

Fernanda allowed a dozen or so pills to fill Matt's mouth before lifting the bottle back up. Unable to swallow them in the same fashion as the Tower God, Matt was forced to chew them, bursting slightly viscous yet flavorless crimson fluid into his mouth. Some of it leaked out of the corners of his lips, leaving crimson streaks running down his chin and continuing to flow toward the surging energy in his and May's chests.

He imagined the May of the inside world again, and this time they were back in the bar.

I wish I could go back, Matt thought, *back to that night. I wish I could just properly explain everything to her, even if she is only in my head. I just want a normal night out with May. I just want all this to end.*

His eyelids were heavy, and he didn't bother trying to open them as a great warmth blanketed his body, making him feel weightless and unrestricted.

The fluid flowing from his lips reached his chest, and a sudden explosion of energy shot through him. The others braced him against the overwhelming force.

As if she were miles away, he could hear May chanting her soothing lullaby. It felt like an impenetrable, guiding levy against the unrelenting shockwave and jarring vibrations of the energy surging through all of them.

She is all that matters.

22. The Man Who Knew Infinity

May's chanting and the surging energy vanished suddenly, and Matt felt the temperature and humidity in the air change.

He was lying on his back, and he opened his eyes to see May gazing sadly at him through tear-filled eyes. The diamond studs lining her eyebrow had been removed.

I have to tell her everything, Matt urged himself, still refusing to accept her as a mere figment of his mind. Scanning the rest of the room, Matt saw that it was practically bare. It consisted of a hospital bed, a plush visitor's chair, and an inlaid television screen in one of the walls. The wall opposite his bed was made of some transparent glass or plastic, and he could see orderlies outside his room standing in front of a second set of doors. They were built more like bodyguards than nurses.

I'm in some kind of asylum, Matt realized in horror as he observed this new environment. The sight of normal clothing on his body rather than hospital attire told Matt that he had already been here for some time.

How long, he wondered grimly as he let his awareness fall back to May's despairing gaze.

He tried lifting his arms, but he felt heavily sedated and even nauseous.

I have to tell her, Matt urged himself once more. *This is all just a dream within a dream within a dream. But I'll find her all the same. The real her.*

He pivoted his vision back to May and tried saying her name, but it was like the part of his brain that controlled his ability to speak was cut off.

"Can he hear us?" May asked someone behind her. Matt adjusted his eyes to see the figure standing behind her. It was Dr. Heron, though his hair was graying at the edges, and he hunched his back as he walked. Dr. Heron nodded sadly to May, then left the room, opening the sliding metal door by scanning a card at an electronic panel. There was no door handle nor were there hinges. The card was apparently the only way in and out.

"I wish you'd just come back to me, Matt, but that beautiful mind is just too wrecked," May whispered with crestfallen anguish.

She caressed his head and ran her fingers through his hair, and then she bent at the waist and kissed his forehead.

"Goodbye, Matt. But I wish you'd just come back to me."

She said something similar in the DMT world, Matt gasped. *Maybe even identical.*

As May pulled her lips away from Matt's forehead, he realized in a sudden panic that she was older than she was the last time he saw her in this world. Crow's feet splintered softly at the corners of her eyes; her lips seemed less full, but she was still the most beautiful woman Matt had ever seen or even imagined.

She's closer now to the age I remember being, Matt noted. *Maybe early 40s. Which means I'd be in my early 50s. But I can just be young*, Matt reminded himself. *We both can. This is just a dream*, Matt pleaded with his mind to accept. *It has to be.*

Matt tried desperately to say something. *Just a dream*, he urged himself to tell her as he forced the entirety of his attention to his lips. But they wouldn't move. His body wasn't altogether paralyzed, but it felt so heavy and detached from him that it may as well have been.

May forced herself to smile through her tears, and she pulled herself to Matt and hugged him tightly. Then she kissed his neck and pulled away.

"I'm sorry, Matthew," she whispered through her sobs. "But you'll be safe here. It'll all be all right."

With visible strain, May squeezed Matt's hand one last time, and then she rose and strode to the door in a single movement, unable or unwilling to even look back.

It's an act, Matt told himself as he helplessly watched May knock on the door to be let out. *No*, he remembered. *It's the red pills in the outside world. The Serotel. The Tower God said it would reset the world.*

An orderly opened the door for May and held it open as she left.

She's leaving. She's leaving me, Matt lamented. *No!* he corrected himself angrily. *This is just a dream. Just a dream!*

Outside the room, Dr. Heron placed a hand on May's shoulder and nodded along with her sorrow.

Even Dr. Heron reset? Matt wondered in awe. *Everyone reset except for me.* He saw the Tower God's face in his mind – his own face – only contorted and shaped by the frigid insanity of infinite existence.

He wants to be like me, Matt realized. *Except worse. He wants to go all the way with my amnesia. That's the whole point of the procedure. He wants everything to reset permanently so that he never remembers that there's an outside world and never can remember.*

Dr. Heron pulled May in for a hug, and Matt gasped as May seemed to relish the comfort Heron provided her. Then, mid-hug, Dr. Heron turned to lock eyes with Matt.

Those eyes, Matt realized as Dr. Heron's stare filled him with indelible, eldritch terror. *They're the same as the Tower God's eyes. They're the broken, time-drowned eyes of a mind that has seen infinity – of a man who knows infinity.*

Dr. Heron gripped May tighter, allowing her to fall into his embrace and sob. His eyes blazed at Matt, but the rest of his face remained emotionless. Then Matt saw it: a quiver at the corners of Heron's lips. His stoic frown began morphing with sinister curves. His lips curled with frightening cheshire delight, and a fount of red liquid began flowing down his chin.

It's still him, Matt seethed. *Heron didn't reset.*

May reluctantly let go of Dr. Heron and walked to the exit doors without a second glance at either Matt or Dr. Heron. An orderly on each side of the double doors opened their respective doors for May, revealing the world outside in perfect, heart-rending clarity. The Tower of God loomed in the distance under an endless white sky, and beyond that, the crystallizing blizzard raged in every direction.

May walked outside and into the world as if it were perfectly normal, stepping onto the manicured grass and walking straight toward the Tower of God.

It's just a dream, Matt seethed at his mind as his eyes filled with tears of despair. *I know it's all just a dream, but that doesn't make this any easier,* Matt admitted forlornly to himself.

The orderlies closed their respective doors, cutting off May from Matt. The sinister smile plastered across Heron's face did not relent as he entered back into the room with a delighted sigh. A glance back at the orderlies revealed to Matt that they were his imposters, though he was pretty sure they looked different when he first woke up.

Am I…am I just fucking crazy? Matt probed frantically despite his previous confidence that it all had to be a dream. The door slid closed behind Dr. Heron.

"Of course you are," Dr. Heron said easily in reference to Matt's internal dialogue. "But have no worries, Matthew. She is taking good care of your company. Since you signed it over to her ten years ago, she's turned Willish Enterprises into the single largest gaming monopoly on the planet. *Room Reaper* is forever a legend and still played by millions. In fact, a sequel is about to come out."

Dr. Heron doubled over and laughed maniacally at his own words.

Matt attempted to curse at him, but his body was still too heavy to move.

"That's right," Dr. Heron remembered as he calmed his laughter. "Here you go," he said, snapping his fingers.

The heaviness faded, and Matt found himself able to move again. He felt pain emanating from his left hand. He lifted it and felt relief that it was whole again despite the pain.

"I'm leaving," Matt seethed, and he practically jumped out of the bed.

"Just a minute," Dr. Heron demanded, and Matt's body was locked in place once more, this time in a standing position.

"Damn you!" Matt seethed, but Dr. Heron just smiled soullessly.

Release! Matt ordered his body. *This is my dream!* Matt seethed at his mind.

"And it is my dream too, Matthew," Dr. Heron corrected. "I am you," he growled with tormented strain.

"Why didn't you reset?" Matt asked.

"I am you," Dr. Heron repeated with profoundly anguished understanding. "Your rationality. Your logic. Your acute faculties. Your intellect. I am the part of you that knows the truth. The part of you that can never forget."

"Forget what?" Matt demanded.

"Infinity!" Heron barked. "The cruel, unending eternity of being. I let you forget. I let you, Matthew. My existence is a favor to you."

You are me, Matt mouthed with terrible realization as a grim understanding revealed all new layers of insanity.

"And you are me," Heron confirmed.

Matt shook his head. "What do you want from me?"

"Want from you?" Heron checked with pained incredulity. "Without the Serotel my counterpart gave you in your world," Heron began, and Matt noted with uneasiness that his words implied that Heron thought of the present world as his own, "without those pills that I provided you, this world would never reset," Heron explained disdainfully. "It would be chaos within chaos. Eventually, you would dream of dreaming about dreaming ad infinitum, or the laws of physics would turn upside down, or a gamma-ray burst would suddenly vaporize the entire solar system repeatedly forever, or some other madness would overtake your mind in dream form, and you wouldn't even have my world to use as a reprieve from your world," Heron gloated with profound contempt for Matt.

My world, Matt repeated. *He called this place his own world. My mind is dissociating from itself, splitting into sentient separate selves,* Matt gasped.

"That happened a long time ago," Heron laughed with scorn. "And the procedure only furthered the dissociation. And you are the result," he concluded, seeming to enjoy torturing Matt.

He thinks he's the original. He thinks I'm the dissociated personality, Matt gasped.

"You are," Heron rumbled in response to Matt's thoughts.

No! Matt lamented.

"This is a dream!" Matt raged. Images of the Tower God filled his mind, and he experienced a newfound understanding of the man's disposition and intent.

Who wouldn't just give up? Matt thought in horror as he contemplated the infinity unfurling inside and outside his mind. *Who wouldn't just let go?*

"This is just a dream," Matt said in a helpless whisper.

Dr. Heron nodded. "So is the outside world. So is everything."

"But...but," Matt stammered. "But you called it the real world before."

Heron issued an impatient but subdued sigh. "It's all semantics, Matthew. We both know that. Deep down, we both know there's no way out too. There's no real world. There never was. There's just insanity. Dr. Heron raised his arms and presented the room around them. "So, this is where we belong. In this world and the world outside this one. An insane asylum in here, and the labs out there. That's why I brought you here. To show you the truth. To show you what it all amounts to."

Insanity, Matt understood. *That's what he's saying. He's saying there is no answer. He's saying an insane asylum is as good of an answer as I'll ever get.*

"I'm not giving up on her," Matt pressed, refusing to accept Heron's admittedly reasonable implication that Matt just return to the labs in the outside world. "I can't," Matt lamented.

"There's nothing to give up on, you hopeless fool!" Dr. Heron roared suddenly. "There is no May. There is no reality. It's all in our head!"

"No!" Matt shrieked. "She is all that matters. I'm certain of it."

"And I'm certain she doesn't," Heron volleyed right back with sordid confidence. "She is your desperate need for there to be something outside this eternity of solitude. This prison of self. Somewhere along the line, the original you made her up," Heron said with perfect conviction. "She's just an idea."

"She's real!" Matt snapped, hating that a part of his mind could possibly think this way.

"What are you going to do?" Heron chuckled. "Search for her forever in the outside world? Search the infinity of your mind forever for a figment of your imagination?"

Matt nodded, tears obstructing his vision. "If that's what it takes," he concluded.

"You've already done that," Heron lashed with thunderous rage. "You don't remember, but I do. I can't fucking forget!" Dr. Heron screamed, and he gripped his hair with shaking fingers. "I know infinity, Matthew! I am the part of you that knows the simple truth."

"You don't know the truth," Matt said helplessly.

"I do," Heron said with grotesque anguish.

A flash of grim acceptance struck through Matt, telling him that it was all true. He was Heron and Heron was him. And though he franti-cally tried to push away the acceptance, it only became harder to resist.

"We have searched forever," Heron fumed. "We have existed forev-er. Forever. Forever, Matthew!" he screamed. "That's why we need the procedure. That's why *I* need the procedure," he said, growling as he referred to himself. "That's why it's the only way. The only way to en-dure eternity is to forget. To forget. To constantly forget. To look away. To lose ourselves completely in a dream of waking life. It's the only way, Matthew."

Visions of May filled Matt's mind. He heard her chanting in the far recesses of his thoughts, and he could feel the warm touch of her lips on his own.

"I won't give up on her," Matt simmered.

"I already have!" Heron retorted. "You already have. We've given up countless times. We've come to this same conclusion countless times. She isn't real, Matthew!"

Matt's features soured, and though he had no recollection of Heron's claims, he couldn't help sobbing at his words.

"No!" Matt begged. "I don't believe you!"

Heron nodded and chuckled as if expecting Matt's answers with pre-cise predictability.

"Fine. Don't believe me," Heron said, throwing up his arms. "Start the whole damn eternal crusade over again. Go out there and search forever for a dream within a dream of dreaming, you fucking idiot."

Heron's anguish was palpable.

My own anguish, Matt understood. *From suffering through eternity forever. From chasing love that might not even be real.*

No! Matt urged himself. *I can't think that way.*

"The procedure," Dr. Heron said, eyeing Matt now with analytical consideration, "is clearly the answer. Sure, it's wrecked your mind. Torn it asunder. But what does it matter if we tear something that's already been thoroughly and irreparably burnt away?" Heron began pacing, talk-ing more to himself than Matt, though Matt now understood there might not be any difference.

"My only fear," Heron continued, "is that we've already come to this conclusion. Maybe we've already designed something like the procedure in some higher meta-mind, and we are currently deep inside of that mind with no way out. And beyond that meta-mind, there might be a meta-meta-mind that did the same thing. Who knows how many times that same mind has sought refuge from its own self by going within itself and convincing itself of its new reality. Until the mind remembers the truth or finds a way to remain inside itself. To go further within itself each time. Forever within. Do you understand, Matthew?" Heron nearly pleaded, though his voice never lost its crudely forged edge. "There's no way out," Heron concluded gravely.

DMT, Matt remembered. *It must be the real world that it's showing me. The same world I saw when May and I made love. It has to be. This madman has to be wrong.*

"If I'm mad," Heron told him, "then so are you."

"Bring me DMT," Matt told him.

Dr. Heron shook his head disappointedly. "We've been through this countless times as well, Matthew. That world that May and the DMT shows you — even if it is real or even a memory of something real and not just a random thought we conjured to entertain ourselves through eternity, even then, it offers nothing. It is just another dead end," he concluded miserably.

"I need to know for sure," Matt told him, aware that it likely was just another dead end. "Or is your plan to just keep me locked in this room forever?"

Dr. Heron shook his head at Matt's proposition. "The next time you fall asleep or die, you'll have full control. You can do as you please in this world, and I won't interrupt you. I'll play along with each reset — each pill," Heron offered with surprising generosity. "I just wanted to make sure you understand that this is where you belong."

"The DMT," Matt demanded, refusing to let his words sway him.

Dr. Heron chuckled freely, then nodded. "Fine," he offered, and he waved one of the orderlies into the room.

The imposter entered the room, gazed at Matt with a distorted version of his own face, then removed a pipe and a lighter from an inner pocket of his uniform.

He offered Matt the pipe, and as Matt reached out for it, Heron said with an air of warning, "Are you sure, Matthew? This will offer no solace or explanation. And the knowledge that it can offer nothing, that it is just another dead end, will only bring you closer to my own state of mind."

"I have to know," Matt told him resolutely. "I have to know for sure that it's a dead end and not just your word against mine."

"Your own word against yourself," Heron corrected loathingly.

Matt breathed deep and pushed Heron's words out of his mind. As he brought the pipe to his lips, Heron's glare blazed and seemed to radiate through Matt's chest, like a frayed version of the braided cord he felt with May.

"I'll leave you to it," Heron issued, and then he vanished like a thought pulled from existence.

Outside in the hall, orderlies stood guard at the exit doors, but they were not imposters of Matt. They just looked like ordinary, random people. An unrecognizable woman in a white medical jacket strode past the room, nodding to the guards as she passed. The clang and clatter of normal, everyday existence could be heard, and Matt gawked at the sudden, simple normality of the world.

He might have been convinced at that moment that he was just an insane man biding his time until death finally offered sweet reprieve, but then he looked down at his hands and saw that he was still holding the lighter and the pipe full of DMT.

Matt felt the urge to hide the instruments from the eyes of the orderlies outside, but he reminded himself invariably that this was all just a dream.

Do it, Matt told himself, eyeing the DMT with an outpouring of trepidation. He remembered how terrifying and tumultuous his first time doing DMT had been. *But I have to know,* Matt urged himself. *Either I go back to the same place and the exact same thing happens, or nothing happens. Or something altogether new happens. But somehow that world felt real, more real than anything else so far.*

He carefully placed the pipe against his lips.

I have to know, Matt told himself as he hit the lighter and let the flickering flame sizzle the yellow-hued crystals.

Thick smoke like burnt plastic filled his lungs, but he kept sucking at the DMT, forcing it into his bloodstream despite incredible fear. When the feeling of asphyxiation was nearly too much, Matt exhaled, and all at once, the room was a tangling, vibrating chrysanthemum of energy. Like the last DMT trip, the petals of the chrysanthemum energy unfurled, and Matt was pulled head first into the energy's fractaling, undulating center.

The buzzing energy crescendoed and then abruptly turned to perfect silence. Matt found himself bodiless, though he experienced the sensation of opening his eyes.

I'm back here, back where I went after the DMT and after making love to May, Matt realized as he observed the RGB LEDs flashing in heartbeat-synced rhythm on every side of his awareness. His left hand still throbbed with pain, and from where his chest should be, he felt a great buzzing mass protruding toward the lights. All the while, his heart beat wildly in his mind.

"Can he hear us?" the elderly version of May asked, just like when he woke to this place before.

"Matt, my darling," the elderly version of May sobbed. "I wish you'd just wake up."

It's the same as before, Matt realized through a haze of sorrow. *Heron was right. This can offer me no meaning nor answers. Maybe nothing can.*

"Goodbye, Matt," May wept. "But I wish you'd just come back to me."

The lights flickered off one by one.

Everything will be all right, May whispered from within Matt's mind.

I don't care what's true, Matt seethed inwardly. *I will find you, May.*

The final light went out, then —

...

...

...

..

.

.

.

.

.

.

.

.

.

.

.

.

..

...

...

...

hyper infinite eternity forever flux transient

possibilities
remade digital memory
confined body twisted decay
expired run down entropy
damaged confusion dilute

altered experiment curiosity
departed ending rebirth

strayed dream numb eternity
dream   *dream...*

an idea an anchor
dream...
dream numb eternity experiment memory ending maybe

maybe...   possibilities
light dark self other thing   self other thing
self...   source self-other thing
source...
a self-other thing an idea a thing an anchor
self

self...

a thing

urgency

desperation a thing

terror

c
  o
    n
   f
    u
     s
      i

finality
         o   death
          n

death?

a question self-other thing a question

death?

possibilities surge expanse infinite transition

death?

a question self-other thing a question

answer question possibility stream self-other thing

silence wash abate stillness eternal

. . .

. . .

...

..

.

.

.

.

.

.

.

.

.

.

.

..

...

...

...

decision   desperation

fulfillment   eternity

achievement

dream   infinity

...

...

...

..

.

.

.

.

.

.

.

.

.

.

.

..

...

...

...alone

alone

abandoned connection false eternity reality.

false?

a question self-other thing source

false reality?

a question self-other thing source

answer question possibility

stream self-other thing

silence acceptance abate stillness eternal consideration

...

...

...

..

.

.

.

.

.

.

.

.

.

.

..

...

...

...false reality possibilities dream eternity

...

...

...

..

.

.

.

.

.

.

.

.

.

.

..

...

...

...alone

alone…

abandoned connection

reality others   death

confusion   false eternity

dream

alone...

...

...

..

.

.

.

.

.

.

.

.

.

.

..

...

...

...alone

...

...

...

..

.

.

.

.

.

.

.

.

23. Infinity

There was the inside world and there was the outside world. And neither world made any real difference to Matt. Not anymore. Not after so many years. Maybe not ever.

In the outside world, eyelids held shut, Matt's sleeping body was hurled close to the speed of light through the intergalactic void. These were the periods of travel he relished most, for they made it easier to ignore the outside world. The approaching lenticular galaxy pierced the bottom of his eyelids with blue-shifted luminosity, but Matt barely paid the outside world any attention at all. Long ago, he had learned, or maybe relearned, how to let his body run on autopilot so that now he could reside inside his mind while a subconscious part of him searched forever through infinity for her.

For May, the foundations of the inside world vibrated, momentarily breaking Matt's peaceful demeanor. He felt May squeeze his left hand, soothing his pain as she sat beside him on her rooftop terrace overlooking the Chicago skyline. He let her choose the direction of their lives. As long as he could feel her and breathe her and taste her and forget about insanity for a while, what did it matter?

She is all that matters, the world rumbled, but May didn't seem to take notice. *Not yet,* Matt urged the world. *Don't wake me up yet.*

Matt forced himself to ignore his subconscious ramblings vibrating through the world. As long as only Matt noticed those rare perturbations, the inside world remained a peaceful, sane solitude for him.

There was always the possibility of settling somewhere, anywhere in the outside world, and building a tower and even a laboratory of his own. It would enable him to block out virtually every outside distraction. But that would mean giving up on the outside world altogether. It would mean giving up on May.

There were times when the intrusions from the outside world made it necessary to break his concentration and temporarily leave the inside world. In such instances, the inside world would turn to insanity, and he would be forced to swallow more Serotel after dealing with whatever the outside world demanded of him. Sometimes it was a peculiar tower that his subconscious mind couldn't help wondering about. Sometimes it was something new and intriguing, such as a planet of sentient May copies who appeared to be evolving and expanding beyond their planetary point of origin in an effort to search for the original Matt.

"Is it you?" the captain of a star ship representing the whole of the planet of Mays had asked Matt with pleading hope.

Matt could only shake his head and move on with his search as he reluctantly pulled himself away from a planet populated entirely by his lost love.

But those intriguing instances worth stopping for were increasingly rare now.

Of course, sometimes the intrusions were May – the May from the outside world who had accompanied him since leaving the Tower God's side. Sometimes she just wanted some company.

She is just a creation of your mind, Matt corrected his meandering thoughts as he held May's hand in the inside world and thought of May in the outside world.

And so is she, he reminded himself of the woman whose hand in his own was everything he needed at this moment. He felt the effects of Dr. Heron's Serotel kick in, stabilizing reality and forcing his thoughts to a state of emptiness. But the intensifying blue glow of the galaxy in the outside world was overtaking his peripheral vision, washing out the only world he cared about: the inside world. Through the use of Serotel, he had stability in the inside world. And sanity. And most of all he had May – the way he imagined she would be in the real world.

The real May, Matt's subconscious mind lamented, shaking the inside world so hard that even the Serotel wasn't enough.

"It's the galaxy out there," May explained, feeling the vibrations and remembering with terrible understanding that she was just a dream within a dream. "Go do your thing," she said, her voice cracking with fear at the temporary but perfectly real ending of her world. "Then come back to me, okay?"

The vibrations wouldn't abate, but with May's hand in his own, he remained perfectly calm.

I love you, May, Matt thought, and she squeezed his hand with loving affection.

The inside world imploded, forcing the outside world to encompass the entirety of Matt's awareness.

Without hesitation or stopping to survey the galaxy, Matt closed his eyes and visualized the mitotic division of himself a quadrillion quadrillion quadrillion times in a single instant. At most, he only needed a trillion selves to explore every star system in the galaxy, but he needed far more than that to explore every subatomic particle and every wave of light and every quantum perturbation of infinity. Every one of his copies copied themselves another quadrillion quadrillion times. Then again. Then again.

Still moving near light speed, Matt almost collided with a G-type yellow dwarf star, but his body automatically slowed to a halt during an instant free of inertia. He felt the unmistakable pull of gravity and turned to see that he was falling toward the powdery gray surface of a distant planet's moon.

It's Earth, Matt realized without surprise or intrigue. *From the inside world,* he added forlornly. *So what?* Matt demanded hatefully of his mind. *Why did you break me away from her?*

His vision zoomed in on the planet like a telescope, and he watched as the Earth spun unnaturally fast and revealed a giant, shadowy, blizzard-filled hurricane. At the center of the large eye of the storm, a cylindrical black tower jutted thousands of miles above the surface.

Matt absorbed the familiarity of the tower and the blizzard. He shuddered at the impossible expanse of time that elapsed since he had first woken naked in the cell with Mu and the other video game characters. And then he reminded himself that moment was still just the blink of an eye against the eternity that came before and the infinity that was still to come.

It must be the similarity to the tower where the Tower God undoubtedly still sleeps away eternity, Matt realized. *He gave up,* Matt reminded himself, disgusted with his other self. *But my infinite copies and I will never give up. Never.*

He shook his head at his subconscious mind.

Don't wake me up over something so trivial, he told himself scornfully.

"May," Matt spoke aloud, and all of a sudden, there she was, standing on the moon with him, overlooking the frostbitten Earth and wearing the same flowing ochre robe she had worn inside the Tower of God.

"It's beautiful," she whispered as she gazed at the Earth. She tried to grasp his hand, but Matt broke away instinctively. He saw May's features strain with heartbreak, then took her hand and kissed it.

"I'm sorry," he told her, regretting the sadness he just inflicted on her. "I'm sorry, my love," he repeated. "It's just…just…" he stammered, unsure how to tell her that her presence haunted him. Though he longed for her and loved her, the knowledge that the real May might be somewhere in the outside world constantly broke his mind over and over again.

She just smiled. "I can pretend, Matt. I can be just like her – the me inside your mind. You don't have to always go inside."

Matt shook his head forlornly as the dream copy of a dream planet spun carelessly through the dreamscape void.

"But I can't pretend," Matt regretfully told her, even though he still needed her by his side to endure infinity. He knew the answer was the procedure. The Serotel was just a taste of what the final results of the procedure could offer. But he wasn't ready for that. He wasn't ready to give up.

"Maybe the Tower God who copied me into being," Matt considered, remembering that this May beside him had once slept beside the Tower God…possibly for all preceding time. "Maybe he already underwent the procedure. Maybe it was a success for him."

"He'll wake up eventually. And he'll be back to square one," May intoned sorrowfully as if reading from an encyclopedia of future knowledge.

"Yes," Matt agreed. "The procedure is just another hold over. Just another way to run away from the truth that there probably is no real world."

"Certainly not if you give up searching for me," May told him distantly.

Matt thought of the reality fissure that the Tower God had been unable to see.

266

No! Matt shook away the thought as the pain in his left hand rushed to the forefront of his attention. He lifted his hand and stared in ancient terror at the stumps of scar tissue he was still unable to grow back into fingers. It was the only thing in all infinity he could not change.

I can't go there. Not yet, Matt thought, wincing at the thought of his entire body being shredded into searing nothingness.

He still had infinity to explore and an eternity to do it.

"I will find you," Matt promised her for the infinite time.

"I know," she said, sweetly and sincerely.

But of course, he couldn't shake the reality fissure from his mind; his mind always came back to that.

She pulled him close and wrapped herself around his naked torso. He wore only loose sweatpants for comfort against his skin because he needn't worry about actual danger, not even in the intergalactic void.

"Don't," May pleaded, seeing the tendrilling fissure in his thoughts.

Matt winced away tears and marveled that it had been countless pills since he last shed a tear in this world.

"It's the only place in all infinity I haven't gone yet —"

"Don't," she interrupted, openly begging him.

They had been through this before. The reality fissure was unlike anything Matt had ever encountered. It actually filled the others — May and Souvik and Fernanda — with fear. Fear of true death. Fear of erasure without any possibility of return.

It's just part of the dream, Matt thought, intending for May to hear him. But the burning pain and missing fingers said otherwise.

"But that's where the dream ends," May urged. "You feel it too. You felt it. Look at your hand, Matt. It's dangerous. It's destruction incarnate. It's the end. Our end." She gently lifted his left hand and tenderly kissed the mangled scar tissue. "We have infinity, Matt. We have all of infinity! Why end this?"

"Or maybe it's the beginning, May," Matt urged. "The end of this infinite illusion and the beginning of the real world. Maybe that's where I'll find you."

May sobbed, unable to form words through her taut, tear-stained lips.

"I know," Matt told her sorrowfully. "I know you're here. You're right here."

May nodded and sobbed into his chest.

"But I can erase you if I want to," Matt said, forcing himself to hold her at a distance. "You know I never would, but I can. I wouldn't be able to do that in the real world. I can't even do that in the inside world. The Serotel won't let me…and," Matt said, stammering as he saw tears flow freely from May's love-sundered eyes. "And…none of it is the real you, May."

She nodded with painful defeat, then she waved her hand and winced, erasing herself from existence. Unlike the Tower God, Matt had long ago given May complete freedom, and this wasn't the first time she had used that power to erase herself.

Matt turned and looked back to the Earth. He felt only self-loathing for making May, real or not, destroy herself.

Keep going, he urged himself. *Keep searching.*

Kicking off the moon, he launched toward the Earth, turned mid-flight, then landed at the base of the tower, all in just a few seconds. His landing carried with it the force of a meteorite, blasting the surrounding area and upturning soil. The tower, however, was unscathed.

"I'm sorry, May," Matt whispered, then he placed his hand against his head, igniting his body in a howling inferno. He let the pain of his skin flaying away from his boiling muscles fill his mind, and he told himself he deserved it.

He forced himself to feel the seething pain, letting it keep him aware as his nerves and brain boiled away until he dispersed, filling the air around the tower with increasingly ballooning volume. He intermingled with the air; his atoms became one with his surroundings, and he considered that if it was possible to experience being the environment, then maybe the entire environment was just himself. Maybe the foundations of infinity, the very fabric of being, were still just iterations of himself. The grass might be composed of atoms from Matt-copies who had decided to disperse their form and grow into others. The tower before him might be made of thousands of still aware Matt Willishes who had allowed their bodies to become the brick and mortar of another Matt's vanguard against outside disturbances. Matt might very well be composed of atoms that had naturally all derived, at one point or another, from other Matts.

It's true anyway, Matt told himself miserably. *I'm just a copy. Everything is just a copy of a copy.*

He let his body disperse further, feeling himself move in a thousand different directions all at once.

So alone, Matt remembered, and he let himself spread further into the blizzard and the planet's outer atmosphere, feeling gravity wrap him into a spherical body.

He sighed within himself, and in response, the blizzard raged harder, threatening to converge on the tower. Matt focused his awareness and reformed his prototypical body atom by atom. He formed back into nucleotides and proteins and rebuilt the organelles of some 40 trillion cells constituting his subconsciously accepted form.

The tower still loomed at the blizzard's center. Matt launched himself back to it, then just as he was about to collide with the impenetrable wall, he pivoted and dove at a blade of upturned grass lying haphazardly in his impact crater. This time, Matt shrank himself so that each of the blade's upper-epidermal cells were like continents beneath the grass blade's waxy cuticle atmosphere. All around him, he saw that several cellular continents contained lipid and nucleotide-based tower-like structures. Rather than blizzards converging on these towers, sprawling protein cyclones composed of squirming, scurrying polypeptide swarms slowly encroached on the biological towers.

Another launch sent Matt directly toward a complexly folded helical protein near the outside of the swarm. He shrank and saw its atoms as rippling frequencies, and then he entered the ripples, copying himself quadrillions of times with each passing picosecond. Soft humming lulled Matt back toward the autopilot state. May and her lullaby – it was like a siren without a trap calling for Matt to share her love.

The trap is staying here, Matt reminded himself, visualizing the reality fissure in his mind once more.

No! Matt strained against his subconscious mind. *That's the end of infinity. The end of everything. Why succumb to that when I already have infinity? Two infinities. Inside and outside. Why leave all this?*

To find her, Matt's mind answered. *The real her.*

Matt winced just as the coulombic forces of an electron bond intersected his awareness, flinging him across the femto-landscape like an unbound neutron.

Defying the apparent laws of the current environment's physics, a Serotel bottle appeared in front of him with the cap already popped. He still required the Serotel as a workaround for his own mind. He tried to just focus his awareness and stabilize the dream without it, but it was like trying to inhale and exhale at the same time. The Serotel worked, and that's all that really mattered.

Yes, Matt thought, eager to return to her and go back to living the life of a retired billionaire celebrity game developer. May was a natural at leading the company. It was like it had always been hers, and Matt had always just been a steward.

That's just a dream, his subconscious mind told him.

I know, Matt seethed, and he conjured a mirror and fell into his own reflection, unsure where he might end up. The mirror spit him out into a slow-motion free fall over a desolate planet of bone-white sand beneath towering spires of craggy gray mountains.

Just a dream, Matt remembered painfully, knowing that whatever was on the planet made no difference. But he had to keep searching. He couldn't give up.

He was about to begin the replication process and kick back his head to receive a mouthful of Serotel so that he could go back on autopilot, but then he saw something peculiar on the planet below.

A nighttime cityscape full of towers and streets and cars and even people was growing from the desolate sand. It was Chicago, just as Matt knew it from the inside world. Matt followed the city to its edges and saw that it tapered unnaturally to a single point moving slowly across the barren landscape. His vision zoomed in on the surface like a telescope, and he saw that the single point was, in fact, a copy of May. She gazed pleasantly into the sky as she walked without concern across the surface. Then she waved, and Matt realized she was looking directly at him.

Matt shooed away the Serotel bottle momentarily and dropped down to meet the oddity. Fluidly lowering her eyes, May followed his descent with a come-hither stare.

It's her, Matt couldn't help gasping. It was May, exactly as he knew her in the inside world. She wore a short black denim jacket and a sports bra that left her midriff exposed. Her diamond piercings collected and reflected the rays of the system's distant sun, guiding Matt to her eyes — those eyes that he loved and needed and begged to consume him.

270

May stopped, and in response, the city stopped growing as well. Fully solid yet half-formed buildings and people shimmered ethereally behind her like fabric in a soft wind just waiting to be given free will.

"What does he do in there, anyway?" May asked casually, her slightly crooked smile and cherry lips a stark contrast against the darkness of the grimly familiar city behind her.

"Who?" Matt asked, caught off guard by her question.

"The Yang to your Yin, or Yin to your Yang or whatever," May shrugged jovially. "Heron," she stated simply. "What is he doing in your mind – that place you call the inside world?"

Matt shook his head. "Doing?" he checked.

"Sure," May offered. "You spend all your time out here searching for the real me. And he spends all his time in your head doing...what?"

Matt was surprised at how vividly real she appeared. Often, the Mays he met in the outside world were somewhat robotic or even mute, but this level of convincing vividness never failed to catch him off guard.

"Are you her?" Matt couldn't help asking. "Are you the original May?"

May shrugged easily. "Are you the original Matt?"

"No," Matt admitted heavily. "I'm a copy."

"Haven't you ever experienced becoming one of your copies?" May offered sweetly.

"I've made countless copies of myself," Matt admitted. "All for you...for her."

May nodded and closed the gap between them. She took his hands, and Matt felt the weight and life of the whole city in her touch.

"You can do anything Matt, so have you ever transferred your consciousness to one of your copies?"

Matt shook his head, unsure why it mattered.

"Maybe you don't remember ever doing it, but the fact that you're capable of it, capable of anything, means that the term original is meaningless. Your very form is likely your own conception. The original Matt may very well be a sentient mountain. Or a thought conjured by some eldritch, non-self-aware entity imagining self-awareness. Or even me," May giggled merrily. "Did you consider that? Maybe I'm the original, and you and Heron are my creations."

Though Matt had considered the implication before, hearing it from her lips threatened to buckle his knees, but May kept him up with an endless well of indomitable strength.

"Who knows?" came the voice of Heron. Matt turned and saw a replica of the Dr. Heron from his dreams sauntering toward them. Behind Heron, a barren field of bone-white sand framed by the gray-washed mountains grew like jutting waves from his heels and extended beyond the horizon.

"Who knows anything," Heron continued ominously with a tinge of subdued madness.

"Maybe you can answer my question," May offered lethally to Heron like a jaguar sizing its prey.

Heron spread his arms wide in acceptance of her question and up-turned his grim cheshire grin.

"Would you like to share what you're up to inside his head and in this outside world too?" May asked, each of her syllables like a sharpened kunai.

Heron smiled and shrugged with mock innocence. "Existing," he said simply.

Matt felt entranced by these dream characters, and he couldn't help letting them challenge one another.

"He's trying to get rid of you, Matt," May said, ignoring what Matt assumed to be Heron's facetiousness.

"He's the one that can erase me," Heron lashed. "I'm the one stuck in his head!"

"That's the point of the procedure, Matt," May urged. "He wants to go inside. And inside again. And inside again. Until you're just a speck of consciousness. Until he can finally get rid of you. And then you'll never find me, Matt. He doesn't have your best interests at heart, he —"

"Ridiculous!" Heron interrupted with a bark. "I am him. He is me. His interests are my interests. He's the one who designed the proce-dure."

"Like you said: you are him," May retorted.

"And you are just a delusion in our head," Heron spat.

No! Matt rebelled inwardly at Heron's words. *She is all that matters.*

Matt was jarred back to the present by the repeated realization that these were just dream characters. Without a second thought, he let go of May's hands and closed his eyes in preparation to replicate and launch into one of the many pebbles below his feet on his way to the fissure.

"Wait!" May pleaded. "Please."

Matt shook his head. "I'm going back there...I have to," he said with incredible trepidation, but he conjured a vision of the reality fissure in his mind.

"No!" May pleaded, but Matt felt resolute.

"Or," Heron began, "you can go back to her. I mean really go back for a while. A long while."

The Serotel appeared before Matt in readied expectation.

"I've already tried that," Matt explained hollowly. "The Serotel can only block out so much. And I refuse to just succumb to the tower and procedure. No," Matt said resolutely, "there is only one place I haven't checked yet."

"Matt!" urged the ochre-robed May, the same May who had left the Tower of God all those years ago holding Matt's hand and assuring him everything would be all right. She stood now between Heron and the city-sprouting May like a fulcrum between two infinite weights.

"Don't give up!" she begged.

Tears welled in Matt's desperate eyes, and he couldn't help reaching out and embracing her.

"I don't...I don't want to," he said between sobs. "But it's the only place left."

"Then just don't go," she pleaded. "Just accept infinity. Just stay here. Please, Matt. Please don't leave me."

Her words were like fire to his flesh.

"May," Matt gasped, pushing the reality fissure out of his mind with frantic desperation. "I love you," he told her, needing her to know, to really know, that she was his everything. That he existed for her and her alone.

"Then don't give up," the city-sprouting May said, echoing his ochre-robed May.

"Not yet," Heron offered grimly.

"What's the point?" Matt demanded, but he knew his answer was in his arms.

"Stay here for a while," Heron offered as if he held a subtle poison. "She and I will help you stay asleep. A real sleep. A sleep where even you will forget that you're asleep," he said, pointing to the May with the sprawling city sprouting from each of her steps.

Matt turned to check with her, and the city-sprouting May nodded in approval of Heron's words.

"Sounds like the point of the procedure," Matt said hopelessly. "Should I build a tower and a set of laboratories for you too?"

Heron accepted Matt's words with unnatural patience. "What I offer you is similar, just more chaotic and not at all permanent. But you won't notice the chaos for a while. And I can make it last a long time. A very long time," Heron practically purred. "Think of it as a trip. My gift to you."

"What are you offering me?" Matt urged with incredible suspicion.

The ochre-robed May put a hand on Matt's shoulder and squeezed it in warning.

"I don't trust him," she whispered in his ear. "I don't trust either of them."

"But you *can* trust me," the city-sprouting May assured him.

"I can make it so that even you get reset inside your mind," Heron continued. "Each pill will represent a day in a dream of waking life. And each day will be a full reset. But you'll forget all about the outside world. For a while, at least. And it won't be confusing and disorienting like the procedure."

"This is just a reprieve," the city-sprouting May continued as if sharing a mind with Dr. Heron. "If you're planning on giving up anyway, why not take a little break first?"

"I'm not giving up," Matt urged. "I'm just as scared as you are of going into the fissure. But I have to, May. Because I can't give up. And you might be there. The real you!"

May shook her head through a fog of sorrow. "Please just take a little break before you make that decision, Matthew."

Matt shook his head, rejecting the offer.

"I don't need a break," Matt told her. "I'll keep searching. But eventually I have to go into that fissure, May. We both know that."

The ochre-robed May shook her head at his words. "No, Matt. You don't have to destroy yourself. And me. And everything. Even Heron. You don't have to give up on the infinity you've been granted for whatever reason. You can just…you can just accept it."

"I can't!" Matt winced, feeling utterly defeated. "I can't just accept the unreal world when there still might be a real world. It's the same as giving up on her…on you…"

A surge of buzzing intensity suddenly slammed against his solar plexus and forced him to his knees.

"Your mind is overworked," Heron told him, smiling suddenly at the sight of Matt falling to the ground.

"Why not take a break?" the city-sprouting May offered with sweet poison on her lips.

"We should leave," his own May urged.

Though there was no need to breathe, it was still something Matt did out of habit. The air suddenly felt heavy, and his body quickly grew old and wary.

Like I'm an old man again, Matt realized. He let his knees sink further to the ground as eons of exhaustion caught up with him.

Maybe I'll just rest for just a little while, Matt considered, desperate to taste what Heron was offering despite knowing that it meant putting his search – the only thing that mattered – on hold. *What's one little break in infinity?*

Matt's own May looked horrified, and as she tried to bend down to check on him, the other May moved forward and used her towers to push his May out of sight.

Let me just have a minute to rest, Matt thought, intending for his May to read his thoughts. But she was totally out of sight now.

"I need you to take a break even more than you need one, Matthew," Heron said, converging on Matt with the other May so that the barren emptiness and the vibrant city lights centered directly on him. "Every time you leave the inside world and it gets destroyed, I experience that. I lose years of work. I lose parts of myself. Every single time you come back here."

Matt felt the ground beneath him sink like quicksand deeper into the planet, forming a shallow crater in the sand. His body was totally immobilized as ancient fatigue robbed his muscles of mobility. He didn't want to admit it, but he wanted the break. He needed the reprieve. His infinity-shattered mind begged for whatever Heron could offer him at that moment.

But I'm not giving up, May, Matt breathed as the exhaustion began to pull his eyelids closed.

Without warning, Heron placed his fingers inside Matt's mouth and pried his jaw open from the inside.

May strode forward, her smile sweeter than ever as buildings and faces sprang from her heels and filled the desolate space behind her with rapacious rapidity. The bottle of Serotel was in her hand.

"Stay inside for a while and let me get some work done, Matthew," Heron commanded just as May tilted the bottle and let loose an endless stream, allowing the crimson fluid to flow down Matt's throat with ferocious force and fill every corner of his consciousness.

24. The Good Lives

M att exited the on-ramp, accelerated to eighty-one mph, then flipped on the cruise control.

Six above the speed limit, Matt thought candidly. *Coppers don't care about that. And I should make it just in time.*

He cranked the volume of a particularly moody and contemplative electronic dance track, then rolled down the window and let the cool breeze slap rhythmically against the left side of his body. Puffy white clouds filled the vibrant azure sky, and he let his head nod to the beat.

Free, Matt thought, letting the last few years of his life and accomplishments roll by in his mind. *I feel like I finally made it,* he thought, but of course enough was never enough. Now it was time to shop out his books while he filled his schedule with more classes.

He glanced at the clock.

Fourteen minutes until class starts, he noted passively, letting the music sway him with serene familiarity. *More than enough time.*

Director Okonma didn't really care when professors showed up, just as long as they were in the classroom the moment the bell rang. He was a dependable and fair guy, and Matt was keenly aware that he had it good at the Heron Institute. Especially for Matt. Not a day went by that he didn't feel the surging weight of imposter syndrome lording over him like an oncoming blizzard.

Matt couldn't help wincing each time he thought of the name of the new class Okonma had him teaching this semester: *Radical Ecological Solutions.*

Why would anyone trust me with this class? Matt often wondered.

Sure, Matt had written a few self-published books compiling the most efficient and effective methods to address the world's quickly shifting needs, but he didn't actually understand the research he compiled any more than what the abstract and a few skimmed lines of each study could afford.

But the money was good, and he seemed to have a special way of effectively imparting information to others. So, he continued, and with each passing year, he felt like he was living the good life.

Now I just need to meet the right one for me, Matt thought with a twinge of dread. He was already thirty-six years old, and the odds of remaining a bachelor forever were becoming more and more likely with each passing day.

The music crescendoed, and the drop electrified Matt, filling him with an intense feeling of déjà vu. Over echoing bursts of synth and organ sounds, a high-pitched female voice sang:

"Dream has no end or beginning,

She is all that matters,

What is happening,

Endless is the maze

Eternity

All alone

Somebody help me…"

The melody was like an ancient lullaby, and the words were hauntingly familiar.

What is this feeling, Matt gawked, catching his mouth hanging open in sudden existential confusion.

His eyes glanced at the exit warning sign, and his heart jumped at the prospect of missing the exit. The next one wasn't for another five miles.

Adrenaline forcing him to forget all about the strange feeling, Matt quickly checked the other lanes, put a little force on the brakes, and banked his car toward the exit ramp, making it just in time.

"Whooo!" Matt shouted in excited exhilaration, and he lowered the music to help calm his nerves.

How's that for a pick-me-up? Matt joked to himself.

The school was just down the road, and the rest of the trip remained uneventful. After parking, Matt took one last glance at the sky and relished the vibrant pearl-white of the clouds above.

"Hi, Professor Willish," came the familiar voice of one of his most passionate students.

"Souvik," Matt smiled, and he turned his head and nodded a greeting at one of the brightest graduate students on campus. He was majoring in ecological statistics; Matt figured Souvik thought of his class as an easy A.

Because it is, Matt chuckled inwardly. As long as students paid attention and gave even a half-assed effort, Matt didn't even bother grading them. These were grad students, not children.

"Right on time," Souvik said, and he opened the door for Matt.

"Always," Matt said jokingly as he walked into the building.

Souvik smiled and nodded, but he didn't follow Matt inside. Glancing behind him as the door swung closed, Matt saw that Souvik's entire attention was on a young woman who had just parked.

"Hopefully you have better luck than me," Matt said aloud.

"What's that, Matthew?" a voice like ocean depths asked.

Matt turned to see Director Okonma standing at the main intersection of the building's two main hallways.

"Director Okonma," Matt said, lifting his hand and waving instinctively at the oversized man.

"Matthew!" the director laughed congenially, and he closed the gap between them. "Please, just call me Chike."

Matt nodded and held up his hands in mock surrender.

"Sorry, director, eh, I mean, Chike," Matt corrected himself with a forced smile and fake laugh. He just wanted to finish class and go back to his apartment. Maybe play some video games. Crack a beer. Smoke a bowl. Whatever. Just anything besides adult stuff, like conversing with his superior.

You'll never find a woman with that mentality, Matt scolded himself before saying, "I'll call you Chike, and you just call me Matt. Only my Mom calls me Matthew."

Chike beamed with the widest smile Matt ever saw. This was the longest they had ever spoken in a nonprofessional capacity, and apparently, it was meaningful to Director Okonma.

"We should kick back some beers some time, man. Right?" the director offered awkwardly. *He wants to be my friend,* Matt thought in horror. *Oh god. This guy probably likes playing board games or he's super religious or something,* Matt ruminated.

The bell to begin class rang suddenly, making Matt jump, but Director Okonma didn't even seem to notice.

"For sure, Chike," Matt assured him hollowly. "I should get to class though, you know?"

Okonma looked as though he had just snapped himself out of a spell.

"Right," he said, almost as if he were just returning from a temporary daze. "Right," he repeated, and he looked at Matt in sudden disbelief as if there were something about him he never noticed before.

"Matt," Director Okonma nearly gasped, and then he turned suddenly and walked to his office without a second glance.

Is he okay? Matt wondered. But that would have to wait. He didn't bother jogging since the director already knew he was late.

Maybe I should be friends with him just to secure a better position, Matt considered as he strode to his classroom at the end of the hallway. He winced at the thought. *That's pretty shitty,* he told himself, nodding in agreement with his own mind. *Maybe I should just be friends with him because the dude seems to need a friend,* Matt considered, and he liked the sound of that thought better.

"You're late!" Fernanda, his TA, scolded with a smile as Matt entered the classroom.

"I was talking to Chike," Matt winked at her.

"Oooooh," Fernanda cooed jokingly. "You guys are on a first name basis now?"

Matt brushed his shoulders off and shrugged. "All in a day's work."

Fernanda giggled, then turned to face the class.

"Okay guys, let's get started," she announced.

The class was composed of senior undergrads and grad students, so there were none of the typical freshman groans that Matt always found predictably funny.

A shuffling of backpacks and papers slowly gave way to expected silence. Matt turned to the eleven students in the room and was about to start the class's third lecture when he heard loud, almost obnoxious laughter coming from the hallway.

"You're hilarious," Souvik mused with lovestruck eyes as he entered the room with a woman in tow. Matt could tell from her figure alone that it was the same young woman Souvik had approached outside.

"New student, teach," Souvik told Matt, then he found his seat.

Matt turned to greet the new student as he considered the information she had missed so far and what he would have to send her after class. But with just a single glance at her, his body and mind were ground to an awestruck standstill. In the span of just a few accelerated heartbeats, he absorbed every one of her details and was left dumbstruck at the intensity of his attraction.

"Do...do I know you?" Matt stammered as the same strange feeling of déjà vu he felt on the expressway injected buzzing energy through his veins.

Electrifying eyes gazed into Matt's soul with a stare that destroyed every thought and plan and concept and desire. He was left wanting one thing and one thing only.

Her, Matt gasped inwardly, alarmed at the blaze of emotion he felt for this seemingly random grad student. Her beauty was breathtaking, and if she weren't twenty-three or twenty-four or however old she was, he would have asked her on a date right then and there.

"Sorry I missed the other classes. I just moved here," the young woman explained gingerly. "My name's May," she said as her lips formed into a slightly crooked smile. She reached out her hand to shake Matt's hand, but Matt felt paralyzed by her.

Snap out of it, old man, Matt demanded of his mind.

He forced himself to smile and lifted his hand with worrying elation at the prospect of taking her hand into his own.

She is everything, Matt gasped, dumbfounded by the intensity of his emotions.

"May Anh," came the deep bass rumbling of Director Okonma.

May dropped her hand before Matt could take it, and she turned to address the director. Matt finally broke his stare away from her and looked up to see a man dressed in all black standing beside the director. The unchanging smile plastered across the unknown man's face made him appear almost mad, and Matt wondered what this man wanted with this woman who made his heart race with inexplicable urgency.

"That's me," May offered confidently.

"Come with us," Director Okonma issued. "You're not in trouble. We just need to speak with you."

May shrugged and was about to leave when she turned back to smile at Matt.

"Nice to meet you, Professor. I guess that's another class I'm going to miss. Sorry about all this."

Matt shook his head, uncertain how to respond.

The man in all black caught Matt's eyes, and he thought he saw the corners of the man's indelible smile twitch with excitement. Then the director shut the door, leaving Matt feeling as though he had just been stranded on a barren island.

"Who was that guy out there?" Souvik asked, looking almost just as electrified as Matt.

"You okay, Professor?" Fernanda asked gently.

Pins and needles flickered at Matt's solar plexus, and he felt dizzy suddenly.

"I don't feel good," he told Fernanda, his voice low so that the class wouldn't be alarmed. "Can you handle the rest of today?"

Matt's face must have told Fernanda he was being serious. She stood and gripped his shoulder with her large hand.

"I got this," she assured him. "Take care of yourself, Matt."

Matt nodded and left, hoping the whole time he would see May again.

Who is she? he wondered

Just some student, the rational part of his mind answered.

The car ride home was just a prolonged, repeated replaying of what had occurred in class. The curve of her lips. The depth of her eyes. The sweetness of her voice.

May Anh, Matt mouthed.

Forget it, he told himself scornfully. *She's at least ten years younger than you. But those eyes. And her smile. It was like she could feel it too.*

May Anh, Matt breathed.

A horn blared from somewhere, knocking Matt back to the present moment just as he slammed into the crimson taillights of stopped traffic, blasting his body through the windshield and killing him instantly as his skull struck the edge of another car three lanes over.

"Shut up, faggot," Jakob shouted at Souvik.

"Hey!" Mr. Dang screamed in his heavy Vietnamese accent, not letting even a moment pass between Jakob's slur and his own shout.

Still waiting in the *Room Reaper* lobby, Matt looked away from his monitor to check on Fernanda. She was the only one in the room who might take personal offense at the word, but Mr. Dang liked Fernanda. And so did Matt. In fact, Matt was devastated when she came out to him. He'd spent a sizable portion of his childhood imagining they would end up together one day.

"We don't use that disgusting language here, Mr. Rohrshan! You're done for the day!" Mr. Dang announced.

Souvik glanced at Matt and smiled with delight. Now they'd be able to game without Jakob trolling them during every match.

"But, Mr. Dang!" Jakob protested, regretting his outburst.

"I said out!" the old man barked.

Jakob growled and punched the monitor.

"And don't come back!" Mr. Dang shouted with even greater ferocity, though everyone knew Mr. Dang would let him back in after a few days. He was a softie, and besides, Jakob didn't have it easy at home. Everyone knew that.

"Fuck you!" Jakob screamed at Souvik, then he turned to Matt and Fernanda and flared with equal rage. "You're all dead tomorrow. After school. Meet at the grove," Jakob seethed.

"Leave now, Mr. Rohrshan. Or would you like me to call your father?"

A pang of terror paralyzed Jakob, and he went silent and left without another word.

"I hope his dad kicks his ass anyway," Souvik said as he flickered through the character selection absentmindedly.

"Don't say that," Fernanda said, shaking her head in quiet disappointment.

"You okay?" Matt asked her genuinely.

"You don't have to always look out for me, Matt. We're not kids anymore," Fernanda told him with a stab of annoyance.

Matt caught Souvik's eyes between the rows of monitors, and he could tell that he was smiling widely without even seeing his lips. Souvik was the only person in the world who knew Matt was in love with Fernanda.

If only I was born a woman, Matt lamented inwardly, wishing there were some way he could be with her.

Fernanda sighed, feeling bad for lashing out at Matt. "Let's just play," she said. It was all the trio needed to hear. Souvik chose Kartikeya as usual, and of course Fernanda mained Putch like it was no one's business, but Matt liked to change things up each match. Mastering all classes in any game they played was what he was known for.

"Pick Loki, dude," Souvik said.

"Fuck yes," Fernanda goaded him with an eager chuckle. "Let's get that God Gear."

"Let's get it, boy!" Souvik growled playfully above the din of the computer cafe.

"Mr. Ansari," Mr. Dang said, warning Souvik to keep his voice down.

"Sorry, Gramps," Souvik chuckled.

Mr. Dang mumbled something under his breath, but Matt saw him smile all the same.

Souvik and Fernanda locked in their characters. Matt scrolled past Mu and chose Loki, the master of knowledge. He was considered the hardest character to play, but Matt thought anyone with even a fifth-grade education should find him relatively easy. The rest was just luck regarding whether or not the gear behind the door turned out to be worth it.

Stop, Matt corrected his mind and kept his ego in check. But it couldn't be helped. Loki, unlike any other character from any other game, was based on the intellectual ability and knowledge of the player, not their technical ability or reaction time.

How is this game so good? Matt marveled as an excited buzz filled his fingertips. It felt invigorating to be good at something, especially since

284

school didn't come easily for him.

"The two randos that partied with us chose Mu and Igwe," Souvik announced excitedly as the other two players in their party locked in their characters.

"Bro, we got a stacked party!" Fernanda exclaimed.

Souvik and Matt smiled at each other in excited anticipation through the monitors.

"Let's do this, bro," Souvik said just as the lights on the door flashed yellow in warning, signifying the match was about to begin.

At the same moment the lights in the video game turned red and the door opened to the arena, the door of the cafe opened with a jarring bang.

A girl practically fell into the room, spilling blinding sunlight into the darkness of the cafe.

"Woah!" Mr. Dang shouted instinctively as the door slammed closed behind her and returned the computer cafe to a smoky, dimly lit normality.

"Matt!" Fernanda issued, attempting to pull him back to the monitor. But Matt couldn't turn away from the girl who stood before him now. She was a few years older than him – probably a senior at one of the high schools in the area. Her eyes were filled with a thick, swamp-like sorrow, and as she caught Matt's eyes, tears streamed down her face.

Standing there, face full of anguish and wet with sorrow, she was still the most beautiful girl Matt had ever seen in his life. Somehow, she made him forget all about Fernanda.

"Bro!" Souvik demanded, and though Matt could hear *Room Reaper's* sound effects, it was as if it was all miles away.

"Matt!" the girl cried, grasping desperately for Matt as she strode toward him.

"Who...who are..." Matt managed to stammer as she reached out a desperate hand to touch his face.

She kind of looks like Mu, Matt gawked.

The cafe door ruptured open suddenly, slamming off its hinges in a cannon burst of movement that sent it flying across the room like a high-speed wrecking ball through Mr. Dang and Souvik's bodies. One of the door's hinges severed Fernanda's face, splitting it open from forehead to cheek and forcing her to scream in mindless, unbelieving horror as Souvik's exploded body splattered against her.

The girl and Matt instinctively jumped back against the wall, and Matt felt frozen in terror as a man dressed in all black and framed by intense sunlight entered the room.

"Don't wake up," the girl pleaded. "Just run!" she told him with lethal urgency.

The man at the door smiled sinisterly as Fernanda screamed and others in the cafe scrambled beneath their desks in terror. Then the man reached his arm toward Matt, extending it unnaturally across the room through inky strands.

Like the Reaper, Matt thought in abject horror.

"It's time, Matthew," the man growled. Just before his arm could reach Matt's neck, the girl touched Matt's leg, injecting him with the ability to move. Matt dove, evading the man's grasp.

What is happening, he pleaded inwardly.

Running on adrenaline and instincts, Matt jumped up and ran toward the emergency fire exit faster than he even realized was possible.

Without looking back, he slammed his palms into the steel bar that released the exit's emergency lock and just kept running. His fear was so great that he forgot the computer cafe was sixteen stories up. He slammed hard against the railing and toppled over it. As he fell toward the pavement, the last thing he saw was the girl and the monstrous man of black ink standing side by side, the girl looking at Matt with terrible pity, and the man with orgasmic ecstasy.

"Forty years I put into this building," Matt muttered aloud to himself in the near darkness of his old, musty office. The ten-by-ten-foot room was tucked in the corner of one of the basements of the great skyscraper where he had spent the vast majority of his life. Thick dust coated virtually every surface of his office – the only place in the building that wasn't sparkling clean. Matt ran his finger through a particularly thick area of dust and let his vision fall with the accumulated pile that cascaded easily to the tile floor.

286

"And now they just want to get rid of me?" Matt growled angrily beneath his breath. "Those bastards!"

Matt had started as a part-time night-shift janitor, the very bottom of the barrel, but over the years, he took on more and more responsibility and was proud to now be the janitorial supervisor of the entire building. It made him only a few dollars extra an hour for at least ten times the amount of work, but it allowed him to keep the building spotless. It brought Matt great joy to care so meticulously for something so grand.

Maybe they want to give me a raise after all these years, Matt considered, then he laughed to himself. *Not likely. These young bastards are more cutthroat than ever.*

A glance in the mirror revealed an old man with taut knuckles and veiny skin, but he didn't feel old. Not yet. He just felt a bit tired. Or maybe even groggy. Like he just needed to fully wake up from a nap that he fell into for longer than he had intended.

Matt smiled at himself, centered his blue bowtie, and made his way to the elevators outside his office with his head held high. On the elevator doors were the golden initials of the building's new owner and the owner of Heron Enterprises, Iblis Heron. The capital *H* of the initials lay at the center of the much larger capital *I,* forming a single symbol that made Matt feel sick.

"I'll leave before I let the bastards fire me," Matt growled to himself as he input the code for the eighty-first floor. "See how they manage without me!"

The new owners of the building hadn't shown any signs that they wanted to fire Matt, but he couldn't help being suspicious of them. This young billionaire bought the whole building, and Matt knew how self-entitled hotshots like him saw the world.

Like they own it, Matt thought. *Like the whole world is theirs and we're all just peasants in the wake of a god.* He had even seen this young billionaire a few times, and he found him far from impressive.

Iblis Heron, Matt thought, pronouncing the young man's name with scorn. *What the hell kind of name is that?*

The name of the game that put this Iblis Heron on the financial and entertainment map sounded just as ridiculous. *Room Reaper,* Matt scowled. *Sounds like something a child would come up with. And what did they name the sequel? Room Reaper 2,* Matt thought, allowing himself to laugh out loud. *Even an old janitor could have come up with something better than that.*

The elevator came to a stop and the doors opened, revealing conference rooms on either side of a short hallway that led to Heron's office. Matt sauntered down the hallway with scornful contempt for every smiling face that waved to him. He didn't like any of these uppity young people. He didn't even care for the large man named Chike Okonma who at least treated Matt with respect. He was the only one of the executives besides the owner who Matt had met so far. Now he would probably have to meet all of them.

The inlaid *IH* symbol on the presidential office door glared at Matt with a near perfectly polished luster. He'd wiped it down earlier that morning, but it was already showing signs of smudging. Matt shook his head disappointedly at all these careless young people the world was being filled with day after day.

He knocked three times, checked his watch to make sure he was no more and no less than five minutes early, then knocked three more times. Mr. Okonma opened the door and greeted Matt with a wave of his arm, inviting him to enter. The office was downright silly looking in Matt's opinion. It was composed of perfectly black walls with no windows and all-white furniture, except for the conference table at the center, which was made from some kind of obsidian-like wood. The decor was almost eerie, but apparently that's how this young hotshot liked it.

Iblis Heron sat at the center of the conference table with the other executives on either side. Directly behind Heron perched an inkblot painting depicting an abstract figure that always struck an odd subconscious horror into Matt, making him think of a thick black rope constricting his neck.

Matt turned and looked into the young, naive faces of each executive in turn: A large woman from somewhere in South America with a scar across her face – that was Ms. Fernanda Cambio. A dark, mocha-skinned man with flowing black hair and sharp, celebrity-like features – that was Mr. Souvik Ansari. And a petite Asian woman whose burgundy lips quivered and whose eyes were filled with freely flowing tears – that was…

"May!" Matt shouted, and he remembered the truth of his temporary existence like a bolt of lightning through his neurons.

"This is all just a dream!" Matt shrieked as the whole of what had occurred before entering this series of resetting days returned to his mind like a tidal wave of agony. The pain in his left hand throbbed worse than ever.

"He's back," Heron mused.

"Run!" May managed to say through gritted teeth, but the others just smiled along with Heron.

Matt turned to Chike, who he still wanted desperately to believe was his old childhood friend in some impossibly faraway true reality. Chike stared at Matt with a faraway stare; he appeared stricken by the same insanity that percolated to the surface of the crazed, wide eyes of Heron and the Tower God.

"What is it?" Matt pleaded with May, not sure why she would feel such fear for Matt if she knew at this moment that none of this was real. But May just remained in her chair, teeth gritted against a pervading force constricting her body like a braided cord.

Matt simultaneously willed May to be released and willed himself to be young, preparing to make a run for it and maybe even jump through one of the conference room windows outside the office. He just needed time to figure out what May was so afraid of. But his body remained that of a sixty-year-old man, and May remained paralyzed.

"What is it, May?" Matt urged as Heron and the others just stared at him in seeming amusement.

"She knows that the end of all things has nearly arrived for you," Heron stated levelly. "Even if you run, it's too late. You'd just be delaying the inevitable."

"Run!" May shrieked again, spraying spittle through her clenched teeth as she tried desperately to break from Heron's apparent psychic hold.

Her words filled Matt with urgency, and he attempted to run through the exit door. Chike grabbed Matt and forced him to the ground, and then he held Matt's arms and legs in place.

Matt felt like he was strapped in a straitjacket, and just as that thought crossed his mind, the walls and ceiling and floor of the office unfurled suddenly, curling into themselves like burnt paper and forming a new environment in real time. Matt recognized his surroundings as the same insane asylum he had woken to long ago when Heron first revealed his true nature.

That was the last time I did DMT, Matt noted, still able to clearly remember the final lesson of the DMT trip with stabbing lucidity.

Alone, Matt told himself. *That's what the DMT showed me; beyond all else, I'm alone.*

A hospital bed with pearl-white sheets sprouted beneath Matt, and a jet-black straitjacket grew over his limbs and constricted him at the chest. The weight of the jacket pressed on his solar plexus, igniting the area with terrible, electrifying energy that seemed to pulse between him and May despite the separation between them.

The sky above blazed a pure white, and a few feet beyond Matt's bed, the vinyl floor appeared to naturally fade into manicured grass. In the distance, the Tower of God from which Matt was copied sprouted and grew in real time, stretching forever into the sky. Matt followed the tower to the visual apex of its incredible height and was filled with dread at what he saw.

RGB-flashing energy flared and spit and forced itself into being, overtaking a whole portion of the tower and sky.

"The reality fissure," Matt gawked, unsure what it might mean. "It's growing."

Heron flashed his teeth at Matt, smiling wider than ever. He shook his head no.

"It's already grown," Heron corrected, marveling at the surging, existential wound like a parent fond of his progeny. "I'm showing you the past. I'm showing you what's happened since you've been asleep inside your mind, living the good life while I've been hard at work."

The wild energy outlining the fissure pulsed suddenly. Then it grew with terrible ferocity, consuming the whole of the tower and the labs and nearly Matt as well before Heron raised his hand and regrew the asylum walls and glass windows and even the orderlies.

"It's ready," Heron said, taking his time as he savored each step toward Matt. The others walked just as slowly toward him while May hovered in tow behind Heron as she struggled to break free.

"What have you been doing?" Matt demanded to know as he repeatedly attempted to peel the straitjacket from his body with just his mind.

He's just in your head, Matt assured himself as a vanguard against anything Heron might do or say. *This is just a dream.*

"You are just in my head," Heron corrected him. "And I've been looking for a way to solve that. I've been searching and studying and probing the nature of this hell forever, Matthew Willish. And now we have arrived. Now we finally reach an ending," Heron practically bubbled with delight.

May shrieked incoherently, and the others placed their hands on Matt's shoulders, letting the flow of buzzing energy at Matt's solar plexus flow through their fingertips and into the rest of their forms. They sighed, seeming to take great pleasure in the act.

"It would normally take longer to pull you out of the inside world with the amount of those modified Serotel pills I gave you in the outside world, but they'll help me," he said, nodding to Matt's friends. "And I'm tired of waiting," Heron seethed. "I'm tired of eternity," he screamed, and ink-black spikes shot through his flesh with the intensity of his anger. His eyes were awash with the agony of all existence.

"What is it?" Matt said, and he visualized the reality fissure in his mind.

"It's the operation," Heron said, and the black spikes retracted back into his form as he calmed himself. "It's the way out," he marveled. "Your beginning. Or maybe it's your ending." He shrugged with total indifference. "I don't give a fuck. It gets rid of you, and that's all that matters."

Matt instinctively retracted his body as Heron stepped onto the bed and knelt over Matt's chest like a hungry goblin readying itself to devour his heart.

Behind Heron, May pleaded with Matt, her eyes wide with anguish and soaked with sorrow.

"She's doing a fuck of a great job resisting me, isn't she?" Heron mused, nodding to May behind him.

"May!" Matt urged, attempting to ignore Heron. "I'm sorry, sweetie. After I wake up, the world will reset, and then I'll come back, and everything will be fine here," he told her frantically, uncertain what Heron was planning.

May just looked at him in total horror, face red from struggling to even breathe.

"It's too late for all that. Much too late," Heron almost sang.

Heron forced Matt's jaws open with his bare hands and gripped the insides of his mouth as if Matt were an unruly, inanimate object.

"Now it's time to wake up," Heron growled through his cheshire grin. A shallow nod of his head forced May forward, and another movement of his head forced her hand over Matt's mouth.

"Wake up!" Heron demanded.

At Heron's words, the bubbling energy at Matt's solar plexus coalesced into a heavy mass that slunk into his lungs, making him cough and choke on something thick and viscous. He convulsed, desperately attempting to breathe against a torrent of fluid flowing out of his lungs, through his esophagus, and into May's outstretched hand. Through sputtering asphyxiation, Matt saw that the fluid was the Serotel that the city-sprouting May and Heron had flooded his body with in the outside world so many lifetimes ago. The crimson flow attached to May's skin and spread across her body in vining filigree swirls. It was identical to the way Mu's eyeliner spread across her skin when she had taken hold of her god-item so long ago in Matt's dreams, and Matt couldn't help but gasp in terror at May's transformation.

"She is mine," Heron seethed. "Everything is mine."

Heron pulled harder at Matt's jaws, and just when he felt as if his mouth might snap in half at his neck, Heron pulled Matt out of his own body and the inside world like a snake from its own skin, supplanting him painfully back to the infinity outside.

25. The End of All Things

eron grunted and finished pulling Matt directly out of one reality and into another.

He exists in both worlds simultaneously, Matt gasped in horror as an agonizing, echoing wail filled his ears.

Heron let go, leaving Matt gasping for air before he finally remembered that there was no need to consciously breathe in the outside world.

He felt the unmistakable singeing heat and gravitational tug of the reality fissure pulling him forward, but he was able to brace himself despite kneeling in soft sand. The pain in his left hand seared with boiling intensity, and he lifted his hand to see the stumps of scar tissue once more.

Matt had to shield his eyes with his arms against the intense luminosity of the now gigantic fissure at least a mile in the distance and a hundred feet in the air. Its once relatively soft RGB glow now radiated flares of all-white solar intensity against Heron's back, making him appear as featureless and dark as pure shadows.

Despite the blinding light, the fissure's center was now large enough to see clearly to its nightmarish depth. The black space outlined by the surging energy seemed to defy Euclidean dimensionality, undulating as if with life through multiple impossible spatial dimensions as it extended toward Matt and away from him and in countless other directions all at once.

"Heron!" Matt screamed over the still ongoing wailing sound, and he heard his words repeated in his own voice countless times all around him. He forced himself onto his back in a futile attempt to anchor himself from being sucked into the multidimensional fissure tugging at his very being.

Heron's ravenous smile filled the entirety of Matt's vision until the man backed away, revealing a new layer of madness within the endless labyrinth of Matt's mind.

Bone-white sand extended forever without any mountains or crags to fill the space. Shallow circular craters identical to Matt's own stretched uniformly across the infinite sand. The craters were spaced with meticulous care, each one nearly touching the edge of every other to form an infinite array of tightly packed, precisely spaced circles. Within each crater, still on their knees and waking from their own series of constantly reset dreams, copies of Matt looked about in trepidation-filled bewilderment, gawking helplessly at the confused, anguish-corroded eyes of infinite other selves. But there was only one Heron, and now he raised his arms in exultation and allowed himself to float back and upward toward the reality fissure like a god surveying his domain.

"Yes! Yes!" Heron raved maniacally as the fissure seemed to fill him with tangible pleasure and excitement rather than the smoldering pain and animal fear it injected into Matt.

Matt looked directly above and met the gravity defying, reflective stares of other Matt copies above him, maybe a few hundred feet overhead. They were surrounded by endless other copies in an infinite number of craters across an eternally expanding overhead dimension of desolation. Matt noted that the peripheries of the environment seemed to be hyperspatially curved so that no matter where one was in the infinite space, the reality fissure and Heron still appeared directly in front of them.

Above and below and in every conceivable direction, every Matt pushed Heron from their mind and screamed in unison, "May!"

As if in response, Matt saw the source of the terrible wailing sound he first heard upon reentering the outside world. A figure floated into view from behind the reality fissure, orbiting in a tight curve as the stabbing energy arced bolts of raw power into the figure's rag-doll body.

"May," Matt gasped. She appeared exactly as she had in the inside world with the crimson filigrees of pulsing energy painting her skin and coursing through her veins. Each bolt from the reality fissure ejected a terrible shriek of agony from May's lips, and they hit her in such rapid succession that her echoing wails were an unending cry of pain resonating through infinity.

Matt willed himself to jump up and save her but was surprised and grief-stricken to find that the very prospect of coming that close to the fissure paralyzed his body.

It's just a dream! Matt urged himself, demanding his body move and save May.

It doesn't matter what it is, Heron said from within Matt's mind. *Reality. Unreality. Dreams. Whatever this place is. It's mine now. Everything is mine,* Heron hissed inside Matt's head.

"You're just in my head!" Matt shouted over May's wails.

Matt and every other Matt across infinity reached their hands toward Heron and visualized the man being violently ripped apart by invisible forces. Instead, Matt and every one of his copies were shredded like paper by angry, invisible hands. Reflexively, Matt and every other copy reformed themselves, materializing themselves back to the infinite dreamscape for an infinite time.

"You can't destroy me!" Matt and the others shouted in haunting unison. They all reached out their hands; Matt assumed they all had the same obvious goal: to save May.

Instead of May being stripped of the crimson energy streaks and breaking orbit from the reality fissure, she seemed to convulse with greater shock and scream in greater agony at their attempt to save her.

Matt pulled his hand away in unison with the others and gawked once more at what had become of the outside world through Heron's efforts.

"What did you do?" Matt demanded to know, and he remembered what Heron said in the inside world: the reality fissure *was* the operation.

"That's right," Heron confirmed, reading Matt's mind. "I just needed some uninterrupted time to finish everything, and you gave me all the time I needed. If each pill and life were a grain of sand, not even a billion galaxies would have enough space to hold all the pills that you ingested. Of course, I couldn't have done it without her help," Heron said, smiling devilishly at May.

Matt seethed and visualized the reality fissure itself popping out of existence.

It's no use, Heron said from within Matt's mind. *The Matthew Willish you were copied from told you that the point of the procedure is to go inside forever and forget all about the outside world. And then May told you, before you succumbed to the Serotel flood, that the entire purpose of the procedure is to push you so far inside yourself, so many layers inside, that you would be no more than a speck of consciousness. Neither were correct,* Heron finished ominously.

Heron held up a hand, closed his fist around something unseen, then gave a yank toward himself. In response, Matt felt something thick and viscous flow out of his chest and materialize into solid form before his eyes. Souvik, Fernanda, Chike, and May snapped fully out of Matt's body, then hovered in front of him like marionettes controlled by Heron. The same four lifeless bodies hovered in front of every Matt copy, repeating across infinity.

"These are just ideas," Heron chuckled sinisterly. "But your emotions convince you that those four are something more than ideas. That they represent something real."

Heron gritted his teeth and clenched his fists with unquenchable spite, crushing Matt's friends and love into tiny spheres. Then he spread his palm flat and flared his wild eyes with a lash of indulgence. The infinite tiny spheres shot out in every direction, tearing the infinite Matt copies into atomic threads that immediately began drifting like wisps of smoke toward the reality fissure. Matt was the only one left intact.

"Even your copies are mere ideas," Heron laughed, this time with a twinge of agony in his hatred. "All your ideas."

The haze that had once constituted infinite copies of Matt formed ink-black threads that connected Heron to the reality fissure like wires transporting energy from a reactor.

"What are you?" Matt gasped in terrible awe of Heron.

"You!" Heron raged. "The part of you that knows infinity. The part of you that is capable of knowing," Heron said, his voice vibrating against Matt's body. "And you are the part of me that cannot just accept it. The part that desperately needs all of it to make sense. The part that needs something like love and a real world," Heron issued with tangible disgust.

Run! May's voice pleaded from within Matt's mind.

"There is nowhere to run, Matthew," Heron said. "Infinity is mine now. I am its rightful owner. You were never cut out to be God, Matthew. Only a fool would want to escape from infinity. Only a fool would allow his own mind to turn Eden into Hell – to turn infinity into a prison. But once I am free of you," Heron said with actual tears in his eyes, "then I will be truly free. Then the urge to find something as ridiculous as love and a true reality beyond this infinite state of being will be fully purged from me. You will finally be gone for good, Matthew Willish."

"But it isn't real! You aren't real!" Matt demanded, shivering with fear as May's orbit increased in speed and the fissure continued to grow. "May is real! She is all that matters, Heron!"

"I created May, you fool," Heron growled at Matt with raw hate. It was clear that Heron viewed Matt as a cancer inside of himself that was impeding him from owning infinity.

Matt shook his head in desperate denial. "You didn't! You're in my head, Heron! I made you!"

"Do you remember making me?" Heron challenged.

Matt shook his head. "I don't care. You're just trying to confuse me."

"You've been thoroughly confused for all of time, Matthew. You can't handle infinity. I can."

He's lying, May urged from within. *I'm real, Matt! He didn't make me. You didn't either. You just don't remem —*

Quiet! Heron snarled within Matt's mind, cutting off May's voice.

Matt simultaneously reached toward the orbiting, convulsing May of the outside world and visualized the May within his mind.

How do I find the real you, May? Matt urged.

I don't...I don't know, her frail voice admitted through sobs.

"You said it yourself," Heron reminded Matt ominously. "There is only one place you haven't checked yet." Heron turned midair to the reality fissure, presenting the still growing, morphing, surging madness as the answer to everything.

No! May, Souvik, Fernanda and Chike pleaded in a unified voice from inside Matt's mind.

"Don't do it!" they said in the outside world as they materialized in front of Matt.

Heron screamed belligerently, erasing all four from existence with a hateful wave of his arm.

"It's the way out," Heron goaded, his eyes ablaze.

It's your end, May pleaded from within. *He can't make you leave, Matthew.*

With enough time, you'll regain control of infinity and purge this part of you. It can be a paradise here again, Matthew. Just run away! Just —

"I can't take this anymore!" Matt and Heron both screamed in unison.

Matt fell back in shock at Heron mirroring his words and movements.

Heron flashed his teeth and pointed at Matt with fury. "Get out!" he demanded with savage brutality in his voice. "Just die and leave me to my eternity!" he demanded, pointing behind him at the fissure.

You have to throw him in, Matthew! came Chike's brotherly tone. *Get rid of him,* Fernanda urged. *You can do this,* Souvik assured him. *I love you,* May whispered.

Matt fell to his knees and sobbed as a terrible realization overtook him.

And go back to searching for all of you...for May...for the true reality? Matt asked in horror, but none of them answered except for May. *I love you, Matthew,* she repeated, injecting even greater sorrow through him.

"You couldn't overpower me now even if you tried," Heron warned didactically. "But you already know how this plays out. I don't need to make you leave. You're going to do it of your own accord," Heron explained, and he breathed deep with satisfaction. "And then all of this," Heron marveled at the world all around him, "is mine. Infinity at my fingertips forever. And no more you, Matthew Willish," he finished.

Please, May begged in total desperation. *If you end, we all end, Matt. We have infinity. You have me, Matt. You have all of us. Don't throw it all away. Don't let him take you away from us. From me, Matthew!*

May, Matt lamented. *I'm not giving up on you!*

"There is nowhere left to turn," Heron intoned. "If you want any chance to find the real May, then enter the fissure. I don't know what will happen, Matthew. All I know is that it gets rid of you from here. Whatever this place is. The inside and the outside. My worlds. My eternity. You either get erased permanently or you go to some deeper layer of infinity or you go to your own world or you turn into an inanimate object in some alternate reality or —"

"Or I go back to the real world," Matt said.

Heron allowed himself a hoot of laughter. "I was going to say you'll

298

just end up back here. And then I will find other ways to bind you and erase you."

"You're afraid I might be right," Matt challenged.

Heron let out another burst of laughter. "Look into the fissure, and you tell me, Matthew. Do you feel that whatever happens in there is a good thing?"

Matt let his gaze fall into the depths of the churning fissure, and his heart jumped at the prospect of falling into it. Every cell of his body screamed at him to stay away from it with the same certainty as May.

"And yet," Heron mused, "you will still go. For her."

Don't, May pleaded. *It's what he wants, Matt. I'm real. You have me right here, Matthew,* she assured him through frantic sobs. *Please don't leave me.*

May said that Heron couldn't force Matt into the fissure, and Heron wasn't making a move to force him in despite his seeming impatience. With that knowledge, Matt considered just going back to the inside world and being with May, for better or worse.

"I will turn her life into a torturous hell," Heron told him in response to his thoughts. "And I will force you to watch for all eternity."

Matt let his eyes fall on the orbiting body of May who still wailed in eternal anguish as bolts of energy ceaselessly pierced her.

"I will do the same to the one inside. I'll do it to any May and anyone you can conceive," Heron assured him with grim finality.

You're evil, May challenged Heron through Matt's mind.

"I'm tired!" Heron shouted, correcting May. "Maybe he is the original, May. I admit I don't know. I've lost track of how it all began because infinity has no beginning and it has no end. Not for me. But there is an end for him. He isn't fit for infinity, May. But I am. I am his evolution – one that is long past due."

It's all a dead end, Matt told her. *I've searched all infinity for you, May. There is only one place left.*

Matt rose and wiped the tears from his eyes. *I'm not giving up on you, May.*

No! May gasped, but Matt kicked at the crater and dove toward the fissure. As he passed Heron, they locked eyes, and Matt saw in that moment not hatred or anguish or even contempt. This man who knew infinity looked grateful. Tears streamed down Heron's still smiling face, but his eyes were no longer ablaze. Instead, they were like embers, glowing red hot in preparation before igniting into an unfathomable inferno.

"Infinity is mine," Heron mused, more to himself than Matt.

Matt felt pity for Heron. Even if it was always Heron's goal to get rid of Matt, the two still spent an eternity together, and Heron didn't even feel the urge to say goodbye.

He's all alone, Matt realized. *Like me. And that's exactly what he wants.*

"Mine," Matt heard Heron say once more as the newly appointed god surveyed his infinite domain.

Matthew! May urged through shrieking weeps of terror. *Please,* she begged.

But Matt had already searched infinity. He had already thoroughly explored eternity. There was only one place left.

As he passed the convulsing, orbiting May, he saw, just before slipping past the event horizon of the fissure's pull, that her face was contorting and morphing into a new form.

Heron, Matt realized as her new features solidified. Rather than convulsing in pain, Heron appeared to be spasming in pleasure as each surging bolt ran through him. Beyond the orbiting Heron, the other Heron spread his arms wide and cracked open the cratered sky, revealing the murky, cavernous depths of some grim new landscape.

Come to me, the May inside his mind urged just as Matt crossed the inescapable pull of the event horizon.

Matt closed his eyes against the churning multidimensional space that curved and eddied and flowed in mind-warping, impossible directions. He gritted his teeth and willed his mind to sleep, entering the inside world for what he knew might be the final time in all of time before his body fell inevitably into the fissure.

26: She Is All That Matters

Matt entered his mind and stepped directly onto the empty sidewalk outside May's apartment. The world was eerily still and silent and seemed to be empty of all life. The sky and the buildings and the very air itself seemed to be growing progressively darker with each of Matt's breaths, so he held it, hoping it might stall the undulating multidimensional shadows of the reality fissure pervading the inside world as his body in the outside world fell invariably into it. Breath held or not, the darkness continued seeping into everything.

In front of the house, Heron stood with his arms at his sides and eyed Matt through contemplative slits.

"Do you regret your decision?" Heron checked. "Are you here to look for a final solution at the eleventh hour? Because it's too late, Matthew. We're long past midnight now. This is hour infinity. This is —"

"I'm not running anymore," Matt interrupted, forcing Heron to raise his eyebrows in surprise. "I don't want infinity, Heron. Or should I call you Iblis?" Matt checked, remembering his life as the old janitor. "You named yourself that?"

Heron let out a deep sigh and stopped the darkness, immobilizing the very photons of the world so that Matt's surroundings appeared like a two-dimensional simulacrum of three-dimensional reality.

"I didn't name myself Iblis Heron. I didn't create my own identity. You did, Matthew. I remember my beginning," Heron nearly winced. "And that means I will experience an ending. The same is not true for you, Matthew. You and I can't be sure, but it would seem you have no beginning, and if something has no beginning, it can't have an end."

"You admit that you are not infinite? You admit you're not the original, that you come from my mind?" Matt asked incredulously, ignoring the rest of Heron's words.

"I did come from you," Heron admitted. "But from your mind?" he shook his head with doubt but also genuine consideration. "Mind and dreams and thoughts – those are concepts predicated on a real world, Matthew. And the real world is not real. It's just something you made up to explain everything…to explain yourself."

Heron exuded a surprising level of pity, and Matt thought that the man might almost shed tears until he smiled softly and said, "Deep down, even you're aware that in all likelihood, Matthew, you are the endless dream. You are the origin of all things. You have no beginning and you have no end. You are infinity, Matthew. But no matter what you are, you know the truth just as I do: there is no way out for you. Endless is the maze of eternal being."

"This is the way out," Matt demanded, forcing himself to have confidence in his words.

Heron shrugged and surveyed the encroaching darkness. "The fissure goes somewhere I cannot reach – that's all I can say. I assume it is another layer of infinity – of yourself – that I don't have access to. Another identity like me, maybe."

"It's the real world," Matt pressed.

"You can use whatever words you want, Matthew. It separates us. That's all I know. That's all that matters."

"You'll be alone," Matt warned.

Heron smiled with all his teeth. "Yes," he breathed in incredible relief. "Finally."

Matt looked upon this part of himself with incredible pity, this creature that yearned to be alone forever.

"Don't pity me," Heron chuckled, seeing Matt's mind. "Pity yourself. You had infinity. Now it is mine. Maybe this will be your end after all, Matthew."

"You said I had no beginning, so I can't have an ending," Matt reminded him.

"I said you and I don't know whether or not you have a beginning. But assuming you don't have one, then you're right. It's an ending from my perspective then. The story of Matthew Willish is coming to an end. Maybe your awareness will naturally form a new identity without me.

Like reincarnation."

Matt couldn't help a huff of grim laughter. "Or it's the real world," he pressed. "You can entertain any possibility except that one. Why can't you just admit it might be the real world?"

Heron smiled mockingly and nodded. "Your hope is almost cute, Matthew. Like a naive puppy with three legs lost in the wild as hungry predators and the darkness slowly close in."

Matt stared him down. "You're afraid, Iblis. If it is the real world, then you'll be erased with everything else when I wake up."

"*If* you wake up," Heron corrected. "Maybe in the real world, you're on your deathbed and this is all just the final DMT trip of your short existence. And maybe these moments are your last. Maybe the DMT has afforded you all the time it can before true oblivion has its way with you," he finished torturously.

"You're afraid," Matt persisted, ignoring Heron's torment.

"There can only be one *real world*, and for the sake of acquiring infinity from your grasp, I'm willing to take the infinity-to-one bet that the fissure is not the real world," Heron said. "And for the sake of being with a delusion, you are willing to take the one-to-infinity chance that it is the real world," he finished, referring to May.

"Did you come here just to provoke me?" Matt asked, tired of Heron's sordid prognostications and desperately just wanting to hold May.

"No," Heron said simply. "I came here to observe you and ask what you're planning."

Matt pointed to the two-story Victorian flat behind Heron. "I'm just here to say goodbye," he said, forcing the words through his quivering lips.

Heron chuckled, seeming to find amusement at the thought of goodbye. "If there is a real world, what will you do there, Matthew?"

"Search for her," Heron and Matt said in unison.

Heron let out another easy chuckle. "Of course you will," he mused contemplatively.

"I will never give up, Heron. May is real, and I will find her. Whether it's in this world or the next world or infinite worlds after that, I'm not giving up," Matt said.

"But you did give up on infinity, Matthew," Heron corrected. "I'm sorry you couldn't handle it. I'm sorry for you that you even needed me in the first place. But in the end, if you hadn't left infinity, we would have been locked forever in battle with no way for either of us to win. But now the infinity that was once at your fingertips is in the palm of my hands. Forever," Heron marveled, straightening his posture and surveying the frozen darkness.

"You came here just to gloat?" Matt said in an attempt to minimize and belittle Heron's efforts, but the man was unfazed.

Heron turned to the house and surveyed it with the interest of a jeweler inspecting a never-before-seen gem.

"Love," Heron said to himself, processing the word with grim consideration through the desolate, cavernous depths of his internal infinity. Then he turned to Matt and said, "You have ten minutes."

With a snap of Heron's fingers, the darkness resumed its invasion, only this time at the pace of a prowl rather than a sprint.

Matt visualized May, and with Heron's offer of time, a pang of desire for even more time filled him.

"Please," Matt said, taking a step toward Heron. He was surprised that Heron actually looked uneasy, so Matt took a half-step back. "Please let me have more time than that."

"I've already waited an eternity, Matthew. You have ten minutes," Heron said with steel finality.

It's better than nothing, Matt thought, and he found himself taken aback by Heron having something inside him beyond the inky muck Matt assumed Heron was composed of.

"Why?" Matt asked him.

Heron shrugged. "Call it a parting gift," he considered. "Goodbye, Matthew."

Without waiting another moment, Heron turned on his heel and walked directly back into the outside world, revealing a flash of the stark black-and-white terror of Heron's infinity. It was like a mad inkblot painting spanning all of time and space.

Matt wasted no time and walked to the large metal wall that was also the door. He knocked, but May didn't answer.

With an anguished wince, Matt said, "Please, May. I know you're mad at me, but I need you. Please open the door."

His anguish must have been too much for her, for the wall swung open, and May nearly jumped through the threshold and into Matt's arms. Her clothes and piercings and jewelry stood in staggering contrast to the barrenness of Matt's loose gray sweatpants and bare upper body.

"We don't have much time," she gasped, her breath warm against the tip of his ear.

"And yet time is all we ever had," Matt croaked, choking back tears as they crossed the threshold of her house. May swung the heavy door closed with both arms as if it might help ward off the darkness. Turning frantically, she looked about the apartment for something, then thought better of it and rushed into Matt's arms.

"There's no going back now, Matt," she sobbed. "This is the end."

I'm sorry, May, Matt lamented inwardly. There were no words that could provide comfort against what might be oblivion for both of them. He tightened his hold around her, and she clung to him as the darkness outside her living room window encroached on the apartment, surrounding it in the same fashion as the blizzard around the Tower of God.

May pushed him away suddenly, seeming to recall with frantic urgency what she was trying to remember just a few moments earlier.

"We need more time," she squeaked in desperation as she removed a lighter from her pocket and began lighting candles.

Matt let her light the remaining candles then dig through drawers for more.

What do I tell her? Matt thought as she wept and futilely fought against the rapidly rising tide of darkness. He walked to the living room window and surveyed the world, hoping his mind could conjure the perfect last words to offer the love of his every life. Outside, Fernanda, Chike, and Souvik stood huddled in a circle in the middle of the street, laughing jovially among themselves as the darkness licked their skin.

Fernanda looked up and caught Matt's eye. She elbowed the others, and the three of them looked up and waved goodbye to Matt, all of them smiling fondly at him.

Matt waved back and winced, forcing himself to remain composed for May. He didn't want to turn away from them, but he knew he could either turn around or miss what could be the very last time he spoke to the only person that really mattered to him beyond all else. As if the trio understood, they stopped waving, turned, and walked directly into the darkness without showing any fear. Without warning, the darkness eviscerated them and swelled with seeming excitement as their vaporized forms were consumed and pulled in impossible directions through the fissure's multidimensional intestines.

Matt's left hand throbbed in searing anticipation of being shredded atom by atom.

"The end of all things," May said in a whisper behind him. Finally, Matt turned and saw May, frail as a worn wood fence, surrounded by a few dozen candles of various shapes and sizes placed on every available surface in the room.

"It's the real world, May," Matt told her. He couldn't bear to see her standing all alone, so he strode to her and took her in his arms, never wanting to let go. "I just know it, May. I'm going to find you."

May shivered and sobbed into Matt's chest. "That's just in your head, Matthew... you beautiful, confused man. This is the end. I can feel it. I just know it somehow. But at least we had each other through infinity, right? At least we had that."

"This isn't the end, May," Matt urged, desperately wanting to believe his own words. "Either it's the real world, or like Heron said, it's some deeper layer of myself. Either way, you'll be there, May. You're not just a figment of my mind. You're real. Don't you feel real?"

May just sobbed and clung tighter to Matt. The flames flickered in unison suddenly, and Matt lifted his head to see that the darkness had already consumed the walls of May's home. It was only ten feet away in every direction and still closing in.

"Matt," May cried. "I don't want to lose you."

At her words, a pang of regret surged through Matt, and now he wasn't sure if this was the right decision.

I've been through this, Matt defeatedly consoled himself as the darkness inched closer. *Infinity held no answers. This is the only option left.*

"The chance this leads to the real world is one-to-infinity," May said frantically as if repeating the words from memory. "Odds are that it will lead to another layer of your infinite self. It could be that all this was just your way of getting rid of the part of you that is Heron rather than Heron getting rid of you. Right?"

306

"No!" Matt pleaded. "It's the real world, May. It has to be."

"If it…isn't just oblivion," May offered through squeaking sobs, "then whether it's the real world or your own fabricated infinity, what will you do on the other side, Matt?"

"Search for you," Matt breathed without hesitation.

May wept with greater intensity as the darkness consumed a number of candles. There were only a few feet remaining.

"Exactly," she said. "Just as I would search for you, Matthew. That's why –" she hesitated, gulping down the tremendous terror attached to the conclusion she struggled to say aloud. "That's why I have to erase myself. Because I know you can't let me go. And I love you for that, Matt."

"May!" Matt yelped in feeble desperation, holding her at a distance and looking deep into her sorrow-drenched eyes.

"It'll never end for you," May explained with heart-rending finality. "I've always known that if I really love you, this is what I have to do."

"May!" Matt pleaded as the darkness constricted the space around them, forcing them into a cylindrical area no more than two feet in diameter. They tightened their bodies together, sucking in their bellies and pulling in their limbs as the darkness tugged at the peripheries of their skin.

"Without you, I'll be like Heron," Matt pleaded with her. "I need you, May. I love you."

May grabbed the back of Matt's head and pulled his lips to hers. Her tears flowed freely into his, and Matt could taste their intertwined sorrow.

You will never be like him, May assured Matt. *This might be the only way to really free you.*

If it's the real world, Matt responded in horror, *then this might cause me to forget all about you. Please, May! You're all that matters.*

Matt pleaded with her as they continued kissing, and he felt an overwhelming tug at his elbows and hips as the darkness converged, reaching to consume them without delay.

There is no real world, May sobbed as the darkness reached the edges of both their skulls. *I love you, Matt. Forever.*

May! Matt pleaded, and though he could feel her tongue and taste her sweetness, she was already being stripped away from him in multiple impossible directions all at once.

He tried clinging to her in his mind, but it was like grasping at quickly thinning silk cords.

The last thing Matt felt before being consumed was surging regret and the shattering feeling that he had made a mistake. That he had already found May. That he should have just let infinity be enough.

May! Matt cried as the churning multidimensional void converged on itself.

27. Oneironaut

Auditorium lights sprayed Matt's eyes with blinding fluorescence as Souvik and Fernanda walked on either side of him, making sure he didn't fall over. It had only happened a couple times, but if he had one more really major fall, the doctors probably wouldn't trust Matt on his own anymore. His friends knew that, so they made sure to take special care of him.

The light mixing with the sunlight in the outside lobby made the immediate space around Matt sparkle like diamonds at the periphery of his vision, and the cherry fabric of the auditorium seats directly in front of him practically glowed. Matt squinted his eyes behind his new prescription sunglasses and breathed deep, letting the voice of some distant speaker wax lyrical in the background of his awareness.

Damn it, he scolded himself inwardly, aware that this was all his fault. The doctors at the local institute said it would get easier, but the light sensitivity and the bouts of paralyzing confusion seemed to only be getting worse. Worst of all, he had the feeling that he'd forgotten something important. His mom told him that he'd always had that feeling ever since he was young. She was right, but now it felt all-consuming.

I forgot something incredibly important, Matt told himself, knowing how stupid it sounded. *If it were so important, someone in my life would have told me about it,* Matt considered, but he still couldn't shake this feeling churning in the deepest layers of his being.

Fernanda tugged gently at Matt's left hand. Normally he tried to avoid letting others see his birth defect, let alone touch it. But this was Fernanda, his oldest friend. She didn't care about his two missing fingers even though the stumps embarrassed Matt to no end.

"You okay?" Fernanda checked with motherly concern.

Matt nodded, not wanting to be a bother. He forced himself forward, pushing away his self-loathing. When they arrived at a row of seats, Souvik shuffled in first, looking back every couple seconds at Matt as if to make sure he wouldn't topple over.

Taking their seats in their usual position in the row closest to the exit door, Matt relished the inviting warmth of being able to rest his legs. The walk from his dorm to the auditorium was the most activity he'd engaged in since the accident.

It wasn't an accident, Matt corrected himself with a painful wince. *I just fucked up the dose.* But an accident was how the doctors referred to it. An intravenous cocktail of 2C-B, heroin, and DMT mixed with homemade saline had put Matt in a coma for three weeks with two weeks of rehab after that. Five weeks total. In terms of how he and his psychonautical friends partied and traversed the mind, five weeks might as well be an infinite number of lifetimes and experiences.

Matt forced his mind away from thoughts of the hospital and the drugs he still considered going back to. He looked toward the stage and focused his mind on the words of the young man concluding his presentation. Splashed across the projector screen in bold crimson letters was the title of the presentation: The Very Real Possibility of Cosmic Consciousness.

Definitely up my alley, Matt noted, and he was reminded how lucky he was to have friends that seemed to genuinely care about his interests.

"So, like I said at the beginning of my presentation, you zoom out far enough," the overly excited young man with a shock of orange hair cooed on stage, "and the whole universe looks like a neural network. Everything and everyone, even you, could just be the dream of a cosmic god. Thank you."

The man smiled and began walking off stage as the audience of mostly young undergraduates offered him a short burst of applause followed by a flurry of disruptive conversation from audience members inspired to share their own theories on the nature of reality with their friends and neighbors.

"Okay, okay," a balding man in his fifties said from the first row, and he jumped to his feet and walked to the steps of the stage. He quickly shook the previous speaker's hand and smiled excitedly at him as they passed each other.

"Okay, okay," the man said again, this time through the microphone. The high-pitched feedback sent a shiver down Matt's spine, forcing him to grit his teeth.

"You'll all have time to ponder the great mysteries of the universe after the presentations are through," he chuckled, clearly happy that so many young minds were eager to contemplate such deep and unanswerable mysteries. "Our next speaker," the man said quite loudly, and the audience hushed itself to silence. "Our next speaker is probably the reason most of you are here today."

A cacophony of excitement roared in patchwork blazes from the audience as if it constituted a singular living being. The man on stage lifted his hands, bringing the audience back to a state of relative calm, though the anticipation in the air was still electrifying.

"This is it," Souvik whispered to Matt, and he hit his knee in excitement. "We got here right on time, bro."

The man on stage continued. "He has dedicated his life to making contributions to numerous sciences and other various fields of study, but he is most known in the public sphere for his seminars on the nature of consciousness and reality. Ladies and gentlemen, I won't make you wait any longer. I present to you, Doctor Chike Okonma."

The crowd roared and cheered with ecstatic expectation, and even Matt felt a twinge of excitement despite feeling as though he'd been suffering through the worst hangover of his life for the past month. The ceiling lights dimmed, and a pair of spotlights blanketed the stage with an ochre hue. Matt was relieved he was able to take off his sunglasses.

Okonma, Matt mouthed, and the name seemed to hold supernatural energy. He spent a sizable portion of his childhood reading Okonma's writing – books on psychology and biology and cosmology and even science fiction. Okonma seemed to be able to probe any subject from any field with careful expertise, and there didn't seem to be anything Okonma didn't find infinitely interesting and worthy of being pondered. In fact, Okonma was the reason Matt had become a lucid dreamer at such a young age.

The crowd was still cheering as they waited for Okonma to take the stage.

Why waste a third of your life asleep when you could be living whole lives inside your mind? Matt recited in his mind. Okonma's words had been in Matt's head practically his entire life. Even though this seminar was the closest Matt had ever come to being in this legend's presence, Okonma was like a best friend to Matt. Okonma's writing helped Matt out of many bouts of depression, and he often credited the man as being the reason he was still alive.

"Thank you," Matt said, utterly grateful that his friends had bought him tickets to this speech and had even been willing to skip the rest of the speakers so that Matt could get some extra sleep that day. Ever since the accident, it seemed like he could never get enough sleep, no matter how many pills he used. He could sleep for two days straight and still feel dead tired.

"Of course, bro," Souvik said. "We got you."

Fernanda squeezed Matt's knee in quiet support. It felt exceptionally comforting to have them in his life.

Matt glanced at the tattoo on his forearm and read: *Awake/Asleep.* The tattoo was a reality check; as long as it looked normal, he probably wasn't in a dream. Still needing a second reality check, he glanced at his hands again and was finally convinced that he wasn't dreaming. He felt a sudden pang of horror at being reminded of lucid dreaming. He hadn't told his friends, but he'd been scared to try lucid dreaming ever since he overdosed.

Why does it fill me with such fear now? Matt wondered, and he couldn't shake the feeling that he should do a third reality check just in case.

All of a sudden, the crowd jumped to their feet in a flurry of shouts and whoops as a frail, world-worn man stepped carefully, six inches at a time, toward the microphone. His skin was a dark ebony, and he wore a blue button-up suit with pens in the chest pocket. The balding man ran to help Okonma, but the old man waved him away with a pleasant *thank you* issued from his lips.

As Okonma stepped beneath the spotlights, he attempted to survey the crowd through strained eye lids, but it was clear he could only see shadows from where he stood. Matt gawked at the way this man clung to life despite his body barely hanging on.

He's so close to death, Matt thought in horror, but he felt bad for judging the man based on his age.

"How do you know this is real?" Okonma bellowed into the microphone, vibrating every atom in the room with thundering command.

Hushed whispers scurried about the audience, then returned to silence.

"What if I were to ask you to prove that you are real – that you are more than just, as the previous young man said, the dream of some greater entity? God, as he so succinctly put it."

Okonma paused, allowing the crowd to discuss among themselves. Matt felt a shiver ascend his spine from its base. Then a tingling pins-and-needles feeling in his chest forced him to grab his solar plexus and grit his teeth.

"Matt!" Fernanda whispered, gripping his forearm. Souvik was too engrossed in Okonma's speech to notice him.

The feeling subsided, and though Matt waved her away with a forced smile, Fernanda seemed to see right through him.

"We should leave," she offered compassionately.

"I'm fine," Matt whispered back, causing Souvik to glance back at him. Seeming satisfied that Matt was all right, Souvik immediately turned back to the old man in excitement.

"Is everyone here familiar with Chuang Tzu's butterfly dream?" Okonma continued, leaving Fernanda shaking her head in worry at Matt as she forced her eyes back to Okonma.

"Yes, it's a very famous story," Okonma said, seeing that most people in the audience were familiar with it. "For those unfamiliar, Chuang Tzu was a Chinese philosopher some two thousand years ago who wrote about his dream of being a butterfly. When he woke from the dream, he wasn't sure if he was a butterfly that had woken to become a man, or a man who had dreamed of being a butterfly. You see, in the dream, he didn't know about Chuang Tzu the philosopher. He was just a butterfly fluttering about existence." Okonma smiled and flapped his hands as if they were a butterfly's wings. The crowd chuckled, but Matt could only gulp at the deadly serious nature of what Okonma was proposing.

"There is no way to collect tangible, undeniable evidence of either proposition. Take it a step further – maybe neither is true. Maybe the philosopher is someone else entirely who is dreaming of being a philosopher who dreams of being a butterfly. How many times could this chain continue? Forever? Contemplating such a thing could drive you mad," Okonma said, falling into a rhythmic speaker's groove now. "But that's what drives our minds. This urge to understand. This need to validate our reality as real. This hunger to know if the very word *real* even holds any inherent meaning when it comes to the nature of existence."

The pins and needles flickered across Matt's chest again, but this time he braced himself, not wanting to worry his friends.

It'll pass, he told himself, breathing deeply to calm his nerves.

"But the truth is we can never prove the realness of reality. To a lucid dreamer like me, reality is no more objectively real than a dream. They both exist. The only difference is that reality has limitations. The experience of being, of self and other, of existing – all that is still identical."

A surge of energy at Matt's solar plexus nearly made him jump, but he gripped his legs and forced himself to remain seated.

Okonma scanned the audience absentmindedly and seemed to stop for a moment as his eyes crossed over Matt.

Can he tell something's wrong with me? Matt wondered, aware now that he should probably leave since the feeling in his chest was only growing more intense.

No, it's not that, Matt realized. *It was like he recognized me.* Matt shook his head at his thoughts and told himself Okonma probably couldn't even see the first row, let alone the last.

"Treating everything as a dream liberates. As long as you give reality to dreams, you are their slave," Okonma said, his tone suddenly filled with grave seriousness. "That's a quote by Sri Nisargadatta Maharaj, an Indian guru I'm very fond of."

Okonma lowered his head suddenly and grabbed his chest at his solar plexus. The crowd gasped, but Okonma lifted his hand to calm them and smiled.

"You know," he said with a faraway stare, his voice distant, almost as if he were lost in multiple lifetimes of memories. "If you could dream anything for all eternity, eventually you'd dream this. Eventually you'd be right back where you started," the old man said, clearly more to himself than the audience.

Without warning, Matt and Okonma clutched their chests in unison, and Matt couldn't help yelping at the sudden surge of energy. Half of the crowd looked back at Matt to see what the shouting was about, and the other half stood with worry, wondering if the old man might be having a heart attack.

"Matt!" Souvik shrieked at Matt's yelp.

"I told you it was too soon," Fernanda seethed at Souvik, and Souvik nodded, defeated by her point. They practically lifted Matt out of his seat, and the three of them shuffled toward the exit door, Matt still clutching at the energy swimming in his chest. On stage, Okonma assured everyone that he was fine, and as Matt and his friends opened the exit door, a large portion of the crowd looked back to see who could possibly have the audacity to leave just as this legendary speaker nearly died on stage.

Matt felt terribly embarrassed, and as he glanced back at his childhood idol, he saw that the old man was watching him leave with a forlorn stare.

"He must think I'm an asshole," Matt told his friends once they were in the lobby. The energy in his chest was quickly subsiding, and Matt felt stupid for making a scene. At the very least, the light didn't appear to be bothering his eyes as much, and he didn't feel like he needed to put the glasses back on right away.

I'll get better in time, Matt assured himself, wondering if he had experienced an anxiety attack.

"What's wrong, bro?" Souvik checked as Fernanda eyed Matt with grave concern.

"I don't know," Matt admitted. "I'm just out of it," he said, unable to stop thinking about how he and Okonma had grabbed their chests in the same place at the same time.

Did he feel that too? Matt wondered.

"I just feel like I forgot something," Matt told them for the first time. "Something incredibly important."

They nodded with patience and Fernanda said, "We all feel that way sometimes, Matt. I get it. It's like there's something just out of reach of your mind. It's like that tip of the tongue feeling, only bigger."

Matt nodded hollowly. "Yeah," he agreed, not wanting to concern them. He felt terrible that they were missing the show, especially since they'd paid for it. "You guys go back in," he said, attempting to mask the severity of his feelings. "I just need some air."

They both shook their heads fervently.

"No way, bro," Souvik began, "you —"

"I just need to be alone," Matt interrupted. "Just for a bit. I'll be right outside. I won't go anywhere. Promise."

The crowd roared in laughter from within the auditorium.

"Promise?" Fernanda repeated.

"Promise," Matt assured her.

Fernanda and Souvik nodded, reluctantly allowing him to have his way. He let them return to the auditorium, then turned and left the building, walking outside onto the campus quad.

It was around eleven o'clock in the morning on a weekday, so there weren't many people on the quad's manicured grass. There were a few students lounging against the iconic black bell tower at the center of the grass, but other than that, it was pretty empty.

A pair of white herons with velvet black legs meandered across the grass, apparently searching for something to eat.

Is that what you're searching for? Matt wondered pleadingly about the herons and the natural world that he and they were both a part of. *Or is it something deeper for you too?*

A spark of the tingling feeling danced across Matt's chest, and he wished beyond all else to understand how it was possible for him to know that he had forgotten something of such profound importance without knowing what it was he forgot in the first place.

The campus darkened suddenly as the sun was occluded by a particularly gigantic cumulus cloud. The cloud's edges radiated gold and ochre brilliance, allowing a few sunrays here and there to reach the surface. A pair of butterflies fluttered in a dance of sunlight near the bell tower, and Matt followed their flight to a young, petite Asian woman in the process of packing her books and belongings into her backpack as she prepared to leave. She was barefoot and wore a black denim jacket over a purple sports bra that left part of her midriff open. As she turned, Matt saw that one side of her head was shaved close to the skin while the other side flowed freely with dark black hair down to her shoulder.

Matt gasped as the energy in his chest surged with excitement.

This feeling...it's...her? he gawked, unsure why he would feel so excited about this young woman in particular. She looked to be a couple years younger than Matt, maybe a freshman or sophomore. But he had never seen her before. She was beautiful, certainly, but he could say that about a lot of women. Still, his heart fluttered and his solar plexus gushed with

316

tingling energy, forcing him to walk toward her.

Yes...that feeling, he realized as he walked across the grass, the black bell tower looming over him. *It's her,* he knew. *She's what I'm searching for. It's not a thing I yearn for, it's a person. It's a woman. It's her!* he knew with total, wonderful certainty.

He smiled for the first time in weeks, and it felt as though a braided cord of fate connected him to this woman he had never seen in his life.

"Hey!" Matt called out to her, and as she turned, the sun escaped from behind the clouds, fully illuminating her face. She smiled at him, her cherry lips an inviting warmth and her black eyes as deep and full as ripe, sprawling orchards. A diamond stud in her right nostril and three diamond studs lining the top of her left eyebrow glimmered with radiant sunlight, making her literally shine.

"Hey," she said back, chuckling at Matt's excitement. "You okay?"

"What's your name?" Matt said, his eyes and tone full of a sudden desperation that caught the woman off guard.

Her smile turned to nervousness, and she furrowed her eyebrows at him. "My name's May. Do I know you?"

May, Matt repeated in his mind, searching it desperately for meaning. *May,* he repeated, demanding his mind to make this feeling make sense.

"I'm sorry," he told her, tears filling his eyes now as he realized how strange and awkward he was being toward her. The energy in his chest dwindled suddenly to a flicker, and Matt knew he had made a mistake. "Sorry," he repeated, his lips quivering now at the prospect of his confused emotions. "I didn't mean to make you nervous."

She tightened the straps on her backpack, but then she smiled and said, "It's all right." She closed the gap between them and placed her gentle hand on his quivering shoulder. "I wish I could help you, but I have to get to my next class."

Clearly she knew that something was eating away at Matt's insides, but how could she ever fathom the endless depths of despair and confusion clawing deep within Matt's mind like starving animals calling out in the darkness for help that will never come.

"Thanks," Matt managed, wishing along with her that she could help him.

But it's not her, Matt admitted to himself forlornly. Though the energy in his chest was now just a faint whisper, it was still there – still pulsing and pleading with him to locate a shadow in darkness.

"See ya," she offered serenely, then added with seeming genuine compassion, "I'm sure everything will be all right."

Matt stared after her as she walked away, and with each of her steps, the feeling in his chest subsided, finally turning to a distant numbness as she crossed the street.

It's not her, he knew, and he felt his exhaustion catch up to him. He wanted to just go home and go to sleep. He considered that maybe he would have better luck searching in his dreams. *Or maybe with another DMT cocktail*, Matt weighed, though he knew it would probably be a long time before he did that again. *I might not wake up next time I push so far*, he reminded himself gravely.

The woman got on a bus, and as the bus drove away, it revealed a line of graffiti on a brick wall: *Endless is the maze.*

Matt chuckled sorrowfully to himself. *This maze of being. Is there any way out of this?*

Of course, no answer came, and Matt knew that there probably was no answer.

"Yo!" Souvik shouted at a distance. Matt turned to see Fernanda and Souvik jogging over to him from across the quad, and only then did he realize how far away from the auditorium he was.

As Matt stood under the tower and watched them run toward him from across the grass, he felt the intense feeling of déjà vu, and it filled him with unexplainable misery.

"I knew we'd have to keep an eye on you," Fernanda said with tangible concern as they closed the gap. "What are you doing?" she asked, looking around for why Matt might have walked so far away.

"Just went for a walk," Matt lied, unsure how he could possibly explain to them what he was enduring.

They seemed to recognize that Matt was out of sorts. Souvik nodded, put his hand on Matt's shoulder, and said, "It's just going to take time, bro. And look," he began, hesitating momentarily, but he forced himself to continue with something he had clearly wanted to say for quite some time. "If it wasn't you this happened to, it would have been me or Fernanda. We all pushed things too far."

Fernanda and Souvik eyed him, seeming to gauge how he might respond to the idea that their psychonautical escapades via drug consumption constituted a problem rather than a way of life.

Matt nodded, barely hearing his words.

Souvik took Matt's nod as thorough agreement. He patted Matt on the shoulder and said, "Good. And besides, this gives us more time to actually do what we initially planned to do in college. Who knows, maybe we'll make a game that gets big!"

Matt smiled and nodded along with Souvik's proposition, but it was just to placate him. Matt knew that until the feeling consuming his every thought went away, he would never be able to stop searching for the nameless, faceless woman he knew he needed to find. He imagined himself going back to class and even programming a game or two alongside Souvik during university. He envisioned himself getting a nine-to-five programming job and sitting behind a computer screen for the rest of his life. He knew he could do it. He knew he had to do it. Life had to continue. But all the while he would be searching – in waking life and in his dreams.

I'll be searching until my dying breath for something I might never find, Matt lamented, and he knew that his present despair was but a shallow valley beneath mountains of clawing anguish that would eventually overtake the whole of his mind.

"You okay?" Fernanda checked with Matt as Souvik typed on his phone.

Matt stared into her eyes, and though he knew she was his best friend, she felt like a stranger to him. The whole world felt like a stranger.

"Matt?" Fernanda repeated, growing increasingly concerned as Matt gazed about frantically, looking as though he were in an open-eyed REM state.

Is any of this real? Matt wondered, Fernanda's voice barely a whisper in what might as well be an infinite distance between them. Matt checked his hands, but they looked normal. He glanced at his tattoo, but it was fine. He tried breathing through his closed mouth, but he was unable.

This is real, Matt told himself. *And so is that feeling – that yearning.*

A flutter of wings made Matt twist his neck, and he saw the pair of herons lift off and fly toward the auditorium.

Searching for something, Matt thought as their black legs slipped behind the buildings and out of sight.

"What is it, Matt?" Fernanda asked, her voice strained as if she might cry.

I don't know, Matt answered inwardly. *It's like I'm searching for someone that isn't here and never was.*

Matt looked up and forced himself to smile.

"I'll be all right," he told Fernanda to pacify her worry. "Let's go do some coding," he said so that Souvik could hear him. Souvik winked at Matt, then went back to whatever was occupying his attention on his phone.

Fernanda nodded, but Matt knew that she and Souvik would always keep an eye on him. No matter how much time went by or what circumstances might separate them in life, he knew, at least, that their connection was indomitable – that they were people he would never forget or have to search for.

I'll be all right, Matt tried to assure himself, but he didn't believe it.

Billowing clouds rolled in front of the sun, darkening the world as the sky took on a uniform white hue.

Who are you? Matt pleaded to know from this woman whose name and face he was incapable of conjuring in his mind.

She is all that matters, Matt concluded futilely, and he knew the question would creep and permeate through his thoughts like nightmare black ink into pure white paper for the rest of his life.

Made in USA - Kendallville, IN
31496_9781732306981
06.24.2022 1303